Lori Foster delivers the goods.
—*Publishers Weekly*

"Known for her funny, sexy writing, Foster doesn't
hesitate to turn up the heat."
—*Booklist*

"One of the best writers around of romantic novels
with vibrant sensuality."
—*MyLifetime.com*

"Foster outwrites most of her peers and has
a great sense of the ridiculous."
—*Library Journal*

"Foster proves herself as a bestselling author time
and again."
—*RT Book Reviews*

"Filled with Foster's trademark wit, humor, and sensuality."
—*Booklist* on *Jamie*

"Foster supplies good sex and great humor along the way
in a thoroughly enjoyable romance reminiscent of Susan
Elizabeth Phillips' novels."
—*Booklist* on *Causing Havoc*

"Foster executes with skill...convincing,
heartfelt family drama."
—*Publishers Weekly* on *Causing Havoc*

"Suspenseful, sexy, and humorous."
—*Booklist* on *Just a Hint—Clint*

Also available from

LORI FOSTER

and HQN Books

LORI
FOSTER

Unbelievable

HQN™

ISBN-13: 978-0-373-77491-3

UNBELIEVABLE

Recycling programs for this product may not exist in your area.

Copyright © 2010 by Harlequin Books S.A.

The publisher acknowledges the copyright holder of the individual works as follows:

FANTASY
Copyright © 1998 by Lori Foster

TANTALIZING
Copyright © 1998 by Lori Foster

This edition published by arrangement with Harlequin Books S.A.

For questions and comments about the quality of this book please contact us at Customer_eCare@Harlequin.ca.

® and TM are trademarks of the publisher. Trademarks indicated with ® are registered in the United States Patent and Trademark Office, the Canadian Trade Marks Office and in other countries.

www.HQNBooks.com

Printed in U.S.A.

CONTENTS

FANTASY

To Judy Flohr, Carolyn Dietsch and Barb Smith, dedicated readers and dedicated friends.

Your friendly faces always make a book signing better, and I can't tell you how much I enjoy our lunches afterward!

Thank you, ladies.

CHAPTER ONE

"GOING ONCE…going twice…"

With anticipation thick in the air, the announcer called out, "Sold!"

And Sebastian Sinclair watched as the man just purchased was led off the stage to the sounds of raucous feminine cheers. Soon it would be his turn.

How the hell did I get myself talked into this? he wondered. Wearing a suit, watching huge amounts of money change hands with no consideration of the cost, being the center of attention—he hated it all. It reminded him of his youth and the fact that he had nothing in common with these shallow blue bloods.

Most of all, he hated the idea of being bought like an expensive toy for the amusement of rich women—regardless of the cause.

He seemed to be the only male not thrilled with the prospect of displaying himself. The others, in ages varying from late twenties to early forties, were smiling, flaunting their wares, so to speak, and generally getting into the spirit of the thing. Only one man remained in line before Sebastian now and judging by the brawn of the guy and his rough-whiskered chin, he wouldn't last long. The women were really going berserk on the macho ones.

Which was probably why the construction workers had on very snug, tattered jeans and T-shirts too tight for men half their size—an adjustment for their female audience, no doubt. There was absolutely no way a man could work comfortably in a shirt that tight.

Likewise, the landscapers wore their work boots and jeans, some of them with no shirts on at all. And the carpenter—he had a heavy tool belt hanging low on his hips. The ensemble was complete with wrenches, a nail pouch and the largest hammer Sebastian had ever seen, no doubt a pitiful attempt at symbolism. Sebastian shook his head and tried, without much success, to mask his amusement.

The announcer, a woman with a very wide, toothy smile, led a man around the stage by one finger hooked in his belt loop. The audience roared, then roared again when she had him turn, showing him to advantage. The spotlight moved over his backside and feminine shrieks filled the air.

Sebastian wondered if any of these rich people realized the seriousness of the benefit, the purpose the money would serve in assisting abused women. He doubted it. To them, it was a lark, not a humanitarian deed to build shelters and help those in need.

To Sebastian, it was much more personal.

The brawny guy ahead of him bounded onstage, anxious for his turn to titillate the giggling masses, and Sebastian was left with a female attendant, waiting for his cue.

As he'd guessed, the bewhiskered fellow went quickly, the last bid coming on a crescendo of womanly squeals and bawdy jests. The attendant took Sebastian's arm and directed him forward.

As he reached the center of the stage, hot lighting flooded over him. He stared out at the audience, satisfied with their reckless spending, but thoroughly disgusted by their careless attitudes. None of them gave a thought to where the money would go or how badly it was needed. They were all the same, full of glitz and shine; shallow, frivolous, concentrating only on their own pleasures. He was disdainful of them all.

And then he saw her.

She stood alone, a small dark-haired woman with huge eyes that dominated her face and expressed her fascination. She didn't smile as he met her stare. She didn't yell out suggestions or a bid as the other women were doing. She didn't laugh or joke; she didn't do anything but watch him. He no longer heard the announcer, no longer felt the heat of the bright lights. His boredom and disinterest seemed to melt away. Her face was upturned, her lips slightly parted, as if in surprise. And he knew—she *couldn't* look away. Somehow he held her physically by the connection of their gazes.

Sebastian didn't dare blink. She seemed awestruck and innocent and he found her utterly irresistible. For some insane reason, because something inside him had stirred and heated at the sight of her, he had no intention of letting her go.

Maybe he wouldn't berate Shay after all. He just might end up thanking her.

SHE WANTED HIM.

Brandi stood in the middle of the floor, right beneath the stage. The men had been coming and going, none of them overly remarkable to her mind, but then, she wasn't here to buy a man. She was only attending this benefit to support her sister, Shay. In truth, she avoided gatherings like this one, where the testosterone filled the air so thick you could choke on it. And there were any number of ways she would have preferred to spend her birthday.

But none of that mattered at the moment. The man onstage was incredible, and once her gaze locked with his, she couldn't stop staring. She felt an irresistible connection to him, and she couldn't seem to find the wit—or the will—to walk away.

The woman handling the bids chuckled at some jest Brandi had missed, then turned to catch the man's arm. Holding a microphone in one hand, she gripped his arm firmly with the other and cuddled up to him. "Such a generous bid!" she called out sounding very excited, though Brandi, deeply involved in her own scrutiny, hadn't heard the exact amount offered. "He's worth every penny, ladies! Come on now, don't be shy. This one is quite a specimen." She squeezed his upper arm, testing his muscle, then made an "oohing" expression to the audience.

The man didn't look overly complimented. He looked disdainful, and rather than work toward drawing more attention to himself as the other men had, he merely crossed his arms and braced his long legs apart. He seemed impossibly tall and strong and masculine in his rigid stance. As impenetrable as a stone wall. Almost barbaric in his strength. And he continued to look at Brandi.

The announcer struggled to gain his cooperation. She tried to force him into a turn, wanting to display him as she had the others in order to raise the already astronomical sum they'd collected. He resisted her efforts with ease. The announcer couldn't budge him a single inch.

And the women loved it. They called out more bids, made explicit suggestions on what they'd do with him and haggled amongst themselves.

Brandi's fascination built. Never before had she felt it, at least, not in eight long years. And before that, she'd simply been too young. But there was no denying the interest surging inside her now. She'd made a decision earlier that day, a decision that would change her life—hopefully for the better. But this? Could she really consider bidding on a man? On *this* man?

In answer to her own thoughts, she shook her head no.

The man gave her a slight, devastating smile that stole her breath—and then slowly nodded his head yes, as if to encourage her. Embarrassed color flooded her face. He couldn't possibly know what she'd been thinking! She shook her head again, more emphatically this time, but that only made his smile widen until he gave her a full-fledged grin.

God, he was gorgeous.

And big. Too big. Much, much too big and imposing and… Brandi felt her heartbeat trip, felt heat wash over her, as if someone had opened an oven. She tried to step back, to break the invisible connection between them, but she couldn't manage it. Never in her life had she been the object of such masculine notice. Her sister Shay was so striking—tall and pale and beautiful beyond words—Brandi naturally faded beside her, becoming a mere shadow to Shay's impressive height and inexhaustible energy.

But now a man—this incredible mountain of a man—had latched onto her with his bold gaze and he wouldn't release her. She felt both alarmed and pleasantly flustered.

At that moment, Shay reappeared at her side. Her slim eyebrows lifted in a question. The man's gaze automatically reverted to Shay, who towered over Brandi.

It wasn't quite jealousy that Brandi felt—she and Shay were very close—it was more like resignation. She had no business staring at a man, inviting his interest when she had no intention of returning it. She *couldn't* return it, not yet, and certainly not with a man like him. Her resolution to start this birthday off differently hadn't yet been implemented. And it never would be with a man like him.

Now that he wasn't looking at her, she could look away, too, and did—with a deep, regretful sigh.

Shay heard that sigh and smiled. "He is gorgeous, isn't he?"

Burdened with her own thoughts, Brandi turned to look up at Shay and asked stupidly, "Who?"

"The man you've been ogling." Then Shay took her arm and led her away from the center of the floor. "Every woman here has been doing the same. But then, he's not exactly the type of man any red-blooded female would fail to notice."

"He isn't enjoying being on that stage."

Shay chuckled. "No, I don't think he is. But did you see how the women are reacting to his disinterest? They're going wild for him."

Feeling choked, Brandi said, "Then I suppose he'll bring in a good amount for your charity auction."

"That's what I'm counting on." Shay slanted Brandi a look. "I could make you a loan, you know."

Brandi stumbled but quickly righted herself. "Good grief, Shay! You're not suggesting...?"

"Why not?"

Such a ridiculous question hardly deserved an answer, but it irritated Brandi enough to give one anyway. "You already know why. Did you look at him? He's bigger than a barn and dark as Satan. Even wearing a suit, the man looks like a disgruntled savage. And so far, he's only smiled once."

"Yes, but that smile almost knocked you on your can. I watched the whole thing. Admit it, Brandi, you like what you saw."

Trying to be reasonable, Brandi explained, "He makes my insides jumpy. That's not a good sign."

Shay's face lit up. "Are you kidding? That's a fantastic sign!"

"No."

"But..."

"No buts." Then Brandi softened her tone. She knew Shay only had her best interests at heart, and she wanted to put her at ease. "I made a decision this morning to get my life in order, to start...circulating again."

"Circulating? As in dating?" There was both caution and elation in Shay's tone.

Brandi smiled. "Yes. I'll probably make a fool of myself, and I'll have to start out with someone safe, someone I know well and can trust and who isn't too pushy or overbearing. But it's past time I got on with my life. I'm going to start acting like a normal woman again if it kills me."

Shay grinned. "Well, I don't think death will actually be a by-product. And I'm thrilled with your decision, I really am. But since you already like the guy onstage—"

They both turned as the announcer began responding to a volley of bids. Things were winding up. He'd be sold any second now. Sadly, Brandy shook her head. Shay didn't understand. No one in her family did. She tried her best not to burden them, so she kept her lingering difficulties to herself and merely replied, "Fine," whenever they chanced to ask how she was doing. So far, that seemed to satisfy everyone.

Brandi turned away from the stage, unwilling to witness the final bid. "I'd never buy a man, Shay. I couldn't do it. You know that."

Shay stared down at her, then straightened to her full, impressive height. "Well, I certainly have no problem with it."

And before Brandi could stop her, before she could get a single word out of her suddenly dry mouth, Shay raised her arm and in a loud, carrying voice called out a bid well above any other they'd heard that night.

Stunned silence followed that astronomical bid, quickly replaced by loud complaints and feminine groans. But no one could go any higher. And after a moment, the announcer banged her gavel with obvious satisfaction. "Sold! To Shay Sommers, and pound for pound, he's a hell of a bargain!"

THE VAGARIES OF FATE were often rather hideous.

Brandi closed her eyes a moment, denying her own despair.

"Well," Shay said, her tone incredibly dry, "that was taken care of rather easily, wasn't it? No one even bothered to counter with a higher bid."

Brandi opened her eyes with that bit of nonsense. "Are you crazy, Shay? Have you totally lost your mind? You can have any man you want, *any* man! You certainly don't need to pay for them."

"But I wanted that man." Then Shay waved an elegant hand, avoiding Brandi's gaze. "This is my event. My project. Everyone expected me to make a purchase."

Brandi made a choking sound.

"Oh come on, Brandi. It's the same as donating the money directly. Only this way, the men on stage get to advertise their businesses to all the press that's here, displaying themselves as concerned businessmen, and the shelter will benefit since every company represented has promised to donate free labor. They'll do painting, concrete work, landscaping…whatever, to help get the newest shelter up and running. They get great publicity and we get free labor. Everyone is happy."

Except me, Brandi thought, feeling categorically unhappy. She wondered what Shay's man would contribute, but in the next instant, decided she didn't want to know. One could only guess what a big, unsmiling barbarian like him did for a living.

"It's a business venture," Shay continued. "Everyone will come out ahead—even the travel agency that donated the Gatlinburg prize packages because it's fabulous publicity for them. And a lot of the people using the packages will be repeat customers. But most of all, needy families will get housing. Do you realize how much money we've made?"

Brandi understood Shay's enthusiasm. Ever since she'd been widowed, Shay had done her best to become involved in the elite Jackson community of Tennessee, trying to pull resources from the wealthy to help those in need. She had her husband's money, which gave her a lot of clout, and she had the energy and wit to put it to good use. Unfortunately, Shay didn't fit the part of the matronly widow, not with her exceptional looks and outgoing personality. Many of the men refused to take her efforts seriously, and many of the women chose to see her as a personal threat.

Brandi knew her sister wanted desperately to find a purpose in life, some way to make use of the fortune her husband had left behind. And Brandi wanted to support her in every way she could.

"Shay," Brandi said, not wanting to dim her sister's overwhelming exuberance, "You don't owe me any explanations. If you want to buy a man…well, you can certainly afford it and I had no business questioning you. I apologize." She *was* sorry—sorry she'd ever come here tonight. Now all she wanted to do was go home, eat her birthday cake in private and forget she'd ever seen him.

Shay grinned. "I just wanted to make certain you understood my motives."

Brandi nodded. She did understand. They'd made a bundle tonight, but then she'd never doubted they would. Whenever her sister set out to do something it got done, in a big way.

This time Shay had bought herself a very expensive man.

Without really meaning to, Brandi asked, "But why him?" There were any number of men Shay could have chosen and each and every one of them would have been thrilled with her as purchaser. So why had she chosen this particular man? The one man Brandi wished she'd had the nerve to buy for herself.

Not that it mattered. Brandi instinctively avoided men like him. He was too large, too dark and too imposing. Even under his suit, she'd been able to see all that hard muscle. The man was a damn behemoth, a huge warrior looking ready for battle. Brandi had no idea what she'd do with him if she had him.

But several ideas, vague in nature, flitted through her mind.

Shay only smiled. "You saw for yourself how in credibly sexy he is."

Sexy didn't even come close to describing him. He'd looked at her, and she'd gone warm and nervous and breathless all at the same time. He hadn't flexed or winked or done any of the things the other men had done. He'd merely stood there, looking magnificent.

And Shay had bought him.

Catching Brandi's hand and dragging her along, Shay led her to where the men were being introduced to the women who'd had the final bids. Brandi tried to hold back, but Shay wouldn't allow it.

"Come on, Brandi. Our guy should be somewhere at the end of the line. He was the last one sold."

Our guy? The heels of her low black pumps left marks on the tile floor as Brandi dug in, refusing to move another inch. "Now wait just a minute, Shay! I don't know what you're up to, but he's not *our* guy."

With a tug, Shay got her moving again. "You're right. He's yours."

CHAPTER TWO

"YOU CAN STOP right now, Shay. I want no part of this."

"Now, Brandi," Shay whispered, leaning way down to reach Brandi's ear. "The press is everywhere, just as I'd hoped. You don't want to give my charity event a bad name, do you? You know how much trouble I already have getting these stuffy old snobs to accept me and to take part in the benefits. If Phillip hadn't left me a very wealthy widow, none of them would even speak to me. And if it wasn't for something so outlandish as an auction, not one of them would have parted with a single additional dime. They couldn't care less about the needy, you know that, but they do love to have their fun. I had to find a way to give them that in the name of charity—to entice them. You know how crowded the women's shelters are here in Jackson. We need this auction to succeed. But if my own sister acts appalled, I'll never be elected to spearhead another event."

Brandi ground her teeth in frustration, but had to admit Shay was right. It was important to show her support, which was why she'd attended the auction in the first place. Ever since Phillip's death, Shay had thrown herself into other activities, but this was the first time she'd made much headway. And the auction was an undeniable success. It would be the event that would open future opportunities for Shay. She wanted to help; she needed to help.

The very idea of women purchasing men had all kinds of connotations attached, just as Shay had predicted. Which was why an abundance of reporters had also attended, titillated and ready to produce a story that would give the auction the publicity it needed.

Brandi couldn't begin to imagine what Shay had in mind for her man. She wasn't sure she wanted to know. For some reason, the idea of Shay alone with him on a quiet, romantic getaway disturbed her. And as much as she hated to admit it, as much as she loved her sister and wanted her to be happy, she felt envious.

"Come on, Brandi. You'll enjoy this."

Extremely doubtful, she thought but it was difficult to take your sister to task when she was so incredibly tall. Compared to Brandi's five feet four inches, Shay's six feet could be rather persuasive.

They finally stopped beside a large crowd of women waiting to claim their "purchases." Brandi looked around, seeing men and women pairing off while photographers captured every move. The women postured, showing off their elegant gowns and jewels, and the men smiled, looking sexy and confident and proud of their success. They were all so natural, so outgoing…so different from her.

Her gaze skimmed the room, taking it all in. Everyone seemed to be having a good time.

All but one man.

Brandi froze, her gaze glued to that intense, unsmiling face. Size alone distinguished him from the other men. But there was also the darkness about him, his straight black hair, his tanned skin. Only his green eyes seemed bright, and they were like fire—watching her.

Already he'd loosened his tie and unbuttoned the top of his white dress shirt. Dark curling hair showed in the opening. Brandi wondered if he was that hairy all over, then flushed with the thought.

Lounging, with one broad shoulder propped against the wall, he affected a casual pose, but Brandi suspected there was nothing casual about it. A panther tensed to attack his prey was a better comparison than casual negligence.

He might as well have been on the stage again, he so completely dominated her vision, her thoughts. A touch of thrilling excitement swirled in her belly.

And then it hit her.

He was now Shay's companion for the next five days, but was singling Brandi out by staring, stalking her with his eyes. Brandi stiffened and let her own black brows draw down in a frown. The man must be a complete cad! Of course, she was searching for reasons to dislike him, to make the situation more tolerable, but still, she had a valid point.

The corner of his mouth quirked in amusement for a split second, then leveled out again. His green gaze, brighter now, but still so very warm, slid over her face, then over the rest of her.

She remembered that look, knew what it meant, though it had been years since she'd experienced it. Experiencing it now made her stomach flip and her muscles tighten. She wondered if her plain black shift disappointed him. It fell to just below her knees, then met with her black stockings. With a barely scooped neck and elbow length sleeves, the dress exemplified her life—plain, uncomplicated, quiet.

Just as she had wanted it to be.

Several women were attempting to speak to him, but he ignored them. He pushed himself away from the wall and started toward Brandi. She considered making a hasty exit, leaving Shay to fend for herself. Watching the two of them get acquainted wasn't something she could anticipate with any degree of outward indifference.

But Shay turned then and followed Brandi's gaze. She placed a restraining hand on Brandi's shoulder, and as the man reached them Shay embraced him with her free arm, kissing his cheek with familiar affection. Brandi could only gawk.

"Sebastian, you did wonderfully—our biggest attraction! For a moment there, I was afraid my bid would cause a brawl. Some of the ladies were very disappointed to be put out of the running." She laughed, then added, "I was right—you are a natural."

"A natural idiot for letting you talk me into this," he said easily, his gaze swinging down to Brandi. He studied her, and his tone dropped to an intimate level. "I don't think I'll thank you for making that last bid, Shay."

Brandi's eyes widened. Was he insinuating that he'd wanted *her* to bid? She opened her mouth to...say what? She had no idea, but then he glanced at Shay again.

"I'd appreciate an introduction," he said, "since you two seem well acquainted."

Shay grinned, making no effort to hide her satisfaction at his interest. "Not only well acquainted, but

related. Sebastian, I'd like you to meet my little sister."
She pressed Brandi forward. "Sebastian Sinclair, meet
Brandi Sommers."

"Sister?" He looked surprised and his eyes narrowed
on Brandi's face, scrutinizing her every feature. Brandi
knew he was drawing comparisons between her and
Shay, and she was bound to come up lacking. She stiffened her spine and scowled at him.

Shay forged on, intent on some course that eluded
Brandi. But somehow Brandi knew she wasn't going
to like it.

"Sebastian is a good friend of mine," Shay said, then
added with a burst of wary enthusiasm, "Happy birthday, honey! I bought him for you."

SEBASTIAN'S FIRST THOUGHT was that the woman
would faint dead at his feet. She'd gone deathly pale and
her mouth had dropped open. Yet when he reached for
her, she jerked back and there wasn't a single ounce of
uncertainty in her expression.

Her glare said plain enough that she wanted nothing
to do with him.

His sense of indignation rose, but he was unsure
what to say. He couldn't pull his gaze away from her
face, regardless of her obvious rejection. Up close, he
could see her huge eyes were a very soft blue, ringed
with thick black lashes. Her nose tipped up on the end
and her small stubborn chin was slightly pointed. There
were hollows beneath her cheekbones giving her a very
delicate appearance, but her jaw was firm. Her lips…
she had a very sexy mouth, he decided, lush and well
defined, even if she refused to smile, even if her expres-

sion now was more shocked than pleased. She wasn't pale like Shay, but rather her skin had a dusky rose hue, and her midnight black hair…it was wildly curly, cut short and framing her face…untamable. He found himself suffering a severe case of instantaneous lust. And yet the woman looked appalled at her sister's generosity. Well, hell.

"I'd never have guessed you were related," he said, trying for an ounce of aplomb in the awkward moment. "You two look nothing alike."

Shay grinned. "I'm adopted, didn't you know? I guess I never told you about that."

"I guess you didn't."

She surprised him with that, enough that he could actually take his eyes off Brandi's face a moment to stare at Shay. "You're not kidding?"

"Nope. My stepparents thought they couldn't have kids, so they took me in. And they've always treated me like their first child."

"You are their first child," Brandi muttered, frowning up at her sister.

"But shortly after my adoption was final, Mom got pregnant." Shay beamed down at Brandi. "She's like a miracle child."

"Hardly a child now," he said, his attention resting on Brandi's pursed lips for a few seconds. He envisioned kissing that mulish expression off her mouth, then had to force that image away before he embarrassed himself.

Brandi rolled her eyes, then crossed her arms over her breasts—small perfect breasts, he couldn't help noticing. She barely reached his collarbone, but she managed to look imposing nonetheless. "You'll have to forgive my sister, Mr. Sinclair. She gets carried away with her generous intentions on occasion. But I don't want…that is…" She fumbled for the appropriate words, which gave Shay a chance to offer more arguments.

"I can afford him, Brandi. And he's the perfect gift!" Brandi stared at her sister, and Shay grumbled defensively, "Well, he is!"

With her face bright red and her posture rigid, Brandi appeared more than determined to send him on his way.

Sebastian interrupted before she could do just that. "When you say 'little' sister, you aren't exaggerating."

Shay grasped the change of topic gratefully. "Brandi looks like the family. Petite and dark. I'm afraid with my gawky height and fair hair, it's me who's the oddity."

"Ha!" Brandy now had her hands on her narrow hips. "A beautiful oddity and you know it." To Sebastian, she said, "Shay is the reining matriarch of the family. She does her best to boss us all around, and usually we let her because she enjoys it so much. It gives her something to do and keeps her out of trouble. But this time…"

He didn't want to be dismissed, so he held out his hand to Brandi and quickly interrupted. "So I'm a birthday present, am I? I suppose I've been worse things in my line of work."

She put her small hand in his large one, gave it two jerky, firm pumps, then mumbled, "Nice to meet you." And in the next breath she asked with a good dose of suspicion, "What exactly is your line of work?"

Shay poked Brandi in the ribs, causing her to jump. As Brandi rubbed her side, scowling, Shay explained.

"Sebastian owns a personal security agency and he does a credible job of taking care of people, watching out for them, protecting them from danger of any kind. It's one reason for all the brawn you noticed."

Brandi's eyes flared and her cheeks flushed. So she'd noticed him to that degree had she? *Excellent.*

She stuttered a moment, then ended with, "I'm going to kill you, Shay."

Shay looked totally unconcerned with the threat. She fluttered her manicured hand in Brandi's direction as if to fan away the anger. "Sebastian has to stay in top shape. His job can be, at times, very physical. But he's up to it. He's real hero material, he just doesn't realize it."

"I do my job the same as anyone else, Shay. There's nothing heroic about it."

"You see what I mean?" Shay asked Brandi, then added in a stage whisper, "Actually he'd be a perfect male if he wasn't such a chauvinist. But Sebastian thinks of all women as delicate and frail and he wants to save them all."

He narrowed his eyes. "Oh, I don't know about that, Shay. I certainly wouldn't term you as delicate. Tough as shoe leather maybe, but not—"

Shay smacked at him, laughing. But Brandi frowned as if she didn't quite trust him, regardless of her sister's romanticized declaration. Then she turned to Shay, and though she lowered her voice, he heard every word. "I don't know what you're up to here, Shay, but it won't work, so stop it right now. You bought him, you can just keep him."

"I don't want him!" Shay said, frowning now herself. "He's a great guy, but we're too much alike. We'd kill each other within twenty-four hours. Besides, I've already been this route and don't intend to go it again."

"But I should?"

Shay shrugged. "You know how it is about a path never traveled. Your weeds are growing tall, Brandi. Pretty soon you won't be able to find the path anymore."

"Oh for heaven's sake," Brandi muttered. "That's the dumbest bit of argument you've ever come up with."

Sebastian was beginning to feel like a stray mutt. Not since he was twelve years old and had begun gaining his height and physical structure had a woman showed such disinterest in his company. He wasn't vain, but then, he wasn't stupid, either. He'd had women argue over him before, plenty of times actually—but never to see who had to be stuck with him. More often than not, women chased him.

But now Brandi wasn't chasing him—she was trying to chase him away. Perversely, he was determined to hang around.

Shay had her hands on her hips, mimicking Brandi's stance, and she looked every bit as determined as Brandi. "I wanted to give you something special for your birthday, Brandi, but I was at a loss. I couldn't think of a single suitable gift. Then, well, you mentioned your new plans, and inspiration struck."

Sebastian bit his upper lip. He didn't understand the part about "new plans," but inspiration was apparently the way Brandi had stared at him while he was onstage. Her sister had interpreted that eat-him-alive look as interest, so maybe he hadn't misread her after all. Maybe it was that her interest hadn't quite encompassed five days alone with him, as the prize package specified.

He didn't understand why—but he was already determined to find out.

Brandi waved a small dismissive hand—the same as her sister had done earlier, only this time it was aimed in his direction. "*He* wasn't part of my plans."

"*He's* perfect for your plans! You're twenty-six today and you never have any fun. Sebastian is fun." She glanced at him and demanded verification. "Aren't you fun, Sebastian?"

"A laugh a minute." But he didn't feel like laughing. He felt like telling Shay to be quiet and stop pushing her sister. Hell, Shay was practically forcing him on Brandi, and she was resisting admirably. It was a new experience—and he didn't like it one bit.

Brandi closed her eyes, then opened them again. "No."

"Now, Brandi…"

It was most likely male pride that motivated him, because he didn't like being rejected any more than the next guy. Especially not after Brandi had managed to intrigue him so thoroughly with her blatant, wide-eyed, somehow innocent staring. He should just forget about the whole thing. He didn't have time to take away from his other commitments. He was in the middle of screening new help for hire at his office, and each room in his home was in some stage of renovation. His free time these days amounted to nil.

But he found himself stepping in front of Brandi and Shay, hiding them from the crowd. That damn *no* had sounded entirely too final, and he'd already determined not to let her say no.

"I'm sorry you're not happy with the arrangement,

Miss Sommers," he said, not quite able to keep the annoyance out of his tone, "but the fact is, neither of us has any choice at this point. The press is ready to snap a shot of anything that even remotely looks suspicious. If you hesitate or look as if you're being coerced, Shay's publicity will suffer. My business will suffer. The women's shelter will suffer."

Turning very slowly, Brandi stared up at him. "You're exaggerating."

"We're next in line for photos. If you look unwilling or unhappy you can imagine how the text will read below the picture. They'll slaughter your sister's intentions, and my business will be given a bum rap. They'll somehow twist it so that you had reason to refuse my company on the trip. This whole event will end up looking like a disreputable scam, and the efforts to provide housing for battered families will lose ground."

After spewing that nonsensical garbage—all of it exaggerated, just as she'd claimed—Sebastian waited. If Brandi Sommers was anything at all like her sister, she wouldn't want to jeopardize the success of the auction. He waited, holding his breath and feeling ridiculous for letting her decision matter so much to him.

After a calming breath, she looked at Shay. "What will happen now?"

A look of relief crossed Shay's features, then she smiled. "Your prize package includes a short trip to Gatlinburg, with all expenses paid." When Brandi started to protest again, Shay added, "You'll be going to a very quiet resort. I picked the place myself. You'll love it."

Reaching out, Sebastian clasped Shay's shoulder,

giving her a silent signal to desist. If he was to be forced on Brandi, he preferred to do the forcing himself. Somehow it seemed less demeaning. "Look at it this way, Miss Sommers. Like it or not, you own me for the next five days."

Her eyes grew so large he had to struggle to hide his grin. That little reminder had certainly gained her attention. "You'll be the one calling the shots. If you want to sit in the cabin the whole time and brood about your pushy sister here, that's your business. I'm just there as an escort if you want or need one." Then he added innocently, "Or for whatever purpose you assign me."

That notion had promise, even though Brandi was proving to be a contrary little wretch. She might be cute, and her unwavering gaze could set a man on fire, but she wasn't the most warm or welcoming woman he'd ever met.

Strange, but for some reason that fact wasn't deterring his interest in the least.

Brandi did look slightly intrigued by the idea, but then she shook her head. "I don't know…."

"Take your time and think about it." He added with a nod at the reporters, "But until we're out of here, it's important that you play along. At least pretend to be an excited, willing participant."

Brandi hesitated again, but she did give in. "Fine. I'll…think about it. But let's get this part of it over with, please. I'd like to get home."

Shay gave her an apologetic smile. "You can't leave anytime soon. The photographers want pictures of the two of you together. There's hors d'oeuvres, drinks. Dancing."

Brandi stiffened up again. For whatever reason, she was determined to resist the attraction between them.

He was just as determined not to let her.

BRANDI CONTEMPLATED muzzling her sister. She was in fine form tonight, at her most autocratic. "We'll do a few pictures, Shay. But you can forget the dancing and drinks."

Shay looked annoyed, but Sebastian accepted her edict. "Fair enough. Are you ready?" He held out his hand to Brandi.

Ready? Good God, no, she wasn't ready. But at this point, Shay had left her little choice.

She really didn't want to touch him again. That one brief handshake had been enough to give her goose-flesh. Just looking at him made her heart beat faster. But she took his hand anyway. It was so large, it swallowed her smaller one. She noticed again that his palm was callused, his skin warm and dry. She actually liked touching him this way. Somehow, the gesture felt right. But she knew getting close enough to that big body to dance—to let him hold her—would be a mistake. She'd probably make a fool of herself and she couldn't bear that. Not with him.

Better to discourage him now; it would save them both a lot of aggravation.

Shay had disappeared after the first picture—she was probably hiding. She'd dumped a volatile situation in Brandi's lap with no warning, and though Brandi knew Shay meant well, Brandi was now in the unenviable position of turning down a sinfully gorgeous, sexy man.

"Mr. Sinclair…"

"Sebastian."

She faltered just a moment, then nodded. "Uh, right. Sebastian." She looked around the room, avoiding his direct gaze. "I can understand the need to protect Shay's reputation by going through with a few harmless photos. But there's no point in carrying this farce any further than that. The idea of a trip together is absurd."

"No, it isn't."

She frowned at his firm disagreement, but he didn't give her a chance to argue. He towered over her, his expression mild, his tone calm.

"Your sister has made me your gift. By now, everyone here knows it. If we tried to avoid the trip, someone would surely find out and the auction would lose its credibility." He tilted his head at her. "Why are you so set against going?"

Since she couldn't very well tell him the truth, she mustered up her most sarcastic tone. "Gee, let's see. I've just met a total stranger and now I'm supposed to go off on a private trip with him."

He only grinned at her, amused by her forced acerbity. Brandi sighed. Well, so much for insulting him. "Mr.... Sebastian. I don't know you. I don't know anything about you."

"Funny, but with the way you stared earlier, I assumed you'd be pleased to have my company."

She drew herself up, which was pathetic given the fact she stood at least a foot shorter than him. "You put yourself on a stage for just that purpose! Besides, I wasn't the only one watching you."

"But you are about the only one who'd cause such a

fuss over a free vacation package! I think just about any other woman here tonight would be happy to go."

"Maybe I should just give one of them my *gift* then, and you can both be deliriously happy."

He stood glaring down at her for a moment, then his expression cleared and he chuckled. He had a nice chuckle…for a mountain. "Damn, I can't believe I'm standing here debating this with you. Talk about a blow to the old masculine ego." He took her arm and, without asking, led her toward a quieter corner. "I suppose if I must be abused, I ought to at least find some privacy so I can salvage a little pride."

Now Brandi felt totally flustered. Abused? She certainly hadn't meant to abuse him. But she also didn't want privacy. She wanted to go home to her quiet apartment and pretend none of this had happened. But looking around, she realized they were drawing notice, so she allowed him to drag her away.

When they stopped in the corner Sebastian motioned for her to seat herself at a wooden bench there. She did, and then he sprawled beside her, taking up too much room, letting his thigh touch hers. Brandi stiffened. "Mr…. Sebastian. I'm sorry if I've insulted you in any way. Really. That was never my intent. It's just that I don't like being forced into a corner."

He stared at her for a moment before he seemed to come to some sort of decision. "I have to tell you, Brandi. Your attitude really surprises me."

"Oh?" She didn't want him delving too deeply into her *attitude,* so she said, "You're used to strange women jumping at the chance to go off alone with you?"

"I wouldn't exactly call you strange. A little different, maybe. But then again… No, don't storm off in a huff." He caught her arm and eased her back into her seat. "I was only teasing."

His smile was so catching, she almost smiled, too.

"You know I'm your sister's friend. I assume you trust her?"

"Of course I do. She's my sister."

"Then you know I can't be a totally reprehensible character or Shay, who has no tolerance for unkindness in any form, wouldn't have bought me for you. Correct?"

Exasperation overrode her annoyance. "Good grief. You aren't exactly a packaged present, for heaven's sake. It's a donation is all. You make yourself sound like a toy to play with."

He chuckled and Brandi felt her face turn hot as she realized what she'd said. He reached out and touched her cheek with his knuckles, softly, just brushing her skin. Brandi almost shot off her seat.

"I don't know how much playing I'm up to, Brandi, but I'll try not to aggravate you too much."

His mere presence aggravated her, but not the way he assumed. She cleared her throat. "I didn't mean to insinuate…"

"I know." He took his taunting knuckles away. "Now, back to dissecting my character. Shay told you I own a personal protection agency. People, the majority being politicians or those with high-profile positions, hire me as a bodyguard, or to keep watch over various functions where they might expect trouble. But I also take on other, more personal cases, with endangered women or children. It never ceases to amaze me how men can so easily brutalize someone smaller than themselves."

Brandi shivered. There was a savagery in his eyes as he spoke that unnerved her. She had no doubt of the contempt he felt for bullies; but then, she shared that contempt.

He seemed drawn into his own thoughts for a moment, then he continued. "I was trained by the military. Spent eight years with Uncle Sam on special assignments that included keeping guard over some big government officials. Then I bailed out, worked for a firm for two years, and now I own my own business. I don't like people who hurt or frighten other people. So I've made it my job to stop people who do."

"How?"

"Excuse me?"

She had to ask. She had to know. "How do you stop them?"

His teeth closed over his upper lip and he pinned her with his gaze, refusing to let her look away. "However I have to. Without violence whenever possible. With extreme violence when necessary."

She shuddered, but otherwise hid her reaction. For some reason, having him give her the unvarnished truth lessened the impact of his ruthless words. Brandi glanced at him, then muttered, "At least you're honest."

"Always."

The drop in his voice nearly did her in. It was almost as if he suffered the same confusing mix of emotions that she did. Of course that was impossible. Her situation was unique to women; a man wouldn't understand.

"I'll always be honest with you, Brandi. As you get to know me—"

"I don't want to get to know you."

"—you'll learn that I never lie."

She wanted to growl in frustration. No man had ever so diligently pursued her. She'd given him options, offered to let him out of the absurd situation. Yet he remained insistent. "What do you get out of this, Sebastian?"

"Other than your sterling company?"

There was that touch of mockery again. She lifted her chin. "Yes. Why would you allow yourself to be sold in the first place? You seemed...disgusted by it all."

"I was, a little." Then he smiled. "Actually, a lot. I'm not one for rich crowds. Especially since my job usually keeps me in the shadows. And throwing money away—"

"On a very good cause."

"I agree. But the battered women's shelter wasn't the motivation for most of the bids. Even without the cause, those people would have been comfortable tossing away thousands of dollars. To them it was no more than a lark, and the waste of it sickens me."

"So, why would you do it if you hated it so much?"

"Because the money is desperately needed. Because the number of battered women and abused children rises every day. I see it in my job, I live with it. And I knew, with Shay in charge, the auction would be a success. She refused my check because she needed bodies to fill the stage. And when Shay sets her mind on something, she can be pretty damn persuasive."

Brandi drew a sigh, then shook her head. He was a likable man, whether she wanted to like him or not. He was mostly polite, even with his arrogance, and his motivations certainly weren't suspect. If anything, she had to admire his sense of obligation. "Shay has always been a bully. I swear, when she wants something, there's no stopping her."

"She's pushy, but she's also a shrewd business-woman."

"You know my sister well?"

"I thought I did. But that bit about adoption threw me. She never let on."

"Shay doesn't think about it all that much, none of us do. She's my older sister. My parents' first child. Besides, it's not something you'd bring up in idle conversation."

"I suppose."

"How did the two of you meet?" Even as she asked it, Brandi knew she was putting her nose where it had no business being. The notion that Shay and Sebastian might have once had a relationship was irrelevant to her. Or at least it should be.

But she didn't retract the question.

"Shay and I've been friends a little over a year now. I had a case where a man threatened his wife. He'd beaten her before, and the hospital had records of the times she'd been in. But she had two kids, no money and no place else to go. Shay had just started work at the shelter. I got the mother and children settled there, then I worked with a few friends on the police force to get the guy locked up. I would have preferred a more personal vengeance, but that wouldn't have solved the problem long-term. As it turned out, we discovered he was dealing drugs, too, so he's out of the picture for a good long while. Anyway, Shay was great, making the family comfortable. We've had joint interests ever since."

Brandi's heart thudded against her ribs. He'd just given

her incredible insight into his character, showing her his morals and his priorities. It was amazing, but she suddenly trusted him. This man was a protector, a man of honor.

And he'd offered to let her be the boss. It was such an intriguing notion—one that worked nicely with her plan to take charge of her life and move forward. She knew now, without a single doubt, he'd abide by her rules.

She hadn't figured out exactly what her rules would be yet, but she had time to worry about that. With a burst of unusual confidence, she decided to take the chance. She thrust her hand toward him and waited.

He looked at her, then at her hand. One glossy black eyebrow lifted, and there was amusement in his green eyes. He took her hand. "What are we shaking on?"

"I'll go to the resort with you."

"Ah." His grin was wide, putting deep dimples into his lean cheeks. "It was the lulling sound of my voice that brought you around, wasn't it? The practiced way I repeat a story? No? Then you were convinced by the way I sprawl so elegantly in a seat?"

She gave him her own grin, feeling somewhat smug. "Actually, Mr. Sinclair, I understand now that you can be trusted to stick to your word. You said I'd be the boss, and that for all intents and purposes, I own you for the next five days. I realized I couldn't possibly pass up such an opportunity. But I won't let you forget, *I'm* the one in charge."

His dark lashes lowered until she couldn't see his eyes, but his grin was still in place. "Believe me, honey. I won't be able to forget."

CHAPTER THREE

THINGS WERE MOVING too quickly. The plane wasn't at all crowded, especially in first class where Shay had put them, but the emptiness only added to Brandi's growing anxiety. Looking out the window, Brandi could see a light rain falling. She hated flying at night. She hated flying, period, but at least this was a rational fear shared by millions.

Which offered her not one bit of comfort.

Flexing her shoulders, she tried to relieve some of the tension, but that only caused her to bump into Sebastian. The man took up too much space with his large frame and even larger masculinity. When he was there, he was…*there,* and it simply wasn't possible to ignore his presence.

Shay hadn't given them much time to prepare for the trip, presumably because she thought Brandi might chicken out. Not that she would have. She was determined to see things through. But Shay wasn't taking any chances. She'd seen to every single detail—and she'd gone overboard in the luxury department.

She'd sent a retainer back to Brandi's house to pack her bags and bring them to the hotel where the auction had been held. The flight had been scheduled only a few hours after Brandi agreed to go. A limo had taken them to the airport, and a limo would await them when they landed, to whisk them off to the resort. There would be a rental car at their disposal.

Sebastian had planned on leaving the auction with a woman, so he'd brought his luggage with him. Before they'd left, he'd changed into a pair of khaki slacks and a black polo shirt. Brandi had been too flustered at the rush to pay much attention to his new attire at first. But now, with nothing to distract her from the impending flight, she looked him over.

His biceps were massive, stretching the short sleeves of the shirt. The dark color caused his green eyes to look even greener and the fit emphasized his broad muscled chest. The pants, stretched taut by his sprawl, emphasized...

Brandi jerked her gaze upward. A black-banded watch circled his thick wrist, and the shadow of his beard was now more pronounced. She jumped when he said her name.

"What?"

He opened his hand palm up on the elbow rest. "Nervous?"

She didn't accept his gesture. She couldn't. To do so would have been admitting to a weakness. And she'd gotten too good at denying her fears to admit to one of them now—not even a small one. "About what?"

"I don't know." His voice was quiet, calming, his expression very intent. She had the feeling he knew exactly how to soothe a person; his movements were too practiced and perfect. "Everything—me, the trip, the flight."

Twisting in her seat she looked at him more fully. Many of the other passengers were napping and had turned out their lights. His face was shadowed, exaggerating the sharp cut of his jaw, the high bridge of his straight nose. The deep awareness in his green eyes.

There was absolutely no chance of Brandi falling asleep.

She frowned in suspicion. "Shay told you how I feel about flying, didn't she?"

"Yeah." He stared down at her. "It's no big deal. I have my own store of phobias. Maybe some day I'll tell you about them."

This hulking mass of muscle was admitting to fears? The mountain had phobias? Brandi couldn't quite believe it. "You're kidding, right?"

"Nope." He wiggled his fingers. "Now give me your hand. It helps, I swear."

The plane began taxiing toward the runway and Brandi hastily slipped her hand into his. His skin felt incredibly hot against her chilled fingers. She looked down in surprise.

Sebastian smiled. "Your fingers are like ice."

"It's cold in here." Dumb, to sound so defensive about such a ridiculous thing. But his heat was seeping into her, making her tingle, making her breathless. She tried to moderate herself and take a more reasonable tone. "I can't believe you're so…hot."

Oh, great going, Brandi. Now she'd amused him. She could tell by his slight smile and the teasing glint in his eyes. Still, he didn't provoke her. When he spoke, his words were soft and even. "Most men naturally have a higher body temperature than women. Probably has something to do with muscle density." He flexed his hand, turning it over so that his was on top. "I've always loved a woman's hands. They're small and delicate, but usually pretty damn strong." He squeezed her hand gently. "Yours is nice."

Brandi stared at him. That low rough voice of his could be lethal, and she suspected he knew it. He examined her hand as if he'd never seen one before. All that attention was making her stomach jumpy again, although now, the feeling was somewhat pleasant. "What are you up to?"

He chuckled. "You think I'm trying to seduce you?"

She blanched. He could fluster her with a look, but the things he said... Feeling like a fool, she shrugged. "I don't know. I'm not...used to this sort of thing."

He smiled. "Actually, I was only trying to distract you while the damn plane got off the ground. And it worked, didn't it?"

Stunned, she turned to look out the window, and found only endless black sky. She drew a deep breath and faced him again. "Yes. Thank you."

"Good." He turned to look at her more fully, unhooking his seat belt with one hand and glancing around to make certain no one could hear them. Since most everyone was sleeping, they had some measure of privacy. Brandi released him to undo her own belt, all the while watching the way he moved, the way his shoulders flexed, how his straight dark hair brushed his collar and fell over his brow. She'd never been so intrigued by a man, by his smallest movement or gesture.

She wanted to hold his hand again. In fact, there were other places she wanted to touch him besides his hands. But it could be so risky....

"Now, about seducing you…"

Good lord, it wasn't a topic to discuss. "Sebastian, really, there's absolutely no need…"

"Yes, there is. I want you to understand that I won't pressure you in any way. I know this vacation is set up to be romantic, but it doesn't have to be if that's not what you want. We can do whatever you like. Take walks, play chess, hell, you can tell me to leave you completely alone if that's what you want. But if you decide you want anything from me—"

"I won't!" The protest sounded panicked even to her own ears.

"You'll have to tell me. What we're doing now, talking and getting to know each other, that isn't about sex, okay? It's about getting comfortable with each other. I know you didn't want to come on this trip, but I'm glad you did. So if I do anything or say anything that in any way makes you uneasy, I want you to tell me. Agreed?"

Again, she chewed her lip, then nodded. He was touching on a topic she hadn't expected to have to face. Especially not this soon. Now that he'd brought it up, though, she couldn't help thinking, wondering what *he'd* think if he knew precisely why she'd been so resistant to the vacation.

He wanted her to tell him if she wanted anything? She'd never have the nerve. But now she really wished she did.

SEBASTIAN'S ARM WAS NUMB, but he didn't mind. He liked having her sleep against his side. The limo rode smoothly, the air was quiet and he liked seeing her this way—relaxed, without those impenetrable mental shields to protect her.

He looked down at her, carefully tucked a wayward curl behind her ear, then touched her smooth warm cheek. Being asleep, she didn't jump away or show her displeasure over his touch.

Having her this close was playing havoc with his libido. She had one leg tucked beneath her, so her dress had hiked up, her knees were peeking out at him and he could see a bit of pale thigh. The sight held his attention for a long moment. One of her shoes had fallen off and he pondered how tiny that foot looked next to his own size fourteens. Her foot was slim, high arched... Good grief, he could hardly believe such a thing could arouse him, but there was no denying the stirring of desire.

He was in bad shape when a woman's foot turned him on.

Warm breath bathed his throat as she sighed deeply in her sleep. Her nose touched just below his jaw, her unruly hair tickled his cheek and one small plump breast pressed into his ribs.

The stirring grew until he had a devil of a time ignoring the reactions of his own body. But she was tuckered out, poor little thing, probably as much emotionally as physically, and he had no intention of waking her. The plane ride had been difficult enough; she didn't need to know how much he wanted her. Especially since the feeling didn't appear to be mutual.

They'd only been in the limo for a little over fifteen minutes when she'd passed out. She didn't fade out gradually like most people did. No, when Brandi went to sleep it was like watching someone faint dead away. One minute she'd been sitting stiff at his side and staring out the window at the moon-shadowed scenery, the next she had slumped into him, giving him all of her slight weight.

He wanted to pull her into his lap, to cuddle her...to kiss her. She was by far the most intrinsically sensual woman he'd ever known. And when she suddenly wakened, stretching along his side like a cat and yawning hugely, he couldn't stop himself from giving her a light hug.

Her eyes snapped open and she jerked away from him. Well, he'd expected as much. She was sexy, but she wasn't interested in him.

Sebastian forced a smile. "I hope the nap helped."

"How long have I been sleeping?"

Her eyes were huge, wary, almost accusing. "About forty minutes. We should be at the lodge soon."

She fussed beside him, smoothing down her hair, tugging at the hem of her dress, rubbing her hands together. Watching her made him want her, so he looked away.

"Are you okay?"

The hesitant question had him turning toward her again. "I'm fine. Why?"

"I don't know. You seem...tense."

Tense and aroused and...almost needy. She'd tied him into more knots tonight than he'd ever experienced while growing up dirt-poor. He'd suffered plenty of rejections as a child and he'd grown accustomed to them. But as an adult, he hadn't allowed anyone to make him feel this way. He *gave* assistance, he didn't *need* it.

But now he wanted a woman who didn't want him

back. The idea didn't sit well with his adult pride. So he gave her only a partial truth.

"I'm not comfortable with all this luxury. The first-class tickets, the limo. The money could have been better spent elsewhere."

For once her expression softened and the look she gave him had him struggling for breath. He had to swallow back a groan. The driver of the limo was silent behind his privacy window, set on his course. The shadowy darkness of the car and the quiet of the night only added to the intimacy of the whole enterprise. And if she didn't quit looking at him like that, he'd lose control.

Brandi didn't appear to notice his trouble. "I'm sure our vacation plan is more extravagant than anyone else's. But then that's Shay—extravagant to a fault, especially with the people she loves. I knew the minute she decided to involve me in the trip, she'd take a personal interest. I wouldn't be surprised if everything was top-of-the-line." Then she tilted her head. "Does it really bother you so much? Most people would love to be pampered with a limo and such."

Undecided on how much to tell her, Sebastian hesitated. It was a rather personal topic, and not the easiest thing for him to talk about. But then Brandi touched his wrist and when he looked at her, his entire body tightened.

"It's all right, Sebastian. I didn't mean to pry."

He went down without a whimper. He wanted to talk to her, to gain her trust. And this was as good a place to start as any. Leaning his head back against the soft leather upholstery of the seat, he said, "I grew up poor."

"I see."

He chuckled. "No, you don't. I'm not saying we couldn't afford a new car, I'm saying we barely afforded food. Half the time the electricity was turned off. Back then, hot water was a luxury, and in our neighborhood a peek at a limo would have been considered prime entertainment."

Brandi watched him, comprehension in her wide eyes. "So, wasting money still bothers you?"

"Bothers me? Yeah, it bothers me. I guess I learned to be especially thrifty—I had to, in order to make the food last. Now, even though money isn't an issue with me anymore, squandering it, even if it isn't mine... Well, it makes my stomach cramp. The only thing I've ever been extravagant with is my house. It gives me a kind of security I can't get anywhere else."

He waited for her reaction. He'd never before trusted a woman enough to share those personal thoughts. Admitting to such a weakness might have detracted from the image women had of him, and could have disillusioned anyone.

But Brandi didn't pull away. Instead, she took his hand, entwining her fingers with his. That one small gesture was so full of understanding, so full of giving that he was prompted to go on, knowing that *she* wouldn't be disillusioned by him or his truths. He wasn't certain why he knew that, but he did.

"My mother was incredible, trying so hard to make everything work. But she'd come home so exhausted from the extra hours at below minimum wage that she wouldn't even think of food. I tried to make certain she ate, but there were times when she was just too tired. There were also times when I couldn't find food to offer her."

"What about your father?"

He made a rude sound and Brandi squeezed his fingers. She was a tiny woman, half his size, but she had one hell of a grip—he felt it all the way to his heart.

"My father was a drunken, abusive bastard who only drank up what money my mother did make." He smiled, but it wasn't a nice smile. "He was the same type of man who keeps the women's shelters crowded. He wouldn't work to better his life. Hell, with the way he drank, he couldn't have kept a job even if he'd wanted to. So he was miserable. And rather than work toward fixing things, he'd turn around and…take out his anger on my mother."

"He hit her?" Brandi sounded appalled, but Sebastian had been pulled into his own memories, so he just shrugged. "I can't even count the number of times I got woke up with my father cursing my mother and her crying. It would last for hours."

Brandi sucked in a trembling breath and pulled away from him. He looked down at her, and froze. Her face shone pale in the dark interior of the car and her hands were fisted in her lap. She didn't look merely shocked—she looked livid. Without thinking, Sebastian said, "Damn it, I'm sorry." And he tugged her close. She was stiff, resisting his comfort, but he needed it as much as she did so he didn't loosen his hold.

"I shouldn't have gone on like that. Hell, I don't even think about it all that much anymore, except for the waste of money. Brandi?" He cradled her head between his palms and turned her face up to him. "Are you okay?"

Nodding, she touched his cheek with a trembling hand. But her dark brows were still lowered and she looked almost ferocious. "I'm sorry, Sebastian. You shouldn't have had to go through such an awful thing."

"Me? It was my mother who had to put up with him."

She shook her head. "And you had to worry about both of them, didn't you?" She sniffed past her anger, a single tear glimmering in her eye.

Her reaction seemed extreme to him. Hell, it had happened long ago. He searched her face, but he saw no pity, no revulsion. There was only complete understanding, which confused him more than anything. How could a woman who'd come from a wonderful loving family really understand the coarse existence he had led?

Slowly, she pulled away from him and moved a few inches over on the seat, putting space between them. She gave him an uncertain look when he continued to watch her. "Do you ever see your father now?"

He made a sound, something between a choke and a snort. "Not a chance. Not when I was the one who chased him away."

"You?"

"When I was about twelve, I decided I'd had enough. I waited for my father with a chunk of broken lumber from the building site down the street. I considered it an equalizer. When he reached for my mother that last time, I stopped him."

"Extreme violence when necessary?" Her voice was a soft, gentling whisper.

He shrugged. "I took a few licks myself that day, but since my father had been disgustingly drunk, I doled out more than my fair share, too. And to a man like my father, it just wasn't worth hanging around if he had to take any abuse himself. He knew damn well, from that day on, he'd have to contend with me every time he showed up. So he left. And he never came back."

"But you saved your mother."

That was how Sebastian had consoled himself over the loss of his father, because despite everything, despite how absurd it seemed, he'd had feelings for the man. He had missed him when he'd just disappeared. For a while, it had been difficult, though those feelings had long since faded. "She never mentioned it, never said if she approved or disapproved. But she smiled more often after he'd gone. And knowing I'd managed to make a difference made me feel good too, even when I had an empty belly."

"My father is the most gentle man you'd ever meet," Brandi said softly. "He spoils us all, going overboard on gifts and affection. He can lecture a body crazy, but he'd never raise a hand against a woman in anger."

"You're lucky that your family is like that."

"I've always thought so." Then she said, "You must be very proud of all you've accomplished since then. You've overcome a very tragic background."

"Not all that tragic, and really, not all that different from what a lot of families live through. But it is what helped me decide on my future. And why I have such a successful business now."

"The personal protection agency?"

"Yes." Sebastian was astounded by how incredibly easy it was to talk to Brandi. Already, she knew more about him than most people did. "I decided I needed a job to help out after my father left, even though we were probably better off without buying his booze and with one less mouth to feed. I'd gained most of my height by then and I was street tough, so I hired myself out."

"You belonged to a gang?"

"I was my own gang." He chuckled now, remembering how full of himself he'd been. "I was a teenager, but I thought I was as capable as anyone. If someone needed protection, I supplied it. I was a big kid and I'd learned to be mean the hard way, by necessity. But I was choosy. I worked as a defense, not an offense. I wouldn't attack, only protect. And I made a bundle doing it."

"Sebastian…" She hesitated, but when he waited, she finally said, "It sounds like you learned how to live with the bad, not how to get away from it."

"True. It's called surviving. But I did finally figure that out, though not before a few scrapes with the law and a few near misses with my general well-being. Which is why I joined the service. College was out of the question. I barely made it through high school by the skin of my teeth. I wasn't dumb, just rebellious. And the service was structured enough to get me straightened out."

"It's incredible how you turned your life around."

Startled, he looked down to see Brandi watching him, her blue eyes wide and intense in the darkness, only an occasional streetlight glimmering across her features. His heart still aching with the memories of his painful childhood, he wanted nothing more than to kiss her, to take comfort and give it. But the moment his gaze dropped to her mouth, she stiffened, and once again he accepted the rejection.

This would probably be the longest five days of his life. Brandi didn't want him—might not ever want him—yet every minute with her made him want her more. He felt an affinity with her that he'd never shared with another person. It didn't make sense, not with Brandi so petite and innocent and sweet—so much his opposite. Yet he felt it, because he felt her understanding, her concern, her giving....

Though he'd had lovers and female friends, none of them had affected him this way. Never had anyone gotten past his guard so effortlessly. Sharing so much time with her alone would be a unique form of torture.

He laughed off the discomfort. He really had no choice. "I'm incredible? Now you're starting to sound like Shay."

She grinned. "Heaven forbid."

When she continued to stare at him, her expression curious, he asked, "What?"

"You're such a…big man. I can't quite imagine you as a little kid. Do you look like your mother?"

"No. She was small, like you, but better rounded."

Brandi chuckled. "Shay is always telling me to eat more. But I could gain twenty pounds and still not be rounded, at least not in the right places."

"You're fine just the way you are. Tell Shay to mind her own business."

He'd said it in a teasing tone, but still Brandi looked embarrassed. "I'd like to meet your mother some day. I imagine she's very proud of you."

"She died years ago, Brandi. But my mother was always proud, even when I didn't deserve it. She used to claim I was the only good thing she had to look forward to. Which, when I look back to my misspent youth, is really pretty sad." Then he grinned, just so she wouldn't see how the topic affected him—how she affected him. "It's a parent's duty to be proud, no matter how you screw up."

In a voice so low he almost couldn't hear her, she said, "My parents haven't always been proud of me."

He stared at her profile, at her downcast expression, and frowned. "That can't be true. You've just said how your father dotes on you, and Shay brags about your mother all the time. They love you a lot."

"Yes, they do. But I've made some pretty terrible mistakes."

He wanted to know what kind of mistakes she was referring to. He couldn't imagine Brandi doing anything irresponsible or reckless. She didn't seem the type. But he also wanted her to confide in him freely. So he didn't ask. His job had taught him patience, especially with women, and he knew that if he bided his time, if he let her get to know him, she'd learn to be more comfortable with him.

She wouldn't look at him, and he had to cup her chin to turn her face up to him. "We all make mistakes, honey. That's part of being human."

"I can't…." She hesitated, not another word forthcoming.

Sebastian gave her a small smile. "It's okay. No pressure, remember?"

She drew a deep breath, then blurted, "I shouldn't be here. You should have had this vacation with another woman. It was unfair of Shay to foist me off on you like this. But it's not too late. Maybe we could—"

"Brandi." She went still as a stone, then blinked up at him. "I didn't want to be here with anyone else. I wanted to be here with you."

"But you don't understand."

"Understand what?" His temper frayed a bit and he struggled to control it. "That you're not interested in getting cozy with me? Believe me, I've figured that out already. And it's okay. I'm still enjoying your company."

"I fell asleep!"

"You were tired. I didn't mind."

"It was rude," she grumbled.

His sigh was long and loud. "Do you realize I've told you more about myself than any of my friends even know?" Her eyes widened. "I don't know why, damn it, I just felt like talking. You listened, so you've heard it all."

"I'm glad."

"And I'm glad you're here with me." He squeezed her shoulder. "We'll make the best of it, okay?"

She drew another deep breath, something she seemed to do when she was nervous, then let it out in a sigh. She peeked at him, her gaze hesitant. "I...I wanted to come. I really did."

"But?"

"I'm just not ready to do this."

He didn't know what *this* was, but several things came to mind. She might be in love with someone else. She might have had her heart broken, or maybe she wanted someone more influential, someone with her background. He didn't care. Whatever the obstacle, he'd overcome it somehow.

He'd been in his business long enough to know what appeared on the surface wasn't always the reality. Brandi seemed like such an enigma—bossy yet sweet, confident yet sometimes unsure. He had five days to learn more about her, to figure her out, and he was looking forward to every minute of it.

He smiled. "Are you forgetting you're in charge of this trip? We do what you want, when you want and how you want."

"I just… I don't like taking chances."

He didn't understand that, either, but it didn't matter, not at this moment. "I think you're ready to take a chance. A small chance," he added, just so she wouldn't stiffen up on him again. "With me."

"That's a rather arrogant assumption, isn't it?"

Of course it was, but he wouldn't admit it. "You know what I keep remembering, what I'll probably remember until I'm old and gray? The way you looked at me while I was on that damn stage. No woman has ever looked at me like that before. I liked it. A lot."

Just as he suspected, her spine snapped straight and her brows came down. But then the driver made a sudden sharp turn that threw her off balance and slammed her up against his side. Where she belonged.

Trying to ignore that vagrant observation, Sebastian slipped an arm around her and held her closer still. Before Brandi could slither away, the driver lowered the divider window. In serious tones meant to impress, he announced that they had arrived at the resort.

Sebastian grinned down at Brandi, seeing that she was flustered and embarrassed and, if he didn't miss his guess, a little excited by their close contact. "So, boss. Are you ready to take charge?"

She narrowed her eyes, not willing to give him the upper hand, even with his teasing. She lifted her small chin and treated him to her direct gaze. "I'm more than ready. I'm…anxious."

"Lord, help me." Sebastian felt his smile slip, but he covered his reaction quickly. "All right, then. Let the vacation begin."

CHAPTER FOUR

SEBASTIAN COULD TELL Brandi loved the opulence of the "cabin" they'd been directed to. But he felt almost rigid with uneasiness. It appeared to be a damn honeymoon retreat, sinfully extravagant and seductive.

The limo had dropped them off at the main lodge where they'd been preregistered. The desk clerk gave them a key and a flashlight then pointed them to a narrow trail that led through the woods, explaining that their luggage would be brought around shortly. A rental car was at their disposal, but wasn't needed to reach the cabin.

Sebastian had held her hand as they walked through the darkened wood, the flashlight beam bouncing off thick trees and rocks. Brandi hadn't said a word. She'd been quiet, introspective, her fingers cold in his grip. But as soon as the cabin came into sight, he'd felt her enthusiasm.

He didn't want to dampen that enthusiasm. It was the first time he'd seen her so excited, and she looked beautiful, her smile wide, her eyes bright in the darkness. Even her wild curls seemed to bounce with energy.

How anyone could call the small rustic house a cabin was beyond him. Set off alone in the woods, it provided picturesque privacy. A floodlight had been left on in front and Sebastian could see an angular deck filled with lavish, well-padded patio furniture. The front room had a skylight over the entrance door and rough quarry stone for a fireplace filled the adjacent outside wall.

With Brandi practically dancing beside him, he had no choice but to unlock the door and step inside.

"It's perfect!"

"It's too much." His grim tone must have reached her, because she swatted his arm.

"None of that now. I know how you must feel, but let's try to enjoy ourselves, all right? After all, Shay went to all this trouble."

But to what end? Without an ounce of subtlety, Shay had dropped them into a honeymoon suite, that's what she'd done. Sebastian kept the thought to himself. Brandi was still skittish with him and he didn't want to damage the fragile bond they'd forged. But how in hell was he supposed to survive this? Every male hormone in his body had been on red alert since he'd first seen her. The ambiance of the damn cabin would only heighten the feeling.

Brandi had already hustled off, peeking into every room and inspecting every corner. "There's a water bed in one of the bedrooms, with a private bath!"

Sebastian was still looking around the front room, but despite himself, her awe brought on a small smile. It had been a long time since he'd been able to feel any passion over needlessly blowing money. With Brandi, all he *did* feel was passion. "Why don't you use that room?"

She stuck her head out the doorway and grinned at him. "I think I will, but only because the other bedroom has a king-size bed." Her gaze dipped over his long frame and she cocked one eyebrow. "That'll suit you just fine, I'm sure."

She disappeared again, this time through the kitchen and after a moment, he heard, "There's a hot tub in the back on an enclosed deck!"

Erotic thoughts and images of warm water and nude female flesh—Brandi's flesh—immediately came to mind. Sebastian had to swallow, and even then, his voice sounded uneven…and very hopeful. "Would you like to unpack and try it out?"

Silence. Brandi came slinking back through the kitchen with her head down and her hands gripped together at her waist. "Um, not tonight. It's late and I'm really tired."

She didn't look at him. Sebastian watched her wrestle with her indecision then finally pry her hands apart in an effort to relax. With a sigh of resignation, he accepted that the Jacuzzi was out for a while. "Maybe tomorrow, then." He stretched, trying to unknot his own muscles with Brandi watching his every move. She jumped when a knock sounded at the door.

"Our luggage." Opening his wallet to retrieve a tip, he said over his shoulder, "Why don't you see what the kitchen has in stock while I carry in our bags? I could use a bite to eat."

But after he'd put the last piece of luggage in the bedrooms—trying his best not to look at the bed Brandi would sleep in—he found her reading a room service menu that had been left on the small dining table. Frowning, he asked, "The kitchen's not stocked?"

Brandi waved a hand. "There's food in there. But I don't feel like cooking. Let's just order something."

He took the menu from her hand and then whistled at the prices. "You've got to be kidding. I could eat a week off what they charge. Besides, it's after midnight. Do you really think they'll serve this late?"

"Well, maybe not. But if it's the money, I can…"

"No. Absolutely not." Appalled by what she'd been about to suggest, Sebastian added, "I can damn well afford it if we decide to order in. It just seems ridiculous to pay those prices if there's food here."

"But cooking is so much trouble. And as you said, it's after midnight."

Without really meaning to, he touched a knuckle to her soft, warm cheek. "You do look exhausted. Why don't you go get ready for bed and I'll get the food together?"

It was probably to escape his touch as much from weariness that she agreed so quickly. "If you're sure you don't mind."

She was already on her feet and heading out, so he chuckled. "I don't mind at all."

He wanted her to leave, before she noticed how she affected him. He was half-hard just thinking of her getting ready for bed, wondering what she'd wear, if she'd shower first.

He heard the water pipes hum and had his answer. It took him several moments before he could get his feet to move, and then he went to rummage in the kitchen cabinets. He found canned soup and crackers and cheese. He also found champagne and knew Shay had struck once again. He would definitely have to speak to her about this propensity she had for wasting money.

After putting the soup on to simmer and slicing a few chunks of cheese, he went back to the living room to start a fire. The cabin was set up in an airy, open way. The living room, tiny dining room and kitchen were all open to each other with two bedrooms at the back of the house. Brandi's bedroom had its own bath, with another full bath at the end of the hall between the rooms.

The ceilings were cathedral with raw wood beams, the floors polished pine with scattered handwoven rugs. A thick cushioned couch and two matching chairs faced the fireplace on one wall, the entertainment center on the other. Ignoring the television and VCR, Sebastian turned on the stereo and found a soft music station.

There was wood already laid in the fireplace and he had a fire blazing in no time. It took the small nip out of the late spring air and added a certain ambiance that belonged in the cabin. The darkness outside was endless. With the floodlights turned off, not even the woods were visible. Inside, the smell of soup and wood smoke scented the air. It was as if they were sealed in together, isolated from the rest of the world, intimate.

He found himself appreciating the cabin, rather than resenting it, because it afforded him the time alone with Brandi that he needed.

Already his stomach was knotting at the thought of the night to come. He would be alone with a woman he wanted more than he could ever recall wanting anyone or anything, yet she froze at his every touch. He had to find a way to breach her reserve, but he didn't know how. One minute she seemed interested, the next repelled. Somehow both reactions only increased his determination to reach her.

When he stood and brushed off his hands, his peripheral vision caught a smidge of white and he turned.

Brandi stood there, looking uncertain and damp and so incredibly sexy he couldn't help but react. If she'd been any other woman, he'd have gone to her, picked her up and carried into the nearest bedroom. He could have spent hours making love to her, alternating between the tenderness she instilled and the hot, primal urges that kept surging through him. He could envision their lovemaking as wild and hard, but also sweet and easy. Either way would do a lot toward satisfying the gnawing need in his gut.

But this was Brandi, and he wanted some kind of emotional commitment from her as much as the physical release. It had never mattered to him before, but then, he'd never met anyone like her. Somehow with her sweetness and caring, she'd gotten under his skin, and the thought of sex without emotion wasn't appealing.

He wanted her. All of her.

He had five days, so he'd be patient—no matter how his body rebelled at the thought. He was a tactician, one of the best. His skill had been honed in the service and on his job. He could ruthlessly plan her surrender with great skill, and she wouldn't know what was happening until it was too late.

But for now, if she noticed the force of his erection and the taut way he barely managed to hold on to his control, she'd find a fast plane back to Jackson.

He cleared his throat. "The soup should be ready in just a minute."

She fidgeted with the belt to her thick white robe. It shouldn't have looked so damn sexy, but it did. Terry cloth covered her from her neck, where she had the lapels folded over so not a hint of skin showed, to the tops of her bare feet. He had no idea what she wore underneath, and that fact almost made him crazy.

She'd washed her hair. The damp curls weren't quite as unruly as before, but somehow, with the small curls clinging to her cheeks and forehead, she looked even more enticing. She'd belted the robe tightly and he could see how tiny her waist was, but other than that, not a single curve showed through the thick material. She still hadn't said anything and he stumbled through more awkward conversation.

"You should have something on your feet. It's a little chilly in here."

"There weren't any slippers in my luggage. Whoever packed must have forgotten."

Her voice sounded strained, breathless, and he stared again, unable to help himself.

"Sebastian?"

"I'll get you a pair of my socks." He left the room, knowing if he stood there a second longer, he'd give himself away. Not even Brandi could have missed the way the material of his khaki slacks strained over his zipper. No female had ever had such a profound effect on him. He felt as though he'd been involved in heavy foreplay for an hour. And all she'd done was change into a robe. A robe for bed. A water bed.

He rubbed the back of his neck and cursed.

When he came back with the socks, his libido somewhat under control, Brandi was stirring the soup. He watched for a moment, appreciating the way her hips moved in cadence with her hand. Barbarian that he admittedly was, he found something intrinsically appealing at the sight of a woman in her bathrobe, barefoot, at the stove. He grinned at the thought. The female population of Jackson would string him up if they could read his mind right then.

Almost in silence, he handed her the socks and while she tugged them on he found a tray. He poured the soup into bowls, added the crackers and cheese while Brandi found two sodas in the fridge. He was grateful she'd ignored the champagne.

They carried the whole thing into the living room. Brandi settled herself on the floor in front of the fire, so Sebastian did the same. He was content just to watch her, the way she tucked her slim legs beneath her, how she fluffed her drying hair. She seemed very introspective, her thoughts deep as she started on her soup without comment. After a few minutes, she looked at him.

"This is great. Thanks. Much better than waiting on room service."

Sebastian only nodded, so turned on he couldn't think of a reply. Soon he'd be demented with lust, he thought.

She bit her lip, then went on. "I've never done this before. I'm sorry if I'm not being very good company." Her cheeks turned red and she bit her lip again. "I...I have no idea what we're supposed to talk about."

"We don't have to talk about anything." Ignoring his strangled tone, he set his nearly empty soup bowl aside. "Brandi, I want you to be comfortable, remember? You're calling the shots this trip. If you want to just sit quietly, that's fine."

She too set her bowl back on the tray. "It's not that.

I mean, I want to talk to you. But…have you ever done this before?"

"This?" His heartbeat picked up rhythm, pumping warm blood to places that already felt too full.

"You know. Sitting alone with a woman in a private place. Eating in front of the fire. Struggling for conversation."

"With the woman in her bedclothes? No, I've never done this before. At least, not when we planned to go to two separate bedrooms. This cabin…"

"I know you don't like it."

"I like it fine. It's just that it's meant as a lovers' retreat." He didn't mention the amount of money it probably cost. That issue was secondary to how he felt right now.

He tried to see her face, to read her eyes, but she kept her gaze averted. "Brandi, I can't pretend I don't want you." His low, husky tone grabbed her full attention. Her head swung around, her expression bordering on shock.

"Damn it." Sebastian stood, then paced a few feet away. When he turned to Brandi again, she looked… almost fearful. He dropped to his knees beside her and tried to ignore the way she cowered back from him. "I'm sorry. Honey, you have to know how difficult this is for me. You don't seem to realize it, but you're a very sexy woman."

"I am not!"

"Yes, you are." He smiled now, some of his frustration giving way to amusement. "And here we are alone, in this love pit."

She raised her brows and a smile hovered on her lips as she, too, started to relax. "Love pit?"

"The water bed? The Jacuzzi? The fireplace? This cabin is meant to seduce. Only I know that's not what you want. And I gave you my word not to pressure you."

"And you always keep your word?" When he nodded, she asked, "I'm the one in charge, right?"

He swallowed, not certain where she was going with her reasoning, but he had a few hopeful ideas. So did his body. "Absolutely."

Her cheeks heated more, and once again her small teeth sank into her bottom lip while she peeked up at him. He wanted those sharp white teeth on him, wanted to soothe her lips himself. Then finally she straightened and looked determined. His thighs tightened in expectation. "All right. I'm in charge. And right now, I think I'd like a kiss."

After making that bold statement, which seemed to take all her nerve, she lowered her lashes and whispered, "That is, if you wouldn't mind? I mean, I know that probably wasn't part of your original agreement, but..."

Sebastian's brain felt like mush but his body was granite hard. He wasn't at all sure he'd heard her right. "A kiss?"

"If you would."

He would all right. Gladly. Even if it killed him, which it just might because a kiss was a far cry from what he wanted, from what he needed right now.

Watching her face for any sign of retreat, he whispered, "There's kisses, and then there's kisses. The kind you want may not be the kind I'm wanting to give you. Why don't you be more specific so I don't screw this up?"

With her fingertip, Brandi drew an idle design over

the rug. She peeked up at him, then away again. "Why don't you just start with the one you think I want…then maybe we can try the one you want to give me?"

BRANDI WAITED, holding her breath, while Sebastian apparently considered her suggestion. He scooted closer and her heartbeat raced with a mixture of dread and excitement. She really wanted to enjoy his kiss and, so far, the only fear she felt was that she might make a fool of herself. The possibility always existed, and she didn't think she could bear it if—

His fingertips touched her jaw, suspending all thought. Gently, he tipped up her chin and her vision was filled by him, the heat in his gaze, the tautness of his expression. Gentleness seemed a part of him, incongruous with his obvious strength, his massive size. The contrasts had intrigued her from the start. She could easily picture him defending a person with lethal skill, then soothing that person with his quiet, sure manner.

It was almost impossible not to trust him, because his power was tempered by genuine caring. All his life, he'd been taking care of others. Brandi wanted to take care of him. She just wasn't sure she knew how.

His eyes closed and hers closed, as well, as she waited breathlessly for his kiss. Then she felt it, the brief, heated touch of his mouth on her own. His breath fanned her cheek, and his lips moved the smallest bit, coasting over hers, teasing.

She wanted to touch him, to put her hands on that broad hard chest, but she was afraid. Afraid of failure, afraid of how he might react. Afraid of how she might react.

Slowly he pulled away, just enough to put space

between them but not enough that she couldn't feel him, his nearness, his heat. Her eyes opened and she saw him watching her, his gaze intent and probing. She swallowed. Her heartbeat knocked against her ribs and there was a queer little tingle in the pit of her stomach, stirred by his hot musky scent. She started to speak, but he laid a finger over her lips.

"That was the kiss you wanted."

Feeling numb, Brandi nodded.

"Do you want to go on?"

It was the sound of his voice that decided her. Rough and grating, like a man on the edge of control. She licked her lips and accidently touched his finger. His expression hardened even more, and before she could deny him, before she had to stumble her way though an explanation she couldn't give, he pulled back.

"No. I don't think we should play this game any more. At least not right now. You might be ready for it, but I don't think I am."

His comment about games distracted her from her worries, so that even though he'd given her an out, she said, "I thought it was my decision to make. I'm the one in charge, remember?"

"I have no intention of forgetting." Then his thick dark lashes lowered and he looked at her through slumberous eyes. "In fact, since you're the one in charge, why don't you do the kissing? Then we'll both know for certain that you're getting exactly what you want."

The idea fascinated her. Sebastian leaned back until his shoulders were braced against the sofa. He stretched out his long muscled legs and crossed his ankles, then folded his arms over his chest. He looked negligent and at his ease—not in any way a threat. Except for his eyes. They shone with heat, the green bright and excited. But instead of fear, Brandi was suffused by her first dose of feminine power.

Rising to her knees, she said, "Don't move."

His jaw hardened, but he nodded. His eyes never left her.

She inched closer, watching him, but he remained in his contained pose. Carefully she placed her palms on his shoulders. He felt so hard, like warm, smooth stone. The muscles bunched beneath her fingers and she dug in just a little, like a cat testing the texture of his body, but there was almost no resilience here. The man was simply hard all over.

He made a small sound, but stayed completely still. Brandi stared at his mouth. The slight growth of whiskers there looked sexy to her, and she wanted to touch his skin, to taste him and luxuriate in his scent. She hadn't known a man could smell so delicious. Instead, feeling like a coward, she leaned down and placed a hard, quick peck on his mouth, then looked to see his reaction.

"That isn't what you wanted, Brandi. Is it?"

Oh, that husky voice, thick with desire, challenging her. Shivering with reaction, she leaned down again. This time she let her mouth linger, each move calculated. Until she forgot what she was doing, until the heady scent of him filled her and she felt drunk and anxious and hot. His tongue came out to glide along her bottom lip and he made a rough sound of pleasure. Brandi gasped. He used that second to lick inside her lips, to explore the edge of her teeth. He kept his hands and body still. Nothing moved except for his mouth, which now slanted against hers.

Brandi leaned a little more heavily into him and he groaned.

Just that quickly, she remembered herself and jerked away. Good grief, she hadn't meant for things to go so far. She'd only wanted to try a simple kiss. But when she saw how dark Sebastian's cheeks had become, how hard his jaw looked, the fierce green of his eyes, she knew she'd gone too far.

She came to her feet in a rush. Still he didn't move, he only watched her. And waited. "I'm sorry. I...I should go on to bed now."

With his arms still crossed over his chest, he slowly nodded. In a slow, deep whisper, he said, "Good night, Brandi."

"I..." She wanted to explain, to try to make him understand.

With a leisurely thoroughness that had her stomach doing flips, his gaze moved over her, and he said, "It's all right. You don't have to say anything."

He shifted slightly, uncrossing his ankles and parting them just a bit. Her gaze was drawn downward. She couldn't miss the sight of his bold erection, pressing taut against his slacks. That part of him looked huge and hard, in concordance with the rest of his big body. Heat washed over her, both from embarrassment and excitement. It seemed impossible to breathe, looking at the length of him, his size. Her lips parted, but no words came out.

She could hear the masculine amusement in his next words. "Like I said, you're a very sexy lady. And I'm not exactly immune."

Brandi gulped. "Good night, Sebastian."

She rushed from the room, but when she peeked back over her shoulder at him, it was to see his head dropped back on the cushions of the couch, one forearm over his eyes. He looked like a man in pain. Or in desperate need.

She didn't like herself for it, but a small kernel of satisfaction swelled inside her. A man like Sebastian…and he wanted her. She had kissed him. She had touched him. She was on her way to a full recovery.

Maybe this vacation wouldn't be so bad after all.

"DO YOU HAVE to buy every damn thing you see?"

Brandi tried to hide her grin as she listened to Sebastian's continual grumping. She'd slept like the dead last night, content with her progress, with her new experimentation. But evidently Sebastian hadn't slept much at all. He looked tired today and his mood could only be described as grouchy.

"You don't like the horse? I think he's kind of cute."

"The damn thing looks ridiculous. The head is too big, and the color is ludicrous. You paid way too much for it."

"It's a souvenir. Of course it cost more than it should."

He made a sound of exasperation, then eyed her shopping bag. "At the marina this morning you bought fake fish, then at the breakfast inn you bought two milkmaid dolls."

"Two very cute milkmaid dolls," she corrected. "And I've had a great time today, Sebastian. Even though it was still a little cold on the lake this morning, I enjoyed the rowboat. I couldn't believe what horrible beggars those big carp were." She knew her gratitude would only annoy him more. Each and every time she thanked him, he frowned.

"This is supposed to be your vacation, Brandi. You're supposed to have a good time."

"And I am. Especially with the shopping." It was the truth, but she had an ulterior motive, also. Since Sebastian was helping her without even realizing it, she wanted to help him, too. She hoped to get him to loosen up a little about money. Like Sebastian, she didn't believe in squandering her cash, but neither did she enjoy putting herself on a shoestring budget, not when she could afford better. Sebastian simply wasn't used to putting his own needs and desires first; his life centered around helping others. It was past time he gave himself some happiness.

"What the hell are you going to do with all that junk, anyway?"

It hadn't been easy, but Brandi had managed to convince him to go shopping along the main strip with her after breakfast. She'd been forced to resort to coercion, reminding him that she was in charge. He'd given in with little grace, and now they'd been at it for hours, not even stopping for lunch.

She'd hoped he'd get into the spirit of it, but obviously the man did not like to shop. He had no appreciation for the many quaint little speciality stores. Brandi, on the other hand, had bought something from almost every shop.

It had rained first thing in the morning, but now the sun was out and shining brightly and the day seemed beautiful to her, though it still wasn't overly warm. She was comfortable in a long denim skirt and loose navy blue sweater. Sebastian wore jeans and another polo shirt, this one dark gray. He looked very handsome, if a bit surly.

Still, even with his attitude turned sour, he was a perfect gentleman. Every time she left a shop, Sebastian took her hand. He protected her from the flow of human traffic and steered her around mud puddles. It felt right to have him so close, to feel his warmth and strength.

"If you must know, I want to take a gift back to each of the kids at the shelter. They get so few presents."

She said it carelessly, but still he looked dumbstruck, then shamefaced. "Damn it. I'm sorry." He rubbed his eyes with his free hand, then sighed. "I know I'm being a bastard today, but I didn't get much sleep last night. How 'bout a cup of coffee? The caffeine will do me good, and your feet have got to be getting tired."

Actually, she felt fine, but he looked ready to drop, so she took mercy on him. "I only have two more gifts to buy. Why don't you go for your coffee and I'll meet you there in a few minutes."

His hand tightened on hers. "I can go with you. I should probably pick up something for the kids, too. I just hadn't thought about it."

Her heart softened and the urge to hug him close almost overwhelmed her. "It's not necessary, Sebastian. I already have plenty of gifts." He didn't look convinced, so she added, "Look, right there on the corner is a café. I'll hit this last shop, grab a few more gifts and then join you. Give me fifteen minutes."

He still hesitated, probably because she tended to spend closer to forty-five minutes in each shop, but she gave him a look of insistence. "Go. I order you. And I'm the boss, remember? Guzzle coffee. Wake yourself up."

Finally he nodded and turned away. She watched until he'd crossed the street and disappeared into the crowd. This vacation was turning out to be a revelation. For such a long time, she'd hidden behind her independence and privacy, never wanting anyone to invade her space, to get too close and ponder her thoughts. But now, she already missed having Sebastian at her side.

It filled her with warmth to think of him, which she did. The whole time she considered small collectibles from the souvenir shop, part of her mind was on Sebastian. Their kiss last night had probably not meant much to him, but to her it had been an accomplishment, a giant step forward. Not since she was eighteen had she kissed a man, or even wanted to. The thought had been nothing less than repellent, the memories stored with it, horrifying. But there was nothing repellent about Sebastian Sinclair. The man could make her tremble with just a look.

With her mind half on her newest purchases, and half on getting back to Sebastian, it was no wonder she almost ran into the men. When she finally did see them, it was too late to step out of their way. Within a second, the two of them had crowded her into the store's brick front.

Brandi felt the visceral panic swell, but she fought it back. They were on a busy street. No harm could come to her. Still, as one of the men gave a long, low whistle, she jerked back, memories assailing her. Both men laughed.

One of them gave her a genuine smile. "You look like you could use some help with that big shopping bag, honey. Why don't I give you a lift to wherever you're going? Or better yet, to where we're going. What do you say?"

She tried to answer, but no words would come, not even a denial. The men were too close, towering over her.

The other one stepped closer still. "She doesn't want you, Josh. Why not give me a chance?" Then he gave her a wide grin. "How about it, sweetheart? You up for a little fun?"

She shook her head, hating her cowardice, the gnawing fear. The first man frowned, looking concerned and he reached for her. She bolted. Feeling foolish even as her legs stretched out, she raced toward the street, her shopping bag clutched to her middle. She heard the men give a surprised burst of laughter at her mad dash, and tears stung her eyes. Frantically, she searched for Sebastian, but didn't see him, which made the panic even worse.

When someone took her arm from behind, she started to scream, but the sound was cut off as she was whipped around and both arms grabbed in a tight hold. "What the hell is the matter with you? What's happened?"

Sebastian. Brandi threw herself against his familiar strength, uncaring that they were drawing notice, or that he might feel her violent trembling. She clung tight to him as she tried to shake the fear. Rather than asking questions, he held her close until she calmed. Several minutes passed in complete silence except for her racing breaths. Sebastian's big hands smoothed up and down her back, and twice she felt the light touch of a kiss to her temple. When she lifted her face from his chest, he surveyed her, then with a grim look, said, "Come on," and started them down the street, his arm tight around her waist. She went with him gladly, not even protesting when he pried her shopping bag out of her numb fingers to carry it for her.

Taking them slightly off the main drag, he urged her toward a low stone fence and then lifted her up to sit. Pink-and-white azaleas bloomed all around them, their sweet scent heady in the air. Sebastian stood in front of her, his legs braced apart, his expression enigmatic. "Tell me what happened, Brandi."

Oh, God, she couldn't. She closed her eyes and shook her head. Sebastian stepped forward until her knees brushed against the front of his body. She didn't dare look down to see exactly where they touched.

"Brandi, you're as pale a ghost."

"And every bit as vapid," she said in disgust.

"You want to tell me what that means?"

"Not particularly." She'd acted the fool, once again. She might as well have been eighteen again, the fear had come back that strong. She was ridiculous and stupid and...

"Brandi? Talk to me, honey, right now. I don't like this one damn bit."

She could hear the genuine concern in his words. Reaching out, she took his hands and held them. "I'm sorry. I overreacted, that's all. Sometimes I can be very silly and foolish."

"Overreacted to what?"

Uh-oh. He sounded ready to do bodily harm to someone. Eight years of military training and hardness sounded in his tone. The barbarian warrior was back.

But no real harm had been done. The men hadn't

even been all that brazen. "It's nothing, really. Two men got a little friendly, that's all. And I…well, it frightened me just a bit. I behaved like an idiot, running off like I did."

He didn't look convinced, but he did correct her. "You didn't run off. You ran to me."

"Well…yeah, I guess I did."

"You felt safer with me."

"I know you, for crying out loud! I didn't know these men. Don't make more of it than it is."

"What did they say to you?"

Now that she was away from them and the panic had ebbed, she couldn't bear to repeat it all. "They were just two men flirting the way men do. They said a few things, and I should have answered them, to put them in their place. But instead, I just ran off."

"To me."

Brandi rolled her eyes. He did seem to be stuck on that small fact. "Yes, to you. Did you expect me to run all the way back to the cabin?"

"I didn't expect you to be running at all or I never would have left you alone. It didn't feel right in the first place. I was just coming to get you when I saw you dashing across the street."

Needing desperately to change the subject, she asked, "Did you get your coffee?"

"No. I saw a sign for an outdoor musical and thought that would work as good as caffeine to wake me up. You want to go? We could grab a hamburger or something there for dinner."

Surprised, Brandi checked her watch. It was going on five o'clock. The morning and afternoon had flown by and they hadn't eaten since breakfast. The idea of an outdoor concert was appealing, but she preferred the privacy of the cabin for dinner. "We can check out the concert, but there's no way I'm going to eat a greasy hamburger. I want real food tonight."

"Fair enough. How about an hour or so of music, then you can pick the restaurant we eat at?"

"No restaurant. I want to go back to the cabin and order room service."

At first, Sebastian didn't answer her. Brandi knew how he felt about the expensive meals the lodge offered, but she needed some privacy tonight, away from the crowds. And she wanted to teach him to take pleasure in the small things, even when they cost a bit more. She half expected an argument from him, especially given his earlier contentious mood. But then he took a deep breath and asked, "Did anyone pack you a swimsuit?"

"I think so. Why?"

"Yesterday you showed some interest in the Jacuzzi." His gaze dropped to her mouth and stayed there. "I thought maybe after dinner you'd want to try it out. It might help to relax you."

Heat uncurled, chasing away the last remnants of embarrassment over her flight of terror. "Do you have a swimsuit?"

"No. But I can just wear my briefs." His gaze held hers, his eyes bright. "As long as you don't have a problem with it."

Brandi knew in that instant exactly where her knees touched him. She felt his body stir, felt his erection grow hard and long and knew it was the thought of being with her that affected him so strongly. But she was

in charge. She could do this—play in the Jacuzzi,
indulge in the special feeling of being alone with him—
with no fear of being pushed and no fear of consequences.

She called all the shots, and she trusted him to abide
by her rules.

Knowing he expected her to refuse, or to at least
look shocked, she lifted her chin and nodded. "All right.
We can try out the Jacuzzi. But dinner first."

Though his expression didn't change, she saw him
draw a deep breath. He lifted her from the wall, then
stood there looking down at her. "What the hell? I think
I'll need to restore my energy with a good meal anyway."

CHAPTER FIVE

WAITING THROUGH THE concert had just about killed him.

Sitting in the grass with Brandi at his side, her body swaying in time to the music, was enough to make him crazy. But what played even more havoc with his male libido was the memory of how she'd run to him. Whatever had frightened her—and he had no doubt there was more to it than she claimed—she'd run to him. Even though she hadn't trusted him enough to share the whole truth, it still had to be counted as progress. No wonder his mood was uncertain today. She kept throwing him off balance. It had all started with that kiss last night, a sweet little kiss that had kept him awake tossing and turning until the early morning. Since then he hadn't been able to get his thoughts gathered.

Something had happened during that brief, all too innocent kiss. And it had to do with Brandi taking control. He'd suggested it as lark, hoping to encourage her. But it had gone beyond that. Somehow, they'd crossed some invisible boundary. He only wished he knew what it was.

Waiting through the concert had been torture enough, but compared to that, dinner was the Spanish

Inquisition. He hadn't even found the wit to complain about the damn T-bone steaks Brandi ordered, steaks that had cost enough to feed a family of four. When she finally leaned back in her seat and pronounced herself finished, he pushed away the rest of his uneaten steak and offered to do the dishes.

She shyly looked away. "No, you did the dishes last night after I went to bed. It's my turn."

He'd taken care of cleaning up and banking the fire just to give himself something to do. But it hadn't worked. He'd still wanted her so much sleep wouldn't come. All because of that one simple but explosive kiss.

He didn't argue with her now, not when he had other things to accomplish. "Fine. You can do the dishes and I'll go take the cover off the Jacuzzi."

Brandi came to her feet, wringing her hands. "You don't think anyone could see us out there, do you?"

"This cabin's pretty isolated. And there's no one around, but we can leave the lights off if you want."

"No!" She blinked, then collected her control. "That is, I like the lights on. Maybe just a few dim ones."

More secrets for him to try to decipher. But he could be patient when the end result was worth it, and this was definitely worth it. "I saw some candles in the cupboard. Will candlelight do?"

Nodding, she whispered, "Yes, that would be fine. Thank you."

He smiled at her formality, then couldn't help but touch her. His fingers drifted over her cheek, then catching one curl and tugging lightly. "Hurry and change into your suit. I'll wait for you in the Jacuzzi."

She looked relieved that she wouldn't have to face

him under the bright fluorescent lighting of the kitchen. The truth was, he'd been thinking of himself. Already, his body was anxious for the sight of her. Being in the water was more to preserve his modesty than hers.

He grabbed three fat candles from the shelf and a pack of matches. Brandi already had the two dishes scraped and returned to the basket they'd come in. All she had to do was place them back on the front porch to be picked up later. She glanced at Sebastian, her blue eyes dark with uncertainty, then smiled and left the kitchen. He went outside to get things set up.

And hopefully to get himself under control.

Fifteen minutes later, while he impatiently waited for Brandi, he realized no amount of warm churning water could ease him. His muscles felt restricted and he hummed with tension. His breathing was thick, his arousal complete. All it would take would be one small smile from her and he'd be a goner. He tilted his head back and stared up at the stars through the glass roof of the enclosed patio. Muted candlelight flickered around the deck, casting a warm mellow glow over the water… over him. But he was far from mellow.

He should have given in and taken care of his need last night. Lying in his bed, he'd given it serious thought. But finding satisfaction without Brandi hadn't seemed right. He didn't want to revert back to the tactics of his youth. He wanted Brandi—over him, under him—any way at all.

He heard a soft sound and his body hardened even more. He was so painfully erect, he hurt. The caress of the bubbling water only served to arouse him more, not ease him. Slowly, he shifted his gaze from the stars to the deck, searching out Brandi's slight silhouette. She stood facing the Jacuzzi, her body curiously still, feet together, hands at her sides. Her skin shone white against the darkness of the early-evening sky and the black of her one-piece swimsuit. She was so tiny, so female. Her curves weren't voluptuous, but they were there, and all the more enticing for being so subtle. Her hips were narrow, only slightly rounded, her legs slim. He saw her tremble and he gave her a smile.

He didn't say a word, only held out a hand. After a long hesitation, Brandi took it. Once she'd stepped down into the water, she released his hand and moved away from him to the other side of the tub. She slowly sank into the warm water, finding the bench that circled the tub. He heard her soft sigh as the heat enveloped her.

Silence dragged on, then Sebastian levered himself up and over to her. Without asking, he positioned himself close beside her. The water sloshed around them before settling into a froth again. Brandi glanced up at him, then whispered, "Sebastian?"

"I'd like to kiss you again." The rough, aroused gravel of his voice didn't embarrass him. He wanted her, and he didn't mind her knowing it.

Brandi dragged her fingers through the water, not looking at him. "I kissed you, remember?"

He smiled, though it pained him to do so. "Will you kiss me again?"

"Will you move?"

Frowning, he asked, "You want me to move away from you?" He didn't understand her, but he wanted to. And this was her show. Much as he'd have liked to call the shots, he was leaving it all up to her.

She still hadn't looked at him, but he caught her chin and lifted her face. "Talk to me, honey. If you don't tell me what you want, what you need, then I can't know. And I want to make you happy."

He felt her sigh, felt her scoot a few inches away from him. The candles afforded enough light for him to see her face, her eyes wide, her lips slightly parted. She looked uneasy, undecided. "Brandi?"

"I want to kiss you," she whispered, her low voice filled with embarrassment…and maybe some excitement. "But I don't want you to touch me."

He searched her face, trying to glean the meaning behind her words. Maybe she was just into control. If she wanted to play sex games, he was more than willing. But he had to know the rules.

When he remained silent, she pulled farther away from him. "Never mind. I'm sorry."

"No, wait." He caught her arm, felt her stiffen and immediately released her. "Just spell it out for me, okay? I don't mind playing."

Now she looked confused, but after several deep breaths, she muttered, "Remember how you sat last night? When I…I kissed you?"

He settled lower on the bench beneath the water's level, resting on his spine. He crossed his arms over his chest and looked at her. "Like this?"

"Yes." She half turned to face him, coming up some on her knees. "Just like that. Now don't move."

His jaw clenched. He didn't know if he could take it. The black suit clung to her small breasts and narrow ribs. Her shoulders gleamed with moisture, the curls in her hair were already damp from the steam. His body throbbed in anticipation as she leaned toward him. He didn't dare close his eyes; never had a kiss meant as much as this one.

Her right breast touched his shoulder and he could feel her stiff little nipple poking at him, making him shudder. He wanted to touch that nipple with his fingertips, tease it with his teeth and tongue, suck her deep into his mouth.

His breathing became choppy, and even though he felt foolish, he couldn't help the instinctive response to her nearness. Her breath fanned his cheek, then his lips and then finally she kissed him.

His groan erupted despite his efforts to remain quiet. But he didn't move. It was a measure of his control that he restrained himself. The touch of her mouth was inquisitive, cautious. He needed so badly to haul her close, to turn her so he could press over her, feel her breasts burning against his chest, feel the part of her slender thighs to cradle his erection.

But he remained immobile, only his panting breaths giving away his excitement. She leaned back.

"Sebastian? Are you okay?"

He half laughed, half groaned. "I'm so damn hot, it's a wonder this water isn't boiling." He bit back the need to touch her and said instead, "You have no idea how much I want you, do you? How close I am to exploding."

Her gaze searched his face, and he saw her incomprehension.

"Brandi, I'm a touch away from coming right here in the damn water. And right now, I'd give just about anything for that touch."

"Oh." Her gaze dropped to the churning surface of the water, searching.

He managed another laugh, husky and deep and persuasive. "You can't see what I mean—but you could feel."

Before he'd finished, she was shaking her head. "No, I can't."

"Why not? You're in charge. You can do whatever you want." He added in a soft promise, "I'm not going to move."

She wanted to. He could tell by her unsteady breathing, by the way she stared at him as if trying to come to a decision. He didn't dare move, afraid she'd choose to leave him. He waited, and it felt like a lifetime before her gaze dropped again and he saw her hand dip into the water.

His body vibrated with a deep groan—a response in anticipation to her touch. Her fingertips bumped against his hard thigh, then shyly slid higher to the smoother skin of his hip. His thighs parted the slightest bit; her hand moved to the inside of his knee.

He knew he was working on a hair trigger. It was no longer a matter of exquisite torture—he had lost his control.

Sebastian jerked away, unwilling to embarrass her, unwilling to be pushed so far over the edge. It was insanity the way she affected him. This wasn't the time or place. He couldn't rush things, not until Brandi was ready to be with him every step of the way. Whatever game she wanted to play, she'd have to play it when he was in better control.

"I thought…"

Her voice quavered, and his irritation with himself grew. "Forget it," he rumbled, "I'm sorry, but the game is over."

He heard a splash and turned just in time to catch Brandi's arm. She crouched on the edge of the Jacuzzi, her face white, her eyes wide, almost wild. *"Let me go."*

Startled by her vehemence, by the sound of tears in her voice, he released her. "Brandi?"

Just like that, she was gone, dashing into the house and leaving the patio door open. Though his body was still tight, his lust had died, banished by the sight of her stricken face. Sebastian frowned, then cursed viciously. The game had been hers, so why was she acting so upset?

It was past time they talked, understood each other. He needed to know what was going on, and he needed to know tonight.

He stepped out of the Jacuzzi and stripped off his sodden briefs, wringing them out and tossing them over the back of a chair before putting the cover back on the Jacuzzi. He found a towel and wrapped it around his hips. When he went into the cabin, silence greeted him. Brandi's door was shut. He started to knock on it, to demand she talk with him, let him explain, but he decided it might be more prudent to face her with pants on and his hormones in check. This turbulent anger was almost as bad as the lust, and he needed the iron control he used on the job, the alert consciousness of every detail that made him so successful at providing personal protection.

By the time he felt he had some measure of control and had dressed again, it was late. He tapped on Brandi's door. When he didn't get any immediate reply, he silently turned the knob and peeked inside.

Brandi lay curled on her side like a small child, her

hands tucked beneath her left cheek, the blankets pulled over her shoulders. She'd left on the bedside lamp.

Darkness. She really didn't like the darkness. He filed away that small bit of information. To the economical man, it was a waste of money to burn a lamp all night long. But this time, his concern for her fear overwhelmed the worry of expense. He didn't like that she had any fears at all. What he disliked most, though, was that, on some level, she seemed to fear *him*.

Closing the door, he decided to put off their talk for the morning. Sleep was the furthest thing from his mind, so he removed his shirt, shoes and socks, then went and settled himself on the small sofa. He used the remote to turn the television on low and found an all-night movie station.

Hours passed, and he was almost asleep, the movie forgotten, when a small, choked scream awoke him. He was on his feet in an instant, his heart pumping adrenaline. But before he could fully react, Brandi's bedroom door flew open. She took one look at him, let out a low pain-filled moan, and came running into his arms.

BEING HELD TIGHT, feeling the solid thumping of his heart, his warm firm flesh, made her feel a little more secure. But the dream had been so horrible, especially since she hadn't suffered through it in so long. She'd prayed the nightmare was gone for good, but it hadn't taken much to revive it. With a sense of despair, she accepted that the horror would never truly be gone— just as she would never truly be the same person again.

She snuggled closer to Sebastian, wanting to crawl inside him, to hide herself away someplace safe. He rocked her gently, murmuring small nonsense words, and it helped so much just having him close. After several moments holding her that way, he tipped her back just a bit and smiled.

"I gather there's no villain in your room? I don't need to go dashing in like the white knight, after all?"

Brandi shook her head, her eyes wide on his handsome face, her mood solemn despite his gentle teasing.

"And no snake came in the window? No spiders under your covers?"

"No. No snakes, no spiders. Just boogeymen."

"So, it was a dream?"

She was so relieved he hadn't said *just* a dream, that she managed a quavering smile, too. But with the smile, she began to feel foolish. It was more than she could bear, constantly playing the immature fool in his presence. She tried to pull away, but his arms tightened. When the dream had awakened her, she hadn't thought about what she was doing, she'd simply gone looking for Sebastian. Now she wished she'd dealt with the dream as she always had—alone.

"Shh. It's all right, Brandi. Don't run away from me again, okay?"

God. After their disastrous Jacuzzi experience, he had to think she was a ninny—either running to him or from him, unable to make up her mind. She dropped her forehead against his chest, fighting against the tears.

His large hand smoothed over her hair, then moved farther down her back, rubbing up and down her spine. There was nothing sexual in the touch, only comfort. "Come here."

Before she knew what he was doing, he'd sat back

on the couch and lifted her into his lap. To her surprise, the position didn't alarm her. It felt secure and warm and cozy. Her long flannel gown was pulled tight over her knees and he lifted her an inch, adjusted her gown with an economical touch, then resettled her again, as if she were a child. It was so amazing to her how different he was from the man who only hours before had been the epitome of raw masculine lust.

With her head tucked under his chin, his arms around her and her legs draped over his own, she seemed to absorb his heat. He was so hot. And his skin… She opened her hand the tiniest bit, feeling his smooth texture, his hardness…. And then she caught herself. She had no business exploring him, leading him on again, when she couldn't do anything about it. He'd already proven earlier tonight that he wasn't interested in her silly brand of timid intimacy. And there was no guarantee she'd ever be able to get past the nightmares, the memories.

She started to pull away, but he gently tightened his hold. She realized he planned to keep her close for a while. She was glad, in spite of herself.

After a soft kiss to the top of her head, he said, "You want to tell me about the dream?"

"No."

She felt his chuckle deep in his chest and some of her grim mood lifted, filled by him instead of the reality of the dream. "But I will. If you're sure you want to hear this. I mean, it wasn't a simple dream."

"I didn't think it would be."

She sighed, wondering where to begin, and decided an apology should probably be first. "I suppose, given the ridiculous way I've acted, I owe you a few explanations."

And he said, "Knock, knock? Brandi, are you in there? How many times do I have to say this?"

She heard the amused exasperation in his words and peeked up at him.

"This is *your* vacation, honey. Yes, I'd like to know you better, to understand you, just like I want you to know me better. But I don't want you to feel pressured. You don't *owe* me anything, especially not explanations. But if you feel up to sharing, if you want to talk, I very much want to listen. Understand?"

Pressing her cheek back to his warm chest, she nodded. The feel of his chest hair was crisp and curly and it tickled her nose. Trying to be inconspicuous, she breathed deep of his wonderful, hot male scent, and almost shivered with the pleasure of it. She could gladly spend the rest of the night just sitting here enjoying the touch and smell of him. She felt relaxed enough to doze off; for once, the nightmare had quickly faded from her mind. But despite what he'd said, there were explanations to give.

Sebastian continued to stroke her, adding to her languor. "You haven't acted ridiculously, Brandi. Granted, I haven't understood everything that's happened, but I never thought you were ridiculous. Don't use that word again."

"Yes, sir."

He gave her a chiding squeeze for her smart mouth, then kissed the top of her head, her temple.

Brandi knew he was waiting, that he wouldn't pressure her. Without thought, she twined her fingers in his chest hair and pressed her nose a little closer while she searched her mind for the right words.

"Brandi?"

"When I was eighteen, I was raped."

It felt as though the world stopped. She probably shouldn't have just blurted it out like that, but how else did you tell such a thing? Sebastian didn't breathe, didn't move. Even the solid, comforting beat of his heart seemed to pause. She was used to that reaction, had felt it with her parents and her sister, Shay. Silent shock, disbelief. A mental distancing, because the truth was ugly and real and people didn't want to share that reality. It left them floundering for the right words, made them uncomfortable.

A familiar lump formed in her throat and she started to shake, but suddenly Sebastian had a hand buried in her hair and it seemed he held her even closer without really moving. His head came down so that his cheek pressed into hers and it seemed as if he were surrounding her, protecting her, as if he could give her his strength.

Brandi drew a shuddering breath. "I know you don't want to hear the details...."

"Yes, I do." His voice was hoarse, and when she leaned back to look at him, his expression was stark. One big, hot hand cupped her cheek, his rough thumb smoothing over her cheekbone. "It's bothering you tonight or you wouldn't have had the dream. That *is* what the dream was about, wasn't it?"

With a tiny nod, she whispered, "I used to have the nightmare all the time, whenever I went to sleep. But over the years, it's gotten better. Now, I hardly ever have it. But I guess with what happened today..."

Sebastian drew a long breath. He lowered his head until their brows touched. His dark lashes swept down to hide his eyes and in a rough whisper, he said, "You mean what I did in the Jacuzzi?"

"No! Well, that is, I didn't like what happened tonight, but the dream was brought on because of those men when we were shopping, not because you rejected me."

His head snapped back up. The light of the television reflected on his face, in his eyes. They were wide-open now and boring into her. "Rejected you? Is that what you think happened?"

She should have been embarrassed, but his incredulous look kept her from feeling anything but defensive. "I know you asked me to touch you. And I would have. I wanted to. But when I took so long, fumbling around and acting like a schoolgirl, you changed your mind."

"God, no." He kissed her forehead, her nose, quick kisses of apology. "No, I just… Brandi, I think there's a lot of things I didn't understand, but none of it was your fault. Hell, I'm supposed to be trained to pick up on stuff. But I've been a typical male idiot, ruled by my hormones and little else."

"I don't know what you're talking about."

His grin was self-derisive. "I thought you were playing a game."

Her eyes searched his. "A game?"

After a big sigh that expanded his chest and drew her attention there again, he said, "We've got a lot of talking to do, I think. Would you like some coffee or hot chocolate?"

She considered that, then shook her head. "I like sitting here. I like…seeing you like this." To explain, she smoothed a hand over his firm broad chest, up his hard muscled shoulders, then to his rough jaw, enjoying the rasping feel of his whiskers on her fingertips.

His eyes closed and he gave her a lopsided grin. "You can stay here all night, okay?" So saying, he sat back on the couch and cuddled her close again. After a second, he laughed, but the sound wasn't one of amusement.

"Brandi, I have to tell you what I thought, so we can clear the air. I don't know any tactful or gentle way to put it, so consider this my apology up front, all right?"

She braced herself for a rejection and nodded. After all, what man wanted a woman who'd been through what she had, who'd been permanently affected by the ordeal? It had taken her years, but she'd gotten her life back in order—all except for the intimacy. And she didn't know if she'd ever be the same as other women in that regard.

With his eyes closed, his head resting back against the couch, Sebastian looked utterly relaxed. "I hope I don't embarrass you, but today in the Jacuzzi, if I'd let you touch me, I'd have come."

Brandi swallowed hard, but thankfully Sebastian still didn't look at her. He shrugged his big shoulders and went on, as if he hadn't just said something so incredibly personal and sexually intimate.

"I didn't want to do that. Not unless and until I was inside you, where I've wanted to be almost since I first set eyes on you." He rolled his head toward her and lazily opened his eyes. "What happened tonight wasn't a rejection, it was self-preservation. You were killing me, being so sweet and seductive and so damn sexy. I can't even look at you without getting hard. By now,

I've been hard so long it wouldn't take much to set me off."

He waited for her reaction, his gaze warm and patient. Feelings swamped her—excitement, anticipation…pride. Sebastian, the most gorgeous, incredible man she'd ever known, wanted her. And then reality and remorse hit her at once. She wanted to look away, to shield herself, but that would be cowardly. So she faced him and gave a small, regretful shake of her head.

"I'm sorry. I don't think I can…. I want to. I love kissing you and touching you. I haven't done that, not with any man, since the rape. The fear…" She stopped to draw a shuddering breath, to compose herself and finish what she was trying to tell him. He deserved to know everything. "It comes out of nowhere, when I don't expect it. I get these panicky feelings. I try to push them back, but I can't."

A gentle smile tipped up the corners of his mouth. "Except maybe when you're in complete control? Like when you kissed me by the fire?"

"Yes. I wasn't afraid then. You said I could call the shots and I trusted you to stick to the deal. When I told you not to move, you didn't. If you had grabbed me, or even held me like this, I might have panicked."

"It doesn't bother you now that I'm holding you?"

"No. We're not kissing. You don't look the same now as you did then."

"You mean aroused?"

She nodded, feeling shy in spite of all that they'd discussed. "You have this look, like you did in the Jacuzzi, as if you want to devour me."

"A damn good description." He lifted his hand to her

cheek again and Brandi noticed that he trembled. She enjoyed the way he kept touching her, so gently, so carefully. And how he'd pressed those soft kisses to her face, not sexual kisses, just…touching. As if he couldn't help himself.

He sat up and cupped her face fully in both palms. "I want you to know, not just for this vacation, not just for the five days, but for as long as you know me, as long as you need to, you'll always call the shots. I couldn't stand it if I made you uneasy. If I do anything, say anything, just tell me. You can be honest with me. But I don't want to have to worry that I'm screwing up and don't know it."

She nodded again, unable to believe what she was hearing. "Does that mean you want to keep on…"

"Kissing you? Touching you? Damn right."

"You're not…disgusted? That I was raped, I mean. Or that I'm still carrying my fears."

"God, no." He hugged her tight. "Brandi, I won't lie and say I don't wish I could find the bastard who hurt you. I'd gladly kill him with my bare hands. But you're not responsible for what he did. And your reservations now seem perfectly normal to me."

"Do you…do you really want to hear about it?"

Still holding her, he said, "I want to know everything about you. What makes you smile, what makes you cry. What makes you happy, what makes you sad. I want to know your dreams and your nightmares, because it's all part of who you are."

She licked her lips, trying to decide where to begin. Borrowing his tactic, she closed her eyes and just said the truth. "There were three men, not one."

"God." His entire body trembled, then tightened around her.

She heard him swallow, felt his deep breaths. But he didn't say anything else, and she had no clue as to how he felt at that moment, how he might actually react to her very ugly truths. She breathed evenly, calming her mind, calming her heart. Then decided, why not? Perhaps learning it all would repulse him, but then at least she'd know, and it would be over with. Somehow, from the beginning, Sebastian had been able to reach inside her to draw out emotions and feelings she hadn't known still existed. If he was going to take those feelings away, it would be easier now than later.

She pasted on a false smile, but she couldn't quite bring herself to look at him. She would hurry through this, get it over with, then accept the consequences.

"My family and I were aboard a cruise ship in the Caribbean—the last vacation I've taken until now. It was supposed to be fun. I was feeling very grown-up—I'd just turned eighteen—almost a woman, so I flirted. With the wrong men. It was exciting, at least until I started to get tired. I left my parents and Shay at a party on the upper deck and went back to our stateroom. I didn't know it then, but the men had followed me. And because I thought Shay would be the only one coming in, I hadn't checked the door. One of my shoes was in the way and it hadn't closed tight. The men didn't even have to knock."

It was getting harder and harder, and it had been so long since she'd rehashed the details. Her chest hurt and her throat felt ready to close. She became aware that Sebastian was stroking her again. She felt his strength and, at the moment, she needed it.

Everything was blurred and she realized that in spite of her resolve, tears had welled in her eyes.

"I yelled and yelled, but they'd slipped in while I was asleep, and I didn't wake up until the door was closed tight behind them. No one heard me screaming. And they were already on me. They…they called me names. And they slapped me, because I wouldn't stop crying and screaming."

Sebastian lifted her hand to his mouth and held it there against his parted lips. She could feel his teeth, the quickness of his breath. He remained silent, though, and she waited. Waited for questions, for suspicions. There were none.

"No one knew what had happened till the next day. Shay and I were sharing the cabin, but when she came in, I couldn't quite bring myself to tell her about it. I should have. It was so stupid of me to just lie there. But I felt numb, almost dead. And so ashamed and dirty and embarrassed. It felt easier to pretend it hadn't happened. Shay assumed I was sleeping. And very early the next day, when we stopped in a port, the men got off. I never saw them again."

Sebastian tapped her knuckles against his mouth, his grip on her hand almost bruising. When at last she looked at him, his eyes were closed, his head bent slightly forward. The muscles in his neck and shoulders were taut, straining. His nostrils flared with every breath he took. But he held still, her hand wrapped securely in his. Her body was bathed in his warmth as he cradled her close on his lap.

It wasn't quite as hard talking to him about it as she'd thought it would be, and she realized with a start that having Sebastian holding her had made all the difference. It wasn't like explaining to the authorities, who had bombarded her with questions while they paced around the room. Or the therapist, who sat there in her chair, looking so cold and detached, despite her sympathetic expression, waiting for Brandi to give away an emotional revelation so she could dissect it and find a *cure*. Even her parents and Shay hadn't been able to just listen. Always they came up with unnecessary apologies and guilt. They'd look at each other, their expressions wounded. She'd always ended up feeling guilty for making them so unhappy.

"At first, my parents were kind of shocked, then so angry. Not at me, but they didn't understand why I hadn't told them what happened. They wanted the men really bad. Thinking back on it, I've decided it was the only reaction they could have had. They made demands of the captain, who asked around and found out I'd been flirting with the men. He didn't accuse me, but he told my parents that I had to learn to be more careful, that you couldn't trust anyone anymore. And he was right. I shouldn't have flirted with strangers. And I should have spoken up right away—but at the time, I just...*couldn't*. Besides, we were in international waters, there was nothing anyone could do."

"Brandi."

There was a wealth of tenderness in the way he spoke her name, but his jaw was rigid, his eyes cold and hard. He looked the same as her parents had—distraught, disgusted. She tried to pull her hand free, but he again pressed it to his mouth, leaving the touch of a hot kiss on her wrist.

Feeling as if she might crumple up and fall away, she asked with a touch of sheltering sarcasm, "Are you happy now that you know it all?"

He wiped a lingering tear from her cheek. "I'm glad you told me, yes. But I'm not happy. I'm probably the most miserable bastard alive."

"Because you're stuck on this vacation with me? No one says we have to spend the time together."

"Oh, Brandi." He shook his head at her in a chiding way. "That's not what I meant."

"No?" Her whole body trembling, she pulled her hand free to wrap her arms around her middle. It was an old habit, one she'd broken herself of, but she fell back on it instinctively. In this situation it was ludicrous, given she was sitting on Sebastian's firm lap. Suddenly she felt cold from the inside out. "I made all the wrong choices, one mistake after another. You must think I'm an idiot."

He ran a hand over her hair, then down her back, moving her just a tiny bit closer to his bare chest. His look was tender and direct and filled with emotion. "The truth, remember?"

She said, "Of course," even though she didn't know if she could bear the truth.

His eyes were sad, but he gave her a small, sweet smile. "What I think is, you're the most incredible woman I've ever met."

CHAPTER SIX

EMBARRASSED BY THE ridiculous compliment, Brandi snorted and said, "You must be awfully easy to impress."

He chuckled. "Actually, no. I'm damn hard to get around, and because of my background, I'm too critical of other people. But after all you've been through, you're still sweet and gentle, not bitter. I think that constitutes a small miracle."

"I may not be bitter, but I'll never be a normal woman again, either."

Sebastian pretended to study her face. "You look fine to me." Then he kissed her cheek, letting his lips linger. "You taste even better. And no 'normal' woman ever pushed my buttons the way you do. If you're not normal, I can only be grateful, because I think you're perfect just the way you are."

She couldn't repress her smile of relief, even though she knew his words were nonsense. "You know what I meant."

Sobering, he said, "Yeah, I do. But it's not true, baby. You're a little more reserved, but you have all the same needs, all the same desires as any other woman." Then he grinned. "You just needed the right man to volunteer his body for your inquisitive mind."

A few remnants of tears were still in her eyes and she wiped them away. He gave her that tender smile again that made her want to stay with him forever.

But there was so much still in the way. "Sebastian, I don't know if I'll ever be able to make love. Just the thought of…" Her voice trailed away. It was more than difficult trying to say such things, trying to express her problem.

"Hey, no blushing now." His voice was low, whispered against her cheek. "You can tell me anything, honey. There's no one here but us."

The night was quiet. Without her realizing it, the television had gone blank, leaving only a dull glow coming from the screen and a soft hum in the air. Her position on Sebastian's lap put her as close to him as she could get. All around her was his scent, his warmth, his concern and his tenderness. He wore only his jeans; his long legs were stretched out in front of him, and his large feet were bare. A dark, appealing shadow of whiskers covered his lean cheeks and sharp jaw. His eyes were slumberous, his dark shiny hair tousled.

To Brandi, he felt safe and sexy and somehow a part of her. She swallowed, then decided to take advantage of the moment. Another one like it might never come again, and she did have so many questions, so many things she'd like to talk to him about. Sebastian was available and willing and she trusted him, even more than she trusted herself sometimes.

"The thought of a man getting on top of me makes me ill. I…I break out in a cold sweat."

He rubbed his chin on the crown of her head and

replied simply, without inflection. "There are other positions, you know."

"But a man is so much stronger. He could always switch positions. And Shay told me once that a man who's really excited doesn't always know what he's doing."

"What?" He tipped her chin up and his frown was fierce. "That's total bull and a miserable cop-out. Men are always responsible for their actions, especially when they're with a woman. Why would Shay tell you such a damn stupid thing?"

His vehemence startled her, but didn't alarm her. "She'd talked me into going on a date. But the guy got…pushy. He didn't really do anything, just tried to steal a kiss."

"A kiss you didn't want to give him?"

"Yes. But I guess he thought he could convince me."

"I hope you slapped his damn face," Sebastian muttered.

A slight grin twitched at her lips as she shook her head. "I wish I had, but instead, I ran. I get panicked and I can't think about anything except getting away."

"Is that what happened today while you were shopping?"

Amazed at how easy it was to talk to him, even through her embarrassment, she nodded. "Two men tried to pick me up."

"I wish I'd seen them."

Brandi laughed at his look of mean intent. She liked it that he felt defensive of her, even though she wanted and needed to learn to defend herself. "It wasn't that big a deal. Shay says I make too much of things sometimes, and she's right. She said that just because a man shows his interest, or steals a kiss, doesn't make him a rapist."

"I'd say she's right. But I'd also say anyone, male or female, should know how to accept no as an answer and to respect another person's wishes. Don't let Shay talk you into doing anything you don't want to do."

"She talked me into this vacation."

"Except for this vacation," he clarified quickly, then gave her a lopsided grin. "In this one instance, Shay was brilliant."

Brandi shook her head. "Actually, I shouldn't have been surprised by what she did. She's made it her personal goal to get my life jump-started. She feels...responsible somehow, for not watching out for me on the cruise. I keep telling her it wasn't her fault. It was my fault."

"No. You were eighteen, sweetheart. You didn't ask to be violated, no more than any woman does. Leaving your door unlocked doesn't warrant blame for you or in any way serve as an excuse for what those bastards did. It was just a small mistake that cost you more than it should have."

"But I had been flirting."

"So? Flirting is something everyone does. It's human nature, not an invitation to brutality. The only people at fault were the men who took advantage of a young woman's innocence."

"I've wished so many times that I'd done things differently."

"We all do. But we're human, and we have faults. That's just something we all have to learn to live with."

Brandi couldn't help but relax. Sebastian was so open and honest in his responses. He didn't seem bothered by the topic, didn't seem hesitant in answering her. She gave him a small hug. "Talking with you is so different from talking with my family."

"How so?"

"They don't really want to hear about any of this. It makes them uncomfortable. They don't know what to say, and they're afraid they'll upset me. Usually they end up apologizing. Again and again. We've made a sort of silent pact not to bring it up, to pretend it never happened. They don't know about the nightmares. I didn't want to worry them or add to their ridiculous guilt, and there's nothing they can do about them anyway. The dreams are just something I have to learn to deal with."

Sebastian cursed softly, confusing Brandi, then he looked at her again. "I'm glad you're sharing it with me, then. And I want you to feel free to tell me anything. Ask any question you want, hold on to me when you need to. Everyone needs to talk. About everything. Keeping things inside never helps."

Brandi hesitated for a moment, uncertain how to verbalize what she was feeling, but she wanted Sebastian to know, to understand how much this time with him meant to her. Usually, with her parents or with Shay, she ended up being the one listening. They needed her to understand that they felt guilt, that they suffered, too, over what had happened. But with Sebastian, he listened and accepted. She could pour out her heart, and it felt good. Somehow, the living nightmares—the ones that stayed with her every hour—weren't quite so overwhelming anymore.

There was no way to put all that into words, so finally she just whispered, "Thank you."

He hesitated, then cautiously, with his lips first on her temple, then her cheekbone, he kissed his way toward her mouth. When his lips touched hers, gently, without pressure, she sighed. So close their noses touched, he looked into her eyes and she could see his smile, could feel the warmth of his incredible green eyes.

"You're welcome." His husky whisper made her tingle.

She had to close her eyes to shield some of the heavy emotions she felt before she could make her next confession. "Sebastian, I like kissing you."

"Do you?"

She smoothed her hand over his bare shoulder again and noticed the muscles were more relaxed now. She looked back to his face and shivered at the sensual heat in his eyes; his masculine interest was so plain to see, so natural. He hid nothing from her, and maybe that was what made it less frightening.

"I've been so curious for so long. But I was afraid to chance getting close enough to anyone to do the things most girls have done by the time they were teenagers. I was a late bloomer. I didn't get asked out much, especially not with Shay around. She's so gorgeous, most of the boys my age were too busy staring at her to even notice me."

"I noticed you."

Brandi grinned. "I know. It still amazes me that you aren't involved with Shay."

He snorted. "Your sister terrifies me. There's no denying she's beautiful, but in a different way from you. Shay doesn't have a subtle bone in her body. She's extravagant and pushy and arrogant."

"She's incredible."

He laughed. "Don't get defensive. I like your sister a lot. And her personality suits *her* to perfection. But Shay has a way of making mincemeat out of the males of our species, and I have no desire to do battle with her."

"You make her sound like an Amazon."

"Close."

Brandi smacked his shoulder. "I'm surprised you escaped. She puts most men under her spell within minutes."

"Including all the boys you knew when you were growing up?"

"Mmm. I was just known as Shay's little sister. It didn't give me much of a chance to experiment when most other girls were getting their first kisses—or more. Then after the rape… Well, I wish now that I'd had at least one boyfriend somewhere along the way."

Sebastian was curiously still. "Are you saying, except for the rape, you're a virgin?"

"Yes. But even more than in the physical sense. I…I'd only been kissed a few times, and those were tiny pecks. But I'd dreamed about doing those things, about finding the right guy and…"

She couldn't put her thoughts into words, but Sebastian understood. "You wanted to experience all that first excitement, the first kiss, the first touch. Necking and petting, but being too cautious to go all the way." As he'd spoken, his fingers had slid up and down her arm over the flannel of her nightgown, giving her goose bumps and making her feel some of what he described.

"I like it when you touch me, Sebastian. And I like

touching you. You feel so different from me." Her hand stroked his collarbone, his warm throat. His flesh there was taut and silky smooth over hard bone and muscle.

Sebastian wrapped his fingers around hers and kissed her palm. Still holding her hand, he lifted it and moved her knuckles over his chin, his jaw. All the while, he watched her face closely. "Have you ever felt a man's beard?"

The hot look in his eyes made it hard to speak, but she managed a nod. "My father's."

His chuckle was deep and intimate. "This is a little different, isn't it?" He skimmed her hand over his upper lip, where a mustache would be in very few days if he didn't shave. His breath felt warm against her palm.

Without conscious decision, she opened her hand and cupped his cheek. His own hands went to her waist, holding her loosely, leaving her free to do as she pleased, without his interference. In a breathless whisper, she said, "Yes, it's different." *And amazing and intriguing and exciting.* "You're always so warm."

He made a choked sound, then briefly pressed his face into her unruly hair. "I have a beautiful, sexy woman on my lap. It's a wonder I'm not on fire."

She didn't pay any attention to his words. She wasn't beautiful, only passably pretty, but he did make her feel sexy. Enthralled, she felt his jaw move as he spoke, as he swallowed. She watched his throat, trailed her fingertips there, feeling the coarseness of his beard stubble, the thickness of his neck, the steady beat of his pulse. She touched the hair at his nape, then touched it again. It felt cool and deliciously silky. "I never thought of men as having such soft hair."

His eyes watched her, never blinking. "My beard is rough, but not the hair on the rest of my body."

That slowed her, making her stomach tingle. It was a pleasant feeling, like a tickle deep and low inside her. She looked at his chest hair, dark and thick, covering his broad chest, circling his small brown nipples. She ran her tongue nervously along her lips, then decided to be daring. She reached out. Sebastian closed his eyes for a moment, then opened them again, pinning her. His nostrils flared on a deep breath and she spread both hands over his chest.

Hard and solid. Incredible heat. And a pounding heartbeat.

"Brandi?" His tone was coarse and low. "I like you touching me, sweetheart."

She felt the drift of his warm breath as he spoke, and then she felt the hardness beneath her bottom and knew he had an erection. Curious, she looked up, meeting his gaze. He smiled, reassuring her with that look.

"I'm not going to move, and I won't touch you unless you ask me to. But I'm a simple man who is very attracted to you. I can't help my reactions."

"I don't think there's anything simple about you." She moved her hands to his upper arms, amazed at his bulk, at the way his muscles clenched and pulled without him seeming to move at all. Even using both hands, she couldn't circle his biceps. He still reminded her of a mountain, all imposing, solid strength. And the heated look in his eyes often bordered on savage.

After a while, she really did feel comfortable touching him, and that surprised her. It seemed so natural to be here with him. And Sebastian, true to his

word, hadn't moved, other than shifting slightly in his
seat and breathing a little harder. She cupped his cheek
again, drifted her fingers over the bridge of his nose, his
brow. Then she touched his eyelids and watched them
flutter shut. He held perfectly still.

"I like how you look at me, with your eyes half-
closed." Before she said it, she hadn't known it was true.
At first, his intensity had frightened her. Then she'd
merely been cautious. But now, she supposed she was
already getting used to it, the way he seemed to see into
her thoughts, the way he looked at her as if no one else
mattered. It made her feel special, but not threatened.
Not anymore.

"What else do you like?"

She didn't hesitate. "The way you smell."

His eyes opened again. They encouraged her, and she
leaned forward until she was very close to him, her nose
nearly touching his throat. The scent of him was enough
to make her toes curl. She nuzzled his throat, along his
shoulder.

He groaned low and deep. When she lifted away
from him, he gave her a cocky smile, but his chest
moved with his deep breaths. "How do I smell,
Brandi?"

She touched the bridge of his nose again and explored
a small lump that accounted for the very slight crook
there. It had probably been broken at one time. There
was a tiny scar at the corner of his mouth and it drew her
fingertips next. Everything about him fascinated her.

"It's hard to describe. You smell warm, very warm.
And like musk and spice." As she touched the small scar,
his lips parted just the tiniest bit. He licked his lips, and

his tongue touched her fingertips. She drew back, shocked at the almost violent sensations that swirled in her belly.

Sebastian stared at her. "Touch me again."

It wasn't a command—closer to a plea. "I…"

"It startled you when you felt my tongue?"

"Yes."

"What did you feel? Inside, I mean." His gaze searched her face, probing, looking for answers. Then his face went carefully blank. "Did I frighten you?"

"No." It wasn't fear that had stolen her breath. But she didn't think she could put it into words. "I've never felt it before, so it's difficult."

"Do you want to continue?"

She nodded, but she wasn't at all certain *where* to continue.

Sebastian settled that problem for her. "How about if I tell you what I felt?"

Her heart raced. The air inside the cabin seemed to be too hot, too thin, even though there was no fire in the fireplace. She felt the tensing of his hard-muscled thighs and squirmed a little, then smiled inside at his reaction. She liked affecting him this way, liked knowing that he wanted her so much.

Keeping his gaze locked to her own, he said, "I felt a rush of heat. Under my skin, inside my muscles. Everything clenched." He grinned. "You're sitting on my lap, so I think you felt it. In my stomach, my thighs. And here." He pressed the back of her hand low on his abdomen. "There's this sweet pressure. Like anticipation that's hot and thick."

Every single thing he mentioned, she felt. Her own belly was tingling with a delicious ache. "You scare me."

He pulled back, but this time it was she who held on. "I don't mean…" Frustrated, she shook her head and said, "It's not fear that I'll be hurt. It's just that I've never felt this way before. Ever."

He brought her hand to his mouth and pressed a tender kiss to her palm. "What happened to you slowed you down a little. You were still too young to have explored your own sensuality before the rape, and afterward, you were too wary. But now, with me, you feel safe." He smiled at her. "Am I right?"

"Yes." But she had to be honest. "To a certain degree."

Nodding he said, "I think I understand your rules now. Earlier, in the Jacuzzi, I thought you were playing a game of dominance, that you didn't want me to move so you could tease me. And I liked it, believe me, I did. But then it was just too much and I couldn't hold back any longer.

"Now I know you weren't playing at all. I understand why it's important for you to be in control." He kissed her again, a quick light kiss that took her by surprise, but thrilled her all the same. "Feel free to satisfy all your curiosity with me. When I first told you that you were in charge, I hadn't exactly had this in mind. Or maybe I had, but not with any real expectations. Just a lot of hope."

Brandi laughed. Bantering with a man, sexual teasing and innuendo, wasn't something she was used to. But with Sebastian, it felt so natural and right, there was no threat, only fun. She grinned and he grinned with her.

As he tucked an errant curl behind her ear, his smile

faded and his look became serious again. "Now that I do understand, I want you to feel free to direct me, to tell me what you want and what you need. You can touch me anywhere you want, however you want. Whenever you want. If you don't want me to move, I won't. If you want me to touch you back, I gladly will. But only if you tell me to. You really are in charge, babe, in every sense of the word."

SEBASTIAN WATCHED as she considered all he'd said. He kept his face carefully masked so she wouldn't know how she'd torn him up inside. At that particular moment, there were any number of people he'd like to light into, not the least of which was her family. Though he had no doubt they'd been misguided by love and their damn guilt, they'd still stifled Brandi's need to talk about the rape, to rid herself of pent-up hurt and anger and fear.

It almost sounded to him as if she'd buried the pain in order to protect them, when it should have been the other way around. But he remembered the guilt he'd suffered for his mother, and knew their lack of understanding hadn't been intentional. Often the victim's loved ones suffered as much—in a different way—as the victim. He'd seen it in his work, as well.

He would have liked to get hold of the men who'd dared to touch her. They'd tried to steal her innocence, her sweetness, but luckily they hadn't succeeded. Despite what Brandi seemed to think of herself, she was simply too strong to lose her will.

But most of all, he felt anger at himself. In his job, he dealt with trauma, both emotional and physical, on a regular basis. He protected women threatened by their abusive husbands, he watched out for the innocent who were stalked for money or political gain. He knew the signs and understood the fears. But he hadn't been himself since first setting eyes on Brandi. He'd let all her signals slip past him, his brain too cluttered with lust and his own vulnerability to see anything else.

He'd actually dealt with rape cases on many occasions. But instead of viewing her caution and curiosity as the residual effects of a trauma, he'd assumed she was playing sex games with him. He'd thought she was using her shyness and need for control as a way to build the sexual tension. Damn his ego.

Now that he knew the truth, though, he had a plan of action. His lust would have to go on hold, but he could deal with that. He *would* deal with it, even if it killed him. Nothing was as important as reassuring Brandi, showing her that she was a woman in every sense of the word.

Her curiosity was starting to bloom, and he'd be damn sure that he was the man who satisfied it. Any amount of sexual discomfort was worth the final reward. But already, he was literally aching with anticipation.

"You want me to…touch you?"

He grinned at her self-conscious expression and rosy cheeks. Perching on his lap in her virginal gown, her dark hair wild and her blue eyes round, she looked more enticing than ever. Her small bare feet were feminine, her scent sleepy and warm and delicious. Grinning hurt, but it was either grin or groan, and he wanted to reassure her, not scare her with his lust.

"Yes, I want you to." Leaning forward, he kissed

her, another light, teasing peck that he hoped would eventually evolve into more. "I want you to feel free to use me. To touch me whenever you want, to kiss me or look at me any way you choose."

"I couldn't."

She said it, but she didn't look sincere. He chuckled. "You already have. And I know if you're this fascinated with my chest, the rest of my body has got to be of interest to you, too."

She gulped, then heaved a big breath. "Are you saying you'd let me..."

"You didn't finish your sentence."

She licked her lips. Her eyes were bright and she had the most adorable expression on her face, a mixture of uncertainty and greed. "I don't know if I could. I mean, I can't predict when the fear will hit me."

The words felt like a blow, erasing all his humor. "I know. And it doesn't matter. If you change your mind, at any time, there's no pressure. Just say no. That's all."

"You say that now. But if we'd already been... involved, you might feel differently."

"And you're afraid I'd lose control?"

"I don't think you'd deliberately hurt me."

He accepted the fact that it would take time to earn all of her trust, but it wasn't easy. Determined to make as much headway as possible in the five days allotted to him, he decided to throw out the only viable solution he could come up with—even if the very idea of it made him uneasy. "If you ever start to worry about me losing control, you could always tie me to the bed."

She stared at him, her eyes wide with incredulous surprise.

"I'm serious, Brandi. I want you to be comfortable with me, and if that's what it takes, then so be it." Seeing her reaction helped firm his resolve and returned his humor. "Of course, you'd have to promise to be gentle with me, to treat my poor body with respect."

She gave him a playful smack while a grin tugged at her lips.

"And absolutely no tickling. I can't stand it."

"So you're ticklish?"

He sent her a mock frown. "I don't like that wicked gleam in your eye. Promise me right now."

"All right. I promise not to tickle you." Then she whispered, "Not while you're tied down."

He pretended to consider her words, while in truth he was thrilled at the easy way she bantered with him. And her tone, when she'd spoken, had been husky with promise, with expectation. More progress. At least, he chose to see it that way.

"All right, we're agreed." Then he reached around her for the remote and switched off the television.

With obvious alarm, Brandi stiffened in his arms. "What are you doing?"

"Not what you probably imagine." He tugged on a glossy dark curl that laid over her temple. "Did you think I planned to stand up and strip off my jeans?"

"I don't know." She searched his face. "None of this is like anything I could have ever expected."

"Well, you can relax. I just thought we ought to get some sleep tonight. It's late."

"Oh." She looked down, but he hadn't missed the disappointment in her expression. She started to rise. "I suppose I should get back to my bed."

His arms tightened around her, keeping her gently in place on his lap. "Actually, I thought we might sleep right here. I'm comfortable, and after holding you this long, the thought of my cold lonely bed doesn't appeal one bit."

He could see how badly she wanted to accept, and tenderness the likes of which he'd never felt before threatened to choke him. She looked up, her gaze wary once again. "I'm not too heavy?" she asked.

"Honey, you don't weigh any more than a blanket."

"I might have another nightmare."

Which was one of the reasons he wanted to keep her close. He'd do his best to protect her, even from her own demons. "If you have a bad dream, you can hold on to me. You won't be alone."

Tears welled in her eyes and he couldn't bear it. He tucked her head under his chin, then stretched out his arm to grab a throw on the back of one of the chairs. He spread the cover over them, propped his legs up on the coffee table and leaned back. Brandi shifted a few times, making him painfully aware of his aroused state, but he gritted his teeth and held in his moan of pleasure.

"Sebastian?"

"Hmm?"

"Good night."

Now, that felt right. Holding Brandi, listening to her gentle breathing, hearing her tell him good-night. It was something he could get used to, something he wouldn't mind hearing for the rest of his life. He pressed his cheek to the top of her head and felt her wildly curling hair tickle his nose. So soft, so damn sweet. "Good night, babe. Rest easy."

She sighed into him. "I will."

And just as she'd done in the limo, she passed out, going boneless within a minute.

It took Sebastian longer to relax. He tried to remember what he'd been like, how he'd behaved, back when he'd first begun experimenting sexually. It was a very long time ago—a lifetime. He didn't like remembering, because those days had been full of poverty and sadness and desolation. He'd started too young, trying to find comfort with the neighborhood women who needed the distraction as badly as he did.

After he joined the service, he'd gotten more particular, and there were times when he'd gone long stretches without the touch of a woman. Most times he hadn't missed it much, but when he had, he'd easily found feminine comfort. And always, he'd stayed in control—no ties, no commitments.

Now here he was, fully committed to Brandi. Knowing she'd missed her sexual maturity filled him with a primitive greed, both emotionally and physically. She was his. Regardless of the rape, he would be her first man, her first lover.

She sighed in her sleep and he smoothed his hand over her waist, then down her hip to her thigh. It had been an automatic touch, not something calculated, but it thrilled him anyway. She felt so slender, so delicate. The flannel gown was soft and somehow suited her perfectly, though he thought her own skin would have suited her even better.

Images filled his mind and he closed his eyes, relishing them. She would be his, he was determined. He still had four days, and he'd make the most of them before his time was up.

First thing in the morning, he would begin.

He grinned, knowing what he planned was a little underhanded, but Brandi needed control, and he wanted to give it to her. The trick was in making her think she held the reins, when in truth she'd be following his lead.

CHAPTER SEVEN

SEBASTIAN CONTINUED TO rub the towel over his damp body even though he knew Brandi stood frozen in the bathroom doorway. He'd been at it for fifteen minutes or more, just waiting for her to show up. Under normal circumstances when alone with a woman he wanted—who he knew wanted him, too—he would have been oblivious to his nakedness, most likely because the woman would have been naked, as well.

Not so with Brandi standing there, her flannel gown dragging the floor, her eyes still puffy from sleep, her soft lips parted in shock. He could feel her curious gaze burning over his body and he wanted to pull her close, to feel the inquisitive touch of her hands, her eyes…her mouth.

He pretended indifference, but in fact he was wound so tight he hurt.

The weather matched his mood, waking him this morning with a powerful thunderstorm. Rain slashed the windows and the sky appeared as dark as early evening. He'd slipped away from Brandi after a loud crack of thunder and he had purposely left the bathroom door ajar as he'd showered. He'd hoped the sounds of the running water would eventually wake her, even though the storm hadn't. Of course, she'd been snuggled up close to him then, warm and secure. He'd felt the chill of the room as soon as he'd left her, and though he'd tucked the blanket around her, he'd thought that the loss of his warmth might be enough to rouse her.

He wanted her familiar with him and his male routine. He wanted her comfortable with his body. The more she thought of him as just a man, male to her female, the less she'd think of him as a dominant counterpart to her feminine vulnerability. The mundane chores of shaving and bathing and eating would help lower him to the status of just another flesh-and-blood person.

Finished drying, he slung the towel around his shoulders and turned to face her with a wry grin on his lips, but Brandi didn't notice. Her gaze was nowhere near his face. He cleared his throat and she jerked. When her eyes rose quickly to meet his, he asked, "You okay, babe?"

"You're naked."

"Am I? Damn, that's right." He mustered up a puzzled look. "I took my clothes off to shower. That's usually how it's done, you know."

Brandi slowly and carefully licked her lips, her gaze now glued desperately to his. "You're…awfully big."

Chuckling, he deliberately looked down at himself— and saw he was thankfully still inattentive to the fact of a very appealing female in the area. "Hmm. And I'm not nearly so impressive as I can be." Then he looked at her. "Does it bother you?"

She shook her head, her dark curls moving around her pale face, and her eyes again went over his body.

She said softly, "I wasn't talking about that. I meant you were just so massive. All over."

"I know. I was teasing you."

"Oh." She looked around, then shrugged. "The door was open."

"I wanted to hear you if you woke up," he said with a straight face.

Brandi nodded. "The storm woke me."

Damn. He couldn't very well stay unenthusiastic if she continued to watch him this way. He had to distract himself, so he moved to the sink and turned on the hot water, then opened his shaving kit.

"What are you doing?"

There was less shocked reserve in her tone, and more natural curiosity, which is what he'd been counting on. He flicked her a glance and saw that she'd stepped a little closer. He treated his nudity as natural, and she seemed to be attempting to do the same.

"I'm going to shave." Then he added casually, "I don't want to scratch you with my whiskers if you decide to do any of that touching or kissing we talked about."

She remained silent, her eyes boring into him, over him. Squirting the shaving cream into his hand, he asked, "Have you ever watched a man shave?"

"No."

"Not even your father?"

"My dad's very private. Besides, he and Mom had their own bathroom."

Flipping down the toilet seat, Sebastian said, "Come on in and sit. I don't mind the company."

"I…um…" He watched as she shifted her feet, her hands clasped together in front of her, then she blurted, "Okay, but could you wait just a moment? I'll be right back."

Before he could answer she darted out. Sebastian chuckled. Of course, she needed a trip to her own bathroom. He only hoped she didn't stop to change clothes. He liked her in the loose-fitting flannel gown with the tiny blue flowers all over it. Its Victorian styling suited her.

He didn't want her to comb her hair or splash her face, either. He liked seeing her all sleepy-eyed and warm and tousled. She looked sexy as hell and so sweet, his stomach muscles ached from being pulled so tight.

She returned a moment later, her hair still wild and disheveled, her gown in place and her blue eyes bright. She rushed forward and took the seat beside him, which put her eyes on a level with his navel. *Damn.* He'd never survive this.

"Go ahead."

He laughed. "Intend to enjoy the show, do you?"

She'd regained enough of her impudence to stretch out her legs, cross her ankles and lean back against the commode. "You offered. It's certainly not something I'll get to see again anytime soon."

"Ah, now, there you're wrong. You can watch me shave any time you like. All you have to do is tell me." So saying, he started by spreading the shaving cream around his face, then went through the contortions all men employ to reach those hard-to-shave places. Brandi sat in fascinated silence beside him. Amazingly, her gaze was as much on his face and the process of removing whiskers as it was on any other part of his body.

He was almost done. As he swiped the razor one last

time across his jaw, Brandi said softly, "You look so hard."

He nicked himself and cursed, but when he turned to her, he saw her staring at his hip where his skin was a shade lighter from being forever protected from the sun. She lifted her hand slightly from her lap, then lowered it again.

Sebastian grabbed up a facecloth and wiped his jaw before turning to face her fully. He couldn't help himself, his body stirred with her interest, and being that he stood there completely naked, hiding his reaction wasn't an option.

Her gaze flicked to his face, then back to his swelling erection. She looked absurdly amazed, and he tried to grin, tried to muster up one ounce of humor, but failed.

"You…you get excited just because I'm looking at you?"

Rather than answer her, he let his own gaze linger over her body as she lounged back in feigned negligence. He could detect the soft mounds of her breasts, the slight curve of her belly, the gentle slope of her thighs. He took his time, letting her *feel* where he looked. She shivered and her cheeks flushed—but not with embarrassment.

"You react when I look at you, too, babe. It's just that your body isn't as obvious as mine. But if a man is smart, if he knows where to look, it's plain to see." His tone was low and gravelly and there wasn't a damn thing he could do about it. Without moving closer to her, he reached out his arm and very gently, with only the barest touch, circled a pointed nipple with his forefinger. Brandi gasped and her eyes closed, but she didn't pull away. "This is a small clue."

Her lips parted while she breathed deeply. "I liked that."

She sounded amazed, not at all repulsed. "Good. Should I do it again?"

Her eyes opened and she stared at him. Biting her bottom lip, she gave a tiny, uncertain nod.

To most people this might have seemed to be the most bizarre situation—a woman covered from neck to toe in sturdy flannel, a man buck naked and on display, leaving himself vulnerable, doing no more than touching one sweet soft breast. To Sebastian, though, it meant he'd made incredible progress. He wanted to shout with his success—Brandi wanted him to touch her in a sexual way. Nothing else mattered to him at the moment.

His hand trembled a bit as he reached out again. He wanted to move closer, to touch her everywhere, to give her unbearable pleasure and hear her moaning his name, hear her crying out in an intense, mind-blowing climax. But he was also afraid of doing one little thing wrong and spooking her. He didn't dare push her too far too fast.

He toyed with her nipple, still using only that one fingertip. He brushed against her, used the edge of his nail for a more tantalizing stroke, circled and flicked until Brandi panted and said in a tiny, almost indistinguishable voice, "Please."

He was so hard, he hurt. His erection pulsed with every heartbeat, but Brandi was now oblivious to everything but her own body. Sebastian licked his lips and whispered, "Both breasts, all right, honey? You'll like this, I promise. But if you don't, just say so."

Not giving her a chance to think about it, he lifted

his other hand and this time he cupped her breasts, feeling them warm and firm in his palms. Her heartbeat thundered. Brandi made a strangled sound and her gaze remained glued to his face. He knew she was watching for any loss of control, so he did his damnedest to hide the level of his arousal. He couldn't remember ever being so primed, so hot. But Brandi's innocence, her trust, was both a powerful aphrodisiac and a potent reminder of who she was to him. More than he wanted anything, including his own pleasure, he wanted hers. He wanted her to trust him enough to let go, to give herself over to him for safekeeping while the pleasure swamped her and left her insensate.

Luckily, his arms were long, keeping him a safe distance from her. It gave her the room she needed to feel secure. It also afforded him an incredible view of her body; the way her stomach muscles fluttered, the way her thighs tightened, how her throat worked and her hands clenched.

He breathed as deeply as she. "Do you like this, sweetheart?"

"Yes."

That one word sounded like a moan, and Sebastian had to clench his jaw to hold in his own guttural sounds of approval. "Honey…I'd like to try something else, okay? No, don't look at me like that. I'm not planning a wicked perversion on your person. You're the boss, remember? I'm just going to make a suggestion."

It took her a moment, but she finally said, "All right."

His appreciation for flannel doubled as he felt her small breasts swell and fill his palms. He continued to pleasure her breasts as he spoke. "You like my fingers and hands on you here. But I think you'd like my mouth even more."

Frantically, she shook her head, her eyes going wide.

"Shh," he soothed, his fingers still taunting, teasing. "Just listen a minute. You could stand on the toilet lid. I'll even put my hands behind my back if you want. And if I do this and you don't like it, you can just say so. No arguments."

He could tell she was tempted and he held his breath.

"I don't want to take off my gown."

"You don't have to."

"Those men...the ones who raped me." Her voice trembled and Sebastian automatically stilled, his heart-beat frozen. "They told me I wasn't much to look at, that I was all bones and no meat. They...they laughed at me. I know I'm too skinny. Shay is always teasing me about needing a few pounds. My mother says I just take after her, that I won't round out until I have kids. But since I'd never thought to do that—have kids, I mean—I figure I'll always be too small."

Goddamn them. Violent emotion slammed through him, making him want to crush those responsible for stealing away her confidence, her self-esteem. And even her family had added to her insecurity. Couldn't they see how they'd hurt her with their careless remarks? They should realize, with what she'd been through, how sensitive she would be.

Shay would be devastated to hear of her part in this, but he damned well ought to tell her, anyway. He knew she loved Brandi and wanted the best for her. It wasn't in Shay to deliberately hurt anyone, especially not those people she loved.

His eyes burned and his head pounded. He must have looked as violent as he felt, because Brandi scurried off the seat and moved around him, toward the door. He didn't turn to her, didn't try to stop her. No sane words came to his mouth. He wanted to howl in anger and frustration. He needed a minute to get his thoughts in order before he tried to explain a few facts to her.

"Sebastian?"

He shook his head. Without meaning to, his hands fisted and his voice came out in a growl. "They're all idiots. Every damn one of them."

Silence. Sebastian turned and found Brandi still standing there, her expression wary as she seemed to consider his words. "Look at me, Brandi." When her eyes met his, he asked, "Do you think I'd want a woman this damn bad if she wasn't sexy?"

"You don't think I'm too small?"

He did shout then, a low, mean sound that made Brandi jump and take a startled step back. Sebastian was too far gone to heed that small message. He stalked toward her. "You can do anything you like this trip, babe. You can tell me to be quiet, to get lost, to stand on my head if that'll make you happy. But don't you dare believe anything those idiots told you. Listen to me. You're small and delicate and feminine. You're also the sexiest woman I've ever met in my life. And despite my own multitude of sins, I'm not an idiot. I know a beautiful woman when I see one."

Surprisingly, she stopped backing away from him. "You really think I'm beautiful?"

"Yes!" He shouted the word, jutting his chin toward

her for emphasis, practically looming over her. He watched her flinch, and then just as quickly, she smiled.

With one more perusal of his body, she said, "I think I'll go get dressed now."

He'd forgotten he was naked. Sebastian nodded, though it was the last thing he wanted. "That's probably not a bad idea."

"Maybe you should get dressed, too."

His eyes narrowed at her teasing tone. "What's the matter? You don't want me strutting around the cabin naked?"

She looked to be considering it and he groaned. "Never mind. Forget I asked." He moved past her and down the hall. With every step, he felt her eyes on his backside. Damn, but this was the most stressful trip he'd ever forced himself through.

Then he thought of the look on Brandi's face as he'd touched her breasts, her nipples. It wouldn't be long now. He had to believe that or he'd go crazy. Soon, she'd belong to him. Very soon.

AMAZING HOW A FEW WORDS or a simple occasion could change everything. Brandi left her bedroom feeling much more in charge, sure of herself and her intentions. Now dressed in the long, button-down denim skirt she wore yesterday, slip-on flats and a light cotton shirt, her hair brushed and her face washed, she was ready to face him again.

She was still shy about following through on her new plans; they kept changing on her, expanding, growing more exciting. But she was also anxious to get started.

She found Sebastian standing in front of the living-room window, looking out at the storm. He'd pulled on jeans and a white T-shirt, but that was all. His bare feet looked as strong and sturdy as the rest of him. His dark, damp hair had only been finger combed. She liked the look. She liked him.

He'd started a fire and the cabin no longer felt chilly. It seemed perfect to her, to be alone with him this way, on this particular rainy day, closed inside together, safe and warm and isolated from the rest of the world.

Brandi walked up behind him, and when he started to turn, she placed her hand on the solid muscles of his back. "Wait," she said.

He went perfectly still, just as she'd known he would.

The sense of power gave her a forbidden thrill. She smoothed her open palm over the massive expanse of his shoulders. He was such a big man, she marveled.

He was also a gentle, sensual man, and he thought she was beautiful.

"I have a few things I want to say to you, Sebastian, and it's easier if you're not looking at me."

He relaxed, shoving his hands into the back pockets of his jeans. "Shoot. I'm listening."

She drew a deep calming breath, then let it out slowly. "What you did for me this morning in the bathroom? I liked it very much. Thank you."

He turned his head a little toward her, then caught himself and faced the window again. "That was my pleasure. Any time you want to do it again, just say so."

"I intend to, but we'll get to that in a minute." She saw his shoulders tighten, heard him make a rough sound of surprise. She smiled to herself. "I feel a little silly, so bear with me, okay? And don't interrupt," she added when he started to do just that. Brandi knew he'd intended to chastise her for feeling silly, but she couldn't help how she felt, and she wanted him to know. For some reason, sharing her thoughts and feelings with him had become important to her.

"I've been thinking about all this a lot. And since you've convinced me you really do want me, I've decided to make the most of this vacation package. It's never been so easy for me to talk to anyone. But with you, it's like I'm finally free again."

"I'm glad."

She heard the tenderness in his tone, and wrapped her arms around him from behind, pressing her cheek into his shoulder blade. She barely reached his shoulders, even when he was barefoot. But his size no longer intimidated her as it had earlier. Now it intrigued her. He was big and hard and he wanted her.

Pressing a kiss to his flesh, she tried to absorb all the ways he appealed to her. He felt so warm and smelled so good. She loved his scent. Without thought, she opened her mouth and lightly bit him. He sucked in his breath, but didn't move. "Will you take your shirt off for me?"

He did, stripping it quickly over his shoulders and tossing it onto the floor. He made no move to turn toward her, but every muscle in his body was now clearly defined.

"Since it's raining, we can't really go out today. And I don't want to anyway. I'd much rather stay here and get acquainted with your incredible body and the wonderful way you make me feel."

"Do you realize you're killing me, honey?"

She chuckled, feeling her cheeks warm and her confidence soar. "I know that means you're aroused. And I'm glad." She began touching him again, loving the hot silk of his taut skin, the firm muscles of his shoulders and lower back. "I'd like to do everything, Sebastian, but I don't think I can. At least not yet. But what you said about…about the bed…"

There was a moment of silence, then he swallowed hard and said, "You want to tie me down?"

His voice was almost breathless, holding a mixture of dread and anticipation. Brandi slid her hand around to his hard abdomen and heard him let out a soft hiss. His stomach muscles were ridged, lightly covered by crisp curls that led from his navel down.

"Yes," she whispered, "I'd like to do that. But in a little bit. Right now, I like this. I like touching you without you looking at me. I can see every inch of you, but I'm not embarrassed, not with you turned away.

"I can't be with you in the dark," she continued. "It frightens me. I don't mind admitting that now. When the men raped me, it was so very dark. It took a long time for my eyes to adjust to the darkness, but the panic made it even more difficult. They seemed to be everywhere, and I couldn't tell where I'd be grabbed or groped next. I didn't know what part of my body to try to protect."

"Babe, don't."

It was the only time he'd ever asked her to stop, and she knew it wasn't the words he wanted to end, because Sebastian let her talk. Somehow he knew that talking about it made it easier for her. She wondered now if someone had been attentive, had listened as closely as he did, if she might have gotten on with her life sooner.

But it wasn't the talk, it was the touch that Sebastian protested. Brandi had dipped her hand down until she felt the long solid swell of his erection under his fly. As she spoke, she stroked him, her fingers dragging up and down the rigid length of him. Sebastian was obviously uncomfortable with the mix.

"This is my time, remember? I want to touch while I talk because feeling you, knowing your body, makes the rest seem unreal and unimportant. That's strange, I know, but I'd always associated this with pain and fear. But with you, touching and knowing your body is just…exhilarating."

He tipped his head back on his shoulders and made an attempt to relax. Brandi stepped closer until her thighs were pressed to the back of his. His legs were so much longer, so much stronger than her own, and for now, she thrilled in the differences. His hands were still in his pockets and she said, "Put your hands up behind your head. I want to touch you everywhere."

He groaned, but did as she asked, slowly, like a man being sent to the gallows. Brandi gave him time to get positioned, then she looked him over.

"You're such a beautiful man, Sebastian. So big and hard and powerful."

As she stroked him, her palms finding his taut buttocks, the steel of his upper thighs, his throbbing arousal, she said, "Do you know what I'd really like?"

"Tell me."

"I'd like to give you pleasure."

His knees locked. "You are, babe. You are."

"No, I mean, *complete* pleasure." This was even more embarrassing than she'd imagined, because now she'd have to face him. But first… She unbuttoned the top of his fly.

"Brandi…"

Her name sounded like a warning, but she ignored it. The sound of his zipper rasping down joined the rasp of his harsh breathing. "Tell me if I hurt you."

Another rough groan was her only answer. She felt the power of him through his briefs, then slipped her hand inside the elastic waistband and touched him. Startled, she whispered, "You feel like hot velvet. But alive, and so hard."

The entire line of his tall body went taut. His hands knotted together at his neck, his elbows pulled forward as if straining against imaginary bonds.

Brandi closed her eyes and enjoyed the feel of him. Her fingers curled around his swollen length, sliding and exploring. Her arms were stretched around him, her body flush against the back of his. Her fingers found the tip of his erection and discovered a spot of moisture. It surprised her, and at the same time gave her stomach an instinctive little curl of pleasure. "Sebastian?"

"Brandi, I can't take much more."

In the face of his need, her embarrassment evaporated. Not looking at him had made this easier, but now she wanted to see his eyes, to judge his reactions, to see him wanting her.

Moving in front of him, she kept her gaze lowered to where her hands touched him, working up the nerve to meet his gaze. Sebastian immediately dipped his head and pressed his cheek to hers, but his arms remained behind his neck. "I want to touch you, too, Brandi. Please."

"I...I'd like that. I really would." She buried her face against his broad, comforting chest.

"You said you wanted to give me pleasure. That would surely do it. I'd die to touch you right now."

She whispered, "I'm very afraid of disappointing you and myself."

"I won't let that happen, I swear. Trust me."

She did trust him, but trust had nothing to do with it. Right now it was safe because she knew he'd respect her wishes. But if they removed all boundaries, what might happen? The fact of her body and her fears was all encompassing, taking over other considerations regardless of how she wished it to be.

Slowly, not startling her at all, Sebastian lowered his arms until his hands clasped her wrists. He pulled her hands away from her fascinated study of his erection and put them on his waist. "Okay?"

Brandi nodded. She did feel okay. A little off balance, but okay.

"I'm going to kiss you now."

Brandi knew it wouldn't be a shy or gentle kiss; that's why he'd warned her. But at the moment, she didn't want shy or gentle. She wanted all his greed, all his desire. She only hoped she could accept what he gave. She drew herself up straight and determination filled her.

Turning up her face, she looked into his beautiful green eyes and said, "I'm going to kiss you back."

Sebastian grinned, but as he very slowly lowered his head to hers, the grin faded. He covered her mouth with his own and Brandi didn't have room in her swirling mix of emotions for fear. His mouth was hot and damp and it ate at hers, pulling in her tongue to gently suck on it, then giving her his, stroking over her teeth, teasing and enticing. He nipped her bottom lip and then slanted his head for better access and made love to her mouth.

Through it all, he held back, careful not to loom over her, making certain not to threaten her in any way. His mouth was devouring, but his hands were gentle, merely holding her, not pulling her closer, making no demands.

When she leaned fully into him, her arms around his neck, her body subtly urging against his, he pulled far enough away to say, "Come to the kitchen with me."

A nervous giggle escaped her. "Don't you mean the bedroom?"

"No. The bedroom seems too blatant to start, though we'll eventually get there. I want to make love to you so damn bad. But I'd rather start safe. This means too much to me to screw it up."

"And the kitchen is safe?"

He nodded. "Will you come with me? Will you trust me?"

She really had no choice. Her body pulsed with wanting him and the thought of stopping now made her ache with dissatisfaction. The fear was still there, but it wasn't as strong as the wanting. "All right."

Sebastian took her hand and led the way. Once in the room, he went to the small round kitchen table and pulled out a chair. Brandi started to sit, but he stopped her. "The chair is for me." He caught her around the waist and lifted her to the edge of the table, facing his chair. "I want you here."

Brandi blushed. When he took his chair, the position put him below her, which she felt certain had been his intent. But it also put him between her legs with her long skirt stretched tight between them. His hands rested on the tops of her thighs and his eyes were even with her breasts. He took advantage of the view, his gaze seemingly glued to that particular spot.

"Is this okay?"

Painfully aware that she'd not put on a bra, Brandi nodded. Already she could feel her breasts tightening, her nipples growing stiff, pushing against the fabric of her blouse.

Sebastian muttered something low, then licked his dry lips. "If you don't like this, tell me."

That was all the warning she got before he leaned forward and his hot mouth closed around the tip of one breast, completely enveloping her swollen nipple.

Her breath came in with a whoosh, but with Sebastian situated so much lower than she and his hands idle on her thighs, she didn't in any way feel overpowered by him. She did feel protectively surrounded by him, though.

Twining her fingers in the silkiness of his dark hair, she closed her eyes and relished the feel of his tugging mouth. Even through her cotton shirt, the stroke of his tongue was exquisite torture.

He switched breasts, tantalizing the other nipple while lifting a hand to the abandoned breast. His fingertips found the damp material of her shirt, smoothing it over and around the nipple, as if to soothe it. The dual assault was more than she could take, and she instinctively started to lie back.

Sebastian's other hand supported her spine, keeping her upright. Brandi whimpered.

"Easy, sweetheart."

His voice was a deep rumble, barely heard through the sound of her own heartbeat thundering in her ears. He nipped the tip of her breast, much like he'd done to her mouth, and Brandi felt the small sting all the way to her womb. Her fingers tightened in his hair. "Sebastian…"

She had no idea what she wanted, only that she needed something. He stood, but kept space between them.

"Let's unbutton this skirt a little, okay, sweetheart?"

The possibility of just such a scenario had entered her mind when she'd chosen the skirt. It hung almost to her ankles, but her legs were bare beneath. She'd pulled it on, thinking how convenient it would be to adjust to his greedy hands, and now the fantasy would be a reality. Brandi slipped her feet out of her flats and nodded.

Sebastian had a way of doing things that made them seem so natural and right. He didn't leer at her, didn't start caressing her. He merely unbuttoned the bottom button, down by the hem, then gave her a moment to change her mind.

She remained quiet, waiting, and after a second, he slipped another button free. All his attention was on his hands and her skirt, so Brandi could watch him freely, without him detecting her bright blush or the anxious fluttering of her pulse.

So this was wanting, and in wanting, she hurt with her need for him. She'd never guessed that it would be so strong, so overpowering. She had to bite her lips to keep from whimpering again, this time in impatience.

It seemed to take a long, torturous time before the skirt hung open above her knees. Sebastian lifted the material to the side and stood there surveying her thighs, parted around his hips and hanging over the edge of the table. Still looking at her uncovered legs, he reseated himself, and now her thighs opened even wider to bridge his upper body, fitting beneath his arms. Brandi knew he could see her plain cotton panties in the open V of her legs. Just once, his fingers contracted on her soft thighs, then relaxed.

But when he looked at her, there was nothing relaxed in his expression. His eyes blazed with heat and desire. "I want to make certain you're enjoying this, Brandi."

"I am." She swallowed, then because she couldn't stand a minute more of this, she said, "Make love to me, Sebastian."

His expression tightened, but he shook his head. "Not yet." He was silent a moment before he asked, "Do you know how to measure your own desire, Brandi? Do you know what happens to your body when you're turned on?"

His gaze was intent, and she stared back dumbly, then shook her head. "I only know I want you. Now."

"But it might not be enough." His hands coasted over her thighs, then stilled. She closed her eyes with a sigh, but opened them again when he said, "Honey, look at me."

His cheeks were flushed darkly and his eyes were heavy lidded. He looked so sexy and compelling, she reached for him. "Sebastian."

His curse was low and strained, and he avoided her kiss. "I don't want to hurt you, babe."

"You won't. Sebastian, please."

"Brandi…I have to make sure you're with me before we go any further." His gaze held hers, fierce and intent, while one hand slid further up her thigh. Brandi gasped.

"Is it easier with me looking at you, or would you rather close your eyes?"

She couldn't help but give a strained smile. "Why don't you close your eyes?"

"Because I want to see you." There was a heavy throb of desire in his tone, ridding her of any humor. She could only see Sebastian, only feel Sebastian. His fingers inched closer and closer up the inside of her leg.

Brandi held his stare, unable to look away. And then his nostrils flared and his palm cupped her and he said softly, "Ah." Sensual satisfaction spread over his features, darkening his eyes, sharpening the line of his jaw. "You are ready for me, aren't you?"

The low growl of his voice sank into her, just as his fingers probed, sliding over her soft panties now dampened with her excitement. The realization that she was wet—and he was touching her—caused her to tighten her thighs. But Sebastian was there, his hard body unyielding.

He stared into her eyes, watching her every movement, her every expression. "Don't shy away from me now, babe. Stay with me."

"I don't think…"

"You don't have to think. Just feel." His fingers worked under the edge of her panties, and slowly, so slowly she panted, one finger parted her and pushed deep.

Brandi cried out. Without her permission, her eyes closed and her head tipped back. She would have gladly sprawled on the table except that once again, Sebastian caught her and kept her upright.

"You feel so good, babe. So hot and wet, just the way I want you." His finger teased, pushing in and then out again. Brandi clutched at him, only marginally aware that he now stood before her, holding her close and kissing her face, her ears, her throat. He loomed over her, and there was a moment's alarm, but then he stepped back the tiniest bit and at the same time pressed a second finger deep.

Her body seemed to be suffering some great tension, growing tighter and tighter. It unnerved her, but she didn't want it to stop. With an arm behind her, Sebastian arched her body. He bent and again took a nipple into the heat of his mouth. Brandi cried. She felt the tears on her cheeks, tasted them at the corners of her mouth. Her hips moved rhythmically against his hand, and even though it embarrassed her, she couldn't stop herself from doing it. She didn't feel like herself, didn't feel in any way familiar.

Sebastian encouraged her, slipping his fingers a bit higher and finding a spot with his rough thumb that made her choke on a scream of pleasure.

"Yes, right there, babe. A little more, okay? Just a little more, Brandi."

She clutched him, her eyes squeezed shut tight, her thighs practically wrapped around him.

"A little more…"

Brandi groaned as a wave of intense pleasure broke over her. Sebastian groaned with her, his arm tight as he murmured and reassured and continued the magic touches. "Yeah, honey, that's right. Come for me. You're mine now, Brandi. All mine."

She heard the soft words, but they didn't make sense. And they didn't alarm her. Not while her world exploded, not while Sebastian held her so close she felt a part of him. And even afterward, when her heartbeat started to slow and her mind reassembled itself, she didn't have a chance to think about the claim of possession he'd made.

Sebastian swept all coherent thought aside by leaning back to smile gently at her, and then asking, "Would you like to tie me down now?"

CHAPTER EIGHT

THE GROWING ACHE in his arms couldn't be ignored much longer, but he truly hated to disturb her. Brandi slept soundly, sprawled out over his bare chest, one leg over his hips, her breath fanning his right nipple.

It was a wonder he'd survived.

He grinned, thinking of how enthusiastically she'd participated once she'd had him secured to the bed. All inhibitions had left her and she'd gone about torturing him thoroughly with her curiosity of his body and how it worked.

She now knew firsthand what made him tick, because she'd had him ticking for hours. He had no secrets from her, and that suited him just fine. Even the touchy subject of the condom—and how to put it on him—hadn't slowed her for long. He'd given instructions, and she'd followed them.

She'd made love to him with the most novel approach, unlike anything he'd ever experienced. Because not only did she discover his body, but her own, as well. And he'd been able to watch every small nuance cross her beautiful features. Wonder and excitement had been there as often as shyness and reserve.

But as much as he'd enjoyed himself, he really

wished she'd remembered to untie him before falling asleep. Once again, she'd merely passed out, and this time her sleep was undisturbed by bad dreams. Sebastian had even managed to doze for a few minutes here and there. But now he was beyond stiff, starving for food, and getting a little cold since the fire had died down and the rain had stopped, leaving an ominous chill in the air.

He lifted his head to look down at Brandi's body. In the late-afternoon light coming through the window, she looked gorgeous. She still wore her shirt, but the skirt and panties were gone. She had a beautiful backside, perfect in shape and texture. The sight of that cute bottom had come close to sending him over the edge several times. He'd wanted to touch her, to squeeze that soft resilient flesh, but by his own suggestion, he'd been helpless to move. It wasn't an experience he wanted to repeat with any other woman. But for Brandi, he'd do it again in a heartbeat. *After* he'd eaten and gotten the circulation back in his arms.

He was just about to say her name, hoping to wake her gently, to soothe her through her unavoidable embarrassment, when a loud knock sounded on the front door. Alarm raced through him. "Brandi? Come on, babe, wake up."

She stirred sleepily. "Hmm?"

Sebastian nudged her with his hips, trying to rouse her. "Damn it, Brandi! Wake up. Someone's at the door."

She lifted her head. "Someone's here?"

She looked totally befuddled and still half-asleep. "Untie me, Brandi."

Rather than doing as he suggested, she sat up, then slipped her slim legs over the side of the bed. She looked around, located her skirt, and started to pull it on.

"Brandi?" His heart thudded heavily as she fastened her skirt. "Untie me."

"Just a minute. Let me see who's at the door first."

"No!" But even as he said it, she started out of the bedroom. *"Brandi!"*

She stuck her head back in long enough to say, "Shh," then was gone again.

Sebastian heard the door open, could hear soft voices, but he couldn't make out what they said. After what felt like an eternity, Brandi returned. She carried a small slip of paper in her hand and she deliberately avoided his eyes.

"It was the front desk. Shay's been trying to get in touch with me. I gather from what the clerk said, she's driving them nuts and she's not happy that we don't have a phone."

He tugged at his bonds. "I don't want a damn phone."

"Me, either. But I suppose I should call her back. Otherwise she's liable to land on our doorstep, just to make certain everything's okay. You know how Shay is."

He lifted his head as far as he could to glare at her. "Don't even think about going to the office without untying me first."

"Oh." She blushed, just as he knew she would. "I wouldn't have done that." Then her gaze made note of his exposed body, and she didn't say anything else, didn't make a move to untie him.

"Brandi?"

"Hmm?"

"I loved every second we spent in this bed, but my arms are starting to get a little stiff now."

"Oh!" She rushed up to the headboard and sat next to his chest. The mattress dipped and he rolled slightly toward her, his body bumping her hip. He inhaled her clean, womanly scent—now mixed with his scent and the scent of sex. The ways this woman affected him! He liked it, but it also scared him half to death.

She'd opened to him more today than any woman he'd ever known. At the same time, she'd needed his inability to move, to react to her, in order for her to feel so free. Protective instincts mixed with raw lust could do any man in, but Sebastian was sensitive to women's issues—and to this one small woman in particular.

She finally freed his right hand and he lowered his arm to let it rest lightly over her thigh and around her waist. She leaned over him, her small, perfect breasts only inches from his nose while she tackled the other knot. He'd pulled fiercely against those bindings earlier, needing the pain to counteract his need to hold her. Brandi had been over him, on him, her face taut with pleasure as she worked awkwardly toward her release, and he hadn't been able to help her, to touch her. Watching her helplessly had been its own form of devilish foreplay. He'd shouted with his own pleasure, but Brandi had been too wrapped up in reaching her peak to do more than gasp.

Thinking about it was getting him aroused again. Luckily she hadn't noticed, because that might have ruined all the headway he'd made. *How* he could get aroused again was beyond him. He'd always been a very sexual man with strong appetites, but he'd never been insatiable. Of course, he'd never known anyone like Brandi.

The knots were probably much tighter now than they'd been when Brandi had tied them, thanks to his struggles.

"I've almost got it."

Sebastian smiled. He could hear the concern in her tone, concern for him. He liked that, too. When the knot was undone, Brandi sat back to smile at him. Sebastian stared at her, not moving one iota, then whispered, "Come here."

Without even thinking about it, she leaned down and kissed him. Sebastian knew she didn't note the significance of the kiss, but he did. They were in a bed, he was free to move, and still she'd come to him.

He'd never played sex games before, but damned if he didn't like it with Brandi.

Still not moving his arms, he opened his mouth, inviting her inside, but she leaned back with a grin. "Oh, no you don't. I didn't untie you only to tie you up again. I have to go the registration desk and see what Shay wants." She smoothed her hand over his chest, her expression soft and warm. "Do you want to come with me?"

He slowly flexed his arms, then bit back a groan. "Yeah, I want to go. Can you wait for me to take a shower?"

"Sure. I have to tidy myself up anyway."

He'd hoped she would offer to shower with him, but she was back to looking shy again. Sitting up beside her, he shifted his shoulders, deliberately crowding against her, seeing how much leeway she'd give him now that they were lovers.

Evidently not much. Brandi shot to her feet, her

hands twisting in her skirt. She started moving toward the door, her grin slipping just a bit. Sebastian caught her hand. "Why don't you change, and we'll try to find someplace nice for dinner. Maybe even a little dancing."

Brandi blinked at him, her nervousness forgotten, just as he'd wanted. "Dinner and dancing? Are you offering to take me to a nightclub?"

"Sure, why not?" He felt a little ill saying it, the thought of the expense and the waste and the time with strangers not really to his liking. But he wanted Brandi happy, and he didn't want her dwelling on what they'd done all day. Not until bedtime rolled around again—when he hoped very much to sleep with her. Not just to have sex, but to sleep, holding her in his arms all night in a comfortable bed, waking with her snuggled close beside him.

Earlier, he'd told her she was his now. She hadn't acknowledged those words, either to deny or accept them. It had been a tactical error on his part, pushing her too fast toward an emotional intimacy she didn't yet feel. But luckily, she hadn't seemed to hear his declaration, which had bordered on possessive.

She looked confused now. "Do you like to dance?"

He shrugged. "I think I'd like dancing with you."

Of her own volition, she stepped up close to him and hugged his naked body tight. Startled, it took Sebastian a moment to carefully return her embrace. With his mouth touching the top of her head, he asked, "Is that a yes or a no?"

"I don't know how to dance."

That damn tenderness hit him again, almost suffocating, and he closed his eyes. Of course she hadn't done much dancing. She'd been a wallflower, over-shadowed by Shay as a teen, then withdrawn from men completely since the rape. There were likely many things she'd never done, and suddenly, he wanted to do them all with her. The cost be damned, because the waste of the money didn't seem like a waste if it made her happy.

"Then we'll definitely go. Trust me, you'll be a natural." He kissed her crown, inhaling her scent and feeling her hair tickle his nose. He loved her hair—the soft, wild curls, the rich dark color. He framed her face with his hands, letting his fingers tangle in those curls, then turned her face up to his. He kissed her gently, trying to ignore the lingering wariness in her eyes.

"We'll do up the town tonight, so wear something sexy."

Laughter replaced the wariness in her beautiful blue eyes. "I don't own anything sexy and you know it."

"Then we'll have to buy you something." Of all the gifts she'd bought, she hadn't purchased anything for herself. She'd only been thinking of the children at the shelter, and he liked that awareness in her. With all she'd been through in her life, she still had room to feel concern for others. She was such a giving, caring woman, it would be all too easy to fall in love with her.

But that thought didn't distress him. He felt good, very good. He'd pick her out a dress more beautiful than anything she'd ever had.

"Sebastian, I don't think…"

He interrupted her, unwilling to listen to arguments. He hadn't felt this enthusiastic about spending money since… Never.

"We've got a lot to do, once you've called Shay. Shopping first, then food, then dancing." He turned her before she could offer more protests, then gave her a light swat on the bottom. "Get going, woman. I'm starved."

SEBASTIAN STOOD BY impatiently while Brandi went through another round of assurances with Shay. She'd been on the phone five minutes now, and from what he could tell from her side of the conversation, Shay wanted a blow-by-blow report of what had gone on, needing to know if she'd made a mistake by rushing Brandi off with a man.

That nettled him. Damn it, he wasn't just any man. Shay knew he had a special sensitivity for women, and she trusted him with many of the situations at the safe houses. So why was she putting Brandi through the fifth degree?

"I promise, Shay, I'm having fun. Honest." Brandi's eyes slanted toward Sebastian, filled with apology and a tinge of embarrassment. "No, it's…it's not like that. He's been…well…"

Sebastian couldn't stop himself. He reached out and plucked the phone from Brandi's hand. She tried to snatch it back, but he held it out of her reach—an easy thing to do given her small stature.

As he put the phone to his ear, drowning out Brandi's muttered complaints, he heard Shay say, "Just remember that he is a man, honey, more man than most. And whether you know it or not, you're a very pretty woman. Don't expect him to keep his distance for the whole trip."

Sebastian rolled his eyes, feeling both annoyance and chagrin. "I'd say she was beautiful, not just pretty, and damn sexy, as well. She can handle any man on her own—even me."

A moment of silence, then: "Sebastian."

"Shay," he replied sweetly.

"I, uh…"

"Warning your sister away from me? And after you donated me to her so nicely. A birthday present, wasn't it?"

"Yes. You were…for her birthday." Then she said in a rush, "I just wanted to make sure I hadn't made a mistake."

He softened, hearing the fretful tone of Shay's voice. He knew she meant well, despite her meddling. Taking charge and running things was simply a part of her. She wouldn't know how to be any other way. "There's no mistake. You trust me, remember."

"Yeah, I trust you. It's just…"

"We've covered it, Shay. Things are fine, and we're having a good time. Both of us." He looked at Brandi and saw her face had gone red. She looked ready to kill him.

He grinned. "I gotta go, Shay. Brandi is anxious to get on with our date." She swung at him, but he ducked and she missed. Chuckling, he said, "If Brandi needs anything, she'll call you. Bye."

"Don't hang—" the receiver hit the cradle and Brandi frowned "—up."

"You don't need her filling you with nonsense." *Or warning you away from me.* "And you don't need her advice. I think we're doing just fine on our own."

She glared at him, but after a moment of him grinning back, her frown smoothed out and she threw her hands up in the air. "All right, I give up. I can't really stay mad anyway, not when I'm secretly glad to be off the phone. But don't ever do that again."

Her frown was back to being fierce, so he quickly apologized. "I was an arrogant jerk. It won't happen again."

She shook her head, then smiled. "I wouldn't go quite that far. Arrogant, but not a jerk. But you were too high-handed."

"You looked embarrassed."

"Um, Shay being insistent is sometimes hard to talk around."

"Next time, just tell her to butt out." He touched her cheek. "Especially when she's questioning your love life."

Brandi laughed. "Are you kidding? With Shay, that would be as good as admitting there was something going on, and she'd have kept me on the phone forever prying for details. Mostly because I've never *had* a love life."

Sebastian took her arm and steered her toward the exit. Very quietly, he asked, "Is there something going on?"

"You know what I mean."

Of course he did, but he needed to know her thoughts. It had occurred to him that while he grew more and more emotionally involved with Brandi she might very well only be using a prime situation to experiment with her sexuality. He'd invited her to do so. And at the time, it had seemed to be enough.

Now he wanted more.

He'd offered her the use of his body, but he didn't want to be used. Not anymore. He wanted to share. He wanted her trust. Maybe he wanted forever.

Brandi had never experienced lust before, so she had no way of knowing how unique the chemistry was between them. Lust existed, more powerful than anything he'd ever imagined, but it was tempered by so many other, more tender emotions. He wanted to teach her to enjoy her body, to enjoy his body, but he didn't want her to take that knowledge and apply it with another man. The mere thought made him furious.

"Sebastian? Is something wrong?"

"No." He shook his head. "Nothing's wrong."

"You look upset."

He glanced down at her as they walked through the doorway and into the dim, damp outdoors. Sebastian breathed deep, filling his lungs with the rain-scented air, bracing himself. "I'd like for you to sleep with me tonight. The whole night."

Brandi faltered. "I don't know…"

He turned to her, catching both her hands, looking down into her wide blue eyes. "Just sleep, baby. I want to hold you all night, and wake up with you beside me in the morning. Trust me."

The look she gave him now was timid, skittering away before he could figure out what it meant. "I want to trust you, but it's not easy. I really don't think I'd be able to sleep."

"Can we at least try?"

"Why?"

She seemed frustrated, and maybe he was pushing her. But he only had a few days left, including the day they'd have to pack and fly home. Once they returned to the real world, with all the outside commitments of family and jobs and life in general, would she give him a chance? Or would she chalk up her experiences here and try to get on with her life? Was it even fair of him to want or expect more? She'd had so little fun and missed out on so much sensual growth, without a single male-female relationship. But he wanted to be the man to give her those things she'd missed; all the flirting and small gifts and new touches.

He could do it. His lifestyle wasn't so inhibited that he couldn't bend a little and buy her flowers and chocolates on occasion. The thought of squandering the money in such a frivolous way had always seemed repugnant, but to make her happy, he'd do it. He would enjoy doing it.

And his house, though set out in the country away from the congestion of rushing people, was adequate in size, even without all the renovations finished. It wasn't fancy, but it was solid and secure. *A good investment.*

He shied away from that thought, that logical reasoning, because it made him feel like an ass. Brandi needed and wanted fun and laughter, not sensibility. And he'd find a way to give it to her.

The sun peeked out, reflecting on all the wet surfaces, chasing away the last of the clouds. Sebastian leaned down and pressed a quick hard kiss to Brandi's mouth, determined despite her resistance.

"I want to sleep with you because you're warm and soft and smell sweet." Her face flamed and she looked away. Sebastian chuckled. "Besides, I think you'll like it. I know I will. It's a nice feeling to be cuddled close all night with someone you care about."

She didn't deny that she cared, though she did chew on her bottom lip in a fretful way. He counted that as a step forward; what the hell? He was an optimist, and if he chose to count almost everything as progress, it was nobody's business but his own.

"If you don't like it, if it bothers you, we'll deal with it, okay? You liked sleeping with me on the couch."

She stopped, looking down at her feet. "The couch is not a bed, and you were sitting. I know it's silly, but it makes a difference."

"Look at it this way. Last week, did you think you'd find yourself sleeping with a man on a couch, regardless of what position he was in?"

"Last week I couldn't have imagined doing any of the things we've done."

"But you don't regret them?"

She shook her head, and her small smile showed her new confidence. Even more than the belated sunshine, it warmed him. He slipped his arm around her and held her close to his side. "We'll just see how it goes. You can even sleep in that long granny gown if it'll make you feel better."

She blinked at him. "Well, of course I'll wear my nightgown!"

Sebastian laughed at her vehemence. She probably didn't realize how damn sexy the gown looked on her slight frame. Sexy and feminine. It draped her body, hinting at curves, and her rosy nipples showed through the material. Just thinking of it made him semierect once again. He had the hair-trigger reaction of a teenager around her.

And unlike Brandi, he slept in the nude.

He looked at the bright sun. There were way too many hours between now and bedtime. And at the moment, he wasn't at all sure he'd last that long.

THE DRESS HAD COST a small fortune, and Brandi had been very resistant to his buying it. But Sebastian had been insistent and he'd made it a birthday present, so she couldn't really refuse. Now, as he moved her around the dance floor, she knew it was the perfect dress for her. When Sebastian had first seen her in it, he'd given his approval with a low whistle and a heated look that spoke volumes.

She felt sexy, but the sexiness came from the simplicity of the dress—and Sebastian's attentiveness. He hadn't tried to coerce her into anything low cut or ultra short. He'd bypassed all the dresses that might have made her uncomfortable and she appreciated his sensitivity.

The dress landed just above her knees and had a two-inch slit up one leg. It hugged what it covered, not tightly, just doing a lot to emphasize her slight figure. The front of the dress rose to her neck, but in the back, it dipped to her shoulder blades. Right now, Brandi could feel the warmth of Sebastian's fingers as they coasted over her skin. The man couldn't stop touching her, and she loved it.

She tried not to think about the coming night, because thinking of it made her queasy. She didn't want to mess things up by behaving like a ninny, or showing her cowardice. And she trusted him now, completely. But that didn't mean she'd be able to rest easy in his arms all night. If she had the nightmare, if she froze up and kept him awake, it would put a damper on their time together, and they only had a few days left.

The music ended and Sebastian smiled down at her. "What are you thinking about?"

He seemed in no hurry to leave the dance floor. That suited Brandi. Now that she felt comfortable dancing, she'd gladly do so all night—with Sebastian. "I was wondering about you. Where you live, if your work takes you away from home very often."

A guarded expression came over his face and he took her hand, leading her back to their table. After seating her, he asked, "Why so curious all of a sudden?"

Brandi didn't know where the questions had come from, or why. It was probably because she wanted to see more of him, in more normal circumstances, even though she knew that was impossible. Their time together seemed magical and unreal. In a way it *was* unreal because they were simply too different to form any lasting relationship. Sebastian was the most vital, energetic, appealing man she'd ever met.

And she was still a timid shadow of a woman. That wouldn't change, no matter how she wished it could.

"Brandi?"

He took her hand across the table—touching her again. She smiled to herself, loving the constant contact with him, and knowing she'd miss it once they returned home. But Sebastian deserved a whole woman, not one bogged down with emotional difficulties from her past.

"You know so much about me, but I don't even know where you live."

He seemed to consider that for a long moment before he answered. Brandi wondered if he thought she was prying, or if perhaps he wanted to keep his life separate so their parting at the end of the trip wouldn't be too complicated.

"I have an old farmhouse I've been renovating. To me, it's beautiful, filled with all natural woodwork and hardwood floors. It's how I spend much of my free time, working on the place. I had to replace a lot of the plumbing and the wiring. The roof was in horrible shape. But it has charm, and it's isolated, away from the congested suburbs and the busy city."

"Does it take you long to get to work each day?"

He shrugged. "That depends. My work differs from job to job, so I never know in which direction I'll be going, anyway. But it's about a forty-minute drive to downtown, where I have my offices. There aren't any other houses around, and I own several acres, so my privacy will always be protected."

"That's important to you?"

He made a rough sound, not quite a laugh "After growing up in tenement buildings where the hallways were always filled with loiterers, vagrants and drunks, and the front steps couldn't be walked on for the bodies resting there, yes, my privacy is damn important." His eyes narrowed on her, bright green and intense. "It's not something I'd ever be able to give up."

There was a warning there, or a message, but Brandi already knew their time was limited. She didn't need him to spell it out. "Do you spend a lot of time away from your home?"

"Occasionally. It's not uncommon for me to be gone for days at a time, but most of my jobs now are contained within the city." He tilted his head at her, as if trying to see into her thoughts. "I could limit my work out of town, if it ever became a problem."

Feeling uncomfortable now, because it was as if he knew she was asking for personal reasons, Brandi added, "I suppose for a single man, it isn't an issue."

"No. I've been expanding my offices, hiring on additional men for surveillance work. But it's a catch-22. Expansion will free up more of my time, but doing the expanding itself requires additional time and commitment."

Brandi couldn't imagine living in isolation, away from neighbors or friends and family. But she could tell by looking at Sebastian that it suited him. "So, you're happy there."

It wasn't a question, but a statement, and one more obstacle to prove their time at the cabin was a fluke, not something that could be extended once the prize package had been used up.

"My home isn't fancy, but it's sturdy, and it's all mine. I enjoy being there, making the repairs myself, watching the house change. It's one of the few concessions with money that I made, buying my home. Buying the land. It's not easy for me to admit, but in a way the house is personal insurance on my security. I know I won't ever be broke and homeless, because I own it outright. And there's enough land to make a profit off any number of ventures if the need ever arose. Having money in the bank adds to security, but not like having a place that's free and clear to call your own. I know I won't ever end up like one of those vagrants sleeping on the front steps."

Brandi knew it was important to him for her to understand his financial independence. And in truth, she was amazed at how well he'd succeeded given his poor start in life. He didn't dress miserly, but neither did he wear exclusive brands or styles. His hair was kept neat—she loved his hair, so dark and straight and fine—but it wasn't salon styled. Brandi pictured him going to a local barber, and she smiled. "It's hard to imagine you worrying about money. You're successful and it shows. And you've been so generous with me."

He shrugged. "The dress wasn't all that expensive, though I admit I have no idea what women's clothes normally cost. Besides, I like seeing you in it. You look sexy as hell."

The thudding of her heart proved how his words affected her. But it wasn't just the compliment. It was that, in some small way, she'd succeeded in helping him overcome his reservations at needless spending. She wanted him to know he couldn't save the world, and there was certainly no crime indulging in a few luxuries for himself. "The dress is beautiful. Probably the nicest thing I've ever owned."

"If you like it, then it was worth every penny."

She wished he could enjoy buying himself things as easily. "It's an extravagant gift." Then she grinned. "Especially since *you* were a gift, which I figured was plenty for one birthday."

His fingers tightened on hers. "I'm glad Shay chose me as the gift, not some other man."

"I'd have refused any other man." It was true. She'd taken one look at Sebastian and found his charm and strength and his smile irresistible. In her heart, she'd already chosen him, and Shay was astute enough to see it. "Besides, Shay had seen my interest in you—a unique thing for me—and I'd stupidly mentioned my new plans to her."

"Ah. I'd forgotten about that. What are these infamous plans of yours?"

Shrugging, Brandi said, "They're not really all that

complex. I just want to get on with my life. I've hidden away long enough, and let the past mean more than it should. It just seemed easier to go it alone than to try to get beyond the problems. Especially when the men weren't exactly beating a path to my door. Not that I minded, since no man appealed to me anyway."

He gave her a crooked grin. "Until you saw me."

"Yes."

Leaning forward slightly, his expression now serious, he said, "I'd like to help with your plans if you'll let me."

"Oh, Sebastian." Impulsively, she lifted his hand to her mouth and kissed his knuckles. The action surprised him, but quickly the surprise changed to an emotion much hotter. His eyes blazed and his features tightened.

Brandi's voice trembled in reaction to that look. "When I said you were generous, I wasn't only talking about the dress. The dress is beautiful, and it was a wonderful gift, but you've given me yourself, too. You made it safe for me to find out things about myself and about lovemaking that I never would have known otherwise."

She no sooner said the words than she felt her face heat. "What we did wasn't exactly lovemaking, though, was it? It wasn't a shared thing, not with you doing all the giving and me doing all the taking."

He shook his head and his gaze held hers, not letting her look away. "Don't think of it like that. What happened today was incredible. *You* were incredible. So, it's not about me helping you. It's about me as a man wanting you as a woman. And finding a comfortable way for us to come together."

She wanted to believe him. But in her heart she knew a man like Sebastian would never have been here with her in the first place if the circumstances hadn't dictated it. And once the vacation was over, she didn't know what would happen. She felt almost desperate at the thought of never seeing him again.

"I wish…I wish things could be normal between us. I wish I could give you as much as you've given me."

In one abrupt motion, Sebastian stood and pulled her to her feet. Startled, Brandi asked, "What are you doing?"

"I think it's time for us to go. I have some explaining to do, and a crowded restaurant isn't the place."

She went willingly as he pulled her out into the night air. It hadn't rained any more, but the air was still thick with moisture, oppressive and heavy with the threat of another storm. Once inside the rental car, he turned to her and hauled her up against his chest.

Only vague moonlight spilled through the windows, leaving the interior of the car very dim. Brandi felt his hands tangling in her hair, pulling her even closer, and then his wonderful mouth covered hers and kissed her for long minutes.

He tasted hot and urgent. When she opened her mouth, his tongue pushed in, stroking and mating with her own. It was a familiar caress now. Many times while they'd been joined on the bed, Sebastian had demanded a kiss or a touch. She'd leaned over him, willing to obey him even though he'd been restrained. She'd let him excite her with his mouth, and kissing him now excited her again.

His lips moved over her cheek, her temple, then her ear. "You're making me crazy, honey."

She thrilled at the feel of his warm breath in her ear, the roughness of his shadowed jaw and his use of endearments. They were a first for her, and she felt special each time he referred to her in such a way. "I'm sorry."

He groaned. "No, don't be. I like your unique brand of torment." He leaned back and gazed at her, his eyes hot in the dim light, his breathing audible. "I also like being tied down and tormented by you."

Brandi found it difficult to breathe with him looking at her so intently. "I didn't mean to torment you."

"God help me if you ever do mean it."

She saw the flash of his white grin, then he kissed her again, hard and hungry. His kisses, no matter how voracious, no longer frightened her.

"Men have fantasies just as women do," he whispered against her lips. "And I can safely say just about every male alive has fantasized being tied and helpless at the hands of a beautiful woman bent on sexual exploration. You didn't hurt me, you pleasured me, almost more than I could bear. Just thinking about it now is making me hard as granite."

Fascinated, Brandi remained stock-still while he kissed her once more. Her brain worked and when he lifted his mouth away, she asked, "What are your other fantasies?"

"Ah, curious, are we?"

"Yes." She felt no embarrassment, not when he discussed things so openly and without shame. The heat of their bodies had caused the windows to steam up, and even if someone happened by, they were well hidden.

In a low gravelly tone, Sebastian said, "Some fantasies are purely sexual and damn basic." He named a few, and she knew her eyes were round with disbelief. She just hadn't ever imagined such things. Sebastian stroked her while he spoke, occasionally licking the sensitive spot beneath her ear, nipping her throat. His voice was deep and husky and aroused.

"Others are based more on emotion. Like being the protector of a woman, having her depend entirely on me for everything, including her pleasure."

"You'd like that?"

"Damn right."

"I thought men these days wanted independent women."

Sebastian chuckled. He kept kissing her, as if he couldn't help himself. They were quick, light kisses over her face, her hair, her throat and ears that teased and distracted.

"We're talking fantasies, Brandi, not real life. To the outside world, I wouldn't settle for anything less than an intelligent woman with a mind of her own. But in the bedroom, it's different. For both men and women. There, everyone has to find their own limits and explore different depths. There's no right or wrong. Only the truth of what turns them on. They have to be open and share their secrets to know what those truths are. We've done that, you know. And it was damn good."

"What other fantasies do you have?"

His big hand cupped her cheek and his thumb smoothed over her temple. "As much as I enjoyed being tied up, the thought of having a woman tied to my bed appeals a hell of a lot, too."

"I could never do that."

"And I'd never ask it of you. Fantasies are something

given, not taken. If you didn't enjoy it, I wouldn't, either."

Despite his reassurance, the panic was still there. She started to speak, but no words would come to her.

"Shhh. It's all right, babe. I wasn't suggesting it as an alternative. You asked and I answered. That's the thing about fantasies. They vary from person to person. So they don't always get met. But there are no bad fantasies, not between two consenting adults. Not between us."

She buried her face against his throat, feeling the heat in her cheeks—and in her body. Somehow, in some distant part of herself, the thought of being at this man's mercy had given her a tiny, forbidden thrill. She still wouldn't do it, because along with the thrill was the fear of being used and hurt. But she acknowledged the idea just the same.

"What about you, Brandi? Do you have any fantasies?"

She shook her head. She'd never given sex much thought one way or the other—except to know she wanted to avoid it. "I don't think so."

"We'll find some fantasies for you. We still have three days left to work on it," he promised in a husky voice, and excitement filled her. Sebastian kissed her again, then turned and started the car. "We better get moving if I'm going to find a pharmacy that's open."

"Why are we going to a pharmacy?"

"I need to buy more condoms."

"Oh." That stifled her, but only for a moment. "I thought you said you just wanted to sleep with me tonight."

As he pulled the car away from the curb, he flashed her a boyish grin. "I do. Afterward."

Brandi kept silent, but on the inside, *she* was grinning, too.

CHAPTER NINE

LYING ON TOP OF Sebastian, feeling his wide chest heave with labored breaths, feeling the heat of his body waft around her, was something to which she'd quickly grown accustomed. His large hand still held her backside, massaging and squeezing. The man seemed to love her behind. She'd learned that he had a special fondness for that part of the female anatomy.

Brandi had a special fondness for him.

It hadn't taken him long to breach her reserves. After that first night of sleeping together, when she had slept more peacefully than she had in years, Brandi hadn't wanted to use her own room at all. Sebastian was always so careful of her, letting her have a dominant position in their lovemaking. They'd done away with the tethers after that one time. Though the ties still lay on the nightstand beside the bed, Sebastian hadn't mentioned using them, so Brandi hadn't, either.

She no longer needed the security of physical binding, not when she trusted him so completely.

After the night of dancing, he'd taken her back to the cabin and begun kissing her as soon as they'd closed the front door. He'd carefully aroused her to where she couldn't see straight, then carried her to the bedroom where he arranged her over his big body and drove inside her.

The added stimulants of his hands and mouth being everywhere had been more than enough to chase away her fears. He never crowded her in bed, always putting Brandi on top. Like a puppet, she moved as he directed, trusting him to know what she would like, what would bring her pleasure. He never failed her.

More often than not, they slept that way afterward, her on top, his arms locked around her keeping her close.

Brandi knew her time with him was something she'd cherish forever, but she'd done the most ridiculous thing—she'd fallen in love with him. Five days ago she would have said a man like Sebastian didn't exist. Now, on their last day at the cabin, she had to admit that a man like him did exist, he just wasn't for her.

Sebastian stirred and she felt him lift his head to gently nip her shoulder. "What time is it?"

Brandi forced her eyes open to see the clock on the nightstand. "Four-thirty."

"You should get to sleep. We'll have to start packing up in a few hours."

His voice sounded gruff, and she wanted to cry. The past five days had been magical. They'd both been changed by the trip to some degree. She and Sebastian had gone shopping, where he'd helped her buy more gifts for everyone—and even a few souvenirs for himself. He didn't seem to mind so much now when he purchased something. He even seemed enthusiastic about it on occasion. Ice-cream cones, Ferris wheel rides, even having his fortune read. Small things, but they gave him enjoyment, and Brandi loved to see him relaxed and happy.

He'd volunteered to help her wrap all the gifts. They'd spent one entire rainy day in the cabin doing just that, then making love afterward in front of the fireplace.

He'd also given her everything she'd missed out on when growing up. He'd taken her parking to show her the dubious joys of making out in a car, and they'd laughed as much as they'd loved, especially when another car had come by and made them both think they'd been caught. He'd brought her wildflowers that now decorated the kitchen table in the cabin. Twice he'd carried her a tray so she could have her breakfast in bed. He'd pampered her and seduced her and wooed her. She loved him for it.

When the nightmare had come again two nights ago, he'd held her close while she struggled with her demons, and he listened while she talked. He hadn't made love to her then, he'd simply let her sleep in his arms. The nightmare had faded away quickly. Soothed by the rhythm of his heartbeat and the security of his touch, Brandi had to wonder if it would ever come again.

They both knew this was their last night, and Brandi clung to him for a moment. Sebastian's hands stilled, then he whispered, "Are you all right?"

"Hmm. I'm just not sleepy."

"Well…" He had that husky tone to his voice that told her he was aroused again. He amazed her with his stamina and his interest. She'd never before thought of herself as a sexual being, but with Sebastian she felt insatiable.

Rising up on her forearms she put her breasts within reach of him. He clasped her waist and moved her upward a bit more until he could carefully catch a nipple between his teeth. Brandi moaned.

"You have the most sensitive breasts."

"So you keep telling me."

"That's because it turns me on so much."

She was grateful that she could give him pleasure, because he'd certainly given it to her. Cupping his cheeks, she pulled him away from her breast and looked at him seriously. "I'd like to make you happy, Sebastian. This is our last night together."

He frowned, then caught her mouth in a ravenous kiss before saying, "I don't want to think about that right now."

She slid to the side of him, then surveyed his long body. With one finger trailing over his chest to his left nipple, she said, "What can I do for you?"

"Brandi…"

She loved his warning tone, the one that told her he liked very much what she was doing. She flicked his nipple, heard him hiss a breath past his teeth, then moved her hand down to his erection. "This part of your body fascinates me."

In rasping tones he admitted, "Your fascination drives me insane."

Brandi chuckled. Sebastian went still, not moving a muscle, and she hated that she caused him to do that, that he had to restrain himself now as much as the bonds ever had. Leaning down, she kissed his rigid stomach muscles, then dipped her tongue into his navel. He groaned brokenly.

"Do you know what I'd like to do?"

The groan turned into a choke. "I know what I'd like you to do."

"I'd like to go the lake."

Sebastian gave a raw laugh. "Aw, babe. You do know how to destroy a man, don't you?"

Brandi pretended not to hear him. She knew what he wanted, and so far she hadn't been daring enough to give it to him. But he'd sparked her curiosity, and she knew this might be her last chance to know all of him.

"I'd like to go to the lake and wrap up in a blanket with you. We could watch the stars and listen to the crickets and...make love."

His fingertips trailed up and down her spine. "Is this one of your fantasies, honey?"

"Yes, I think it is."

Sebastian had encouraged her to think of any fantasy she wanted, anything that appealed to her. And he'd made each and every one of them come true. But what he didn't understand was that the fantasies were all about him, not about time or place or position. Certainly not about any other person. And Brandi couldn't tell him, because she knew even though her fears seemed to have been put on hold, it was only because Sebastian was so careful with her.

He was a man, and how long would it be before the enforced caution bored him? Or worse, before he became annoyed with her and the restrictions? He deserved a woman as alive and open as himself, a woman unafraid to share herself in every way.

Not a woman with hang-ups that would eventually drive them apart.

Sebastian sat up and pulled Brandi into his lap. He nuzzled his whisker-rough cheek against her own soft cheek. "I can arrange this one, no problem. But are you sure you won't get cold?"

Sebastian seemed impervious to the chills that often affected her. She could be freezing, and he'd be comfortable. As he'd told her in the beginning, his body temperature was degrees higher than hers. She'd count on that temperature—and her own excitement—to keep her comfortable.

"It's been warm all day. I'll be fine. Let's just take some blankets. I want to stay to watch the sun come up."

The small lake was located close to their cabin. They'd been there several times while exploring, taking long walks and picking flowers and watching the occasional rabbit or squirrel. After that one night when Sebastian had spent a small fortune, Brandi tried to make certain they stayed close to the cabin. When they did go out—during her second shopping spree—she'd requested lunch at an inexpensive diner. Sebastian seemed to think she was accustomed to more luxury than she was. Like him, she lived a simple life, especially compared to Shay. The one picnic lunch they'd had at the lake had been her favorite meal of all. There just wasn't any way to convince Sebastian of that. He seemed intent on spoiling her, when it wasn't necessary at all.

Sebastian didn't complain as he pulled on jeans and a T-shirt, then gathered up quilts. Brandi put on her robe, tying the belt securely, but leaving herself naked beneath. If this was to be her last night with Sebastian, she intended to make the most of it. She could sleep anytime.

Sebastian was patient with her while she led the way

to the lake. He even waited silently, his wide shoulders propped against a tree, while she took her time choosing a spot to spread the largest quilt. But when she untied the belt to her robe, he straightened.

"Brandi?"

The robe slid to the ground, leaving her naked in the pale moonlight. She'd never before so blatantly exposed herself for his view. Shyness had prevented her from being so bold, just as desperation now forced her to it. If this was to be her last night with him, she wanted everything, with no barriers between them.

There was no doubt he liked it. His gaze traveled over her in the shadows of the night, and she heard his low groan. Typical of Sebastian, though, he didn't move; he waited for her to direct him. Not once had he taken the control from her, which was probably why she'd been able to let loose as much as she had.

"Come here, Sebastian."

He kicked off his shoes and stepped into the center of the quilt with her. When he reached for her, Brandi took his hands, kissed each palm and then put them back at his sides. "Take your shirt off for me."

The shirt went over his head in record time. Brandi took it from him and laid it by her robe. She would have liked to completely undress him herself, but he was too tall for her to pull his shirt off. That was, however, the only concession she was willing to make. His jeans were very reachable.

She slid her cool fingers over the hard, heated skin of his abdomen, then under the first button of his fly. A soft breeze blew around them, bringing with it the scent of the lake, the azaleas and the dew-wet grass. The air was silent except for the rustle of leaves and their mingled breaths.

The first button slipped free. Brandi dropped to her knees and kissed the small patch of hair-rough skin she'd exposed. Sebastian sucked in his stomach on a startled breath.

The next button was a little more stubborn, but then the third and forth came undone with no difficulty. Sebastian hadn't bothered with briefs, and she could now circle the hot, hard length of his shaft with her hands. Brandi nuzzled his erection against her cheek.

His hand touched her head, then fell away. "Brandi," he groaned. "Honey, you're killing me."

She began working the jeans down his thighs to his knees. Her mouth trailed in the wake of her fingers, drifting over his inner thigh. "I love how you smell, Sebastian."

His hands hung in fists at his sides. In a strangled rasp, he asked, "How do I smell?"

"Warm and musky. Sexy. Very male."

"Brandi, why don't we lie down now?"

"No. Not yet." She wanted this night to be special to him, and she wanted it to be enough to carry her for the rest of her life. There would never be another man like Sebastian. He'd given her back herself, shown her how to be a woman again. But she'd never be woman enough to keep him happy. Though she loved him, he deserved so much more than she could give.

The thought caused her heart to ache, but she banished reality by leaning forward and drawing him deep into her mouth.

Sebastian cursed and groaned and for one instant, his

hand tangled almost painfully in her hair. Brandi started to pull back, fearing he'd lost control, but he released her and locked his hands behind his neck.

"Sebastian?"

He panted. "Sweetheart, what you're doing… I like it very much."

Brandi licked her lips, still tasting him. "If I do it wrong…"

He laughed, a hoarse sound of disbelief. "There is no wrong way, babe. Not between me and you. Just please don't quit on me."

"No. I won't do that." Then she leaned forward. "Do you like this?" She licked the very tip of him and heard him gasp. "And this?" Her mouth slid slowly down the length of him until she couldn't take any more into her mouth. Sebastian's only answer was a broken moan.

She realized there was another fantasy she wanted to fulfill, and she went about working toward that end. She knew her movements were awkward, but he didn't complain. Far from it. He begged and cursed and praised. And finally, after his entire body had started to tremble in taut expectation, he pulled away from her and quickly kicked free of his jeans.

"Sebastian?"

Swearing, he knelt down and dug in his pocket until he found a condom, but his hands shook too badly to put it on, and Brandi took it from him. She hadn't finished what she'd started, but she wanted him too much to quibble. Deftly sliding the condom over his swollen member, she reacted to his urgency. Sebastian heaved beside her, and his hands were hard as they grabbed her around the waist and lifted her onto his lap.

He drove into her with one smooth, powerful thrust, and came almost simultaneously. Brandi was so excited herself, knowing she'd driven him to such a degree of desire, she only had to continue to move on him a half minute before she, too, exploded, then slumped against his chest.

Long minutes passed in silence while they held each other, and Brandi wondered if Sebastian, too, was already feeling the loss. She didn't want to go back, but she knew it was inevitable. She had a job and a family. He had his work and his house.

She'd never get to see his house, she realized. In her mind, she'd pictured it, how it would look, how it might be improved even more with a woman's touch. Only she would never be that woman.

Surely they would run into each other again. After all, he was a friend of Shay's, helped her with the shelter, and Brandi spent much of her time with Shay working on getting donations and assistance for the shelter.

But when she did see him, she wouldn't cause a scene. She'd be mature, and friendly. Never would she make him regret his generosity. Never would she make him uncomfortable for having given himself to her.

They spent the rest of the morning at the lake, not talking, just holding each other. And when the sun came up, Brandi did her best not to hate the coming day. Sebastian kept her warm, wrapped in his heat and a blanket. Just as dawn broke, he made love to her again. It was probably just her heart breaking, but his movements seemed as desperate as her own.

Three hours later, they caught a plane for home.

WITH EACH PASSING SECOND, Sebastian grew angrier. Damn it, how could everything just end as if none of it had ever happened? Yet that was evidently what Brandi wanted. On the plane, she'd distanced herself from him, only holding his hand during takeoff and landing. She'd even suggested they take separate rides home, to save him the time of going by her house. Luckily, Shay had sent the limo after them, giving him a good excuse to refuse her offer.

He'd wanted to shout then, but he'd held himself back. Hell, he'd been holding himself back from the start. She didn't even know him, because he hadn't wanted to hurt her, hadn't wanted her to be disappointed by the fact that she'd given herself to him. He also hadn't wanted the Gatlinburg trip to be the end of their relationship.

Several times he'd started to tell her how he felt, only to draw up short. It probably had something to do with the poor kid still in him, but he didn't want to risk her rejection. She'd had a whole new world opened up to her, and she deserved a chance to explore that world. On the other hand, everything basic and primal in him demanded he claim her, that he make her understand she belonged to him and only him. He tried to convince himself it was only the erotic sexual circumstances of their time together that was making him feel so territorial. But he'd been with plenty of women, and he'd never felt this way before.

He knew it would never happen again.

She hadn't asked to see him, hadn't mentioned furthering their relationship. For Brandi, it seemed to be over with already, and she wasn't even home yet.

He felt the tension building with each mile that passed. He had to do something before he lost his head and transformed into a barbarian. Turning to Brandi, he asked, "Will Shay be coming by to see you?"

She sent him a small smile. "No doubt. She's probably waiting on my doorstep."

Sebastian wondered if Brandi would tell Shay about them. Not that it would matter. Brandi was her own woman, independent despite her reserve. He remembered first meeting her— it seemed like months ago, rather than days. She'd been adamant and outspoken in her desire *not* to go anywhere with him. She hadn't wanted him, not even as part of a luxurious prize package. She had no trouble leading her own life.

She'd only needed him for sex.

He'd given her that, even though their intimacy had been controlled. It should have been enough, should have been the ultimate fantasy, but now it made him feel empty. Rather than being anxious to get back to his house, and to the job he loved, he dreaded each minute that passed. It put him one minute closer to losing her.

He cleared his throat, trying to chase the panic away. "When will you go to the shelter?"

"First thing tomorrow. I can't wait to give the kids their presents."

He forced a smile. "I'm sure they'll be excited."

"I appreciate all the help you gave me, picking out the gifts and wrapping them."

"I enjoyed myself."

Brandi hesitated, her hands twisted together in her lap. "Sebastian…"

Hoping to hear an invitation, some clue as to how she felt, he held his breath and waited.

"I want you to know how much this trip has meant to me."

The anger hit him, but he controlled it. Trying not to sound sarcastic, he said, "No problem. It wasn't exactly painful for me."

Brandi looked confused, her gaze darting over his face, then away. Her voice dropped and he heard a slight tremor in the tone that hadn't been there moments before. "It was very special to me. And I'll never forget it."

He'd hurt her feelings and now he despised himself for it. Damn her new freedom, her rights. Yes, she deserved some time to sort out her feelings, but that didn't mean he wanted to let her go cold like this. He put his arm around her and tugged her closer to his side. Her face turned up to his, her expression wary, and he whispered, "We're…friends, babe. I hope you'll call me if you ever need to talk or visit."

She blinked, looking pleasantly surprised by his offer, and she gave him a shaky smile.

Then he added, "Or if you ever need this." And his mouth closed over hers. He didn't care if the limo driver watched, he didn't care if the whole world saw them.

Brandi's fingers dug into his shoulders, not to push him away, but to hold him close. His tongue slid along her lips, then inside. He ate at her mouth, devouring, consuming. He wanted her to remember him, he wanted her to realize this was special, not something she'd find with any other man.

Not something she could toss away.

He pressed her back against the seat and heard her

soft moan as his fingers found and toyed with her nipple through her dress. He wanted her in his mouth. He wanted her naked beneath him.

He wanted her.

Realization came slowly, but the stillness finally penetrated his brain. The limo had stopped. Sebastian lifted his head and he scanned the area. Brandi's house. It was over.

He looked at her and saw her damp parted lips, her eyes still closed. With a gentle kiss he whispered, "You're home, Brandi."

Her thick lashes lifted and she gazed at him a moment before comprehending. "Oh." She tried to straighten herself and Sebastian couldn't help but smile as she tucked dark curls behind her ears and they immediately sprang forward again to frame her face. He loved her hair. Loved her face. He loved everything about her.

The driver had been busy unloading Brandi's bags from the trunk. He carried them up to her front steps and Sebastian started to get out to help. She caught his hand and stopped him.

"I'd rather say goodbye right here."

He settled back into his seat, staring at her hard. He couldn't let her go like this, not without giving her fair warning. He wouldn't commit himself, but he had to at least let her know things weren't over, no matter what she thought.

"For the past five days, I've let you call the shots, Brandi. And I don't regret one second of it. But the trip is over and from now on, I'm playing by my own rules."

Her eyes widened and her voice was weak. With arousal? "I don't understand."

Sebastian grinned. Having made up his mind to take the decision away from her, he felt much better. Patience no longer suited him well. "Sure you do." He cupped her cheek and smoothed his thumb over her kiss-swollen lips. "There is no goodbye, Brandi. Not between us. You may not realize that yet. But you will. Soon."

She stared at him in confusion and, if he didn't miss his guess, excitement. Then she scurried from the limo and hurried up the walk to her front door. Sebastian watched her, waiting. At the last moment, she turned to look back at him.

He'd give her twenty-four hours to think about things. Then he was staking his claim. Maybe he was a barbarian, after all.

CHAPTER TEN

"ALL RIGHT, SHAY, where is she?"

Shay bit her bottom lip, but her back was straight and she was so tall she nearly looked him in the eye. "I can't tell you."

He cursed, a colorful, explicit curse that had Shay lifting her beautiful eyebrows and pursing her lips.

Sebastian was at the end of his tether. He'd meant to give Brandi one day to get settled back at home, to get accustomed to the idea that he intended to pursue their relationship. But he'd gotten called away on a case, one he couldn't hand to anyone else because he'd been previously involved and knew the history. As much as he'd wanted to see Brandi, he had obligations that he couldn't ignore—not when it came to a woman being stalked by her ex. The woman couldn't afford to hire anyone else, and Sebastian already understood the situation. He'd wanted to call Brandi beforehand, but it had been so late. And by the time he'd gotten back, none of his calls got answered.

Now, a week later, he still couldn't reach her and his anger had grown steadily with each passing hour. He'd had more time away from her than with her, and the thought nettled him. So even though it was the dinner hour, and he might have been intruding, he'd gone to

Shay's house. He wanted answers, and she was the only one who might be able to give them to him.

"You're playing some game here, Shay, and I don't like it. I need to talk to Brandi. Tell me where she is."

"I'm sorry, Sebastian, really. But she made me promise."

"Why?"

At that point Shay lost her temper. With one finger poked into his chest, she stood on her tiptoes and looked him dead in the eye. She shouted, "That's what I'd like to know! What the hell did you do to my sister? She hasn't been the same since she came back. One minute she looks ready to burst into tears, then she's smiling like she has some damn secret to keep, and then she informs me she needs a vacation! She just came back from Gatlinburg! She won't tell me a single thing that happened there."

"Maybe because it's none of your business."

"We share everything!"

"Even guilt?"

Shay went still, her eyes wide. "What are you talking about?"

Sebastian regretted the words as soon as they'd left his mouth. There was no point in rehashing the past. It wouldn't solve anything, and in fact, might make matters worse. He intended to be around from now on, and he'd make certain things changed, that her family understood Brandi better.

He needed to divert Shay, and he sighed. "Do you intend to leave me standing in the doorway, or can I come in and sit down? I'm beat."

Her frown softened, and then she sighed, too. "Come on. We can go into my study and talk there."

Sebastian looked around in amazement as he entered Shay's home. Luxurious, rich, expansive—all the things he'd expected but seeing them now made his gut twist. How could he ask Brandi to come to his modest home when she had this in her family?

"It's a great house," he said when he noticed Shay watching him.

"It's an empty house and terribly lonely at times." She opened a thick oak door to a large parlor done in rich shades of burgundy and hunter green. "Brandi has no use for it. She thinks I ought to buy something more homey. She calls it a depressing mausoleum."

Sebastian stared hard at Shay, wondering at her words and how much truth was behind them. "Brandi actually said that?"

Shay nodded, looking around the room with a poignant half smile. "And I'd even agree with her, except that this is where my husband chose to live, and since his death this is all I have left of him. Besides, after a while, the place kind of grows on you."

Shay was such a young, beautiful, vital woman, it was often difficult to think of her as a widow. He reached out and gave her hand a quick squeeze. "I'm sorry."

He'd said it before, countless times to countless victims. It always felt less than adequate and left him feeling hollow, as it did now.

Shay ran her fingertips over a mahogany desk, and Sebastian could see the memories in her eyes. "Don't be. I'm content with my life and the choices I've made. But I want Brandi to be happy, too, and something just isn't right with her."

He scrubbed his hand over his tired eyes. Shay looked unhappy as hell, her worry plain to see, and he decided right then he wouldn't tell her how she'd innocently added to Brandi's burden. It wouldn't happen again, because he'd be there, making certain it didn't.

He intended to make Brandi happy, and to keep her that way, so the point was now moot. "I didn't mean to let this much time pass before seeing her again, but I was called away. I just got back in town this morning. I tried calling her twice while I was gone, and several times since I've been home, but I couldn't get an answer."

"She was probably avoiding you."

Well, that was typical of Shay to be so blunt. Sebastian dropped into a chair and leaned his head back. "I ought to strangle you for getting me into this mess."

"Is that what it is? A mess?"

"What the hell would you call it? You send me off on an innocent trip…only it wasn't so innocent."

"Uh, I hesitate to ask, but what exactly are you telling me?"

He couldn't help but laugh. "Not what you think. I was supposed to entertain your sister for five days, but instead, I fell in love with her in one. The rest of the trip was pure torture, and even though I kept telling myself she deserved a second chance at life without a possessive Neanderthal like myself hanging around, I can't just let her go."

Shay blinked twice. "You love Brandi?"

His voice softened at her amazement and he said simply, "How could I not?"

Shay's smile was blinding. "Exactly! She's perfect, isn't she?"

"No, she's beautifully flawed and I want her. Where is she, Shay?"

"It might not be that easy. You see, I get the impression Brandi doesn't think she's good enough for you."

That volatile anger roiled in his stomach, giving him cramps. It was worse than worrying about money, because Brandi made him feel more secure, more valued, than money ever could. He contemplated Shay's statement, and his eyes narrowed. "Where did she get that harebrained idea?"

"From you evidently, so you can just stop glaring daggers at me. Right now, Brandi thinks you walk on water. To hear her tell it, you're the perfect man."

Emotion swelled inside him—pride and need and lust. "She said that?"

"Not the part about you being too good for her. I just figured that out on my own, given the solemn way she sang your praises. Let me see, you're gentle and confident and understanding and caring and... Oh, yeah. Strong." Shay punched his shoulder and winked. "But then any woman with a pulse can see that on her own."

"You're a terror, Shay. When you snag a man, he'd better have a will of iron so you don't trample him into the mud."

"Ha! Been there, done that. I have no intention of getting involved—much less married—ever again."

"Spoken like a woman on the brink of a great fall."

Shay made a rude sound. "I'm too sturdy to fall. Brandi's the one who's fallen, and I want to know what you're going to do about it."

All traces of fatigue left him. He'd spent four days in surveillance, two in wrapping up an attempted assault which he physically prevented. The ex-girlfriend of the assailant had bordered on hysteria, and it had taken him a long time to calm and reassure her. He'd been on and off planes for more hours than he cared to count, and he'd had nothing but broken, disturbed sleep on any given night. An hour ago he'd felt bruised, physically and mentally tired, and ready to collapse. But now his anger made him ready to burst with adrenaline. He needed an outlet, and Brandi with all her stubbornness seemed like a prime target.

How dare she think she wasn't good enough for him?

He stood to tower over Shay and his tone emerged as a low, mean growl. "I'm going to take care of everything. As soon as you tell me where she is."

Shay backed up. "I know you're inclined to be a little autocratic on occasion. And I appreciate the fact that with your job, it's probably necessary. But you aren't going to do anything…well…uncivilized, are you?"

He snorted. Shay knew him well enough she shouldn't have been worried at all. "I'm going to make your irritating little sister see reason, that's all." *After* he made love to her a couple of dozen times. When he'd finished, she'd know for certain just how much she meant to him.

Shay grinned and patted his arm. "I'll get you the address." She went around her desk to open the top drawer. "But I'm counting on you to make this work out, Sebastian. I don't want to have to deal with Brandi's temper if she comes back here alone."

"She's not going anywhere without me."

"Ohhh. A forceful man. Be still, my heart." She fanned her face with a small square of white paper.

Sebastian grabbed the slip of paper from her hand. "Ha. You're too damn bossy to ever put up with a forceful man and you know it. You'd have him begging for mercy within twenty-four hours."

Shay shrugged. "Damn right. But I can have my fantasies."

As he started out, he said over his shoulder, "Yeah, we all do." And Brandi was about to fulfill his, whether she liked it or not.

BRANDI STEPPED OUT onto the front porch of the small rental cabin, and opened her arms to the feeling of being wrapped in a big black sky filled with diamonds. There wasn't a cloud in sight to block the stars and the moon was a fat orb that glowed softly. She wondered if this was how Sebastian felt when he stood in the isolation of his own home; at peace, lulled by his surroundings. Then she felt keen regret, because she would never know.

This cabin was rustic compared to the elegant one she'd shared with Sebastian. She preferred it here, though, if she had to be alone, because this cabin had a gentle familiarity to it, a hominess that she needed to mend her broken heart.

He hadn't called. He hadn't come to see her.

Though she knew it was for the best, for a short time she'd hoped for more. Sebastian had seemed so determined to continue their relationship, that a secret part of her had hoped he would force the issue, that he would take her choices away. But then those first few days had passed and she hadn't heard from him. After that, she'd accepted what was right for both of them.

Still, she missed him terribly. Everything she did,

everywhere she looked, she thought of him. The nights were the worst. There wasn't a repeat of the nightmare, just the endless loneliness, and the knowledge of what she was missing. It had only been five days—the same length of time as the mundane workweek she usually put in—but time enough for her to fall completely, irrevocably in love.

It wasn't a mere infatuation with her first lover; no infatuation could be this strong, this all consuming. She had no doubts about the depth of her feelings. She loved him, and that wasn't going to go away.

It was Sebastian she had to wonder about. Was it possible for a man to be so gentle and considerate and not be emotionally involved? Could he have been using the situation only to gratify them both sexually? He'd always had her best interests at heart, she knew that as well as she knew her own limitations. Sebastian hadn't used her. But he'd admitted the circumstances were a fantasy for him, for almost any man. And what normal, healthy man would turn down the invitations she'd given? Now that the trip was over, maybe he'd decided to find a woman with fewer inhibitions, someone who could meet his high level of sexuality without faltering.

Moving to sit in an old wooden rocker, she closed her eyes and immediately the fantasies began to intrude. She had never considered fantasizing about a person before, but Sebastian had been so open about it, so natural, that his fantasies were now her own. In her mind, she could clearly see his bare, powerful body drawn taut on the bed, his expression hard and heated as she gently, endlessly rode him. The sounds of pleasure he made, the way his breath rasped, the thrusting of his hips as he struggled against his bonds. A tingle started inside her, and she felt the ache more keenly than ever.

She knew now what she was missing, and the knowing hurt. But she wouldn't have gone back to her ignorance for anything, her memories of the time with him were too precious to regret.

Disgusted with herself and her obsession with a man she couldn't have, she started to rise. An unfamiliar sound made her hesitate; tires crunched on the long gravel drive, then braked to the side of the house. With her entire body straining with the effort, she listened to the sound of a car door slamming, the noise carried easily on the still night air.

No one knew she was here, so she certainly didn't expect any visitors. Unless Shay had come to check on her, which was possible. But the stomping footsteps that rounded the house weren't made by a woman, and just that quickly, all her old fears returned, choking her, slowing her heartbeat. She was alone, vulnerable....

A familiar figure bounded onto the porch and Sebastian stood there, overwhelmingly big and strong, making the small porch seem even smaller. Relief, yearning, confusion—they all swamped her at once. She sat frozen, unsure what to do, how to react. He didn't notice her sitting so quietly in the corner. He had his hands on his hips and a fierce frown on his face. To Brandi's eyes, he looked incredibly gorgeous.

Then one large fist raised to pound on her door. In the next instant, he bellowed her name in demand, the sound echoing dully around them. Brandi had no doubt he was angry.

She spoke quietly from her shadowed corner. "What are you doing here?"

He whirled toward her, his eyes searching in the darkness. When he located her, he stepped close. He wrapped his long fingers firmly around her upper arms and half lifted her from the chair.

"I came for you. Why the hell are you hiding from me?"

"Hiding?" His tone was antagonistic, almost brutal. Brandi didn't understand his mood at all.

"Yes, damn it. I've been trying to reach you. I had to threaten Shay to find out where you were."

He had frightened her half to death coming out here this way, and now he accused her? In the week since they'd parted, she'd suffered ten kinds of hell, missing him, wanting him. *Needing him.* And he verbally attacked with his first breath. She tried to pull away from him, but he held firm, so she did her best to stare him in the eyes. She had to tip her head way back to do so. "I'm not hiding, you big jerk. I'm relaxing. And why shouldn't I have gone away? You said you were going to call, but then you didn't."

She hadn't meant to make that accusation. It served no purpose, except to show the measure of her hurt. Pride made her stiffen. As much as she wanted him, she wouldn't humiliate herself.

Muttering, she said, "Shay should have kept her mouth shut. She promised me."

"Yeah, well, she buckled under my threats."

Brandi snorted. "Shay doesn't buckle under to anyone."

"Okay, so she was more reasonable than you." He shook her gently, and his tone was urgent. "I explained to her I was called out of town on an emergency, and she believed me."

"You were out of town?"

He made a rough sound of exasperation. "*Yes*. I had to deal with a case where only I knew the history. I couldn't hand it over to anyone else."

Just looking at him made her heart beat faster. She licked her lips, more aware than ever of the differences in their heights, their strengths. "Was it a woman you had to help?"

He ran a hand through his hair. "Yeah. But it's over for good now. The jerk harassing her had a prior of petty theft. This time he had robbed a small convenience store. They had him on film. After she contacted me, I got the police involved and we set him up. The damn fool tried shooting at the cops."

Brandi swayed, and automatically she reached out to touch the solid strength of his chest, verifying that he was still in one piece. "You could have been hurt."

He shook his head. "I'm fine."

For the first time, she noticed the exhaustion in his eyes, apparent even in the dim moonlight. Being a hero was tiring work. Yet he'd come after her. Tears clouded her vision and she didn't know what to think.

All the differences between them had never seemed more magnified. He was close to a Superman figure, but she was certainly no Lois Lane.

"I tried to call once I got settled in a hotel, but you didn't answer your phone."

"The phone rang really late a couple of times. I

thought it was Shay. She's driving me nuts, wanting to coddle me, and at the same time trying to pry details out of me. She's not being at all subtle."

Sebastian's grin shone very white in the darkness. "I'm relieved that's all it was. Shay told me you were avoiding me."

This time, she really would strangle Shay once she got home. "No, I wasn't doing that." Then she shrugged. "I didn't think there was any reason to avoid you. You hadn't called. I thought it was over."

His fingers tightened on her arms, not hurting her, but letting her feel his strength. "No."

That one word held a wealth of determination. Very carefully, Brandi pulled away from him. Not because she was afraid, but because she needed time to think. She stepped behind the rocker. "Sebastian, I'm sorry if I misunderstood. But it was for the best anyway. We can't continue where we left off."

"Bullshit."

Shocked, Brandi curled her fingers over the wooden slats of the chair. Her anger simmered. "I'm trying to be honest here," she shouted in frustration.

"Then be honest and admit you want me! I'm too damn tired for more games."

Knowing she was only reacting to his anger, Brandi tried to find a measure of calm, but she couldn't. Sebastian was simply being too brutally provoking. "We're not suited to each other," she insisted.

"I'll warn you right now, honey," he said, his tone hard and low and rasping, "if you give me any nonsense about not being good enough for me, you probably won't like the consequences."

"I'll always have the fears, Sebastian, and eventually, they'll come between us!"

He cursed again, loudly, and Brandi's temper rose to match his. "Quit cursing at me! Do you think this decision has been easy for me? I'm trying to do what's best for both of us. So go home and leave it alone." Tears stung her eyes. In disgust, Brandi turned away and stomped into the house. Sebastian followed.

With only one light on in the tiny kitchenette, the interior of the cabin was dim. "Don't walk away from me, Brandi." He caught her arm and swung her around. Lowering his face close to hers, he said, "I've given you as much space as I can. From the very first, you've wrapped me around your little finger. But I'll be damned if I'll let you end it this easy. *I care about you.*"

Brandi had given this a lot of thought, and she was prepared to be reasonable, even noble, despite the volatile mood. She squared her shoulders and stated, "Sebastian, you're a hero."

With a hoot of rough laughter, he sneered and said, "Is this a new fantasy, Brandi? Hey, I'm game, you know that. But I need to know the details if you want me to play the right role."

He looked dangerous, and Brandi imagined this was how he looked when he worked. He seemed poised to jump on her, but she knew he wouldn't. She trusted him. Still, her own anxiety made her tone as harsh as his. "Damn it, Sebastian, will you just listen?"

He looked ready to snarl in anger, but finally he nodded.

Brandi drew a steadying breath, but she couldn't calm herself. The truth of what she was losing, of what she was chasing away, made her angry. "You've been rescuing women for years, starting with your mother, then in your business. You've always seen women as small and vulnerable. Being a protector is as much a part of you as your sexuality."

His low growl reverberated in the quiet cabin. "I don't think of women as inferior people, Brandi."

"I know you don't." She tried to keep her voice even, desperate to make him understand. Still, her words came too fast and too hard. "The reality of your size and strength in comparison to a woman's is obvious in everything you do. And more than most men, you're aware of that reality. It's ingrained in you, with your job, your background. And you…you probably viewed me, with the circumstances of my rape, as a woman in more need of rescuing than most."

He shook his head. "I wasn't initiating a rescue attempt when I let you tie me down. I was answering a sexual need. I was hot, and you were the answer."

Brandi took a step forward, her eyes narrowed. He was deliberately being crude, trying to embarrass her. In low tones, she said, "Good. Because you don't have to rescue me. The five-day fling is over. Your obligation is over."

His snarl was loud and ferocious. "Damn you! Is that all you think it was? An *obligation?* I've got plenty of obligations, lady, but I don't usually handle them in bed."

Brandi felt her cheeks heat, but refused to look away from him. "Our situation was unique."

"Damn right it was. You used me, and now you're through, is that it?"

Her breath caught painfully. *"No!"*

"Listen to me, Brandi, and listen good." He still

frowned, but now his expression was intent, filled with cold determination. "My house will never be fancy, nothing like Shay's, but it's mine, and it's not something I can give up. Anything else is negotiable but that. I have enough money put away that you can redecorate as many times as you like. And I've already decided to limit the cases that take me out of town. The house is isolated, but you won't be alone there very often. I'll even hire a maid, if that'll make you feel better. It's not a mansion, but you'll adjust."

Tears blinded her, and without thinking she struck him hard in the chest. It felt like hitting a stone wall, and she gasped with the pain of it, cradling her hand to her chest. Sebastian blinked, his anger replaced by surprise, but other than that, he didn't show any sign that the blow had registered.

Brandi went on tiptoe to try to look him in the eyes. "Damn you, Sebastian, this isn't about money! It isn't about a house or maids or decorating. It's about *you*."

She tried to strike him again, and this time he caught her fist and held it against his chest. "Stop that. You're going to hurt yourself."

Brandi snarled with her anger. "I don't care about money!"

"But I do. A little too much."

"Ha! What about the cases you don't charge for? You made it sound like it was an isolated case here and there, but Shay told me there were a lot of people who needed you, and you do the work gratis."

He stiffened, as if he didn't want that part of his life examined too closely. "Not everyone with a need has that kind of money to spend. I make a more than sufficient income on the bigger cases."

"That's exactly my point! You don't hoard your money. You're not oblivious to those in need. God, you're the most generous man I've ever known."

"Brandi…"

"No! You listen to me this time. I love you, you big jerk. You're an amazing man, considerate and sexy and strong and gentle and…" She faltered, the words choking her. She cleared her throat and stared up at him. "You can have any woman you want, Sebastian. You don't need me."

His eyes suddenly blazed with a savage expression. *"Like hell I don't."*

"Sebastian…"

"I need you and I want you." He jerked her up against his hard, hot body. "Right now."

She glared and actually stomped her foot. "You are *not* going to sidetrack me with sex!"

Sebastian caught both of her wrists and used them to control her, holding her just tight enough to let her know she couldn't escape him. A slow grin suddenly spread over his face. "You are so damn beautiful."

Brandi gasped. "Aren't you listening to me? Have you heard a word I've said? This would never work out between us. You deserve everything a woman has to offer. But I can't give it to you, because part of me is forever gone. You deserve so much more than I can— *Umpf!*"

Sebastian jerked her hard into his body and his mouth muffled her protests. He kissed her, letting her feel his anger, his lust. When he pulled away, Brandi was dazed.

"I warned you not to do that, not to put yourself down. Don't you ever belittle yourself, do you hear me?" He kissed her again, a quick hard kiss, then whispered, "I love you, Brandi. I accept all your flaws, just as I hope you'll accept all of mine. Having you makes me feel more secure than any amount of money ever could. And you might as well know right now, I'm never letting you go."

Before Brandi could form a coherent argument—if indeed she would have—Sebastian picked her up and carried her to the only bedroom. It housed a double bed, and as he lowered her to the mattress, his mouth came down on hers again, stifling any complaint she might have made. Brandi struggled against him, especially when he started pulling off her T-shirt. Nothing had been settled yet!

He misunderstood and said against her lips, "It's just me, babe. Only me." His head lowered to her breast and he sucked her nipple gently into the heat of his mouth. Brandi arched up off the mattress with a harsh cry of pleasure.

Lowering his full weight onto her to keep her still, Sebastian trailed his mouth over her breasts, kissing the other nipple, then moving down to her ribs. Brandi writhed beneath his comforting weight, loving the feel of him over her, surrounding her. Her earlier fantasies, combined with his sudden appearance and her raw emotions, left no room for anything other than need. She could no longer focus on fear, regrets or what might be right or wrong for the future.

Sebastian growled and his hand slid between her thighs, seeking, probing. He didn't hold back now, didn't temper his desire or his urgency. Brandi moaned.

"I need you, babe. Right now."

"Yes." Brandi said the word mindlessly, her hips lifting into his, pressing. He unsnapped her shorts and jerked them open. His long fingers caught at the waistband, and he stripped her shorts down her legs, taking her panties with them. Sitting poised between her widespread legs, he looked at her. The heat in his eyes should have brought on her wariness, but instead, it thrilled her.

He was back, and he wanted her. He'd said he loved her.

"Sebastian?"

"I'm sorry, sweetheart, but I can't wait."

Brandi screamed when his mouth pressed against her sensitive flesh. His tongue touched and explored; he suckled and nipped with his sharp teeth, and through it all, he held her legs spread wide with his rough hands. Brandi had almost no time to adjust to the unfamiliar caresses before she felt her climax building. Her body arched high, pressing her closer to his mouth, closer... She felt suspended with intense pleasure for long seconds before the feelings began to diminish.

When she slumped into the mattress, her breathing still harsh and her heart thundering against her ribs, Sebastian leaned back and quickly fumbled with his belt and the closure of his slacks. The zipper came down and he eased the restriction of clothing away from his erection.

Balancing on his arms above her, he positioned himself, then gently probed against her slick folds. He made a low sound of pleasure. "You feel so hot and wet." He slid in an inch, pacing himself, then squeezed his eyes closed. "Tight."

Brandi wrapped her legs around him. She loved him. And she needed him now. *Sebastian.*

He thrust forward, and this new position, with him planted firmly between her thighs, left her helpless to counter his thrusts. The sense of being totally vulnerable to him—feeling him so deeply inside her, stretching her—enhanced her pleasure rather than inhibiting it. They both groaned.

When he gruffly apologized, Brandi knew he had meant to be slow and gentle. But their mating had turned urgent. Unlike the lovemaking that Brandi had controlled, this was wild and primal, and so beautiful she cried.

Within minutes, she came again, but it was better this time, the feelings more intense, deeper, because Sebastian was a part of her. She wrapped herself around him and screamed with her pleasure. Sebastian's low growl followed, while his shoulders tensed and his hips pumped wildly. Then he slumped onto her, his body limp, sated.

Brandi drew her fingers up and down the long expanse of his back, solid with muscle, warm and damp from his sweat. She loved him, every big gorgeous inch of him, from his hair-rough legs to his whiskered chin. He was the most incredible man, and if she could believe his words, he was hers.

Smiling, she said, "You were wrong."

He stiffened, then carefully levered himself upward. Brandi felt tears sting her eyes at his look of uncertainty. She raised her head enough to kiss him, letting her lips play lightly over his. "You told me I wouldn't like the consequences—but I liked them very much."

Sebastian grinned, then dropped his forehead to hers. "I love you, Brandi. Don't ever leave me again."

"I won't. Not if you really love me."

"I love you so much it terrifies me."

Everything seemed perfect, but she had to make certain. "The nightmares might not be gone."

"Nothing that emotional is ever completely gone. I'll always have a soft spot for people in need, and feel sickened by financial waste. I'll always take part in charities, needing to help as much as I can. Things become part of us, molding us, making us the people we are. Good and bad, we just have to adjust and be who we are."

"I love who you are, your scruples, your dedication, your morality. I think you're a wonderful person."

"I love you, too. We'll deal with anything that comes up. Together."

He kissed her, long and sweet, then not so sweet. "I forgot to use a condom."

Brandi chuckled at his chagrin. "Is your house big enough for a baby or two?"

His eyes turned a fierce, bright green. "Yeah, it's plenty big enough. And there are trees in the yard that would be perfect for a playhouse, or a tire swing. And a creek around the back of the property where we could catch crawdads and minnows and tadpoles."

The tears overflowed her eyes, but she managed a wobbly smile. "I'd say it sounds like life with you will be perfect."

He cupped her face. "Will you marry me?"

"I think Shay would probably insist on it."

He chuckled. "And if Shay wasn't around to force the issue?"

Widening her eyes in mock alarm, she asked,

"You're not thinking of doing anything nefarious with my sister, are you?"

"No way. I owe Shay big for setting us up together in the first place." He pushed his hips against her, reminding her that he was still inside her—and aroused once more. "Now, will you answer me?"

She moaned, her eyes closing as his gentle thrusts stole her thoughts.

"Brandi?"

"Yes, I'll marry you. Just please don't stop what you're doing."

Sebastian grinned past his own desire. He slid one hand between their bodies, finding her heat and making her moan loudly. Now that he'd been partially sated, and the desperate need to get a commitment from her had been appeased, he could take it a little easier, go a little slower. Tease a little more.

Brandi looked beautiful with her incredible dark hair wild around her face, her lips parted, her cheeks flushed. She wanted him and she no longer felt any shyness in admitting her need. He kissed her nipple and felt her internal muscles squeeze him.

"Brandi?" he whispered, his lips against her soft skin. "Did I ever tell you the fantasy I have about owning a sex slave?"

Her eyes opened slumberously and she smiled. "No. But I think I'd like for you to tell me about it right now."

He showed her instead.

* * * * *

TANTALIZING

To Bonnie Tucker: Funny, caring, a very special friend—you're all these things, Bonnie. Your Sunday long distance calls are a tonic that keeps me smiling for hours.

I look forward to them, just as I do to each of your hilarious, loving books. Thank you.

CHAPTER ONE

TUGGING AT THE HEM of her miniskirt, Josie Jackson came the rest of the way into the noisy room. Seeing to the end of the bar was almost impossible in the near darkness with blue gray smoke clouding everything. But she finally spied a man, his back to her, sitting on the end bar stool, just where he was supposed to be.

Brazen, she told herself, trying to get into the part she needed to play. *Daring, sexy, confident.* She'd scare the poor man to death and he wouldn't be able to leave quick enough.

Josie had chosen the busy singles' meeting place, hoping that would end it right there. But he'd surprised her by agreeing with her choice. At least, her sister claimed he'd agreed. But her sister had also said he was "perfect" for her, which almost guaranteed Josie wouldn't like him. Susan had described him as responsible. Mature. *Settled.*

Josie was so tired of her sister setting up blind dates, and she was even more fed up with the type of man her sister assumed she needed: stuffy, too proper and too concerned with appearances. Men who didn't want anything to do with romance or excitement. All they wanted was to find someone like them so they could marry and get on with their boring lives.

She was twenty-five now and had spent most of her life working toward her goals, pleasing her sister with her dedication. Well, she'd reached those goals, so it was time for other things. Past time. She deserved to have some fun. Bob Morrison may be interested in a nice little house in a nice little neighborhood with a nice little family, but Josie Jackson had other plans, and if the location for this meeting hadn't put him off, one look at her would.

She sauntered toward him. There was a low whistle behind her, and she felt heat pulse in her cheeks. The next thing she felt—a bold hand patting her bottom— almost caused her to run back out again. Instead she managed to glare at the offender and stay upright on her three-inch heels. No small feat, given that she normally wore sturdy, rubber-soled shoes. She *could* do this, she told herself, she could…

All thought became suspended as the man turned to face her.

Good heavens. Her breath caught somewhere in the region of her throat and refused to budge any farther. She stared. *Well. He certainly doesn't look stuffy, Josie girl, not in those nice snug jeans and that black polo shirt. This can't be the right man.* For once, he seemed too…right, too masculine and attractive and sexy. Definitely sexy. Fate wouldn't be so cruel as to actually send her a gorgeous, stuffy man. Would it?

She forced herself to take another halting step forward, hampered by the tight miniskirt, the ridiculously high heels and her own reservations. "Bob? Bob Morrison?"

His dark eyes were almost black, as was the shiny, straight hair that hung over his brow, unkempt, but still very appealing. His gaze went from a slow, enthralled perusal of her mostly bared legs to her midriff where he paused, looking her over from chest to belly, his look almost tactile in its intensity, then he reached her face. He drew in a long breath, apparently feeling as stunned as she did. She waited for him to speak, to do or say something that would prove her assumptions had been correct, that he wasn't what she wanted in a man, that he was another typical offering from Susan who was supposed to further domesticate her life.

But then he stood, towering over her, six feet of gorgeous, throbbing male, and he smiled. That smile could be lethal, she thought as it sent shivers deep into her belly. The man exuded charm and warmth, and there was absolutely nothing stuffy or uptight about him. In fact, she felt like Jell-O on the inside. Nothing stuffy about that.

He held out his hand—a large hand that engulfed her own and seemed to brand her with his strength and heat. With the type of voice that inspired fantasies, he said, "I'm…Bob. It's very nice to meet you, Josie."

HE WASN'T USUALLY a liar.

Nick Harris took in the exquisite female before him and forgave himself. Lying was necessary, even imperative, given the fact he was faced with the most gorgeous, sexy woman imaginable—so close, and yet, not for him. He'd tell a hundred lies if it would keep her from walking out. Bob wouldn't appreciate being impersonated, of course, but then, Bob hadn't wanted anything to do with her. He'd been more taken with her sister, that rigid woman who had conspired the entire meeting. What Bob saw in Susan Jackson was beyond Nick, but now he could only be glad. Bob's preferences in women had Nick sitting here on a Saturday night, prepared to make excuses for his friend and partner.

Thank God he'd agreed to do it. If he hadn't, he might have missed her, and she was well worth the football tickets he'd wasted. She was well worth giving up *all* sports.

She looked surprised, as surprised as he felt, her green eyes wide, her soft mouth slightly open. Her full lips were painted a shiny red, and he could see her pink tongue just behind her teeth. Damn, the things he'd like to do with that tongue…

Belatedly his manners kicked in. "Would you like to sit down?" Normally he was known as a gentleman, as a reasonable man, sane and intelligent and given to bouts of outstanding charm. But he felt as though he'd just been poleaxed. And it only got worse as she flipped her long silky red hair over her shoulder, shrugged, then lifted her shapely bottom onto the bar stool next to his. That bottom held his spellbound attention for a few moments, before he could finally pull his gaze away. Her very short black skirt, hiked up as it was, revealed slender thighs. She crossed her legs, swinging one high-heel clad foot. He swallowed, heard himself do it and told himself to get a grip. He couldn't let her see how she'd affected him.

"Can I get you something to drink?"

She hesitated, and he could almost see her considering, but then she shook her head. Those sexy green eyes of hers slanted his way, teasing, flirting, causing his muscles to twitch. "There's a lot of things I do, but drinking isn't one of them."

It took him a second to recover from that look and the outrageous words she'd spoken. He hoped to hell he'd interpreted them right. "Oh? Religious reasons? Diet?"

Her lips curved and her long lashes lowered. "I just like to have control at all times. I want to know exactly what I'm doing, how I'm doing it and who I'm doing it with. Alcohol tends to muddle things."

As she spoke, a pink flush spread from her cheeks to her throat to the top of her chest, where the scooped neckline of her blouse showed just a hint of cleavage. Light freckles were sprinkled there, like tiny decorations, making him wonder where other freckles might be. He'd heard things about redheads, but he'd always discounted them as fantasy, nothing more. Now he had to reassess. This redhead seemed to exude sensuality with her every breath. And he was getting hotter than a chili pepper just looking at her.

He'd have to wrest control from her, despite her just-stated preferences, if he wanted to survive. Never had he let a woman get the upper hand in any situation, not since he'd been a teenager and his stepmother had taken over his life. He didn't intend to let this little woman, no matter how appealing she was, call the shots. Not even if those shots might be to his liking.

She'd temporarily thrown him, but now he was getting used to looking at her, to breathing her musky scent and hearing her throaty, quiet voice. And she kept peeking looks at him, as if she were shy, which couldn't be, not looking the way she looked. Or maybe she was feeling just as attracted as he was. That should work to his advantage. At least he'd know he wasn't drowning alone.

He ordered two colas, then slowly, giving her time to withdraw, he slid his palm under hers where it rested on the bar. Her eyes widened again, but she didn't pull away. Her hand was slender, frail. Her fingers felt cold, and he wondered if it was from being outside, or from nervousness. But there didn't seem to be a nervous bone in her luscious little body.

"You're not exactly what I expected." With Bob's usual tastes in women, he'd thought to find a conservative, righteous prude, someone who resembled the sister, Susan. That woman could freeze a man with a look—and she'd tried doing just that to him when she'd first come to him and Bob for an advertising campaign. The woman had taken an instant dislike to him, something about spotting a womanizer right off, so he'd left her to Bob. And when the date had been engineered, he'd expected to find a woman just as cold, just as plain and judgmental. He'd expected mousy brown hair and flat hazel eyes. A quiet, circumspect demeanor.

But Josie Jackson was nothing at all like her sister. It was a damn good thing Bob hadn't come. He might have had a heart attack while running away.

The thought inspired a grin.

"It makes you smile to get the unexpected?"

She sounded almost baffled, and he chuckled. "This time, yes. But then, you're a very pleasant surprise."

Small white teeth closed over her bottom lip. He wanted them to close over his lip. He wanted them to close over his—

"You're not what I expected, either. Usually my sister lines me up with these overly serious, stuffy, three-piece-suit types. They're always concerned about responsibilities, their businesses, appearances." Her eyes met his, daring him, teasing him. "You wouldn't be like that, now would you?"

He stifled a laugh. She thought she was taunting him, he could tell. But at the moment, responsibilities and business were the furthest thing from his mind, and he hoped like hell she wouldn't expect him to worry about appearances. He never had.

Bob would, but he wasn't Bob.

"No one has ever accused me of being stuffy." That was true enough, since Bob usually lamented his lack of gravity. Come to think of it, maybe it was his casual attitude that had made the sister dislike him so much. Not that he cared. Formality had been his stepmother's strong suit, so he naturally abhorred it. He believed in keeping the business sound, but he didn't think it had to rule his life. Evidently Josie agreed, though she looked shocked by his answer. Interesting.

Not willing to wait another minute to hold her, he stood and pulled her to her feet. "Let's dance."

She balked, her legs stiffening, her expression almost comical. She tried to free her hand, but he held tight, determined.

"What's the matter? You don't dance, either?"

"Either?"

"Like the drinking." He rubbed his thumb over her palm, trying to soothe her. He didn't want her bolting now, but if he didn't get her in his arms soon, he was going to explode. He'd never been hit this hard before, but damned if he didn't like it.

"I dance," she said, then looked down at her feet. "But not usually in heels like these."

He, too, looked at her feet. Sexy little feet, arched in three-inch heels. Tugging her closer he said, "I won't let you stumble." His voice dropped. "Promise."

As he led them onto the dance floor her throat worked, but she didn't deny him. It was crowded with gyrating dancers, bumping into each other. He used that as an excuse to mesh their bodies together, feeling her from thigh to chest, holding her securely with one arm wrapped around her slender waist, his hand splayed wide on her back. She felt like heaven, warm and soft, and incredibly he felt the beginnings of an erection. His thighs tightened, his pulse slowed.

Even in her heels, she was only a little bit of a thing. His chin rested easily on the top of her head, and he felt the silkiness of all that hair floating around her shoulders, curling around her breasts. Wondering what it might feel like on his naked chest, his belly, made him clench his teeth against rising need. It was almost laughable the reaction she caused in him. But it was like his own private fantasy had come to life before his eyes. From her long lashes to her freckles to her shapely legs, he couldn't imagine a woman more finely put together than her. Or with a sexier voice, or a more appealing blush.

The blush was what really did it, with its hint of innocence mixed with hot carnal sexuality. *Damn.*

His hand pressed at the small of her back and he urged her just a bit closer. Her small, plump breasts pressed into his ribs, her slender thighs rubbed his. She sighed, the sound barely reaching him through the loud music. But the softening of her body couldn't be missed.

His lips touched her ear and he inhaled her scent. "That's it. Just relax. I've got you."

And he intended to keep her. At least for now.

He wondered how he could get around Bob and her sister. There was no doubt Susan Jackson wouldn't appreciate him being with Josie. She'd been very open about her immediate dislike and distrust. They'd spoken for a mere fifteen minutes, him using all his charm to soften her, before Susan had made her opinion of him known. Of course, maybe he had poured the charm on just a bit thick, but then prickly, overopinionated, pushy women like Susan Jackson irritated him. They reminded him of his stepmother, who had been the bossiest woman of all.

At what point should he tell Josie who he really was? Bob had claimed she would be crushed by his inability to meet her, that she was a wallflower of sorts who counted on her sister to set up her social calendar due to a shy nature and a demanding career. But the woman moving so gently against him, neither of them paying any attention to the beat of the music, in no way resembled a wallflower or a driven, career-minded lady.

There was the possibility Bob might want to reset the date once he realized what he was missing, despite his ridiculous requirements for a woman and his initial interest in Susan. But of course, Nick wouldn't allow that now. Circumstances had decreed that he meet Josie first. And finders keepers, as the saying went. Bob could damn well concentrate on the contrary Susan for his future wife. Why Bob was so determined to court a wearisome little housewife-type anyway didn't make sense to Nick. Especially not when there were women like this one still available.

Putting one foot between hers, he managed to insinuate his thigh close to her body. She jerked, startled, then made a soft sound of acceptance. He felt her incredible heat, the teasing friction on his leg as they both moved, and he shuddered with the sensations. With a little dip and a slow turn, he had her practically straddling his thigh. She gasped, her breasts rose and fell and her hands tightened on his chest, knotting his shirt. Such a volatile reaction, he thought, feeling his own heartbeat quicken.

"I'm glad I came tonight." The words were deep and husky with his arousal, but he wanted her to know, to understand how grateful he felt to Bob for bailing out. Things were going to get complicated, of that he was certain, but he didn't want her to misunderstand his motives.

The smile she offered up to him made his gut tighten. "Do you know, I thought you'd be horrified by this place."

He looked around, not really enjoying the busy singles' bar, but not exactly horrified, either. Located on the riverbank, with a restaurant downstairs and the dance floor and bar upstairs, it was a popular meeting place. "Why?"

They had to shout to be heard, so he began moving them toward the corner, away from the other dancers and out of the chaos. He wanted to talk to her, to know everything about her, to understand the contrast of her incredible looks and her shy smiles. He wanted to taste her, deep and long.

"From what my sister told me about you, I gathered you were a bit…sedate."

Bob was sedate. Hell, Bob was almost dead, he was so sedate. *He was Bob.* Cautiously he asked, "What else did your sister say about…me?"

"That you were dependable."

They reached the edge of the floor, and he snorted. "Dependable? Makes me sound like a hound."

Her soft laugh made him change his mind about the corner and lead her to a balcony door instead. It was chilly enough in early September, with the damp breeze off the river, to deter other dancers from taking in the night air. As they stepped out, he released her and she wrapped her arms around herself for warmth.

Below the balcony, car lights flashed as traffic filled the parking lot and navigated the narrow roads around the bar. Boat horns echoed in the distance, and a few people loitered by the entrance door, waiting either to come in or go out. Their voices were muted, drowned out by the music. He turned to face Josie, seeing her eyes shine in the darkness, that red hair of hers being lightly teased by the wind. He reached out and caught a long curl, rubbing it between his fingers.

"Are you disappointed that I'm not dependable?"

"You're not?"

"No." He owed her some honesty, and his outlook on life was something he never kept from a woman, any woman. Not even one that he wanted as badly as he did this one. "I'm safe. Trustworthy. You don't have to be afraid of me." She grinned and he tugged on her hair until she stepped closer, then he released her and looked over her head at the night sky. "I'm a nice guy. I'm secure. But I'm not the type of man you want to depend on, Josie."

She lifted a hand to brush her hair from her cheek and studied him. "Are you fun?"

The epitome of temptation, she stood there looking

up at him, her eyes huge in the darkness, her body so close only an inch separated them. He touched her cheek and felt her softness, the subtle warmth of her skin. "Do you want me to be fun?"

She stepped away, moving across the balcony and bracing her hands on the railing. Eyes closed, she leaned out, arching her back and letting the wind toss her hair. Turning her face up to the moon, she said, "Yes. I think I deserve to have fun. I want to do things I haven't done and see things I haven't seen. I want to put work aside and enjoy life for a change."

Looking at her, at the way her stance had tautened her bottom in the snug skirt, her legs braced with the high heels putting her nearly on tiptoe, her hair reaching down her back... He couldn't resist. He stepped up to her until his legs bracketed hers, his groin pressing into her smooth buttocks. She would feel his erection, but he didn't care.

With a soft push, he acknowledged her shock, her surprise and her interest.

Leaning down, he kissed the side of her neck, her ear. He spoke in a soft, intimate whisper. "I can show you lots of ways to enjoy yourself, Josie."

There was a split second when he thought she'd draw away, and already his body grieved. But then she leaned her head back to his chest and tipped it to the side to give his mouth better advantage. He tasted the sweet heat of her skin, his tongue touching her, leaving damp kisses behind that made her shiver. He flattened one hand on her abdomen and his fingers caressed her. His heartbeat drummed, the pleasure twisting, escalating.

"Yes."

The word was caught in a moan, and Nick closed his eyes, not sure he'd heard it. "Josie?"

Turning in the tight circle of his arms, the railing at her back keeping her from putting any space between them, she flickered a nervous, uncertain smile and said again, "Yes. Show me."

Excitement mushroomed. Already his body throbbed with sexual heat. Slowly he leaned down, keeping her caught in his gaze, letting the anticipation build. He heard Josie drawing in choppy breaths and knew she was as turned on as he. His mouth touched the softness of hers and she made a small sound of acceptance, her hands curling over his shoulders.

Her lip gloss tasted of cherries, and he licked it off, slowly, savoring her every breath, her sighs. She tried to kiss him, but he sucked her bottom lip into his mouth, nibbling, until her lips were lusciously full from his administrations, begging for his kiss.

Her tongue touched his and he covered her mouth, unable to resist a moment more. She was so hot, so sweet.

And it took him about thirty seconds of incredible kissing to figure out she was damn innocent, too.

She didn't return his kisses, or his touches. She only accepted them, clinging to him, a sense of wonder and expectation swirling around her. He led, but although she was willing, she didn't quite follow. In fact, it seemed almost as if she didn't know how.

With a groan, he pulled back, dragging his gaze over her body, so sexy, revealed in the short tight skirt and low-cut blouse, her hair wild and free, her smile shy but inviting. *Inviting what?* His heart threatened to punch through his ribs, and he silently cursed in intense frustration.

Josie Jackson was a little fraud. Despite all the packaging, despite the seductive words and gestures, she was probably more suited to Bob. But that idea made Nick half-sick with anger and he swore to himself Bob would never touch her. He wouldn't allow it.

He knew women, had been studying them since he'd first become a teenager. He knew the good in them, the gentleness and pleasure they could offer. And because of the feminine members of his family, his stepmother and his mother, he knew the bad, the ways they could manipulate and connive.

This little sweetheart was up to something. But then, no one had ever accused Nick Harris of turning down a challenge—especially not one this tantalizing. Mustering a grin, he let his fingers fan her cheek, her temple. "We both know what we want, honey, so why don't we get out of here and go someplace quiet?"

He waited for her to refuse, to call him on his outrageous bluff. Then she'd explain, and he could explain, too, and they could start over, taking the time to get to know each other. And for a second there, she looked like she would refuse.

Instead, she knocked him off balance by nodding agreement, and whispering quietly, shyly, "You can lead the way."

Oh yeah. He'd lead the way all right. Right into insanity. He wasn't in the habit of rushing women into bed, certainly not only minutes after meeting them. He wasn't an idiot. But all the same, he took her proffered hand and started back toward the exit. Excitement rushed through his body with every step.

Excitement and the sure knowledge that he was about to make a huge tactical mistake, one he'd likely live to regret, but he was helpless to stop himself.

CHAPTER TWO

"Did you drive?"

"No, I, ah, took a cab." Because her car was as sensible and plain as she was, and would have given her away. Her plan wouldn't have worked, she would have lost this opportunity. She closed her eyes on the thought.

"I'll drive, then."

"Okay." Josie could hardly speak for the lump of excitement in her throat. She'd started out acting a part, and now she was going to get to live it. With this gorgeous, sexy man...*her sister had found?* Incredible. Maybe Susan was finally starting to understand her better. She'd have to thank her... No, she wouldn't. She still didn't want people meddling in her life and setting up blind dates. It was past time she put an end to that high-handed habit. Besides, if her sister knew how incredible Bob Morrison was turning out to be, she wouldn't want Josie to see him anymore. She certainly wouldn't approve of them slipping off together to do...all the wonderful things she'd never dared to dream about.

Josie wasn't even certain *she* approved of herself. Things like this just didn't happen to her. Men didn't notice her, and she'd always accepted that. But now everything felt so right, so instinctive. She'd never considered herself impulsive, but then, she'd never had the attention of a man like Bob. And it wasn't just his sexy looks. It was his smile, a tilting of that sensual mouth that made her feel special, and the fact that since they'd first met, he hadn't taken his eyes off her. He held her gently, and she'd felt a trembling in his hands that proved he was affected by the madness too. When he spoke, his voice was deep and husky, his words persuasive, telling how much he wanted her.

She had only to look at him and her stomach took a free fall, as if she'd just jumped from a plane and didn't care where she landed. All her life she'd been cautious and circumspect, first pleasing her parents, and after their deaths, trying to please her sister. Susan took Josie's failures personally, so Josie had made certain to always succeed. She made Susan proud with her respectability and propriety, her overachiever attitude. And she had found a measure of happiness in the structured stability of that role.

But now she had a chance to taste the wild side, to sow some wild oats and experience life. And it was so exciting, being spontaneous for a change. Nature summoned, sending all her hormones into overdrive, making her hot and shaky and anxious. For once, she was going to let nature have its way.

"Don't you even want to know where I'm taking you?"

Josie paused, stung by his apparent irritation. From one second to the next, he'd gotten quiet and surly. When he turned to look at her, she saw that his dark thick brows were low over his eyes, his mouth a thin line. So far, that mouth had done nothing but smile at her and give her the most incredible, melting kisses imaginable, but now he was angry. She took a cautious step back. "What's wrong?"

He held her gaze, then with a growl of disgust, raked a hand through his midnight hair, leaving it disheveled. "Nothing. I'm sorry." He reached his hand toward her, palm up, and waited.

Josie bit her lip, uncertain, but the feelings, so many different feelings, were still curling inside her, demanding attention. It felt new and wonderful wanting a man like this, knowing he wanted her, too. After the blow of losing her parents, she'd drawn into herself and let Susan, with her natural confidence and poise, take over her life, direct it. And as the big sister, Susan was determined to give Josie every advantage, to protect her. She'd helped Josie through high school and then college, giving up her own education so Josie could have the best. She'd helped Josie start a career, and now, evidently, her goal was to help Josie get married to a suitable man.

If it hadn't been for Susan, Josie would have been alone in the world. The knowledge of what she owed her sister was never far from her mind. But she didn't want to settle down with some stuffy businessman. She wanted all the same things other women wanted—romance and excitement and fun—only, she was a little late in recognizing those desires.

He'd said he was a safe man, trustworthy. And she had to believe it was true, because Susan never would have set her up with a man who couldn't be trusted. Susan's standards were high, nearly impossible to reach, so he had to be a very reliable sort, despite his comments to the contrary. She smiled and put her hand in his.

His fingers, warm and firm, curled around her own, then he lifted her hand to his mouth, his gaze still holding hers, and kissed her knuckles. Just that small touch made her tummy lurch and places below it tighten. His tongue touched her skin, soft and damp, dipping briefly between her middle and ring fingers and she felt the touch sizzle from her navel downward. She almost groaned.

The look he gave her now was knowing and confident, hot with his own excitement. "Come on."

Josie licked her dry lips. "You haven't told me yet where we're going."

"Someplace quiet. Someplace private. I want you all to myself, Josie."

Prudence made her pause again. He wanted control of the situation, but this was her night, the only fantasy she was ever likely to indulge in. "I'd like to know, exactly, where we're going."

He looked down at her, then his large hands framed her face. He seemed almost relieved by her questions, like he'd been waiting for them, expecting reluctance. "Scared?"

"Should I be?" She wasn't, not really, but that didn't mean she held no reservations at all. She'd led her life on the safe side, never even imagining that such a turmoil of sizzling emotion existed. It would take a lot to make her turn away now, especially since Bob was the first man who'd ever tempted her to be so daring. The ruse she'd started was over. Now she was only doing as she pleased, being led along by her feminine instincts. And enjoying every second.

His thumb touched the side of her mouth, moved over her bottom lip and then ran beneath her chin, making her shudder, her breath catch. He tipped her face up, arching her neck and moving her closer to his tall strong body at the same time. "Open your mouth for me, Josie."

She did, parting her lips on a breath. His mouth brushed over hers, light, sweet, his tongue just touching the edge of her teeth, coasting on the inside of her bottom lip. "Don't ever be afraid of me."

"I won't." She clutched at his shirt, wishing he'd do that thing with his leg again, pressing it against her in such a tempting way. "I'm not."

He smiled, his look tender. "Not afraid, but I can feel you shaking."

Quaking was more like it. Her legs didn't feel steady, her heartbeat rocked her body and little spasms kept her stomach fluttering. His mouth came down again, his teeth catching gently on her bottom lip, nipping, distracting. Josie closed her eyes, wanting him to continue. He couldn't know that this was all new to her, so she confessed, "I'm not afraid. I'm excited."

"By me."

Two simple words, so filled with wonder—and with confidence. "Yes. I…I want you." Saying it made her skin feel even hotter, and she tried to duck her head, knowing she blushed. But he wouldn't let her hide. Catching and holding her gaze, he gave her an intense study, as if trying to figure her out. Josie wondered how much more obvious she could be.

The wind blew, damp and cool, and it ruffled his thick, straight hair. When she shivered, he broke his

stare to gather her close, holding her to his warm chest
and wrapping his arms tight around her. Being held by
this man was a singular experience. She'd never
imagined that anything could feel so *safe*. Or that she
needed—wanted—to feel that way.

"You might not be afraid, Josie, but I am."

That startled her and she pushed back from him
again. "You're not making any sense, Bob." He flinched
and she took another step back, separating their bodies
completely. Frowning with possibilities, with hurt and
embarrassment, she whispered, "If you don't want me,
just say so."

That got her hauled back up against him, his mouth
covering hers and treating her to a heated kiss the likes
of which she hadn't known existed. His tongue stroked;
he sucked, bit, consumed. It made her toes curl in her
shoes, made her nipples tighten painfully. She gasped
into his open mouth and pressed her pelvis closer. The
thick, full bulge of his erection met her belly, making a
mockery of her notion that he might not want her.

As if he knew how her body reacted, she felt his
thigh there again, giving pressure just where she needed
it. One palm gripped her hip, keeping her from retreat-
ing, and his other slowly covered her breast, caressing,
dragging over her nipple then gently stroking with the
edge of his thumb. He made soothing sounds when she
jerked in reaction. She couldn't bear it, the feelings
were so wildly intense. She moaned and clutched at
him.

"Damn." His head dropped back on his shoulders, his
eyes closed while his throat worked. He kept Josie
pinned close and his nostrils flared on a deeply indrawn

breath. "Let's get out of here before I lose my head completely."

He showed no more hesitation, moving at a near run, making Josie hobble in her high heels trying to keep up with him.

He led her to a shiny black truck and opened the door. But the minute she started to step up into the thing, she realized she had a definite problem. "Uh, Bob…"

He made a sour face that quickly disappeared. "Hmm?"

"I, ah, I can't get into your truck."

Reaching out, he tucked her hair behind her ear, cupped his hand over her shoulder, caressing, soothing. "I've told you I won't hurt you, Josie. You can trust me."

A nervous giggle escaped her and she was mortified. She never giggled. "It isn't that. It's, well, my skirt is too tight."

His gaze dropped, then stayed there on the top of her thighs. She saw his broad shoulders lift with a heavy breath. "Looks…good to me. Not too tight." He swallowed, then added, "Perfect, in fact. You're perfect."

Perfect. Josie knew then, there was no changing her mind. No man had ever told her she looked perfect. No man had ever given her much attention at all. Of course, she'd never given them much attention, either, or dressed this way before. She'd only done it now to discourage Bob from liking her, thinking him to be another prig, a suit with an image to protect and a family-oriented goal in mind. But seeing as he *did* like her like this, she vowed to be more flashy every day, because she liked it, too. It made her feel feminine and attractive and… She still couldn't manage to get into the dumb truck.

"Bob, I can't step up. And your seat's too high for me to reach."

He blinked, his gaze still lingering southward, then he chuckled. "I see what you mean. Allow me." He picked her up, swinging her high against his chest with no sign of effort. He hesitated to set her down inside.

"Bob?"

He groaned. "Don't… Never mind. I think I like holding you. You don't weigh much more than a feather." He pulled her close enough to nuzzle her throat, her ear, to kiss her mouth long and deep before reluctantly putting her down on the seat and closing the door.

When he climbed behind the wheel, Josie decided to be daring again. "So, you like small women?"

"I never did before."

Leaving her to wonder what he meant by that, he started the truck and drove from the lot. "I was thinking, why don't we go to your place? We could drink some coffee and…talk."

Uh-oh. Josie shook her head. There was no way she could take him to her condo where her functional lifestyle and boring personality were in evidence everywhere. In her furniture, her pictures, her CDs and books. Nursing magazines and pamphlets were on her tables. Nostalgic photos of her deceased parents, along with photos of her and Susan together, decorated her mantel. He'd see her with her hair braided, her turtlenecks and serious, self-conscious mien.

That wasn't the woman he wanted, and she couldn't bear it if he backed out on her now.

"I don't think that's a good idea."

He glanced at her curiously as he wove through the traffic. "Why not?"

Why not? Why not? "Um, my neighbor, in the condo complex, was planning a big party and I bowed out. If she sees me, she might be hurt, or insist I come to the party after all." It was only a partial lie. Most of the condo owners were nice, quiet, elderly people, living on retirement and Social Security. They were her friends, the only people she felt totally comfortable with. They loved her and appreciated whatever she did for them, no matter how insignificant. For them, she didn't have to measure up, she could just be herself.

Until recently, there had never been parties at the condo. Now, with Josie's encouragement, Mrs. Wiley was known for entertaining—but hers certainly weren't the type of parties Josie would be comfortable taking Bob to. Mrs. Wiley could be affectionately referred to as a "modern" grandma.

Bob nodded his understanding, his brow drawn in thought.

She squirmed, then suggested, "Why don't we go to your place instead?"

"No." He shook his head, shooting her a quick look. "Not a good idea."

"Why?"

"I, um… You know, I hesitate to suggest this, because I don't want to insult you."

"Suggest what?" Her curiosity was piqued. And she couldn't imagine any suggestion on his part being an insult, not when they both knew what it was they wanted, what they planned.

"My father has a small houseboat docked on the

river, not too far from here. It's peaceful there. And quiet. Just like home, only smaller. And floating."

How romantic, and how sweet that he feared insulting her. "I think it sounds like heaven, but…I thought Susan told me both your parents were dead."

"My…" He turned his face away, his hands fisting on the steering wheel.

"Bob?"

Now he groaned. When he did finally look at her, he appeared harassed. "They are. Gone that is. Deceased. But they left me the boat and I guess I…still think of it as theirs?"

He'd ended it on a question, as if he weren't certain, which didn't make any sense. Unless he was still dealing with the loss of them. She herself knew how rough it could be. It had taken her months to get over the shock of her parents being gone, and by the time she realized how selfish she was being, Susan had just naturally taken control, cushioning Josie from any other blows. Even though Susan was older, it had still been a horrendous thing for her to deal with on her own.

It was obvious Bob had a difficult time talking about it. Josie sympathized. "My parents died when I was fifteen. Susan took on the responsibility of being my guardian. It hurts sometimes to remember, doesn't it?"

His gaze seemed unreadable. "Does it hurt you?"

"Yes. I still miss them so much, even though it's been ten years. And…I feel guilty when I think of everything Susan gave up for me. We have no other relatives, and because she was nineteen, she was considered an adult and given legal custody." It wasn't as simple as all that, but Josie didn't want to go into how hard

Susan had fought for her, the extent of what she'd given up.

He reached for her hand. "I doubt Susan would have had it any other way. She seems…determined in everything she does."

"You're right about that. She's a very strong person." Josie smiled, then decided to change the subject. "Tell me about the boat."

His fingers tightened. "No. Talking about taking you there makes it damn difficult to drive safely."

He never seemed to say the expected thing. "Why?"

"Because I wish we were already there." He glanced at her, his look hot and expectant. "I want to be alone with you, honey. I want to touch you and not stop touching. I want—"

She gasped, then mumbled quickly, "Maybe we shouldn't talk about it." She fanned herself with a trembling hand and heard him chuckle.

After a minute or two had passed in strained silence, he said, "Okay. I think I've come up with some innocuous conversation."

Relieved because the silence was giving her much too much time to contemplate what would come, Josie grinned. "Go ahead."

"Tell me about where you work."

"All right. But I assumed Susan had already told you everything. I don't want to bore you with details. I know she can go on and on with her bragging. Not that there's really any reason to brag. But she does act overly proud of me. As I said, she rightfully takes credit for getting me through college and giving me a good head start."

His mouth opened twice, without him actually

saying anything. He shrugged. "I'd rather hear it from you."

She supposed he just wanted words flowing to distract him from what they were about to do. She knew it would help her. She'd never felt so much anticipation and yet, she suffered a few misgivings, too. Spontaneous affairs weren't exactly her forte. The fear of disappointing him, and herself, made her stomach jumpy. So far, they'd been moving at Mach speed. What would happen if she faltered, if her inexperience showed? She couldn't even contemplate the idea. The fact of her nonexistent love life was too humiliating for words.

"I do home-nursing care. I started out working for an agency, but I hated the impersonal way they functioned. I always got close to the people I worked with, and they became friends, but as soon as they were released from care, I wasn't supposed to see them ever again. So I decided to start my own business. Susan already knew, through the experience of starting her flower shop, how to go about setting things up, and she helped a lot. It took me a while to get everything going, but now I'm doing pretty well."

"You like your work?"

"Yes. So far it's been the only thing I've been really good at, and it gives me comfort."

She knew her mistake instantly when Bob frowned at her. "What exactly does that mean?"

"It means," she said, measuring her words carefully, "that I'm trying to make changes in my life. I'm twenty-five years old, and I've reached most of my business goals. So I've set some personal goals for myself. Things I want to see happen before I'm too old to enjoy them."

He gulped. "Twenty-five?"

"Does that surprise you? I mean, I know Susan must have told you all about me, what I do, my supposed interests, my normal appearance."

He rubbed one hand over his face, as if in exasperation. Shifting in his seat, he cast a quick glance at her. "Uh, yeah. She did." His voice dropped. "But you're even more attractive than I thought you'd be. And you seem more…mature than twenty-five."

"Thank you." Josie wondered if much of her maturity came from spending all her free time with the elderly. They were so caring and giving, offering her a unique perspective on life.

"You mentioned personal goals. Tell me about them."

He sounded so genuinely interested, she hated to distract him. But it wouldn't do for him to learn *he* was a personal goal. If he discovered the reserved life she'd lived, how sheltered her sister had kept her, would he decide against taking her to the boat? She wasn't willing to run the risk.

"Everyone has personal goals. Don't you? I think I remember Susan saying something about you trying to double your company assets within the next five years. Now, that's a goal."

He mumbled something she couldn't hear.

"Excuse me?"

"Nothing."

Turning down a narrow gravel drive that headed toward one of the piers, he slowed the car and gave more attention to his driving. But he kept glancing her way, and finally he said, "It's my partner who's actually into building up the company. I'm satisfied with where we are for now. We're doing well, and to expand at the rate he wants, we'd have to start putting in tons of overtime. That or take on another partner. I don't want to do either. Work isn't the only thing in my life. I want to have time for my grandfather. I want to see other people and pursue other interests. Work is important, but it isn't everything."

Marveling at the sentiments that mirrored her own, she said, "I can't believe this. My sister mentioned your partner, but she said only that he was arrogant and she didn't like him. She said his only goal seemed to be joking his way through life. In fact, I think she refused to work with him, didn't she?"

Even in the darkness, she could tell he flushed, the color climbing up his neck and staining his cheekbones. "Yeah, well, she took an instant dislike to…Nick. I couldn't quite figure out why—"

"Susan claims he tried to schmooze her, to charm her. She can pick out a womanizer a mile away, and she said that Nick is the type who draws women like flies with his *false charm*."

With a rude snort, he glared at her. "That's not true. And besides, Nick is very discreet."

"He's evidently not discreet enough. Susan is very liberated and doesn't like being treated any differently than a man. From what she said, I assume your partner is a bit of a chauvinist. 'Pushy and condescending' is how she described him."

He muttered a short curse. "Yeah, well, Nick doesn't particularly like pushy women, either, and your sister is pushy!"

Josie didn't deny it; she even laughed. "True enough. I consider it part of her charm."

A skeptical look replaced his frown. "If you say so. Anyway, it was easier for her to work with…me."

Josie laughed. "Susan said you had the best advertising agency in town. And she showed me the ads you worked up for the flower shop. They're terrific. She's gotten a lot of feedback on them already." Josie patted his arm. "Susan claims you're the brains of the agency, while this Nick person only adds a bit of talent. But I'd say you're pretty talented, too. And not at all what I expected."

"Oh?" He sounded distracted, almost strangled.

"I'm beginning to think finding me dates is Susan's only hobby, and I would have wagered on you being another guy like the last one."

That got his attention. "What was wrong with the last one?"

"Nothing, if you like men who only talk about themselves, their prospects for the future, the impeccability of their motives. He laid out his agenda within the first hour of our meeting. He actually told me that if I suited him, after about a month of dating, he'd sleep with me to make certain we were compatible, then we could set a wedding date. Of course, he'd require that I sign a prenuptial agreement since he worked for his father, and there could be no possibility of me tinkering with the family business." She laughed again, shrugging her shoulders in wonder. "Where Susan finds so many marriage-minded men is beyond me."

After muttering something she couldn't hear, he turned to her. "I hope you walked out on him at that point."

"Of course I did. And then I had to listen to a lecture

from Susan because I didn't give him a chance. She claimed he was only nervous, since it was our first date and all."

He grunted, the sound filled with contempt. "Sounds to me like he's a pompous ass." He tilted his head, studying her for a moment. "You know, it strikes me that your sister doesn't know you very well."

Josie didn't know herself, or at least, the self she was tonight, so she couldn't really argue. "No. Susan still sees me as a shy, self-conscious fifteen-year-old, crying over the death of our parents. Afraid and clingy. She put her own life on hold to make certain my life didn't change too much. She's always treated me like I was some poor princess, just waiting for the handsome prince to show up and take me to a mortgage-free castle. Now she thinks of it as her duty to get me married and settled. She's only trying to see things through to what she considers a natural conclusion to the job she took on the day our parents died. It's like the last chapter in my book, and until she's gotten through it, I'm afraid she won't stop worrying about me long enough to concentrate on her own story."

"You're hardly in danger of becoming an old maid. Twenty-five is damn young."

"I know it, but Susan is very old-fashioned, and very protective. Convincing her to let up isn't going to be easy."

"You're pretty tolerant with her, aren't you? In fact, you're not at all like she claimed you to be."

"I can imagine exactly how Susan described me." Josie couldn't quite stifle her grin, or take the teasing note out of her words. "Probably as the female version of you."

He shifted uneasily as he pulled the car into an empty space right behind a long dock where a dozen large boats were tied. He turned the truck off and leaned toward her, his gaze again drifting over her from head to toe, lingering on her crossed legs before coming up to catch her gaze. "We're here."

She gulped. Her stomach suddenly gave a sick little flip of anxiety, when she realized that she didn't have a single idea what she should do next, or what was expected of her.

"Josie." His palm cradled her cheek, his fingers curling around her neck. "I want you to know, I'm not in the habit of doing this."

"This?" The breathless quality of her voice should have embarrassed her, but she was too nervous and anxious to be embarrassed.

"I'm thirty-two years old, honey. Not exactly a kid anymore. I know the risks involved in casual sex, and I'm usually more cautious. But you've thrown me for a loop and…hell, I'm not even sure what I'm doing. I just know I want to be with you, alone and naked. I want to be inside you and I want to hear you tell me how much you want me, too."

Her words emerged on a breathless whisper. "I do."

He held her face between both hands, keeping her still while he looked into her eyes, studying her, his gaze intense and probing. "I can't remember ever wanting a woman as much as I want you." He kissed her briefly, but it was enough to close her eyes and steal her breath. "This can't be a one-night stand." He seemed surprised that he'd said that, but he added, "Promise me."

She nodded. She'd have promised anything at that point.

"Tell me you won't hate me for this."

That got her eyes open. "I don't understand."

His forehead touched hers. "I'm afraid I'm going to regret this, because you're going to regret it."

Her hand touched his jaw and when he looked at her, she smiled. "Impossible." She'd never been so sure of anything in her life.

He hesitated a second more, then opened his door with a burst of energy and jogged around to her side of the truck. She'd already opened her own door, but he was there before she could slide off her seat. It seemed a long way down, hampered by her skirt, so she was grateful for his help. But he didn't just take her hand. He lifted her out and didn't set her down, carrying her instead.

He didn't have far to walk. The boat he headed for was only partially illuminated by a string of white lights overhead, draped from pole to pole along the length of the pier. His footsteps sounded hollow on the wooden planks as he strode forward. Holding her with one arm, he dug in his pocket for a key and fumbled with the lock on the hatch, then managed the entrance without once bumping her head. She barely had a chance to see the upper deck, where she glimpsed a hot tub, before he began navigating a short, narrow flight of stairs. When they reached the bottom, he paused, then kissed her again, his arms tightening and his breath coming fast.

He lowered her to her feet by small degrees, letting her body rub against his, making her more aware than ever of his strength, his size, his arousal. It was so dark inside, Josie couldn't see much, but she didn't need to. He led her to a low berth and together they sank to the edge of the mattress. When he lifted his mouth, it was to utter only one request.

"For tonight," he said, "please, call me anything but Bob."

CHAPTER THREE

HE'D LOST HIS MIND. That could be the only explanation for making such a ridiculous comment. Not that he'd take it back. If she called him Bob one more time, he'd expire of disgust—that or shout out the truth and ruin everything.

But now she'd gone still, and he could feel a volatile mixture of dazed confusion and hot need emanating from her. Damn it all, why did things have to be so confused, especially with this woman?

"I don't understand."

The soft glow of her eyes was barely visible in the dark interior of the boat as she waited for him to explain. But no explanation presented itself to his lust-muddled mind, so he did the only thing he could think of to distract her. He kissed her again, and kept on kissing her.

Night sounds swelled around them; the clacking of the boat against the pier, the quiet rush of waves rolling to the shore, a deep foghorn. Her lips, soft and full, parted for his tongue. He tasted her—her excitement, her sweetness, her need. She pulled his tongue deeper, suckling him, and he groaned.

What this woman did to him couldn't bear close

scrutiny. He didn't believe in love at first sight; he wasn't sure love existed at all. Certainly, *he'd* never seen it. But something, some emotion he wasn't at all familiar with, swore she was the right woman, the woman he needed as much as wanted. Her scent made him drunk with lust, her touch—innocent and searching and curious—made him hungrier than he'd known he could be. She presented a curious, fascinating mix of seductive sexuality and quiet shyness. She spoke openly and from her heart—leaving herself blushing and totally vulnerable.

Lord, he wanted her.

Working his way down her throat, he teased, in no hurry to reach a speedy end, wanting to go on tasting her and enjoying her for the whole night.

If she'd allow that.

He listened to her sighs and measured her response, the way she urged him. He wanted this to be special for her, too. If later she hated him for his deception, he needed to be able to remind her of how incredible the feelings had been. It might be his only shot at countering her anger, of getting a second chance. It might be the only hold he'd have on her. So it had to be as powerful for her as it was for him. And with that thought in mind, he rested his palm just below her breast. Her heartbeat drummed in frantic rhythm and he realized she was holding her breath suspended while she waited.

With his mouth he nuzzled aside her blouse and tasted the swell of her breast, then moved lower, drawing nearer and nearer to her straining nipple. His progress was deliberately, agonizingly slow.

Using only the edge of his hand, he plumped her

flesh, pushing her breast up for his mouth, for his lips and tongue and teeth. He kissed each pale freckle, touched them with his tongue. Josie squirmed, urging him to hurry, but he knew the anticipation would only build until they were both raw with need.

"Please…" she begged, and the broken rasp of her voice made him shudder.

"Shhh. There's no hurry," he whispered, and to appease her just a bit, his thumb came up to tease her stiffened nipple through her bra, plying it, rolling it with the gentlest of touches. Her back arched and her fingers twisted in his hair. He winced, both with the sting of her enthusiasm and his own answering excitement. The tip of his tongue dipped low, moving along the very edge of her lace bra, close to her nipple, but not quite touching.

"Bob."

"No!" He lifted his head, kissing her again, hard and quick. "Shush, Josie. You can moan for me, curse me or beg me. But otherwise, no talking."

"But…"

Through the thin fabric of her blouse and lace bra, he caught her nipple between his fingers and pinched lightly, feeling her tremble and jerk and pant. Her response was incredible, as hot as his own, and it had never been this way before. He tugged, his mouth again on her throat, lightly sucking her skin against his teeth, giving her a dual assault. She cried out, and the interior of the small cabin filled with the begging words he wanted to hear.

"Oh, please…"

It was a simple thing to ease her backward on the berth until she was stretched out before him. Knowing she lay there, his, waiting and wanting him, was enough to make him come close to embarrassing himself. The possessiveness was absurd, but undeniable, even after such a short acquaintance. Looking at her, his hunger was completely understandable. His erection strained against his jeans, full and hot and heavy, pulsing with his every heartbeat.

His fingers stroked over her cheek. "Be still just a moment."

He fumbled behind him, looking for the small lantern they used for fishing. He wanted to see her, but he didn't want harsh light intruding on their intimacy or maybe bringing on a shyness she hadn't exhibited so far. As he lit the lamp and turned the flame down low, the soft glow spread out around the cabin, not reaching the corners, but illuminating her body in select places—the rise of a breast, the round-ness of a thigh, a high cheekbone and the gentle slant of a narrow nose. Those wide, needy eyes. Nick dragged in another deep breath to steady himself, but it didn't help.

Never had he seen a woman looking more excited, or more inviting. Her hands lay open beside her head, palms up, her slender fingers curled. She watched him, her eyes heavy and sensual and filled with anticipation. One leg was bent at the knee which had forced her skirt high—high enough that he could just see the pale sheen of satiny panties.

Nick stood, then jerked his shirt over his head. His gaze never left her, and as she looked him over, taking in every inch of his chest, he smiled. Her eyes lingered on places, so hot he could almost feel their touch, and her body moved, small moves, hungry moves. Impatient moves.

Guilt over his lies filled him, but he knew he'd do the same again. He'd do whatever was necessary to get to this moment, to have Josie Jackson—such a surprise watching him in just that way, waiting for him.

Susan Jackson could think whatever she wanted, as long as Josie accepted him.

The shoes came off next, then his socks. He unsnapped his jeans and eased his zipper down just enough to give some relief. His eyes closed as he felt his erection loosened from the tight restraint. He took a moment to gather his control.

"What about your pants?"

The throatiness of her voice, the rise and fall of her breasts, proved how impatient she was becoming.

Lowering himself to sit on the edge of the cot again, he smiled and touched the tip of her upturned nose. He wanted to gather her close and just hold her; he wanted to be inside her right this second, driving toward a blinding release. The conflicting emotions wreaked havoc with his libido and made his hands tremble.

"Fair's fair. You have some catching up to do."

He leaned down, bracing himself with an elbow beside her head while his free hand began undoing the tiny buttons of her blouse. He kissed her again, soft teasing kisses that he knew made her want more. But he wouldn't give her his tongue, just skimming her lips and nipping with his teeth while she strained toward him. When she reached for him, he caught her wrists and pinned them above her head. "Relax, Josie."

A strangled sound escaped her. "Relax? Right now?"

His chuckle was pure male gratification. "You said you wanted some fun, some excitement. Will you trust me?"

"To do what?" Rather than sounding suspicious or concerned, she sounded breathless with anticipation.

Her blouse lay open and he pulled it from her skirt to spread it wide, exposing her lace bra, which did nothing to hide her erect little nipples. He couldn't pull his gaze away from them. "To give you as much pleasure as you can possibly stand." As he spoke, he carefully closed his teeth around one tight, sensitive tip, biting very gently, then tugging enough to make her back arch high and her breath come out in a strained cry.

"You have sensitive breasts." He shuddered in his own response.

"Please…"

Licking until her bra was damp over both nipples, making them painfully tight, knowing how badly she needed him, he showed her just how much pleasure she could expect and the extent of his patience in such things. He loved giving pleasure to a woman, loved being the one in complete control, but never before had it been so important. This time wasn't just to make being together enjoyable, but to tie her to him, to make her need him and what he could do for her. *Only him.* He had to build a craving in her—a craving that only he could satisfy.

He had to believe this explosive chemistry was as new for her as it was for him. Knowing women as well as he did, her inexperience was plain. She hadn't touched him other than to desperately clutch his shoulders or his neck when she needed an anchor. And her surprise had, several times now, showed itself when he'd petted her in a particularly pleasurable place. Thinking of all the places he intended to touch her tested his control.

He caught her shoulder and turned her onto her stomach. Lifting her head, she peered at him over her shoulder, but he only grinned and began sliding down the zipper that ran the length of her skirt. The skirt was still tight, hugging her rounded bottom and distracting him enough that he stopped to knead that firm flesh, filling his hands with her and hearing her soft groan. He bent and kissed the back of her knee through her nylons. She squirmed again, her body moving in sexy little turns against the berth.

His mouth inched higher, bringing forth a moan. She buried her face in a pillow, her hands fisting on either side of the pillowcase.

She'd worn stockings, fastened with a narrow garter belt. *He loved stockings.*

Such a little flirt, he thought, forcing away all other musings because he didn't want to get trapped in his own emotional notions. Using two fingers, he unhooked a stocking and moved it aside so he could taste soft, hot flesh. Her thighs were firm, silky smooth, now opening slightly as he nuzzled against her.

"Bob..."

He gripped her skirt and yanked it down. She squeaked, and buried her head deeper into the pillow. The silky panties slid over her skin as he caressed her rounded buttocks, then between, his fingers dipping low, feeling her dampness, the unbelievable heat, her excitement. His heartbeat thundered and he retreated, afraid he'd lose himself in the knowledge she was ready. *For him.*

He kissed her nape, down her spine. The bra unlatched and he pulled her arms free, then turned her again.

Even in the darkness he could see her crimson cheeks, and the way she held the bra secure against her breasts gave him pause. Josie wouldn't know how to use her body to get her way. She had no notion of the power women tried to wield over men; everything she felt was sincere. His hands shook.

In no way did he want to rush her, or coerce her into doing anything she didn't want. Her body might be ready for him, but emotionally she was still dealing with the unseemly rush of their attraction.

Stretching out beside her, he pulled her into his arms and simply held her, stroking her hair and back. He wanted to give her time to understand what was happening, to accept it. She needed to know he would never force her into anything, that she could call a halt at any time—even though it might kill him.

So he held her, passively, patiently. But he couldn't control the pounding of his heart beneath her cheek, or his uneven breaths, or the tightness of his straining muscles as his whole body rebelled against the delay.

"What…what's wrong?"

He sighed. For whatever reason, she had planned this. There was no other explanation for the way she'd come on to him, her verbal innuendoes, her willingness to come to the boat with him. But she was also very unsure of herself—amazing considering her natural sensuality and her allure, how completely she responded to his every touch.

He took her small hand and flattened it on his

chest, holding it there. "Josie, are you certain you want to do this?"

She reared up, staring at him with something close to horror. "Don't you?"

The laugh emerged without his permission. Her innocence delighted him. "Honey, I think I'd give up breathing to stay in this boat for a week, loving you day and night—and twice in the afternoons." He touched her face, tracing her brows and the delicate line of her jaw. "But I don't want you to do anything that bothers you. There's no hurry, you know. If you'd rather…"

She frowned and said with some acerbity, "I'd rather you not torture me by stopping now." Then, after a second of lip-biting, she released the bra and it fell to the bed.

Nick halted in midbreath. Damn, but she had pretty breasts. Full and soft and white. He didn't move, but he forced his gaze from her luscious breasts to her face. "What do you want, Josie?"

"I want…" Pink spread from her cheeks to her breasts, and he half expected her to shy away once more. Instead she said, "I want you to kiss me again."

Very softly, in a mere whisper, he asked, "Where?"

Her nipples were pointed, pink, tempting him. Already he could almost taste them on his tongue. When her hand lifted, hovered, then touched exactly where he wanted his mouth to be, he groaned. "Come here."

He stayed perfectly still, leaving it to her to make the next move—a small salve to his conscience for being so manipulative. But he did open his mouth, his gaze on her breast, and with a small sound of excitement she leaned over him.

Her nipple brushed his lips, and he lifted a hand to guide her, to keep her close while he enclosed her in the heat of his mouth and suckled softly. Her arms trembled as she balanced above him, and her harsh breathing, interspersed with moans, made his jeans much too tight and confining. He felt ready to burst. Her pelvis bumped the side of his hip, then again, more deliberately, pressing and lingering. She pushed her heat against him, trying to find some relief, and he groaned.

His patience, his control, were severely strained by the taste of her and her generous reaction to him. Only the sure knowledge that this had to be perfect, that she had to believe they were magic together, kept him from losing control.

He slid both hands into her panties and dragged them down her legs while he switched to give equal attention to her other breast. With slow, unintrusive movements, he stripped her, never interrupting his ministrations to her body. When she was finally naked, he shifted to put her beneath him, then shucked off his jeans. Holding her gaze, he led her hand to his erection and guided her fingers around him, silently instructing her to hold him—hard. She whimpered and he cupped his hand over her mound, only stroking her, tangling his fingers in her tight curls, his explorations soft and soothing.

Her movements were clumsy, but so damn exciting, he couldn't bear it. Especially with her expression so dazed, so dreamy, locked to his, letting him feel everything she felt, letting him touch her in ways no other woman ever had. It added unbearably to the physical excitement.

He couldn't take it. Her scent filled him and he

pressed his face into her throat, his mouth open, her skin hot. She reluctantly released him when he moved down in the bed, trailing damp kisses over her breasts, her ribs and abdomen, her slightly rounded, sexy little belly. Then to where his fingers teased over hot, damp feminine flesh.

"No!"

"Yes." Never had he wanted anything as much as he wanted to know all of her. Her scent, powder fresh and woman tangy, was a mixture guaranteed to make him crazed. He kissed her, holding her thighs wide and groaning with the excitement of it, with the taste of her. She was deliciously wet, softly swelled, and he groaned again, his tongue delving deep, his open mouth pressed hard against her. Her hips shot upward and she cried out. Pressing one hand to her belly, he held her still and continued. With each thrust and lick of his tongue, she shuddered and wept, begged and cursed. Knowing his control to be at an end, he closed his mouth around her tiny bud and suckled sweetly, his tongue rasping, and two fingers gently pushed deep inside her.

He felt the contractions build, and he reveled in it, using every ounce of his experience to see that her orgasm was full and explosive. He'd never heard a woman cry so hard, or be so natural about her response, without reserve, without pretense, raw and intense and so very real. It fired his own imminent climax, and he pressed his erection hard into the berth's mattress as he rode along on her pleasure. When she quieted, spent and limp, her legs still sprawled open to prod his excitement, he had only seconds to locate a condom from his discarded jeans and enter her before he knew he'd be lost.

His thrust was deep and strong, and froze him. With a small, weak cry, her body stiffened in shock, and he stared at her, not sure he wanted to believe the unbelievable. She was twenty-five. She was gorgeous and sexy and so responsive, she could make a man nuts. His pulse went wild. "Josie?"

Her body shuddered and he felt the movement all through him, making him squeeze his eyes shut tight.

She took several deep breaths before saying, "I—I'm okay."

He pressed his forehead to hers, straining for control, trying to keep his hips perfectly still, his tone soft and calm. "You're a virgin?"

"I…was. Yes."

But not anymore. Now she was his. His heart thundered with the implications, ringing in his ears, making his blood surge with primitive satisfaction. But his brain couldn't decipher a damn thing, couldn't even begin to sort through it all. Discussions would have to wait until later; his body took over without his mind's consent.

Very slowly, measuring the depth of his stroke against the smallness of her body, he thrust, his lower body pulling tight as he pushed into her. Josie arched again and groaned around her tears.

His second slow thrust had her crying out—in startled pleasure. A third, and she wrapped around him and continued to hold him tight while he growled out his release, pressing himself deep inside her, becoming a part of her, making her a part of him. When finally he collapsed over her, she squeezed his neck and kissed his ear, his temple. Her breath was gentle against his heated skin. He shuddered with a fresh wash of unfamiliar, unsettling sensation, something entirely too close to tenderness.

After several minutes had passed and they could both breathe again, she stirred and whispered against his ear, "You are the most incredible man I've ever met."

The wonder was there in her tone, nearing awe. He started to smile, wanting to echo her words, wanting to kiss her again, to start all over. She was special, and she needed to know that, needed to know that somehow they'd been destined to meet, destined to be here, locked together in just this way, with him a part of her. He was thirty-two years old, and in his entire lifetime, never had a woman made him feel this way, hungry and tender and touched to his very soul by her presence. It should have scared him, but it didn't. Not yet.

She'd given him a precious gift, not just her virginity, which was a rare thing indeed, but her honesty, her openness. She went against everything he believed, every truism he'd ever taught himself over the years through endless empty relationships. Holding her left him...content. What he felt was somehow special; he knew that instinctively. He needed to make her understand it, too.

But then she smoothed her hand over his hair and kissed his shoulder, and added in a shy whisper, "Thank you, Bob," and he felt reality smack him hard in the head.

Damn, maybe the time for explaining had finally come, because he didn't think he could bear one second more of hearing her call him by another man's name, not after what they'd shared, not after he'd concluded they were meant for this night—and many more nights like it. And what better way to ensure she listen to him, that she give him a chance to reason with her, than to keep her just like this, warm and soft and spent beneath him.

He leaned up and saw her small smile, the glow in her eyes, the flush of her cheeks. The need to kiss her soft lips was intense, but he held back, knowing his responsibility now. "Josie—"

She lifted her hips, causing an instant, unbelievable reaction. He should have been near death, should have been limp as a lily in the rain, but it took only one small suggestive squirm from her and he was back to the point of oblivion, of not caring about anything but her small body and the way she held him. Her hands, having been idle before, now dug into his buttocks, keeping him a part of her, urging him deeper, and she smiled. "Do you think we could…start all over? I'm afraid I might have missed a few things the first time around."

Her frank, innocent way of speaking made his head spin. "Oh?" He winced at his own croaking tone and the weakening of his resolve. "Like what?"

She seemed to touch him everywhere, her fingers dragging through his chest hair and gliding innocently over his nipples, sliding downward to explore his hips and thighs. "This time, I want you to tell me where to touch you. And where to kiss you. And where to suck—"

Her words broke off as he devoured her mouth, and he thought, *Tomorrow. I'll confess all tomorrow.*

But for tonight he would drown her and himself in pleasure. And with her moving beneath him, urging him on, it seemed like the very best of plans.

JOSIE KNEW THE SUN was coming up by the way the light began to slant in though the slatted shutters. It might become a beautiful fall day, but she wouldn't mind spending it inside this very cabin, with this very man, doing exactly what they'd done throughout most of the night.

Poor Bob. He slept like the dead, but no wonder, considering the energy he'd expended all night. The bed they rested on was very narrow, and not all that comfortable. Of course, out of necessity, she'd spent most of the night resting on him, her head on his shoulder, her breasts against his wide hairy chest, one thigh over his lower abdomen. The man was so sexy, she could spend all night, and the whole day, just looking at him, trying, without much success, to get used to him.

How long this fantasy could last was her only troubling thought. She wasn't the woman he'd made love to repeatedly last night, the woman who threw caution to the wind and lived for the moment.

She was a sensible woman, with a responsibility to her job, to those who relied on her—to her sister. She led a quiet life in a quiet condo, had an understated wardrobe and tidy hair. Her car, a small brown compact, was paid for and got good gas mileage. She had a sound retirement plan at the local bank. Other than last night, she'd never been in a nightclub. She bought Girl Scout cookies religiously, and kept emergency money in an apple-shaped cookie jar at home. Most of her social life was spent in the nonthreatening company of people over the age of sixty-five.

The wild woman who'd indulged in the outrageous

night of sex would have to confess sooner or later to being a complete and utter fraud.

Her palm drifted over his chest, feeling the crisp dark hair, the swell of muscle and the hardness of bone. *Let it be later,* she silently pleaded, not wanting it to end, not wanting to own up to her own deceptions. Knowing she should let him sleep, but unable to help herself, she pressed her cheek against his throat and breathed his delicious, musky, warm-male scent. It turned her muscles into mush and twirled in her belly. Possessiveness filled her, and she wanted to scream, *He's mine.*

Instead, she pushed reality away and continued to explore his undeniably perfect body.

Heat seemed to be a part of him, incredible heat that seeped into her wherever she touched him, heat that moved over her skin when he looked at her or spoke to her in that sexy deep voice. She hadn't needed a blanket last night, not with him beneath her, giving off warmth and securing her in his arms. She inhaled again, and marveled at the scent of him. His skin was delicious, musky and inviting, stretched tight over muscle and bone, covered in sexy places with dark, swirling hair.

His nipples, brown and flat and small, hid beneath that hair. And his stomach, bisected by a thin line that grew thicker and surrounded his penis with a perfect framework, drew her fingers again and again. She'd never really looked at a man before; she'd never been this close to a naked man.

She could have looked at Bob forever.

Curiosity drove her to bend over his body, examining that male part of him in some depth. Thick and long and rock hard when he was excited, but now merely resting in that dark nest of hair, it looked almost vulnerable.

Her chuckle woke him and he stirred. To her fascination, it took only a split second before he changed, before he grew erect, filling and thrusting up before her very eyes.

Her gaze shot to his face and was caught by the intensity, by the seriousness of his stare.

"I died and went to heaven last night, right?"

His voice was thick with sleep, his midnight black hair mussed, his jaws shadowed by beard stubble. He was a gorgeous male, and she suddenly wondered how awful she might look after a night of debauchery.

He lifted a hand to her cheek and his fingertips touched her everywhere—her nose, her lips, her lashes and brows. In that same, sleep-roughened voice, he whispered, "You have to be an angel. No woman could look this beautiful first thing in the morning."

Josie blushed. She wasn't used to hearing such outrageous compliments, or seeing such interest in a man's eyes. His fingers sifted through her hair, feeling it, dragging it over her shoulders, then over his chest. He lifted a curl to his face and inhaled, smoothed it over his cheek.

"Come here."

Ah, she knew what that husky tone meant now. She'd heard it many times last night. She'd be dozing, enjoying the feel of him beneath her, when suddenly his lips would be busy again, touching and tasting whatever part of her skin he could reach. His large, wonderfully sensitive hands would start to explore, innocently at first, then with a purpose.

He'd roused her several times in just that way throughout the long night. And each time she'd look at him, he'd say those words. *Come here.*

She wanted to hear him say them every morning, for the rest of her life.

Still holding a lock of her hair, he tugged her down until her lips met his, until he could steal her breath with a kiss so sweet, it brought tears to her eyes. He shifted, prodded and urged her body until she was arranged to his satisfaction—directly on top of him.

"Mmm. You're the nicest blanket I've ever been covered by." His large, rough hands held her buttocks, pressing her firmly against him. His stubbled cheek rubbed her soft cheek, giving her shivers. "And you smell good enough to be breakfast." His voice was thick with suggestion as he nuzzled the smooth skin beneath her chin.

Thoughts of the things he'd done to her, the shocking way she'd responded, made heat rush to her cheeks with the mixed meanings of his words. The bold things he said, and the way he said them, made her body pulse with excitement.

She kissed the bridge of his nose and wondered how to begin, how to start a confession that well might put an end to the most wonderful experiences she'd ever imagined. She had no doubt he'd tell her not to worry, that it wouldn't matter. At first. But when he got to know her, when she was forced to revert back to Josie Jackson, home-care nurse, community-conscious neighbor and responsible sister, he'd lose interest. She couldn't be two people, no matter how she wished it. And the woman he'd made love to all night would cease to exist because despite the isolation of it, she loved her job and cared about the people she tended.

She opened her mouth to explain, to try to find the words to rationalize what she'd done, the insane way she'd behaved. But he forestalled her with his questing fingers, tracing the space where her thigh met her buttocks, then gently pushing between. She should have been shocked, and hours ago she would have been. But no more, not after the pleasure he'd shown her. She trusted him to do anything he wished, knowing she'd enjoy it. And she did.

If the sound of quickened breathing was any indication, he liked touching her as much as she liked being touched.

With his free hand at her nape, he brought her mouth to his again so that words were impossible anyway. And unwanted.

When again she lay over him, so exhausted and replete she could barely get her mind to function, much less her limbs, he said, "We need to talk, honey."

True enough. They hadn't had too many words between them last night. She pressed a kiss to his heart and lifted her head until she could see him. His expression was worried. And serious. Very serious.

She started to wonder if he'd already realized she was a fraud, when she was distracted by the loud hollow thumping of footsteps on the pier. Bob turned his head, his brows now knit in a frown. A voice broke the early-morning stillness and they both jumped.

"Nick!" Pounding on the wooden door accompanied the shouting. "Damn it, Nick, are you in there?"

Josie stared at Bob, dumbfounded. In a whisper, she asked, "Does Nick use your parents' boat, too?"

With a wry grimace, he said, "All the time. But he never brings women here. Remember that, okay?" He lifted her aside. "Stay still, honey. And be real quiet. I'll be right back."

She was treated to the profile of his muscled backside and long thighs while he stepped into his jeans, zipping them, but not doing up the button. He looked sexy and virile and too appealing for a sane woman's mind. When he turned back to her, his gaze drifted over the length of her body. He grabbed up the sheet and reluctantly covered her. More pounding on the door.

"I know you have to be in there, Nick!"

"It looks like our magical time is up, sweetheart." His sigh was grievous, but he pressed a quick kiss to her lips. "Promise me you won't move."

"I promise."

"Nick!"

He closed his eyes briefly before shouting back, "Hold your horses, will you?"

He was out of the cabin, the hatch shut firmly behind him, before Josie could form a second thought.

CHAPTER FOUR

As SOON AS NICK stuck his head out the door, Bob pounced. "I've been hunting all over for you." He looked harried and unkempt, very unlike Bob who prided himself on his immaculate appearance. Nick had a premonition of dread.

"Shh. Keep it down, all right?" He took Bob by the arm and led him down the pier toward the parking lot. He kept walking until he was certain he'd put enough space between Bob's booming, irritated voice and the boat. He didn't want Josie to overhear their conversation. A cool damp breeze off the river washed over his naked chest and he shuddered. "Now tell me what's wrong."

Bob stared at him, disbelieving for a moment. Then his expression cleared and he barked, "*What's wrong? What do you mean, 'what's wrong'?* I want to know what you did with Josie Jackson!"

It was a fact that Bob, even though he was a grown man, was much too naive to actually be given the full truth. Besides, what he'd done with Josie was no one's business but his own. This time Nick didn't mind lying in the least. "I haven't done anything with her."

Without seeming to hear, Bob paced away and back again. "Susan's almost hysterical. She's been phoning her sister all night, and finally she called me this morning to see how our damn date went. She thought *I'd* done something with her! I didn't know what to say."

Though the morning sun glared into his eyes, Nick decided it was way too early to have to deal with this, especially since all he wanted to do was get back to Josie. The image of her waiting for him in bed made his muscles tighten in response. "What exactly did you tell her?"

Bob's face turned bright red. The wind whipped at his light brown hair, making it stand on end, and he hastily tried to smooth it back into its precise style before stammering a reply. "—I told her business caused me to cancel at the last minute."

"Damn it, Bob—"

"I couldn't think of a better lie! And I couldn't just come out and tell Susan she's the one I'd rather be seeing, that I canceled because of her."

"Why not?" When Bob had first suggested Nick break the news to Josie for him, and why, he hadn't been overly receptive to the idea. He'd imagined Josie would be a lot like Susan, and he hadn't wanted another confrontation with an irrational female. Susan had disliked him on the spot; he remembered being a little condescending to her, just as Josie had related, but he'd had provocation first. The woman was rigid, snobbish and demanding. Not at all like Josie.

Bob had hit it off with Susan right from the start. To Nick, it was obvious they were kindred spirits, the way they formed such an instant bond. So he'd tried not to be too judgmental, and he'd done his best not to cross her path again.

But his largesse was limited. He hadn't wanted to do her any favors by meeting her wallflower sister.

Thank God he'd changed his mind.

"I've told you a dozen times, Bob. Susan will likely be flattered by your interest. You should give her the benefit of the doubt."

Susan's like or dislike of him no longer mattered to Nick, though her disparaging him to Josie had been tough to accept. Nevertheless, the desire to defend himself had been overshadowed by the need to keep Josie's trust.

And after last night, he considered any insult he'd suffered more than worth the reward. He owed Susan, so maybe he'd give her Bob.

"Ha! I'll be lucky if she ever speaks to me again. She was outraged that I would cancel on her sister." Bob rubbed both hands over his face. "I told her Josie had mentioned spending some time alone, and suggested she maybe wasn't up to talking right now. Susan decided Josie was depressed because I cancelled the date, and that made her even angrier."

Nick's grin lurked, but he hid it well. Poor Bob. "Josie wasn't depressed."

"Obviously not. But I never dreamed you'd bring her here and keep her all night."

"What makes you think she's here?"

Bob clutched his heart and staggered. "Oh, Lord, she is, isn't she? If she's not with you, then where would she be? Susan will never forgive me, I'll never forgive myself, I—"

Nick grabbed Bob and shook him. "Will you calm down? Of course she's here. And she's fine." More than fine; Josie Jackson was feminine perfection personified. He thought of how she'd looked when she'd promised not to move, and he wanted to push Bob off the pier.

He hastily cleared his throat and fought for patience. "The thing now is to get Susan interested in you."

Bob was already shaking his head, which again disrupted his hair. "She's convinced I'm perfect for her little sister. She won't stop until she pushes us together."

"Trust me." Nick kept his voice low and serious, determined to make a point Bob wouldn't forget. "You and the little sister will *never* happen."

Bob blinked at what had sounded vaguely like a threat. "Well, I *know* that." He waved a hand toward the boat and added, "The fact that she's here, after meeting you just last night, proves she's isn't right for me—"

He gasped as Nick stepped closer and loomed over him. "Careful, Bob. What you're saying sounds damn close to an insult."

"No, not at all." He took a hasty step back, shaking his head and looking somewhat baffled. After a moment, he smoothed his hands over the vest of his three-piece suit and straightened his tie. "I only meant…well…" He looked defensive, and confused. "You're acting awfully strange about this whole thing, Nick. Damn if you're not."

Nick made a sound of disgust. Behaving like a barbarian had never been his style, and he certainly didn't go around intimidating other men. Especially not his friends.

And he usually didn't feel this possessive of a woman. This was going to take a little getting used to.

He clapped Bob on the shoulder and steered him toward his car. "Forget it." When they reached the edge of the gravel drive, Nick stopped. He was barefoot after all, and in no hurry to shred his feet. Not when he had much more pressing issues to attend to. "Now my advice to you is this. Give Josie a little time to call her sister. I'll let her use my cell phone. Then go see Susan. She'll want someone to talk to, to confide in. She's been worried all night, and you can play the understanding, sensitive male. Pamper her. Try to let her know how you feel. Ease her into the idea. But don't tell her Josie was with me."

Bob had been nodding his head in that serious, thoughtful way of his, right up until Nick presented him with his last edict. Then he looked appalled. "You want me to lie to her?"

"You've already lied to her."

"When?"

Nick shook his head at Bob's affronted expression. "You allowed her to believe you did her ad campaign when I'm the one who did it."

"She wouldn't have worked with us if she'd known you were doing it. She doesn't like you much, Nick."

Bob acted as though he were divulging some great secret. "You also lied to her when you told her why you didn't meet with Josie. What's one more lie?"

"But last night she was so upset, I just drew a blank. I didn't mean to lie. Now it would be deliberate."

Nick's patience waned. "Do you want Susan or not?"

"She's a fine woman," Bob claimed with nauseating conviction. "Dedicated, intelligent, ambitious, with a good head for business."

Nick made a face. "Yes, remarkable qualities that could seduce any man." She sounded like any number of other women he knew. Driven and determined. "She'll take over your life, you know."

Frowning at Nick's cynicism, Bob protested, "No, if I'm lucky, she'll share my life. And that's what I want."

"It's your life. Just don't say I didn't warn you."

"Damn it, Nick—"

"Okay, then." Bob wasn't an unattractive man, Nick thought, trying to see him through a woman's eyes. He was built well enough, if not overly tall. He wasn't prone to weight problems and he didn't drink to excess or smoke. He still had all his hair, and at thirty-six, he might be overly solemn, but he wasn't haggard. He was tidy and clean.

Susan would be lucky to have him. "I've got a deal for you."

Eyeing him narrowly, Bob moved back to put some space between them. "What sort of deal?"

"Will you quit acting like I'm the devil incarnate?" They'd often been at odds with each other, both personally and professionally, due to the differences in their lifestyles and outlooks on things. But in business and out, they managed to balance each other, to deal amicably together. They were friends, despite their differences, or maybe because of them, and for the most part they trusted each other. "I want to help you."

"How?"

"I can get Susan for you, if that's what you want." Nick didn't quite understand the attraction, but he'd always lived by the rule To Each His Own. If Bob wanted Susan, then so be it. Maybe Bob could keep her so busy she wouldn't be able to find the time to make insulting remarks about him to Josie.

"I can find out from Josie exactly what Susan likes and dislikes, what her fantasies are—"

"Susan wouldn't have fantasies!"

The bright blue morning sky offered no assistance, no matter how long Nick stared upward. When he returned his gaze to Bob, he caught his anxious frown. He felt like a parent reciting the lesson of the birds and the bees. "All women have fantasies, Bob. Remember that. It's a fact that'll come in handy someday. And it'd be to your advantage to learn what Susan's might be. I'll help. Within a month, you'll have her begging for your attention." And he and Josie would have had the time together without interference.

There was no doubt of Bob's interest. He couldn't hide his hopeful expression as he shifted his feet and tugged at his tie. "Okay. What do I have to do?"

"Just keep quiet about Josie for the time being. You know Susan doesn't exactly think of me as a sterling specimen of manhood. If she knows I'm interested in her sister, she'll go ballistic. She'll do whatever she can to interfere. I get the feeling Susan has a lot of influence on Josie." Or at least, she had in the past. For twenty-five years Josie had remained a virgin—the last ten under Susan's watchful eye. But last night, she had decided to change all that—with *him;* it still boggled his mind.

A sense of primitive male satisfaction swelled within him, along with something else, something gentler. He assumed it was some new strain of lust.

After glancing back at the boat, he decided he'd spent enough time with Bob. "Go home. Give Josie about an hour to contact Susan." An hour wouldn't be near long enough, but he'd have to make do. He could be inventive. And he had a feeling Josie would appreciate his creativity. "After that, go over to her house."

"I can't just drop in."

"Trust me, okay?" He gave Bob a small nudge toward his car. "Tell her you were concerned about her. She'll love it."

Bob peered at his watch. "She's probably at the flower shop now. I suppose I can drop in there."

"Great idea." Nick gave him another small push to keep him moving. "Let me know how it goes, okay? But later. Call me later."

Bob left, mumbling under his breath and thinking out loud, an annoying habit he had, but one that Nick had no problem ignoring this morning. He heard Bob drive away, but still he stood there staring down the dock. Confession time had come, much as he might wish it otherwise. With mixed feelings he started toward the boat. Josie would understand; she had to. He hadn't had near enough time with her yet.

His relationships, by choice, never lasted more than a few months, but he was already anticipating that time with her—and maybe a bit more. He wouldn't let her cut that time short. But first he had to find a way to get through to Josie, to gain control of his farce and make her understand the necessity of his deception. As he neared the boat, he went over many possibilities in his mind.

Unfortunately, none of them sounded all that brilliant.

JOSIE HEARD THE FOOTSTEPS first and froze. Her heartbeat accelerated and she tried to finish fastening her garter, but her fingers didn't seem to want to work. Stupid undergarment. Why had she chosen such a frivolous thing in the first place? At the time, she certainly hadn't suspected that anyone would ever know what she wore beneath her suggestive clothes. But it had felt so wickedly sinful to indulge herself anyway. And she'd felt sexy from the inside out. Maybe that had in part given her the courage to do as she pleased last night.

She would never regret it, but last night was over, and she wanted to be dressed when Bob returned. At first, she'd sat there waiting, just as he'd asked her to. But after a few moments she'd gotten self-conscious. She'd read about the awkward "morning after," and though she'd never experienced one herself, she knew being dressed would put her in a less vulnerable position. And she needed every advantage if she was to make her grand confession this morning.

Then suddenly he was there, standing in the small companionway, his hands braced over his head on the frame, looking at her.

He was such a gorgeous man, and for long moments she simply stared. His jeans, still unbuttoned, rode low on his lean hips and his bare feet were casually braced apart, strong and sturdy. She could see the muscles in his thighs, the tightness of his abdomen.

His dark hair, mussed from sleep and now wind tossed, hung over one side of his forehead, stopping just above his slightly narrowed, intense dark eyes. He wasn't muscle-bound, but toned, with an athletic build. Curly hair spread over his chest from nipple to nipple, not overly thick, but so enticing.

Not quite as enticing as the dark, glossy hair trailing from his navel southward, dipping into his jeans. She knew where that sexy trail of hair led, and how his penis nested inside it. Josie had intimate knowledge of his body now, and she blushed, both with pleasure and uncertainty.

"You moved."

The whispered words caused her to jump, and her gaze shot back to his face, not quite comprehending.

"You promised you'd stay put, naked in my bed."

He sounded accusing and she managed a shaky smile. Though she wasn't exactly what one would call *dressed,* with only her stockings, bra and panties on, she still felt obliged to apologize. "I'm sorry. You were gone so long…." Her voice trailed off as he gazed over her body. Feeling too exposed in only her underthings, she shifted nervously. "Bob?"

She saw him swallow, saw his shoulders tighten and knew he must be gripping the door frame hard. "You have a very sexy belly."

"Oh." She looked down stupidly, but to her, her belly seemed like any other. She cleared her throat. "Is everything okay, then?"

He hummed a noncommittal reply.

"Should I take that as a 'yes'?"

"What? Oh, yeah, everything's fine. Just a misunderstanding. Forget about it." He stepped into the room and knelt before her, and everything inside her shifted and moved in melting excitement.

He lifted her hands from her thigh, where she'd been fumbling with the garter. Wrapping his long fingers around her wrists like manacles, he caged them on the berth, one on each side of her hips. "I'm not sure last night was real, Josie. I've been standing outside, trying to think of what to say, of where we go from here. But to tell you the truth, I don't want to go anywhere. I want to halt time and stay right here alone with you. To hell with the world and work and other people."

She started to speak, to tell him even though it was Saturday and she wanted nothing more than to stay with him, she had a few patients she needed to check on. But he leaned forward, releasing her hands so he could cradle her hips. He kissed her navel and her mind went blank. Hot sensation spread through her belly as his tongue stroked, dipped. She wound her fingers into his silky hair and held on.

"Did you find the head okay?"

"Hmm?" It took a moment for the whispered question to penetrate, hummed as it was against her skin. The head? Then she remembered that was the nautical term for the toilet. "Yes, yes, thank you."

"Are you hungry?" He rolled one stocking expertly down her leg while pressing hot kisses to the inside of her knee. "There's some food in the galley, I think. And coffee."

Each whispered word was punctuated with a small damp kiss, over her ribs, her hip bones, between. No, she didn't want food.

Gasping, she tried to speak, to tell him, but only managed a moan.

"Josie, are you sore?" He kissed her open mouth, gently forcing her back until she lay flat on the berth with her legs draped over the edge. He knelt on the floor between her widespread thighs, his hard belly flush against her mound, his chest flattening her breasts. His fingers trailed over her skin from knee to pelvis and back again, taunting her, making her skin burn with new sensitivity.

"I'm...fine."

Cupping her face to get her full attention, he said, "How is it you were a virgin, sweetheart?"

She didn't want to talk about that now. She wasn't sure she ever wanted to talk about it. She tried to shake her head but he held her still.

"Josie?"

Sighing, she considered the quickest, easiest explanation to give. A confession might be appropriate, but she didn't want it to intrude right now, to possibly halt the moment, which seemed an extension of the night, so therefore still magical. It was all so precious to her, and she wanted to keep it close, to protect it.

"I started college young, when I was barely seventeen." She drew a shuddering breath, speech difficult with him so close. "I've always been something of an overachiever, which always made Susan proud. But because I was young, and she had to be mother as well as sister, she naturally kept an extraclose eye on me. Not that it was necessary. My studies were so time-consuming, I didn't have room for much socializing anyway. We had clinicals at seven o'clock most mornings, plus the regular classwork. It took all my concentration to get my BSN."

"And since college?"

She shrugged. "I spent two years working in a hospital, then two years gaining home health-care experience so I could open my own business. There were so many federal and state licenses to get, so much red tape, again I had little time for anything else. Now I work with the elderly. The...opportunity to meet young single men just isn't there. So, bottom line, I've been so wrapped up in getting Home and Heart started, I haven't had time for dates. And with my job, the dates can't find me anyway. That is, if they're even looking."

"They're looking, all right. Trust me."

She gave him a smile, which seemed to fascinate him. With gentle fingers he touched and smoothed over her lips, the edge of her teeth. He kissed her—featherlight, teasing. She had to struggle to follow their conversation. "Maybe I'm the one who didn't know where to look, then."

He didn't smile. "But you found me last night?"

No way would she admit her guise had actually been to discourage and repel him, not after the very satisfying outcome. She feigned a nonchalant shrug. "Susan is always attempting to fix me up with dates. Most of the guys are total duds, at least for what I want out of life." She smoothed her hands down his back. "But you were perfect."

"I'm so glad I was the one." He pressed his face into her neck and gave her a careful hug. "And I still can't imagine how a woman as sexy as you remained a virgin for so long."

Trying to laugh it off, she said, "I'm discriminating, so it was easy."

He licked the smile off her lips. "I want to make love to you again, Josie. I want to be inside you and hear you make those sexy little sounds, feel your nails on my back."

For the longest moment, words failed her. Finally she managed, "Me, too."

He shook his head. "I need to talk to you first."

Josie felt dread at the serious tone of his voice. His brows were lowered, and he looked regretful, almost sad. A slow panic started to build, making her stomach churn and her chest tighten. She tried to sound casual as she made her next suggestion. "Why don't we save the talking for later?"

Using his words against him, she dragged her nails slowly, gently, down his spine, holding his gaze, seeing the darkening of lust on his face. She slipped her hands inside his jeans and felt his firm, smooth buttocks.

"Josie…"

It sounded like a warning, which thrilled her. "Do you really want to see me again?"

"Damn right."

Slowly his hips began the pressing rhythm she'd grown accustomed to last night. Even through his jeans, she felt the heat of it, the excitement.

She could hardly believe he was still so very interested—it simply wasn't the reaction from men that she was used to. She wasn't about to give up such an opportunity. "How about Sunday? We could get together to talk then. Right now, I'm not at all sure I can listen." She had some morning calls to make, but the rest of her day would be free, and tomorrow was soon enough for confessions, soon enough to see her fantasy end.

With his lips against her ear, he whispered, "Just give me a time."

"Noon."

"I think I can manage to wait until then." He raised up to look at her. One hand cupped her cheek, the other cupped her breast, plying it gently. She drew in a long shuddering breath and his fingers stroked her nipple while he watched her face, judging her reaction. "But remember, Josie." He pinched her lightly and she moaned. "It's your idea to wait to talk until then. Promise me."

Struggling to follow his logic and his conversation, she said, "I promise."

He kissed her, then, and they both knew she hadn't a clue as to what she'd just promised. They also knew, at the moment, it didn't matter.

"MAYBE YOU SHOULD call your sister."

Nick gazed at Josie from across the cab of the truck. She looked sleepy and sated, and he wanted to turn around and take her back to the boat. Damn, he'd never met a woman who affected him so strongly. But he had promised Bob.

He reached down and picked up the receiver in his truck, then handed it to her. "Here. Why don't you call her now?"

"A car phone?"

"Hey, we're a growing company. We have to stay up-to-date."

She smiled, that beautiful killer smile that showed all her innocence and her repressed sensuality. *All for him.* He couldn't remember ever sleeping with a virgin before. Even his first time had been with an older, experienced girl. Somehow Josie didn't epitomize the squeamish, whimpering image of a virgin he'd always carried in his mind. He eyed the miniskirt and high heels she wore, and grinned. No, she was far from any woman he'd ever known, but she was exactly what he might have visualized in an ideal fantasy.

Before she could use the phone, he took her wrist. "I've been thinking."

She politely waited for him to continue, and he cleared his throat, praying for coherent words to come through. "Last night took me by surprise, Josie."

"Me, too."

Damn, that soft, husky tone of hers. He felt his body stir and cursed himself for being ruled by his libido. It was brains he needed now, and a little old reliable charm.

"What we've done, I know it's out of the norm for you, but I want you to know it wasn't exactly the typical conclusion to one of my dates, either. I'm not in the habit of having sex with women I barely know."

He peered at her, trying to judge her reaction to his words, but her eyes were downcast, her hands gripping the phone in her lap.

"You're beautiful, Josie. I want to see you and make love to you again, but other people might not understand."

Her head snapped up. "Susan said you were conservative, but…you're dumping me because of what other people would think?"

The truck almost swerved off the road. "No! That's not what I'm saying at all. I just don't want us to…share what we've done. I don't want the world and its narrow-minded views to intrude."

She frowned, apparently thinking it over. "You want to keep our relationship a secret?"

Damn, why couldn't he have said it so simply? He couldn't recall ever stammering over his words this way. "Would you mind? At least for a little while?"

A shy grin tilted the corners of her mouth. "No. Actually I was wondering what in the world I was going to tell Susan. She wanted us to hit it off, but I'm certain this wasn't exactly what she had in mind."

He tipped his head in agreement. Susan would want to cut his heart out, he had no doubt. "You're probably right."

"I'm not ashamed that we were together, but she'd never understand or approve."

He stiffened, already anticipating Susan's interference. "Do you need her approval?"

"No, of course not. But it's important to me because *she's* important to me. If she knew where I was last night, she'd be upset. She would never judge me harshly, but she'd worry endlessly and I'd never hear the end of it. I'd like to avoid that."

He'd like to avoid it, too. At least until he got everything straightened out.

Cautious now, he made a necessary suggestion. "You could tell her we didn't hit it off, and that you canceled. From what you told me, that shouldn't surprise her. And then she wouldn't ask you tons of questions that you'd feel awkward answering."

Laughing, she punched in her sister's number. "No, she won't be surprised. It's what I usually do. But I can't outright lie to her. That wouldn't be right."

Before he could say anything more, Susan had answered, and even Nick could hear her frantic voice booming over the line. He kept one eye on the road, and one eye on Josie. He half expected his cover to be blown at any moment. Then Josie would look at him with those big green eyes. She'd detest him and his damn deception and she'd forget her promise to let him explain on Sunday.

But Josie grinned and her look was conspiratorial as she explained to Susan that she'd had a change of plans last night—an understatement if there ever was one— but that she was perfectly fine.

"I've asked you to stop worrying about me, Susan. Please. I'm a big girl now. If I choose to stay out late, or to unplug my phone, that's my own business. You can't panic every time I don't answer one of your calls."

Nick reached across the seat and took her hand. She hadn't lied, but she'd hinted at an untruth, and he suddenly felt terrible for putting her in such a position. As Susan claimed, he was a reprobate; lying came naturally to him. But they were never lies that hurt anyone, and he'd never lie to his grandfather, the only close family he had. Yet he'd forced Josie into a corner. He'd find a way to make it up to her, all of it.

"I'll pick up something for lunch and come over to the shop after I finish my rounds today. We can chat." There was a moment of silence, then Josie winced. "Susan, I'm sorry. Really. I didn't mean to make you worry. No, I'm sure he really is a terrific man." She grinned at Nick. "I suppose I can think about giving him another chance, but let's talk about that later, okay? Yes, Susan, I'll honestly think about it. I have to go now. No, I really do. I'll be by later. Love you, too."

She hung up and then began giggling.

"What's so funny?"

"She came to the automatic conclusion that I stood you up. You should have heard her. She sounds half in love with you herself. You're intelligent and conscientious and you have a good mind for business. Strong praise coming from Susan."

Nick remembered his promise to Bob. Given the way the two of them echoed their appreciation of each other, it shouldn't be hard to fix them up together. It might not even take the entire month he'd allotted to the project. "Is that what Susan likes? I mean, are those the qualities most important to her?"

"Yes, but in some ways, she's a fraud. Susan pretends to be all seriousness, but she's a sucker for a box of chocolates or a mushy card. I think deep down, she's hoping for someone to rescue her from herself."

He slowed the truck and glanced at her as Josie directed him at a turn. "What do you mean?"

"She rents every mushy movie in the video store. She'd never admit it, but I've found romance novels by the dozen hidden in her house, under couch cushions and her bed pillows. Of course, I've never said anything to her. It would embarrass her to no end. But I think she'd really like some guy to come along and share a little of her load. She's had to shoulder so much responsibility at such a young age."

Intrigued, Nick wondered if he could ever get Bob to sweep into Susan's life. Already, he was forming plans in his mind. Maybe this would be even easier than he'd thought. "So you think Susan would be impressed with a man who treated her gently? That wasn't the impression I got. If I remember correctly, I—that is, *Nick* tried to show her some old-fashioned courtesy and she bristled up like a porcupine."

"You'd have to understand Susan and all she's struggled for. She was only nineteen when our parents died, just starting college herself. The authorities wanted to take me away from her, to put me with someone more established, more mature. She had to fight to keep me with her. It made her angry, the inequality between men and women, and it wasn't just because she was young, but because she was female.

I think she went overboard trying to prove her independence and her worth, but I can understand her feelings. She likes to be treated with respect, and she hates to be patronized."

The image of Josie as a frightened little girl whose parents had died, and whose sister had to struggle to keep her, disturbed him. Neither her life nor Susan's had been easy, and his appreciation for Susan grew. He decided to urge Bob to start wooing her now, to send her a small gift. She deserved it.

They stopped for a red light and he turned slightly toward Josie. Pushing sad thoughts from his mind, he lifted her hand to his mouth and kissed her knuckles. "What about you?" He wouldn't mind sweeping this woman off her feet for a romantic weekend. The idea held a lot of appeal. "Do you read romances?"

Josie shook her head and her red hair fell forward, curling over her breast. Deliberately he stroked the long tress, letting the back of his hand brush her nipple.

She sucked in a breath and blurted, "No."

"No?"

"No, I don't read romances. Horror stories are more my speed." She spoke quickly, her voice rasping from the feel of his hands on her body again. He liked it. He liked her easy response and her eagerness.

Now wasn't the time, though, so he removed his hand and pulled away with the flow of the traffic. "Horror stories?"

"Mmm-hmm. The more gruesome, the better. I have all the classics—*Frankenstein, Werewolf, Dracula*. And all the modern authors, like King and Koontz. I'm something of a collector."

Her small, earnest face beamed at him, guileless, sweet, as she described her interest in the macabre. Somehow the images wouldn't mesh. "Horror?"

She laughed at his blatant disbelief. "It fascinates me, the way the human mind can twist ideas and stories, that ordinary men and women can write such frightening things. It's incredibly entertaining. I'll be appalled and frightened the whole time I'm reading, ready to jump at every little sound. And when I get to the end, I just have to laugh at myself. I mean, the ideas are so unbelievable, really. But still, I wish I had that kind of talent. Wouldn't it be wonderful to write a book like one of King's and have it made into a movie?"

He couldn't stop the wide grin on his face. "You're something else, you know that?"

Again she ducked her head, hid her face. "I'm sorry. I've been going on and on."

"And I've enjoyed every minute."

It wasn't long before Josie directed him into her condo complex. The ride hadn't taken nearly as much time as he'd wished for. He started to get out, but she stopped him.

"If we're going to keep things a secret, my neighbors probably shouldn't see you. You know how gossip spreads."

Anxiety darkened her eyes and he wondered at it. He looked past her at the large complex, wondering which condo she owned. "They'll see me tomorrow when I pick you up."

"I was thinking I could just meet you somewhere."

He wanted to say no. He wanted to insist on seeing her home, to try to gain some insight into why she'd suddenly decided to cut loose, to throw her caution to the wind. He wanted to know all her secrets.

But he had secrets of his own to keep, at least for the time being, so he couldn't very well push her without taking the chance of exposing himself.

He considered his options. The boat was out; they'd never get around to talking if he took her there again. And he still couldn't let her in his house until he'd given her a full explanation. Then it struck him.

"There's a monster-movie marathon at that little theater down the street from my office. Right next door to it is a small café. Meet me there. We can grab a sandwich and talk, then take in a few movies." He hadn't exactly planned to have his confession in an open forum, but perhaps it would be better in the long run. Josie didn't strike him as the type to cause a public scene, so she'd be more likely to stay put and hear him out if there were curious spectators about. At least he hoped she would.

Her face had lit up with his first words. "I read about that marathon. I had promised myself I'd find the time to go, even if I had to go alone."

His heart twisted in a wholly unfamiliar way and he pulled her forward for a brief, warm kiss. His lips still against hers, he spoke softly. "Now neither of us has to go alone."

Unexpectedly she threw her arms around him. He held her tight, wondering at her apparent distress. He was the one with the damn secrets; he had a feeling everything would explode if he let her out of his sight.

"Tomorrow," she said, swallowing hard. "Tomorrow I have to explain a few things to you."

That was his line. He kissed her again, first on her rounded chin, then her slender nose, her arched eyebrows. "Then we'll both explain a few things. It all went so fast, I guess we're both still off-kilter. But I swear, it will be all right, Josie. Do you believe me?"

"I want to. But tomorrow seems a long way off."

"Much too long."

She stared at him a moment, then opened her door. "I have to go. I have the feeling that if I don't I'll attack you right here in your truck for all the world to witness." She laughed as she slid off the seat, but he couldn't find a speck of humor, not with his body reacting so strongly to her words.

Before closing the door, she turned to face him and her cheeks pinkened. She looked shy again, and much too appealing. "Last night was the most wonderful night of my life."

He smiled.

"Thank you, Bob."

She slammed the door and hurried up the walkway, hobbling just a bit in her high heels.

His forehead hit the steering wheel with a solid *thwack*. The most perfect woman he'd ever met, sweet and sexy and open and *real*. She made him smile, she made him hot. She intrigued him with this little game she played, looking the vamp while being the virgin. She was every man's private fantasy, not just his own.

And damn it, she thought he was Bob.

Could life get any more complicated?

CHAPTER FIVE

"TELL ME THE TRUTH! Did you cancel or did he?"

Josie opened her mouth, but Susan cut her off. "If he canceled, I'll give him a piece of my mind. That's what he first told me, you know. That he was the one who'd backed out. But I found that so hard to believe. I mean, he's so conscientious and he did promise me."

"I canceled."

Susan's frown was fierce. "I don't suppose I'll ever know the full truth, will I? You're both telling such different stories. But never mind that."

She sat across from Josie and stared her in the eye. Josie almost winced. She knew that sign of determination when she saw it.

"You have to give him a chance, Josie. He's different from the rest. He's…wonderful."

Josie stared at the limp lettuce in her salad. She didn't have an appetite, hadn't had one all day. All she could do was think of Bob and miss him and wonder what he was doing right now, what he'd say tomorrow when he learned she wasn't the woman he thought her to be. She wasn't exciting and sexy and adventurous. She was dull and respectable; all the things she claimed to disdain.

She could just imagine what a man like Bob would

think of her. She wanted to change things; she wanted to go places, be daring and fulfill every fantasy she could conceive. She'd been such a coward, living a narrow life while sinking everything she was, everything she wanted to be, into her business. She'd escaped the grief of losing her parents, of being a burden to her sister, despite Susan's disclaimers. She'd escaped any risks of being hurt—and any chance of enjoying life. But she wanted to change that, now.

Last night had been an excellent start.

But her sister wouldn't think so. "I don't need your help picking my dates, Susan."

"What dates? You never go out!"

The outfit she'd worn for Bob was the only one like it she owned, and she'd bought it to repel him, not attract him. What would he think of that? What would he think when he saw her in her standard comfortable wardrobe, meant for visiting the elderly and running errands?

She needed to find some middle ground somewhere between the woman she was and the woman he thought her to be. And she only had until noon tomorrow to do it.

"Are you listening to me?"

Josie pulled her thoughts away from the monumental task she'd set for herself and smiled at her sister. "Yes, Susan, I'm listening. You think Bob is wonderful." Privately she agreed. More than wonderful. Incredible and sexy and... She sighed. Such a very perfect man—who thought she was a different woman.

"I do. Think he's wonderful, that is. And you would, too, if you'd just stop being so stubborn. He's perfect for you, Josie."

Amen to that. Now if only she could make it come true.

"And handsome—not that it matters in the long run what a man looks like. It's his integrity and responsible attitude that are important. But he really is an attractive male. Proud, intelligent. Courteous. And a brilliant businessman. He did such a fabulous job on my ads. Business has been pouring in."

Something in Susan's tone cut through Josie's distraction. She shoved her salad aside and contemplated her sister's expression. Susan had leaned forward on the counter, her own take-out lunch forgotten. She had both hands propped beneath her chin and a starry look in her hazel eyes.

That look was the one normally reserved for expansion plans for the flower shop, or matchmaking. Josie drew a deep, thoughtful breath. The heady scent of flowers and greenery filled her nostrils. The air inside the shop was, by necessity, damp and rich, heavy. As an adolescent, Josie had always loved the shop. It had been a one-room business back then, catering mostly to locals, but with Susan's hard work and patience, it had grown considerably over the years. This was a special place, where Josie had always felt free to confide in her sister. Many serious talks had occurred at this exact counter.

This time, however, Susan seemed to be the one in need of a chat.

She sighed a long drawn-out sigh, and Josie felt a moment's worry at the wistful sound. "What are you thinking?"

Susan jumped. Normally her thoughts would be on a new business scheme to implement in the shop, a moneymaker of some sort. Or a way to get Josie's life headed in the direction Susan deemed appropriate. Not this time. "I was thinking of how apologetic Bob was for how things turned out. *He* was sorry for making me worry so much."

Josie was startled. "You talked with him?"

"Of course I did! Haven't you listened to anything I've told you? Bob stopped by earlier and apologized for causing me concern. He admitted he should have called me himself last night, to explain about the change in plans. He's promised me it won't happen again. Now, when do you think the two of you can reschedule?"

Josie narrowed her eyes, her thoughts suspended. Bob had been here, talking to Susan? Why would he ask her not to say anything, but then risk calling on Susan himself? It didn't make any sense. "He told you he would reschedule?"

"Yes. We, um, talked for quite some time as a matter of fact. You know, he has big plans for the advertising agency. Someday he'll be a very prosperous man, a name to be recognized. You wouldn't have to continue working if things went well between the two of you."

Josie couldn't help but grind her teeth. Bob had told her he wasn't all that interested in expanding the company. Had he lied, or had Susan misunderstood? She felt buried in confusion and conflicting emotions. "I like my work, Susan, and I'm not ever going to give it up."

"Josie, you know how proud I am of you. I think it's incredible all that you've accomplished. And I love you for all your hard work and dedication." Susan patted her hand. "But it's a terrible job for a young single woman. You never have an entire weekend free, and I can't remember the last time you took a vacation. It's no wonder you never meet any nice men."

"Like Bob?" Josie whispered.

"Exactly!" Susan looked flushed again, and she averted her gaze. "We discussed the problem of your work, how you can't keep any regular hours, and Bob suggested that he wouldn't mind if his wife had a job like my own, running her own shop, meeting new people. A nice nine-to-five job where you'd be home in the evening to share dinner with him, and be there on the weekends to spend time with the kids. Maybe he could help you hire someone, so you wouldn't have the full load yourself...."

Susan's words trailed off as Josie jerked to her feet, hitting the fronds of a large fern with her elbow and almost smacking the top of her head on a hanging philodendron. She cursed, surprising both herself and Susan.

How dare Bob discuss her life with her sister? He had no right to make plans for her behind her back, or to even think of trying to rearrange her life.

She felt as though Bob had betrayed her, and it hurt. Damn it, it hurt much more than it should have. It took two deep breaths to calm herself enough to speak. "Susan, I appreciate your concern, you know that. But you're meddling in my life and you just can't do it anymore. I'm a grown woman. I *like* what I do, and it's important to me. I'm not giving up my work for anyone, *Bob* included."

"Well." Susan looked subdued, but just for a moment. "We were only thinking of the future, wondering how you're going to fit a family into that hectic schedule of yours."

Josie growled, appalled at Bob's arrogance. Just because she'd slept with him, he thought he had the right to start rearranging her life? "Family! I've barely gotten started on the dating."

"Not for lack of trying on my part!"

"Susan." She said it as a warning, long and drawn out. Having her sister fuss over her was one thing; she loved Susan, so she could tolerate the intrusion. But Josie couldn't have Susan discussing her, planning her life, with every man she deemed marriage material.

"All right. I can take a hint." Susan made a face, acting much aggrieved. "But I hope you'll agree it's worth your time to pursue this association."

"Relationship. Time spent between a man and woman, outside of business, is called a relationship, not an association."

Susan waved a dismissive hand. "The point is, you need to compromise a little, Josie, if you ever hope to marry a man as perfect as Bob. He has his life all planned out, down to the last detail. All his business expansions, the house he'll build, even the names he'd like to give his children. Believe me, he's worth your efforts."

Josie straightened her shoulders and stared at Susan, shocked. Realization slowly dawned. For the first time in memory, Susan seemed genuinely attracted to a man. And not just attracted; but totally enthralled. Maybe even *in love*. Josie swallowed, trying to sort through her own muddled feelings to see the situation clearly.

"Did you ever stop to think, Susan, that Bob might be worth *your* effort?"

Blinking owlishly, as if she'd never heard anything

so preposterous, Susan stood and began clearing away their half-eaten salads. "Don't be ridiculous."

"Why not?" Josie summoned the necessary words past the lump in her throat. "It seems to me you admire him a great deal. Admit it, you want him for yourself." She wouldn't think of Bob, of what they'd shared last night. She couldn't.

Josie drew a deep breath. "Since I...don't want him, there's no reason for you to deny yourself." She went to Susan and took her hands. "I love you, Susan, you know that. But you have the most irritating habit in the world of thinking I deserve the very best of everything—even if it's something you want for yourself. You've been doing it since the day Mom and Dad died, putting my needs before your own. You sold the house, then used all the money for me to go to college while you dropped out. You bought me a car when I graduated, when you had to take the bus."

Susan looked away, embarrassed, but Josie only continued in her praise. Susan deserved it—and much more. "You've been the very best of sisters. I can't tell you how much I appreciate all you've done for me, for being there when I didn't have anyone else, for being my best friend and my mother as well as my big sister." Josie swallowed back her tears, and ignored the wrenching heartache.

She squeezed Susan's hands, her gaze unwavering. "You don't have to do it anymore. I can take care of myself now. If you're attracted to a man, to..." She swallowed, then forced the words out. "If you're attracted to Bob, let him know. You deserve to give it your best shot."

Before Susan could respond, the bell over the door

jingled and a man walked in carrying a fancy wrapped package. "For Miss Susan Jackson?"

Susan stepped forward, eyes wide, one had splayed over her chest. "For me? Oh my goodness, who's it from?"

Josie tipped the delivery man and then peered over Susan's shoulder while she fumbled with her package.

"It's chocolates!" Susan peered at the box, holding it at arm's length. "I can't imagine who it's from."

Josie had a sick feeling she knew exactly who had sent the extravagant gift. Her knees felt watery and she perched on a stool. "Read the card."

Looking like a toddler on Christmas Day, Susan tore the small envelope open with trembling fingers. She read the card silently, her lips moving. When she turned to Josie, she bit her lip in indecision.

"Well?" Josie urged.

"It says…" Susan cleared her throat, and her cheeks turned pink. "It says, 'With all my regard, Bob.'"

How…prosaic. Josie would have thought Bob could do better than *that*.

Susan halted, her smile frozen. "It doesn't mean anything, Josie."

Very gently Josie said, "Of course it does."

"No. He knew I was worried about you last night and this is his way of showing me he understands."

"I think it's his way of showing you he's as interested as you are."

"No! Don't be silly. He's simply a very considerate, kind man. He's always thinking of others, even that disreputable partner of his, Nick something-or-other. Now, there's a man who can't be trusted! I could tell just by looking at him, he's entirely too used to getting his own way. But Bob is different. He's scrupulous and…"

While Susan droned on and on, trying to convince Josie while simultaneously pulling open the silver ribbon on the box, Josie did her best to keep her smile in place. Her stomach cramped and her temples pounded. She'd made such a colossal fool of herself, and possibly damaged something very precious to her sister. The problem now was how to fix things.

Susan went in the back room to put the chocolates in the refrigerator and Josie did the only thing she could think of to do. She grabbed up one of the little blank cards in the rotating stand by the cash register and filled it out. It would be easier to write the words than to face Bob and say them out loud. In fact, if she had her way, it'd be a long, long time before she had to lay eyes on him again.

She added Bob's name to the outside and attached the card to a basket of dieffenbachia and English ivy, spiked with colorful tigridias. The plants were supposed to help filter the air of chemicals, and right now, she thought the air needed a little cleaning. She stuck a large bow wrapped with a wire into the middle of the thing along with the yellow address copy from an order form. She shoved it up next to the other plants due to be sent out in the next half hour.

After dusting off her hands in a show of finality, she reseated herself. She didn't really feel any better for having made the break clean, but at least it was over. If her conscience wasn't clear, at least it *was* somewhat relieved.

The hard part would be trying to forget what it had been like, being with him, feeling his heat and breathing his scent and… No. She wouldn't think about it. Not at all.

When Susan came out humming, looking for all the world like a young girl again, Josie lost her composure.

Self-recrimination was all well and good, and probably deserved. But what she'd done, she'd done unknowingly. Bob should have said something. So she'd more or less thrown herself at him? With his looks and body and charm, it probably happened to him all the time. He could have resisted her, could have been gentleman enough to tell her the truth, to explain that her own sister was interested in him. Susan certainly deserved better treatment than that. And not for a moment did she imagine Bob to be oblivious to Susan's interest. The man wasn't naive, and he had to have firsthand knowledge of female adoration.

As to that, why was he even accepting blind dates? He surely had his pick of women.

She thought about everything now and saw things in a different light. He'd said, several times, that they needed to talk. But she'd kept putting him off. Had he intended to tell her that what they'd shared had been no more than a wild fling for him? Just as she'd cut loose for once, maybe he had, too. Could she really fault him for that, when she knew firsthand how difficult it was always to be circumspect and conservative? Perhaps he'd even planned to explain the truth to her tomorrow. She hoped so, for Susan's sake. With all she knew now, she realized how ideally suited Bob and Susan were for each other.

When the delivery truck pulled up to collect all the flowers, Josie decided it was time to go home. Susan never noticed the extra basket. She merely signed the inventory form, moving in a fog as she made repeated trips to the back room for more chocolate in between singing Bob's praises. Josie gave the deliveryman an extra ten to make certain Bob's basket got delivered right away. She hoped he was still at the office, as Susan assumed, because she wanted him to get the thing today.

Susan stood staring out the front window, a small smile on her face. Josie couldn't help but smile, too. As heartsick and disillusioned as she felt, she was glad for her sister. Susan deserved a little happiness, regardless of the cost. "Hey, sis? Anyone home in there?"

Susan turned to her, one brow raised. "I'm sorry. I was thinking."

"Gee, I wonder about what."

Seeing Susan blush was a novelty. Normally Josie would have teased her endlessly. Today she just didn't have it in her. "Will you call him and thank him for the candy?"

Susan's blush vanished and her brows drew together in that stern look she had. "Of course not. Why don't you just thank him for me when you reset your date?"

"Susan…"

"Now, Josie, you promised you'd give him another chance. Don't back out on me now."

Josie rolled her eyes, trying to cover her discomfort. Susan could be so stubborn once she'd got her mind set. "Just once, why don't you do what *you* want instead of thinking about me?"

Susan looked nonplussed. "Why, because you're my sister, of course. And he'd make you the perfect husband, Josie. I just know it."

Josie quelled the churning in her belly and smiled. "You can't dictate love, Susan. It happens when you least expect it." If her words sounded a little uncertain, a little sad, Susan didn't notice.

"But you haven't even given him a chance!"

Josie closed her eyes, not wanting Susan to see the guilt there. She hated lying to her sister.

Susan huffed. "For the life of me I don't understand your attitude, Josie. He's a terrific man."

"I know. Perfect."

"Well, he is!" Susan crossed her arms over her chest and glared. Josie knew what that meant. "At least go out with him once. Just once. If you're truly not interested, then I'll accept it."

Though she knew it was a mistake, Josie saw no way around it. "And you'll admit that you're the one who's attracted?"

"I didn't say that."

"Susan." There was pure warning in Josie's tone.

Throwing up her arms, Susan conceded. "Oh, all right. If nothing comes of your date, I'll…consider him for myself. But trust me, Josie, you'll adore him. It's just that you don't know what you're missing."

But Josie did know. She only wished she didn't.

"I'M GLAD YOU DECIDED to come in for a few hours."

"A few minutes, not hours." Nick went past Bob, who was lingering in the lobby of the building that housed their offices. Each of them had his own space, connected by a doorway that almost always remained open. They shared access to the numerous pieces of computer and graphic equipment they used. "Do I look like I'm dressed for the office?" he added.

Bob eyed his tan khaki slacks and polo shirt. "Not particularly, but with you I'm never sure."

Nick thought about being offended, since he always wore a suit to the office, but he didn't bother. At present, he had other things on his mind. "I'm only going to pick up the Ferguson file. I thought I'd look it over tonight and see if I come up with any ideas."

Bob trailed behind him, a fresh cup of coffee in his hand. "We don't have to make a presentation on that job for some time yet."

"I know, but I have the night free." Nick caught Bob's censuring look and shook his head. "Lighten up, Bob. It's Saturday. The work will still be here come Monday."

"Actually, I was amazed you have Saturday night free. That's a rare occurrence, isn't it?"

Nick shrugged. He had no intention of explaining to Bob what he wasn't sure he understood himself. Josie hadn't in any way asked him to restrict his dating habits, but he'd done so anyway. And in the back of his mind lurked the worry that she might not be so considerate. He wasn't used to worrying about a woman, and he didn't like it. What pressing business did she have between now and Sunday?

Not that knowing would alter his decision. He didn't want to see anyone except Josie, and besides, after the day's activities, he was too tired to go out, but too restless to sleep. And sitting in his house had about driven him crazy. He kept remembering everything about her—her hot scent, the incredible feel of her skin, the way she moaned so sweetly when he—

He jerked open another drawer and shuffled files

around. He was damn tired of torturing himself with those memories. He needed a distraction in the worst way and the Ferguson account would have to be it.

With his head buried in a filing drawer, he heard a knock and then Bob opened the outer door to speak to someone. Nick twisted to try to see who had entered, but only managed to get a peek of a large basket of flowers and greenery. He blinked, lifted his head and smacked it hard on the open drawer above him. "Damn it!"

"You okay?"

"I'll live." Rubbing the top of his head, he sauntered over to where Bob stood opening a small envelope. "What's this?"

Bob grinned, still holding the card. "I sent Susan some chocolates. I guess she decided to send me flowers."

"Flowers, huh?" He looked at the basket with interest. No woman had ever sent him flowers. He fingered a bright green leaf, intrigued and a tad jealous. "Hey, the plants are alive. What do you know?"

"Umm…" Bob hastily stuck the card back in the envelope. "I think these were meant for you."

"Me?"

"Yeah. The card says *Bob,* but Josie sent them. I take it you didn't come clean with her yet?"

Half pleased over the gesture of the plant, and half embarrassed to still be caught in his lie, Nick rolled back on his heels and looked at the ceiling. "I tried. But she didn't want to do any serious talking. The timing wasn't right. We decided we'd clear the air tomorrow afternoon. We're doing lunch and a movie."

"But that's when we play poker. You've never missed a Sunday!"

Nick was well acquainted with his own routine; he didn't need Bob to run it into the ground. "I'll miss it tomorrow."

"But…this is unprecedented! You never change your plans for a woman!"

Nick ground his teeth, frustrated with the truth of that. And it wasn't even Josie who had asked him to change his plans; he'd done so on his own. But he didn't regret it. And that was the strangest thing of all.

Bob was staring at him, assessing, and Nick forced a shrug, not about to reveal his discomfort. "So tomorrow will be a first."

It took him a second, and then Bob managed to collect himself. He looked away, and mumbled, "Maybe not. Here, you should probably read this."

Nick watched Bob hustle out of the room after thrusting the card at him. He discreetly closed the door behind him. Nick looked at the plant again. A live plant with flowers somehow stuck in it. It was pretty and he felt absurdly touched by the gesture.

He opened the envelope and began to read.

Dear Bob,
Yesterday I wasn't myself. If you ever met the real me, you'd understand what I'm telling you. It wouldn't be right for me to see you ever again. If you truly want a continuing relationship, I suggest you call on Susan.
All my best,
Josie

He read it twice, not quite believing the little fool would actually do such a thing, then he cursed. Storming out of the room, he went after Bob. He found him behind his desk, pretending to look over an ad campaign. "You sent Susan candy today, right?"

"Well…"

"And you had them delivered to her at her shop, am I right?"

"Well…"

"And you put your own damn name on it, instead of leaving it as a secret admirer like I suggested. *Right?*"

"Well…"

"Damn it, Bob, do you know what you've done? Do you know what that plant is? I'll tell you what it is. It's a damn *kiss-off* plant. I'm getting dumped because Josie thinks I'm you and she apparently thinks I want Susan!"

Bob shot to his feet. "Well, whose brilliant idea was that? Not mine. I told you to tell her the truth."

"And you promised me you'd give me a little time. If you'd gone with our original plan and played the secret admirer, none of this would have happened."

"I'm no good at that stuff and you know it. I'd have been blushing every time I looked at her. It wouldn't have taken Susan five minutes tops to figure out the candy was from me. Then I'd have looked plain stupid."

"You would have looked like a romantic."

"Which I'm not. And I'd have ended up in the very position you're in right now."

He had a point. Nick supposed every speck of fault could be laid at his own big feet, but that didn't help him to figure out what to do next. A sense of panic began to swell around him. He had to do something. "I should go see her."

"Who, Susan?"

Frustration mounted. "No, not Susan." He ran a hand through his hair, leaving it on end. "That woman hates me, remember? I meant Josie."

"Do you know where she lives?"

"I know which condo complex she's in, but not which condo." He looked at Bob hopefully. "You could get her exact address for me."

"Forget it. Susan already thinks I should be interested in Josie, not her. The woman doesn't understand her own appeal. It took me forever this afternoon to get her to soften up a little, but she's still determined to get me and Josie together, no matter how I try to divert her. If I start asking for Josie's address now, she'll decide her intuition was right, and Susan will never give me the time of day. It'd be like taking three giant steps backward."

God, what a mess. Nick thumped his fist against the desk. "Think about it, Bob. Susan wants you to pursue Josie, but you want Susan. I want Josie, but she thinks I'm you and courting her sister." He groaned, his stomach knotting as he thought of how Josie must feel, how hurt she must be right now. Would she think he'd merely used her last night? Hell, she probably hated him, and he couldn't blame her. He'd been a total ass.

"So how are we going to fix things?"

Nick closed his eyes wearily. "You can't ask Susan for Josie's address because she'll think you're hung up on Josie. I can't very well ask her for it, because odds are she wouldn't give it to me. I suppose I'll just have to go over there and start knocking on doors."

"You're kidding, right?"

Nick glared at him. "No, I'm dead serious. Unless you have a better idea?"

"As a matter of fact, I do. I remember Susan mentioning a woman who heads up the decision committee for the condo. She has a nephew who does the yard work, and she monitors all the problems in the complex. She wanted some advice on inexpensive advertising for a small business she's recently started. She could probably tell you which condo is Josie's."

Nick rubbed his hands together, finally feeling a little of the bizarre panic recede. Things would work out. They had to. No woman had ever thrown him off balance this way, and he wasn't used to it. He didn't know how to react, that's all. He needed just a little more time.

He wanted to make love to her, to touch her. Her effect on him was unique, but considering how explosive they were together, it was understandable. At least to him. Hell, he got hot just thinking about her—yet she'd done the unprecedented and dumped him. "Give me her number."

"I can do better than that." Bob rummaged in his drawer and then withdrew a pink business card. He handed it to Nick. "That's her address in the complex. From what I understood, she knows Josie pretty well. She can tell you which condo Josie lives in."

Nick snapped the card twice with a finger, then slipped it into his pocket. He felt filled with relief, and iron determination. "If you wouldn't think ill of me, I'd kiss you."

Bob pretended horror and ducked away. But Nick

still managed to clap him on the shoulder, nearly knocking him into his desk.

Josie Jackson didn't stand a chance. She might think things were all over—damn her and her ridiculous *Dear John* plant—but she was in for a rude awakening. She'd started this game with her short sexy skirt and taunting smile and unmistakable come-on. She could damn well finish it. But this time they'd play by his rules. No more holding back, and no more being called by another man's name. He'd find out exactly why Josie had showed up in the bar looking like an experienced femme fatale, when in truth she was as innocent as a lamb. He'd find out why she'd chosen him, of all men, to be her first lover. And then he'd take over.

That had been his first mistake, giving up control. He'd let her think she was calling the shots and hadn't been up-front with her. Things had gotten way out of hand. But no more.

He went back to the inner offices, collected his plant with the big bow and colorful flowers and saluted Bob on his way out.

He left the Ferguson file behind.

EVERY NEIGHBOR in the complex had come to stare at him sometime during the day. But he hadn't buckled under, he simply stared back. They had the advantage, though, because most of them, he figured, had to be myopic—being stared at wasn't as personal for them, or as unsettling. That's if they could see him at all. Some of Josie's neighbors wore thick glasses, most of them had watery eyes of a pale shade.

Not a single one of them was under seventy.

At first he'd loitered around Josie's door, waiting, wishing he could peek in through a window, but not willing to risk having the neighbors converge on him in righteous indignation. But she hadn't come home. So he wandered around outside, looking at the neatly kept grounds, the symmetry of each building. He'd drawn too much attention there, so he'd waited for a while in his car. That got too hot, causing his frustration to escalate.

Where the hell was she? Mrs. Wiley, that little old white-haired grandma who wanted to advertise her Golden Goodies home parties for seniors, hadn't minded in the least if he waited. In fact, she'd wanted him to wait with her while she explained her home-sale ventures. He'd made a red-faced escape, unable to discuss with any dignity the prospects of advertising her product. She'd managed to press a colorful catalog on him before he got out, but he hadn't really looked at it yet. He couldn't quite work up the nerve.

Mrs. Wiley had seemed innocent enough, pleasantly plump in a voluptuous sort of way, with neatly styled silver-white hair and a smile that had probably melted many a man in her day. She'd used that damn smile to get him to agree to work on an advertising plan for her. Something simple and cheap, she'd said, and he'd known she was using her age to her advantage, trying to look old and frail. Nick had fallen for the ploy, hook, line and sinker. But how the hell did you advertise seductive novelties for the elderly?

He was sitting on the front stoop, staring out at the sunset and still pondering the issue of Mrs. Wiley's problem, when Josie finally pulled into the parking lot. He almost didn't recognize her at first, not in her small dull-brown car, with her hair pinned up and no makeup. She looked like a teenager, young and perky, not hot and sultry. He gawked, knew he gawked, but couldn't do a damn thing about it. In no way did she resemble the male fantasy that had turned him inside out last night.

He quirked a brow. In many ways, he admitted, she looked even better.

Josie Jackson made one hell of a good-looking frump.

He cleared his throat and stood. She hadn't yet noticed him. Stepping back from her car in her jeans and white sneakers, her arms filled with grocery bags, she looked like a typical homemaker. Not a sex symbol.

His muscles tightened. "Josie."

She stopped, but she couldn't see over the bags. Motionless for several moments, she finally lowered one of the bags enough to glare at him. Her expression didn't bode well. "What are you doing here?"

"Setting things straight."

Her cheeks colored and her beautiful eyes narrowed. "Didn't you get my message?"

His nod was slow and concise. "I got it. But I'm not letting you dump me with a damn plant."

The bags started to slip out of her arms and he made a grab for them. "Here, let me help you. We need to talk."

"There's nothing to talk about."

He took the bags despite her resistance. "Yes, there is. And we might as well do it inside rather than out here entertaining our audience."

Audience referred to three older women hiding behind some bushes and two men who pretended to be chatting with each other, but were keeping a close watch. Josie didn't seem to notice any of them. She looked blank-faced and flustered and hostile. After she closed up her car, she lifted one hand to her hair, but curled it into a fist and let it drop to her side. She seemed equal parts confused, angry and embarrassed.

"Josie?"

Her shoulders stiffened. "You've, um, taken me by surprise."

He grinned. "So I have." His voice dropped to an intimate level. "I missed you, honey. You look wonderful."

She snorted at that and started off for the condo at a brisk marching pace. He kept up, enjoying the sight of her backside in tight jeans, her exposed neck and the few stray curls that bounced with her every step. By the time she reached her door, a spot now very familiar to Nick, she had slowed to a crawl. She stood facing the door, not speaking, not looking at him.

His heart thudded and his determination doubled. "Unlock it, Josie."

Still with her back to him, she muttered, "The thing is, I really don't want you inside."

Brushing his lips against her nape, he felt her shiver. "I like your hair up like this. It's sexy." He kept his tone soft and convincing, reassuring her. "Of course, you could wear a ski mask and I'd think you were sexy."

A choked sound escaped her and she stiffened even more. "You're being ridiculous. I look like a…a…"

"A busy woman? Well, you are. Nothing wrong with that."

Her shoulders stiffened as she drew a deep breath. "I don't want to see you again."

The bottom dropped out of his stomach, but he pressed forward anyway. "I think I can change your mind. Just give me a chance to explain."

"You're not going to go away, are you?"

It was his turn to snort.

"Oh, all right." She jerked out the key and jammed it into the lock. "But don't say I didn't try to discourage you."

He stayed right on her heels in case she tried to slam the door in his face, and almost bumped into her cute little behind as she bent to put her purse on an entry table. He remembered that bottom fondly, petting it, kissing the soft mounds, gripping the silky flesh to hold her close.

He stifled a groan and followed her into the kitchen to put the bags on the counter. Josie stood with her arms crossed, facing him with an admirable show of challenge.

He looked around the condo, then nodded. "Waiting for my reaction, are you?"

She lifted her chin and tightened her mouth.

Her home was interesting. Domestic. Neat and well organized and cute. Everything seemed to be done in miniature. The living room had a love seat and a dainty chair, no sofa. The dinette table was barely big enough for a single plate and there were just two ice-cream parlor chairs, which looked as if they'd collapse under his weight.

The wallpaper design was tiny flowers and all the curtains had starched ruffles. A bright red cookie jar shaped like a giant apple served as a focal point.

"In a way I suppose it suits you."

Josie rolled her eyes. "You don't even know who I am, so how can you possibly make that judgment?"

He stepped close until mere inches separated them.

Slowly, with the backs of his fingers, he stroked her abdomen. "I know you. Better than any other man."

Her eyes closed and she trembled. His fingers brushed higher, just under her breast. He was losing his grip, but couldn't stop. "Josie?"

She bit her lips and then caught his hand. "You have to listen to me, Bob. Yesterday was a mistake."

"No."

"Yes, it was." She waved a hand at the kitchen and beyond. "You see all this, and you think I'm as domestic as Susan, as conservative and contented as she. But I'm not content. I wanted—"

She broke off as he tugged her close, ignoring her frantic surprise. He tilted her chin and kissed her hard, without preamble or warning of his intent. When he thrust his tongue inside, he groaned at the same instant she did. Sliding his hands down her back, he cupped that adorable bottom and squeezed gently, lifting her up to her tiptoes and snuggling her close to his growing erection.

"You feel so good, Josie." Before she could object, he kissed her again, more leisurely this time—tasting, exploring, seducing her and himself. When he pulled back, she clung to him. "And you taste even better. Sweet and hot."

Slowly, she opened her eyes, then shook her head as if to clear it. "This will never work."

He saw the pulse racing in her throat. "It's already working."

"No." She tried to pull away, but he held her fast. "I want freedom, Bob. No ties, no commitments. I have no interest in marriage or settling down or starting a family. I—"

"Neither do I."

She frowned and her mouth opened, but he cut her short.

"And I'm not Bob, so please don't call me that again. I hate it."

Her expression froze for a single heartbeat, and then she jerked away. She stepped around the small table, putting it between them and glared at him in horror. "What are you talking about?"

He decided to take a chance on one of the little chairs. Tugging it out, he straddled it and then smiled at her. "I lied. I'm not Bob, I'm his partner, Nick."

She blinked, her lips slightly parted, her face pale.

"Thanks for the plant, by the way, but I refuse to get dumped. It's an experience I hope never to undergo."

"You're not Bob?"

"Naw. Bob is hung up on your sister. That's why *he* visited her this afternoon. I'm his evil partner, the no-talent, no-brain reprobate your sister took such an instant dislike to."

Her mouth fell open, but then instantly snapped shut. "You lied to me deliberately?" Her hands trembled, but it wasn't embarrassment causing the reaction. "All night last night, you let me believe you were a different man!"

"I hadn't intended to." He watched her eyes, fascinated with the way they slanted in anger, how the green seemed to sparkle and snap. Her cheeks were no longer pale, but blooming with outrage, making her freckles more pronounced. Her mouth was pulled into an indignant pout. He wanted to kiss her again; he wanted to devour her.

"Josie, I'd only gone to the bar to break the date for

Bob because he wants Susan, not you. But when you showed up, looking so damn hot and sexy, my brain turned to mush and I just went for it. A typical male reaction. I'm sorry. It wasn't my most sterling moment, but it's the truth you threw me for a curve."

She took a menacing step forward. "You lied to me deliberately."

"Uh, I thought we already established that." He eyed her approach, wondering what she would do. "I'd like to get to the part about your little deception."

She came a halt. "My deception?"

"That's right. You led me to believe you were experienced when you were a virgin."

"I did no such thing."

"The way you looked, the way you spoke? No one would have guessed you could be innocent. Then you led me to believe you simply hadn't had the time to indulge your inclinations. You gave me that long story about being too busy studying and setting up your business." He looked around the condo again for good measure. "But it seems to me like you're some sort of Suzy Homemaker. I bet all your towels match and your shoes are lined up neatly in your closet. Am I right?"

The flush had faded from her face. Now she just looked angry. And determined.

Nick settled himself in to learn more about her.

She sent him a wicked smile that made his abdomen tighten in anticipation. "There was no deception, not really. You see, I was busy. Too busy. But I've decided to live on the wild side for a time. I want to be free, to date plenty of men, to expound on the realm of sensuality we touched on last night. Yes, I've led a quiet life, and it suited me for a while, but that's over now. I want fun, with no ties."

He spread his arms, benevolent. "Perfect. My sentiments exactly."

But Josie slowly shook her head, her smile now taunting. "You were just my starting point, so to speak. The tip of the iceberg." She tilted her head back, looking at him down her nose. "I intend to branch out."

He couldn't tell if she was serious or not, or if she only meant to punish him for lying. Women could be damn inventive in their means of torturing a man. They seemed to take great pleasure in it. He'd learned that little truism early on in life.

When she continued to smile, not backing down, he came to his feet and pushed the chair away. He'd intended to take control, and it was past time he got started. "Like hell."

"You have no say over it, *Nick*."

"Like hell." He sounded like a damn parrot, but nothing more affirmative came to mind. She was mad and making him pay, and doing a damn good job of it. When he thought of another man touching her, a pounding started in the back of his skull, matching the rush of blood through his temples. It filled him with a black rage. Never in his life had he been jealous over a woman. He didn't like the feeling one bit.

Then finally salvation descended on him and he developed his own plan. He stared at her, working through the details in his mind, expounding on his idea. He nodded. "I'll make you a deal."

"What kind of deal?" She leaned against the counter, the picture of nonchalance—until he started toward her.

Holding her gaze, he stepped close until no space separated them. He could feel her every breath and the heat of her. She might be angry with him, but her body liked him just fine.

With the tips of his fingers he stroked her face, watching her, waiting for her to bolt. But she didn't even blink. His lips skimmed her forehead, then her jaw. His words were a mere whisper in her ear. "This is the deal, Josie. Are you listening?"

She gave a small nod.

"I'll show you more excitement, more sensual fun than your sweet little body can handle, honey. Every thrill there is I'll give to you until you cry mercy."

His fingers slid over her buttocks, then between, stroking and seeking before he nudged her legs apart and nestled himself between them. He levered his pelvis in, pinning her, pushing his erection against her soft belly in a tantalizing rhythm that made heat pulse beneath his skin and his muscles constrict. "I can do it, Josie. You already know that. I can show you things you haven't even imagined yet, things we both know you'll love. I can make you beg, and enjoy doing it.

"But it has to be exclusive. Just me. For as long as we're involved, for as long as we're both interested, there's no other men. You want something, you want to experiment or play, you come to me."

He held his breath, waiting, his body taut with lust, his mind swirling with a strange need he refused to contemplate. He didn't share, plain and simple.

She touched his chest, then her hands crept around his neck. With a small moan, she said, "I think we have a deal."

CHAPTER SIX

WITHOUT EFFORT, Nick lifted her to the top of the counter. Josie felt his fingers on the hem of her T-shirt, tugging it upward, and she shivered. This was insane, outrageous, but she didn't stop him, didn't change her mind.

"Nick?"

"Finally." A rough groan escaped him and he squeezed her tight. "You don't how bad I hated being called another man's name." His mouth closed over her nipple through her bra and she dropped her head back, gasping. The gentle pull of his mouth could be felt everywhere, but especially low in her belly. When he pushed her bra aside, she knew she had to stop him before she was beyond the point of caring.

Panting, she managed to say, "I have a stipulation."

He surprised her by saying, "All right." Then he added, "But tell me quick. I'm dying here."

He lifted his head to look at her and she saw that the tops of his cheekbones were darkly flushed, his eyes slumberous but bright with heat. He looked so incredibly sexy, she almost forgot what she wanted to say. But it was important. He had lied to her and made a fool of her. When she thought of how she'd gone on and on about his partner, Nick, she wanted to crawl away into a dark hole. And he'd let her discuss him as if he hadn't been sitting right beside her. He'd *let* her make a fool of herself.

She'd tried bluffing her way out of the embarrassment by claiming a determination to experiment, to experience life—and men—to the fullest. Only, he'd called her on it and made a counteroffer she couldn't possibly refuse. She knew how easily he could fulfill his end of the bargain, and knowing made her want him all the more. When he left, it would hurt; she didn't fool herself about that. But now, for at least a little while, she could have everything she'd ever dreamed of—all the excitement and whirling thrills. If she didn't grab this opportunity for herself, she'd regret it for the rest of her life.

But if she was going to play his game, then she had to have control, to make certain he would never again be in a position to deceive her. She'd take what he freely offered—but on her terms, not his.

Nick toyed with the snap on her jeans. "Is this your idea of foreplay, honey? Making me wait until I lose my mind? Believe me, with the way I feel right now, the wait won't be too long. After what I've been through today, insanity is just around the bend."

His teasing words brought her out of her stupor. "I have to be in charge."

He lifted one dark brow and his fingers stilled. "In charge of what?"

What kind of question was that? She tried to keep her chin raised, to maintain eye contact, but his slow grin did much to shake her resolve. "Things. What we're doing."

"So then this—" he dragged his knuckles from the snap of her jeans, along the fly and beyond until finally he cupped her boldly with his palm "—is what you would be in charge of? You want to control our relationship, what we do and don't do, where we do it…how we do it?"

She gulped, words escaping her. The man was every bit the scoundrel her sister accused him of being. Too blatant, too outrageous, too incredibly sure of himself and of his effect on her, probably on all women. She could feel his palm, so hot and firm against her, not moving, just holding her and making her nerve endings tingle in anticipation. And that tingling had become concentrated in one ultrasensitive spot.

"No? Did I misunderstand?" His gaze searched her face and she could see the humor in his dark eyes, the slight tilt of his sensual mouth. With his free hand, he took hers and kissed her fingers—then pressed her hand against his erection. He no longer smiled, and his expression seemed entirely too intent. "You want to control me like this, Josie?"

He felt huge and hard and alive. Instinctively she curled her fingers around him through the soft material of his khaki slacks.

"Women have been trying to control men since the beginning of time. This is the most tried-and-true method."

Her fingers tightened in reaction to his harsh words. She felt the lurch, the straining of his penis into her palm, and heat pounded beneath her skin, curled and uncurled until she felt wound too tight, ready to explode.

In a voice low and gravelly, he asked, "Is that what you want, sweetheart?" His breath came fast and low. "Because in this instance, I have no objections. Just lead the way."

Frozen, Josie could do no more than stare down at her hand where she held him. She licked her lips, trying to think of what to do, trying to remember her original intent in this awkward game.

"Josie?"

"I…" She shook her head, then carefully, slowly stroked him. His eyes closed as he groaned his encouragement. "I concede to your experience."

The sound he made was half laugh, half moan.

"But I want to do everything there is to do."

"Damn." His fingers flexed, teasing her. "I want that, too. Sounds to me like we're in agreement."

She shook her head. "You called what we have a a relationship. But that's not what I'd consider it."

His answering gaze was frighteningly direct. "No?"

She looked away. "I'd call it a…a fling. With no strings attached." When he got tired of her and walked away, she wanted him to know it was with her blessing. She was out of her league with Nick, coasting on dangerous ground. It was too tempting not to play, but she was too prudent not to take precautions.

She drew an unsteady breath. "I want—need—to be free to come and go as I please. No ties at all." He was the only person she'd ever felt tempted to do this with, but the same wasn't true of him. He'd been with many women, and he'd be with many more. She'd be a fool to expect anything else. "I can't agree to this exclusive stuff," she said. "I need to know you won't object if I decide to explore…elsewhere."

"Oh, but I do object. In fact, I refuse." His mouth smothered any comeback she might have made, not that she could think of any. The nature of his seduction suddenly became much more determined, almost ruthless. He lifted her off the counter and skimmed her shirt over her head.

"Nick…"

"I like hearing you say my name. Especially the way you say it." Her bra straps slipped down her arms when he unhooked it, then clasped her nipple with his hot and hungry mouth, sucking hard.

Her knees locked and her entire body jerked in reaction. *"Nick…"*

He switched to the other breast while undoing her jeans, and he hurriedly pushed them down to her knees. "Tell me you want me, Josie."

She made a sound of agreement, coherent words beyond her.

He dropped to one knee and kissed her through her panties—small, nipping kisses that had her gasping. Her legs went taut to support her, her fingers tangled in his dark silky hair. With a growl, he pulled her panties down and spread her with his thumbs, then treated her to the same delicious sucking he'd used on her nipple, only gentler, and with greater effect.

It was too much, but not quite enough, and she sobbed, pressing closer, her eyes squeezed shut. His tongue rasped and she arched her body, tight and still, then suddenly climaxed with blinding force when he slid one long finger deep inside her.

The sharp edge of the counter dug into her back as she started to slide down to the floor. She needed to sit, to lie down; her limbs trembled, her vision was still fuzzy. Nick caught her against him and pressed a damp kiss to her temple. "Damn, that was good, Josie." His voice shook, low and sexy. "So damn good. For a virgin, you never cease to amaze me."

"I'm not a virgin anymore." The words sighed out of her, laced with her contentment.

His chuckle vibrated against her skin. "Ex-virgin, then."

Limp, she let him hold her for a few seconds, until he gently turned her to face the counter. She didn't understand what he was doing. Looking at him over her shoulder, she saw him smile. He took her hands and planted them wide on the countertop.

"Open your legs for me, Josie. As wide as your pants will allow."

The rush of heat to her face almost made her dizzy. He was looking at her behind, his hands touching, exploring, exposing, urging her legs even wider. She struggled with her embarrassment and the restriction of her jeans.

He made an approving sound. "That's nice. Now don't move." After laying his wallet out, he unsnapped his pants and shoved them down his hips. Josie stared at his erection, her pulse pounding. "You've seen me before, honey. But I don't mind you looking. In fact, I like it."

He clasped her hips and brushed the tip of his penis against her buttocks, dipping along her cleft. He held her tight and pressed his cheek against her shoulder. "I like it a lot. Too damn much."

With a groan, he pulled a condom out of his wallet and slipped it on. Fascinated, Josie concentrated on holding herself upright, despite the shaking in her knees, and watched him closely so she didn't miss a thing.

But with his first, solid thrust into her body, she forgot about watching and closed her eyes against the too-intense pleasure of it.

"Ah. So wet and hot. You do want me, don't you, sweetheart? *Just me.*"

She rested her cheek on the cool countertop and curled her fingers over the edge, steadying herself. Nick's hand slid beneath her, then smoothed over her belly before dipping between her thighs.

"No…" She gasped, the pleasure too sharp after her recent orgasm, but he wouldn't relent. He continued to touch her in delicate little brushes, taunting her, forcing her to accept the acute sensations until her hips began to move with him.

He groaned with pleasure. "That's it. Relax, Josie. Trust me." He moved with purpose now in smooth determined strokes that rocked her body to a tantalizing rhythm. His forearm protected her hip bones from hard contact with the counter while his fingertips continued to drive her closer to the edge. Suddenly he stilled, his body rock hard, his breathing suspended. Josie could feel the heat pouring off him, the expectation of release.

He wrapped around her, his chest to her back and he hugged her tight. His heart pounded frantically and she felt it inside herself, reverberating with her own wild heartbeat. "Josie," he said on a whispered groan. And she knew he was coming, his thrusts more sporadic, deeper, and incredibly, she came with him, crying out her surprise.

Long minutes passed and neither of them moved. Josie was content. His body, his indescribable scent, surrounded her in gentle waves of pleasure. She could feel the calming of his heartbeat, his gentle, uneven breaths against her skin.

"Woman, you're something else."

She wondered how he could talk, even though his words had sounded weak and breathless. She relished his weight on her body, the soft kisses he pressed to her shoulders and nape and ear. He made a soft sound and said, "I could stay like this forever."

Mustering her strength, she managed to whisper, "That's because you're not the one being squashed into the cold counter."

He chuckled as he straightened and carefully stepped away. "Hey, you were the one in charge. You should have said something if you didn't like it."

Her sigh sounded entirely too much like satisfaction. "I liked it."

"I know."

She smiled at his teasing and forced herself to stand. "This is a downright ignominious position to find myself in."

She heard him zipping his pants, but couldn't quite find the courage to face him. Her fingers shook as she struggled with her panties, which seemed to be twisted around her knees.

"I think you look damn cute. And enticing." He patted her bare bottom with his large hand, then assisted her in straightening her clothes. "Are you okay?"

That brought her gaze to his face. "I'm...fine." She could feel the hot blush creeping up to her hairline. After all, she was still bare-breasted, and her hair was more down than up. She started to cross her arms over her chest, but hesitated when he covered them himself with his hot palms.

"I wish I had planned this better. But I only had the one condom with me."

"Oh." Her blushing face seemed to pulse, making her very aware of how obvious her embarrassment must be. He was so cavalier about it all, like making love in the kitchen was something he'd done dozens of times. And maybe it was, she admitted to herself, not liking the idea one bit.

Nick grinned, enjoying himself at her expense. "Of course, I could give you more pleasure, if that's what you want. I'm stoic and brave and all those other manly things. And we did have an agreement. I'll sacrifice my needs for yours if you're still feeling greedy. If you're in the mood for a little more *fun*."

She didn't quite know how to deal with him. He was all the things Susan claimed—arrogant and cocky, used to female adoration. She pulled away and slipped into her bra and T-shirt, then turned to the sink. As she ran water into the coffeepot, she could feel his gaze on her back, moving over her like a warm touch.

She drew a steadying breath and glanced back at him. "I think I can manage to be as stoic as you. But since you're here, we might as well get a few things straight."

His smile disappeared. "What things?"

"Our agreement, of course."

Disbelief spread over his face. "Little witch."

She ignored his muttered insult and measured out the coffee grains. Mustering her courage, she blurted, "Did you laugh at me after we made love on the boat?"

"As I remember, I was too busy trying to devise ways to keep from tripping myself up to find any humor in the situation."

Josie considered that. "You know, now that I think about it, a lot of things make sense. The way you kept insisting I not call you by name, your hesitance to take me to your house. Your surprise that I was willing to go with you at all."

"I thought you'd back down. Bob had repeated Susan's description of you—and you didn't look a damn thing like what I expected. It's for certain you didn't act the way I thought you would."

Knowing Susan, it wasn't difficult to imagine the picture she'd painted. "I thought you would be the way my sister described Bob. I expected you to run in the opposite direction when you saw what a wild woman I was."

He came to stand directly in front of her, and his large hot hand settled on her hip, his long fingers spread to caress her bottom. "A million ideas went through my mind when I first saw you, and running wasn't one of them." He leaned down and kissed her, gently, teasing. "Are we done talking now? I can think of better things we could be doing."

She faltered at his direct manner and provocative touch, but had the remaining wits to mention an irrefutable fact. "You said you were out of condoms."

He spoke in a low rumble against her lips. "I also said there were other things we could do, other ways for me to pleasure you without needing protection." His eyes met hers, bright and hot. "Right now, I'm more than willing to show you all of them. Tasting you, touching you, is incredibly sweet. Giving you pleasure gives me pleasure. And I love the way you moan, the way your belly tightens and your nipples—"

A soft moan escaped before she managed to turn her face away. "Nick."

With a huge, regretful sigh, he looped his arms around her and held her loosely. "All right, what were you saying?"

She gave him a disgruntled frown. "I don't remember."

"Oh, yeah. You thought I was Bob. And he probably would have been horrified to see you. Horrified and frightened half to death."

"That's what I figured."

"He's hung up on your sister, you know."

Having Nick so close made it difficult to carry on the casual conversation. But he seemed to have no problem with it, so she forged ahead; they really did need to get things straightened out. "He's the one who sent Susan the chocolates?"

"Yup."

"And he's probably the one who told her he didn't approve of my job."

"That'd be Bob. But I doubt he really cares one way or the other what you do. He's just willing to say anything to agree with Susan."

"Susan likes him, too. She was so pleased with his gift. When it arrived, she was all but jumping up and down."

Nick touched her hair, winding one long curl around his finger. "And what did you do?"

She wasn't about to tell him how hurt and betrayed she'd felt. That wouldn't have been in keeping with her new image. "I wasn't sure what to do, except that I knew I couldn't see you again."

"Hmm." He kissed her quickly and stepped away. "Finish the coffee and let's go sit in the other room. I don't trust these tiny kitchen chairs you have. I'm afraid they might collapse under me."

Josie eyed the delicate chairs and silently agreed.

It took an entire pot of coffee and a lot of explaining before they sorted out the whole confusing mess. By the end of the explanations, Nick had Josie mostly in his lap on the short love seat and he'd removed the pins from her hair so that he could play with it. In one way or another, he touched her constantly, his hands busy, his mouth hungry.

"I want to see you tomorrow, Josie. Will you go to the movies with me?"

She shook her head. As soon as she'd left Susan's shop, she'd accepted an invitation from one of her clients. She could have cancelled if she'd wanted to, but with everything she'd just learned, including his deception and her volatile reaction to him, she didn't trust herself to be with him again so soon. He was playing games while she was falling hard. She needed time to think, to regroup. "I already made other plans, Nick."

Through narrowed eyes, he studied her face a long moment, his gaze probing, then looked down at her clasped hands. "What about Monday?"

She shrugged helplessly. "I can't. Mondays are late nights for me."

He seemed disgruntled by her answer. Josie had the feeling few women ever turned him down. She almost relented; seeing the disappointment in his sensual gaze made her feel the same. But she had a responsibility to her patients, and as tempting as he was, her responsibilities took precedence over her newfound pleasure.

"How late?"

"It depends on who needs what done. But I can't rush my visits. For many of my clients, I'm the only company they get on a regular basis."

He sighed, obviously frustrated but willing to concede. He cupped her cheek and stared down at her. "You're pretty incredible. Do you know that?"

"It's not so much. I enjoy their company, and they enjoy mine."

"Does it involve much traveling?"

"Some. A lot of the people I work with now or worked with in the past live in this complex, which is one reason I bought here. It's easier to keep an eye on things."

"You know, I did wonder about that. I had all these old folks staring me down, looking at me like I was an interloper. I didn't understand it at first."

"Young people in the complex are always a curiosity. I'm surprised Mrs. Wiley didn't come out and question you."

"She didn't need to. I went to her to find out which condo you lived in." He pulled the rolled catalog from his back pocket. "She gave me this and I promised to try to come up with some kind of inexpensive advertising promotion for her."

Josie stared down blankly at the Golden Goodies catalog, which had fallen open to show pictures of various-size candles and love-inspired board games. She couldn't quite manage to pull her fascinated gaze away, even though she'd seen the thing dozens of times. The difference now, of course, was that she wondered if Nick would enjoy playing any of the inventive games, winning prizes that varied from kisses to "winner's choice." She had a feeling she knew what his choice would be.

Josie cleared her throat. "A supplier gives her the catalogs and fills the orders, then the selling is up to her. And she's pretty good at it. But I suppose she does need a wider audience than the complex allows."

Nick turned the page, perusing the items for sale. He looked surprised. "Why, that old fraud. This stuff isn't X-rated. The way she carried on, I thought she was selling something really hot."

Tilting her head, Josie asked, "Like what?"

He opened his mouth, then faltered. "Never mind."

She smiled. "For most older folks, scented lotions and feather boas are pretty risqué. They love Mrs. Wiley's parties. It makes them feel young again, and daring."

"Have you ever been to one?"

Without looking at him, Josie flipped to another page, studying the variety of handheld fans and flavored lipsticks. "Once or twice." She cleared her throat. "There was a party here the night we met. I think I mentioned it—remember? That was one of Mrs. Wiley's."

"Ah. So that's the reason you didn't want to come back here."

Josie didn't correct him. But the truth was, she hadn't wanted to return because she hadn't wanted to see his disappointment when he realized what a domestic homebody she really was. She'd talked her way around that, but the risk was still there, because she knew from Susan's dire predictions that no man would tolerate her demanding schedule for long—certainly not a man used to female adoration, like Nick. Hopefully, before he grew tired of her harried schedule, she'd be able to glut herself on his unique charms and be sated. For a while.

Nick brought her out of her reverie with a gentle nudge. "Have you ever bought anything from her?"

"A few things."

His eyes glittered at her. "Show me."

"No."

He laughed at her cowardice. "Before we're through, I'll get you over your shyness." His taunting voice was low and sensual, and then he kissed her deeply.

Before we're through... Josie wondered how much or how little time she'd actually have with Nick. When he lifted his mouth from hers, it took her several moments to get her eyes to open. When she finally succeeded, he smiled.

"Sometime, if it's okay, I'd like to go with you to visit your friends."

That took her by surprise. In a way, his interest pleased her, but it wouldn't be a good idea to introduce him to too many people. The more he invaded her life, the harder it would be when he left, which would be sooner than later. Sounding as noncommittal as possible, she murmured, "We'll see."

He nodded. "Good. Now, what about the rest of the week? When will you be free?"

"What do you have in mind?"

"We could go back to the boat, and this time I promise to show you the river at night. It's beautiful to look at all the lights on the water, to smell the moisture in the air and hear the sounds." He put his mouth to her ear and spoke in a rough whisper. "We could make love on the deck, Josie, under the stars. Mist rises off the river and everything gets covered in dew. Your skin would be slippery and…"

She shivered before she could stop herself, then remembered how he'd told her his parents were dead. Annoyance came back, but not quite as strong this time. Not with him so close. "Is it your boat?"

"I'm making love to you and you want to know who the damn boat belongs to?"

His feigned affront didn't deter her. "I'm just trying to figure out what's true and what you made up."

With an expression that showed his annoyance, Nick gave the shortest possible explanation. "It still legally belongs to my father. But when my parents divorced, it more or less became mine to use."

The sarcasm couldn't be missed, and Josie felt stung. Nick didn't want her to delve into his past, into his personal life. Their time together would center only on the physical. It was what she'd claimed to want, but now she felt uncomfortable. She started to rise, but before she could move an inch, Nick's arms tightened around her.

"Damn it, Josie, do we really need to discuss this?"

She blinked, surprised by his outburst. "Of course not. I didn't mean to pry."

He reached for her hand and held it. "You're not prying. It's just… Your parents died when you were fifteen, and mine divorced. The effects were damn similar. They fought for years over everything material, and eventually, the boat was bestowed on me for lack of a better solution. Mother didn't want my father to have it, because then he might have shared it with Myra, the woman he married three months after the divorce became final. And my father didn't want my mother to have it because he was still too angry over her foisting me off on him."

"What…what do you mean?"

Nick sighed, then leaned his head back, his eyes closed. Josie realized he was shutting her out to some extent, but still he answered her question. "My mother thought it would be a cute trick to saddle my dad with me while he was trying to start a new life with his new wife. He saw through her, knew what she was doing and pretty much resented us both. He tried to send me home, but Mom wouldn't let him."

Josie stared, speechless. She couldn't imagine him being treated like an unwelcome intruder by the very people who should have loved him most. For her, it had been just the opposite, and she suddenly wanted to tell Susan again how much she appreciated all she'd done. Careful to hide her sympathy, she asked, "That must have been pretty rough."

He shrugged, still not looking at her. "Naw. The only really tough part was putting up with Myra. For the most part, my mom and dad ignored me once everything was settled. But for some ridiculous reason, Myra saw me as competition. And she hated everything about me. She tried to change my friends, my clothes, even the school I attended. And she tried to make certain I stayed too busy to visit my grandfather."

"Why? What did it matter to her?"

"My grandfather had no use for her. And it bugged her. I used to spend two weeks every summer with him. But after Myra married my father, she convinced Dad that I needed some added responsibility and insisted I take on a summer job. It wasn't that I minded working, only that I missed Granddad."

"She sounds like a bitch."

He laughed with real humor, then opened his eyes and smiled down at her. "Myra wasn't unique. I haven't met a woman yet who didn't think she could improve me in one way or another."

Josie stiffened. "I like you just the way you are."

He didn't look as though he believed her. "I fought with Myra a lot, and likely made her more miserable than she made me. Graduation didn't come quick enough to suit either of us. The summer before my first year of college I moved out on my own. That's when I met Bob and we roomed together to share expenses. He got a job as an assistant to an accountant, and I got a job with the college newspaper. I did the layout on all the ads." He flashed her a grin, his pensive mood lifting. "And as your sister can attest, I'm damn good at what I do now."

It took her a moment, and then the words sank in. "Susan said Bob was the talented one. That he's solely responsible for making your business so successful."

Rather than looking insulted, he grinned. "Yeah, well, Susan refused to work with me. If she'd known I was handling her file, she wouldn't have given us her business."

Josie gasped. "You've lied to her, too! Oh my God, when Susan finds out you did her ads, she'll be furious. We'll all be running for cover."

Nick winced, though his grin was still in place. "Is it truly necessary to tell her, do you think? I mean, right now, she likes Bob, and he likes her. I wouldn't want to cause them any trouble."

Josie gave him a knowing look. "You just don't want Susan biting your face off. You're not fooling me."

"Your sister is enough to instill fright in even the stoutest of men." He kissed her, but it was a tickling kiss because he couldn't stop smiling. "She already despises me, Josie. If she knows I talked Bob into tricking her, she'll run me out of town. Is that what you want?"

As he asked it, his large hot hand smoothed over her abdomen and Josie inhaled. "No."

"Good. Then let's make a pact. We'll do all we can to get your sister and Bob together—before we drop any truthful bombshells on her. Okay?"

Since he was still stroking her, she nodded her agreement. Besides, if Susan knew the full truth, she would do her best to talk Josie out of spending time with Nick. That decided her more than anything else. "I don't suppose it will hurt to wait. As long as you eventually come clean. But Nick, you have to know, when she finds out Bob isn't all that's perfection, she won't be happy."

"Why don't we let Bob worry about that? Besides, he may not be perfect, but he is perfect for her. At least that's what he keeps assuring me."

"I hope he's right, because I don't want to see her hurt."

"Everything will work out as it should in the end." He smoothed the hair from her forehead, kissed her brow. "Now tell me about yourself."

"What do you want to know?"

"Everything. Yesterday we didn't exactly get around to talking all that much. I think we should get to know each other a little better, don't you?"

Josie blushed. Yesterday, words hadn't seemed all

that important. "Do you really think it's necessary? I mean, for the purposes of a fling, do we need to know personal stuff?"

His expression darkened. "I don't like that word— *fling*." She started to reply to that, but he raised a hand. "Come on, Josie. Fair's fair. I confided in you."

She supposed he was right. But her story differed so much from his, she hesitated to tell it. She started slowly, trying to keep the focus on Susan's generosity, rather than her own grief. "After my parents died, Susan wouldn't even consider me getting a job. She sold our house so we'd have enough money for me to continue my education. It was a big, old-fashioned place with pillars in the front. It used to be our great-aunt's before she died and left it to my mother when we were just kids. We both still miss it, though Susan won't admit it. She doesn't want me to know how much it meant to her, or how hard it was for her to let it go."

With a thoughtful expression, Nick nodded his approval. "Susan did what any good big sister would do."

And Josie thought, *I had Susan. But who did you have?* Rather than say it, she touched his cheek and smiled. "Do you ever see your family now?"

He pretended a preoccupation with her fingertips, kissing each one. "Not often. Mother is always busy, which is a blessing since she's not an easy person to be around. And Myra still despises me, which makes it difficult for my father and me to get together." He sucked the tip of one finger between his teeth.

Feeling her stomach flutter, Josie wondered if she'd ever get used to all the erotic touching and kissing. She hoped not. "I imagine you must resent her a lot."

"Not really. If it hadn't been for Myra, I might never have hooked up with Bob, and he's great as both a friend and a partner. He's the one who suggested we go into business together. In fact, he's the one who got things started."

He deliberately lightened the mood, so Josie did the same. "Ah. So, Bob really is the brains of the operation?"

He bit the tip of her finger, making her jump and pull away. Josie glared at him.

He grinned. "Sorry. But I hear enough of that derision from your sister."

"No doubt you'll hear a lot more of it from her when she finds out we're seeing each other."

He made a sour face. "Couldn't we skip telling her that, too?"

"You must not know my sister very well if you think I could keep it from her. She's like a mother hen, always checking up on me."

"Well, as I said, I'm stoic. I can put up with anything if the end result is rewarding enough." His thumb smoothed over her lips. "And you're definitely enough. Now, can you find any spare time this week to go to the boat with me?"

When Josie thought of all the women he must have taken there over the years, she couldn't quite stifle a touch of jealousy. She looked away, wondering how many women had observed the stars from the deck, the moisture rising from the water.

"Josie." As if he'd read her thoughts, he hugged her close again. His hand cuddled her breast possessively, and rather than meet her curious gaze, he stayed focused on the movement of his fingers over her body.

"Do you remember me telling you on the boat that I never take women there?"

"You took me there."

"And you're the only one. That wasn't a lie."

She wanted to believe him, but it seemed so unlikely.

Before she could decide what to say, Nick shook his head and continued. "I'm not claiming to have been a monk—far from it. I've always used the boat when I wanted to be alone. There's something peaceful about water, something calming, and I never wanted to share that with anyone, especially not a woman. With all the fighting that damn boat caused between my parents, it has a lot of memories attached to it, and most of them aren't very pleasant. I've never found it particularly conducive to romance." He made the admission reluctantly, his voice sounding a bit strained. He raised his eyes until he could look at her and that look started her heart racing. "Until I met you. Now I don't think I'll be able to see it any other way."

Emotion swelled, threatening to burst. Susan was wrong. Nick wasn't a self-centered womanizer. He wasn't a man without a care who would tromp on people's feelings. The special fondness he felt for his grandfather was easy to hear when Nick spoke of him. And his dedication to Bob went above and beyond the call of duty to a partner, to the point of silently accepting Susan's contempt. She'd accused him of having no talent; he *was* the talent. Nick had even agreed to work out an ad campaign for Mrs. Wiley, despite his reservations about her business. Though his adolescence had obviously been bereft of love and guidance, he was still a kind and generous man.

It would be all too easy to care about him.

"What are you thinking?" Nick smoothed the frown from her forehead.

"I'm thinking that you're a most remarkable man, Nick Harris."

He made a scoffing sound and started to kiss her, but Josie was familiar with that tactic now. Whenever he wanted to avoid a subject, he distracted her physically.

Teasing, he said, "I'm a scoundrel and a man of few principles. Just ask your sister."

"But Susan doesn't really know you, does she?" His gaze swept up to lock with hers. Josie lifted a hand to sift through his hair. "She's given me all these dire predictions, but I don't think you're nearly as reckless and wild as she'd like to think."

His expression froze for a heartbeat, then hardened. Before Josie could decipher his mood, he had her T-shirt pulled over her head and caught at her elbows, pinning her arms together, leaving her helpless. He studied her breasts with heated, deliberate intensity. When he spoke, his words were barely above a whisper.

"Don't, Josie. Don't think that because I had a few family problems, I'm this overly sensitive guy waiting to be saved by the right woman." His hand flattened on her belly and she trembled. "I want all the same things you want, honey. Fun, freedom, a little excitement. With no ties and no commitments. It'll be the perfect relationship between us, I promise you that. You won't be disappointed."

She wanted to yell that she was already disappointed. No, she hadn't ever considered a lasting relationship. But then, she hadn't met Nick. All by himself he was more excitement than most women could handle. And despite what she'd claimed, she wanted more out of life than a few thrills. So much more. But Nick had read her thoughts, and corrected them without hesitation. She'd dug a hole for herself with her own lies and deceptions, and she wasn't quite sure how to get out of it. She couldn't press him without chasing him away—and that was the very last thing she wanted to do.

Nick bent, treating one sensitive nipple to the hot, moist pressure of his mouth, and she decided any decisions could wait until later. He seemed determined now to show her all the ways he could enjoy her without the need for precautions, and at the moment, she didn't have the will to tell him no.

Minutes later, she didn't have the strength, either.

NICK WHISTLED as he entered the offices. He hadn't felt this good in a long time, though he wasn't sure exactly *why* he felt so content, and wasn't inclined to worry about it. Right now, he had better things to occupy his mind—like the coming night and the fact that he'd be alone with Josie again. His entire body tightened in anticipation of what he'd do with her and her sensual acceptance of him. It had been too long.

She hadn't been able to see him Tuesday, as he'd expected, because that, too, was a late night for her, and the needs of her patients came first—a fact that nettled since he wasn't used to playing second fiddle. So even though he'd had other plans for the night, he'd canceled them. Again. Josie didn't know he'd changed his plans for her, and he didn't intend to tell her. She might get it into her head that she could call all the shots, and he liked things better just the way they were.

Josie wanted to use him for sex, wanted him to be a sizzling male fantasy come to life, and if that wasn't worth a little compromise, he didn't know what was. It sure beat the hell out of anything he could think of.

Besides, she had given him a request, and it was to assist her in exploring the depths of herself as a woman, not to skim the surface with mere quickies. He could be patient until her time was freed up. He wanted to sleep with her again, to hold her small soft body close to his all night, to wake her up with warm wet kisses and the gentle slide of his body into hers. He shuddered at his own mental image.

As he entered the building, the sound of arguing interrupted his erotic thoughts. It was coming from Bob's office, and he started in that direction but drew up short in the doorway when he recognized Susan's virulent tones.

Since he enjoyed pricking her temper, and had from the moment he met her, he asked pleasantly, "Am I interrupting?"

Two pairs of eyes swung in his direction. "Nick," was said in relief at the same time "You!" was muttered with huge accusation.

Ignoring Bob for the moment, he directed his attention to Susan. "Miss Jackson. How are you today?"

"How am I?" She advanced on him and Bob rushed around his desk to keep pace with her. Nick had the feeling Bob intended to protect him. The idea almost made him smile.

"I was fine, that is until Bob confessed the rotten trick you played on my sister."

Turning his consideration to Bob, who looked slightly ill, Nick asked, "Had a baring of the soul, did you?"

"Actually," Susan said, staring up at him with a frown, "he did his best to cover for you after I forced him to confirm that you're seeing Josie. He's been explaining to me that you're a *reformed* womanizer, that you truly care for my sister. Not that I'm believing it." She pointed a rigid finger at his chest. "I know your kind. You're still a die-hard bachelor just out for some fun, and that's not what Josie needs in her life right now."

"You make *fun* sound like a dirty word," Nick muttered, but there was no heat in his comment. He was too distracted for heat. Did Bob really see him as *reformed?* The idea was totally repellent. For most of his life, certainly since Bob had known him, he'd avoided any attempts at serious relationships. Not because he was still troubled over his parents' divorce, or his father's remarriage. And not because his psyche had been damaged by his mother's rejection. Mostly he'd avoided attachments because he hadn't met a woman yet who didn't want to change everything about him. They'd profess unconditional love, then go about trying to get him to alter his life. His stepmother had been the queen of control, but at least she hadn't ever tried to hide her inclinations behind false caring.

No, he'd had enough of controlling females, and his life was as he wanted it to be. He didn't intend to change it for anyone. But he did want Josie, and he'd have her—on his terms, not Susan's.

Not about to explain himself to the sister, he halfheartedly addressed Susan's sputtering outrage, going on the offense. "You don't really understand Josie at all, do you?"

"She's my sister!"

"Yeah, but you would have hooked her up with Bob."
He warmed to the subject, seeing Susan's face go red
while Bob blustered in the background. He'd been
coaching Bob for the better part of a week, getting him
to send cards, to make phone calls late at night. To
whisper the little romantic things women liked to hear.
Susan appeared to be melting faster than an iceberg in
the tropics. Though she hadn't as yet admitted it. According to Bob, all her considerable focus was still aimed at
getting Josie *settled*. Damn irritating female. Josie didn't
want to settle, and that suited Nick to perfection.

He grinned, feeling smug over the way both Susan and
Bob glanced at each other. "I'm sure you realize now
what a mistake that might have been, for both Josie and
Bob."

Susan thrust her chin into the air. "So she and Bob
wouldn't have worked out. That doesn't mean I want
her seeing you."

Softly he said, "But that's what Josie wants."

Susan bristled. "Josie is just going through a phase."

Damn right, he thought. A sensational stage of dis-
covering her own sexuality, and he'd been lucky enough
to be there when she'd decided to expand her horizons.
He kept his expression serious. "She's discussed that
with me, Miss Jackson. Josie and I understand each
other, so you have no reason to worry." Nick not only
understood, he encouraged her.

Agitated, Susan paced away. When she faced Nick
again, her look was more serious than aggressive. "You
think you understand, but you can't know what Josie's
been through. When our parents died, everything
changed. We lost our house, our car. There was never

enough money for her to do the things most girls her age were doing. She didn't shop with her friends for trendy clothes, attend dances or school parties or date. At first she just became withdrawn. It scared me something fierce. But then she started college, and she put everything she had not just into succeeding but excelling. She's worked very hard at shutting out life, and now that she's ready to live again, she deserves the best."

"And to you, that means someone other than me?"

"Josie needs someone sensitive, someone who's stable and reliable."

His chest felt tight and his temples pounded. Susan was determined to replace him, but he wouldn't let her. For now, Josie wanted him, and that was all that mattered. "I won't hurt her. I promise."

"Coming from you, I am not reassured!"

Surely he wasn't *bad* for Josie, he thought with a frown. He was an experienced man, capable of giving her everything she wanted, and right now that meant freedom and excitement and fun, not love everlasting. He wasn't prudish and he wasn't selfish; he hadn't lied when he said he enjoyed giving her pleasure.

Susan assumed she knew what Josie needed, but Josie claimed the opposite. She'd made it clear she didn't want attachments, so he'd assured her there would be none. That had been her stipulation, but he'd gone along with the idea, even emphasized it, to keep her from backing out. Josie wanted a walk on the wild side, and he was more than prepared to indulge her. Especially if it kept her from seeking out other men, a notion he couldn't tolerate.

Susan was still glaring at him, and he sighed. "I'm really not so bad, Miss Jackson. Just ask Bob."

Bob nodded vigorously, but Susan ignored him. "Bob is sincere in what he does. His intentions are always honorable. But I'm finding he can be rather biased where you're concerned."

At that particular moment, Nick wanted nothing more than to escape Susan's scrutiny. But he had no intention of walking out on Josie now, so gaining her sister's approval might not be a bad thing. He sifted through all the readily available remarks to Susan's statement, none of them overly ingratiating, then settled on saying, "Bob is the most ethical and straightforward man I know."

Susan made the attempt, but couldn't come up with a response other than a suspicious nod of agreement.

"And yet he keeps me as his partner and his closest friend. Can you imagine that? Surely it says something for my character that Bob trusts me? Or is it that you think Bob is an idiot?" He waited while Susan narrowed her eyes—eyes just like Josie's, only at the moment they were filled with rancor rather than good humor. Bob sputtered in the background.

Through clenched teeth, Susan replied, "It might show that Bob is too trusting for his own good."

Nick almost laughed. Susan wasn't a woman to give up a bone once she got her sharp little teeth into it. Finally she sighed. "Though I don't think you're at all right for Josie, I'll concede the possibility that you might have a *few* redeeming qualities, Mr. Harris."

He gave her a wry nod. "I'm overwhelmed by your praise." Truth was, Susan had him worried. If she decided to harp on his shortcomings, would Josie think twice about seeing him? And if Susan kept marching marriage-minded men in front of Josie, would she one day surrender? He knew Susan had some influence on her—after all, Josie had been a twenty-five-year-old virgin!

He was distracted from his thoughts of being replaced, which enraged him, when Susan cleared her throat.

"Before I leave, Mr. Harris, I do have one last question for you."

He noted that Bob had begun to tug at his collar. Nick raised a brow, then flinched when Susan produced the damn catalog Josie's neighbor had given him.

She held it out by two fingers, as if reluctant to even touch it, and thrust it at his face. Her foot tapped the floor and she stared down her nose at him. "If you're truly as reformed as you claim, why do you have this floating around the office?"

She looked triumphant, as if she'd caught him with a girly magazine. Obviously she hadn't looked at the catalog or she'd have realized how innocent it was.

For a single heartbeat, Nick thought he would laugh. But he glanced at Bob and saw how red his face had turned. He grinned. "Bob's birthday is next month, you know. I was trying to find him something special. If you need any ideas on what to get him, feel free to look through the thing. I believe he might have dog-eared a few pages."

Susan stared at the catalog, stared at Bob, then amazingly, she flipped to the first bent page. Nick knew what she would find. After all, he was the one who had cornered the pages while searching for a hook on an ad campaign.

There was nothing even slightly offensive displayed on the pages, but Susan's eyes widened and she dropped the catalog on Bob's desk. "I...uh, hmm."

"Find anything interesting?" Nick asked with false curiosity.

Susan made a small humming sound. "Ah...possibly."

With a weak smile and a hasty goodbye, she made an unsteady exit.

"I'm going to kill you."

Nick slapped Bob on the shoulder. "Did you see her face? Sheer excitement, Bud. Take my word for it. She'll think about that damn catalog, and your romantic tendencies all night. It'll drive her wild."

Bob picked up the catalog and peered at the page Susan had turned to. He groaned. "Leopard-print silk boxers?"

Nick raised his eyebrows, chuckling. "Real silk, by the way. I was thinking of buying a pair." He turned to go into his own office. "But they'll look much cuter on you."

He barely ducked the catalog as it came flying past his head. Seconds later, he heard Bob cross the floor to pick it up again.

It seemed his efforts to bring Susan and Bob together were finally paying off. Maybe Bob could distract Susan from her campaign to marry off Josie. He didn't want Josie married. He didn't want her exploring elsewhere, either.

He decided he needed to ensure his position, and he

could do that by driving her crazy with pleasure. After he finished, marriage and other men would be the furthest things from her mind.

CHAPTER SEVEN

"TELL ME IT'S NOT TRUE."

Josie had barely gotten the door open before Susan wailed out her plea.

"Uh—"

Susan pushed her way in and closed the door behind her, then fell against it in a tragic pose. "He's not Bob, Josie. He's not a man meant for a woman like you."

Josie didn't know if she should laugh at Susan's theatrics or wince at the unwelcome topic. "I take it we're talking about Nick."

"Yes!" Susan pushed away from the door. "Why didn't you tell me you were seeing him? Oh, this is all Bob's fault! If he hadn't stood you up in the first place, none of this would have happened."

"Then I'm glad Bob didn't show!"

They had both resorted to shouting, and that rarely happened. Susan blinked at Josie, then sank onto the edge of the couch. "Oh, God. You're infatuated with him, aren't you?"

Infatuation didn't come close to describing what she felt. But it wouldn't do to tell Susan that.

"Josie?"

Glancing at the clock, Josie realized she only had a

little time left to get ready before Nick arrived. She wanted tonight to be special, for both of them.

She settled herself next to Susan and took her hands. "Susan, I know you mean well. You always do. But I'm not going to stop seeing Nick. At least, not as long as he's willing to see me." Susan shifted, and Josie squeezed her hands, silencing her automatic protest. "And yes, before you say it, I know what I'm getting into. Nick has been very up-front with me. I know he's not the marrying kind, and I can handle that." She would have to handle it; the only other option was to stop seeing him, which was no option at all.

"Can you?" Susan's smile was solemn. "When he walks away, do you have any idea how you'll feel?"

She had a pretty darn good idea, but she only smiled. "It'll be worth it. Even you have to admit, Nick is exactly the type of man any red-blooded woman wants to enjoy, with or without a wedding ring. And I plan to do just that, for as long as I possibly can."

Susan's blush was accompanied by a frown of concern. "You've always lived a sheltered life. You don't know his kind the way I do. They're arrogant and insufferable. They want everything their own way, and they don't care who they hurt in the process."

"Nick is different."

Susan snorted, causing Josie to smile.

"He may not want any permanent ties, but he's the most charming man I've ever met. If you got to know him, you'd probably like him. He's sweet and funny. He listens when I talk and he understands the priorities of my work. He doesn't pressure me, but he's so complimentary and gracious and attentive. He acts like I'm the only woman alive. He's...wonderful."

"Ha! He's a wolf on the prowl, so of course he's attentive. None of what you've said surprises me. It's just his way of keeping you hooked."

Josie knew it was true, knew Nick probably behaved exactly the same way with every woman he had an intimate relationship with. But for now she felt special, and almost loved. "Susan..."

"I don't want you to romanticize him, Josie. You'll only get crushed."

"That can only happen if I let it. But I know what I'm doing." Josie had at first been torn by mixed emotions. She wanted Nick, the excitement and the romance and the sexual chemistry that seemed to explode between them whenever they got close. It was so thrilling, making her feel alive and sexy and feminine. But she knew she wasn't the type of woman who could ever hold Nick for long. Her life was mundane and placid. She was a very common woman, while he was a wholly uncommon man.

But at the same time, the very things that made her and her lifestyle so unsuitable to him were things she wouldn't want to change. The friendship and kindness she received from working with the elderly, knowing she had made a difference in their lives, letting them make a difference in hers. All her life, Susan had been playing the big sister, taking care of her. But with the elderly, Josie got to be the caring one, the one who could give. They welcomed her into their homes and their hearts. They didn't judge her or frown on her conservative lifestyle. They didn't expect anything she couldn't give.

And there was the fact that Susan would never approve of Nick. But Susan had given up her own life for Josie, without complaint or remorse. She was the only family Josie had left, and she loved Susan dearly.

"I know this is all temporary, Susan. I won't be taken by surprise when Nick moves on. I have no illusions that I'll overwhelm him with my charms and he'll swear undying love."

"And why not? Nick Harris would be lucky to have you!"

Emotion nearly choked her. Though at times Susan could be abrasive, Josie never doubted her loyalty. "I know you can't approve, but will you please try to understand?"

Her sister's sigh was long and loud. "I do understand. Maybe I wouldn't have before meeting Bob, but now I know what it is to get carried away. Bob is very special to me." She grinned. "I have to admit, I'm glad you didn't settle on him."

Josie laughed out loud. "So, you two are getting along?"

Susan shook her head. "No, right now I'm furious with him. I do understand how you feel, honey, but I can't help worrying anyway. And I know if Bob hadn't lied to me from the start, if he'd gone to see you himself instead of sending Nick, we wouldn't be having this conversation."

Though she had promised Nick, Josie thought it was time to clear the air. She made her tone stern while she gave Susan a chiding look. "Do you even know why Bob lied?"

Susan lifted a brow.

"Because he cares about you. Bob did everything

he could think of to keep you around. He even…" She hesitated, wondering if Susan would understand Bob's motives.

"He what?"

With a deep breath, Josie blurted, "He even told you he was the one who created your ads, just because he knew you didn't like Nick."

Susan's nostrils became pinched and her expression darkened. "Are you telling me Nick Harris is responsible for my advertisements? Are you telling me he's the one I should be grateful to?"

"Yes, that's what I'm telling you. Rather than let you go, Bob contrived to keep you around. And Nick, whom you seem to think is a total cad, let you revile him even though he could have taken credit all along."

"You're kidding."

"Nope. You can ask Bob, though I imagine it would embarrass him to no end."

Susan jerked to her feet. "I will ask him. But I have no doubt that damn partner of his is behind this somehow! That man is nothing but trouble."

With that, she stormed out of the condo, and Josie winced in sympathy for Bob. She hoped Susan wouldn't be too hard on him, but she had a feeling it was Nick who would feel the brunt of her anger.

Josie looked around her apartment, thinking how quiet it seemed without Susan there shaking things up. Her apartment always seemed empty, but somehow lonelier to her now. Before meeting Nick, she'd enjoyed her solitude and independence. But now, too much time alone only served to remind her of how she'd wasted her life, what a coward she'd been. She knew, even though Nick would never love her, she was doing the right thing. Her time with him was precious, and it filled up the holes in her life, the holes she hadn't even realized were there until recently. When he went away, she'd still have the memories. And for now, she had to believe memories would be enough.

An hour later, when the doorbell rang again, Josie was in front of her mirror, anxiously surveying herself. Knowing it was Nick, she pressed a fist to her pounding heart. She felt so incredibly nervous, this being the first time she and Nick would have extended time alone since that first night.

Moreover, it was the first time she'd dared to dress to please him. Though he hadn't said they'd be going anywhere except the boat, she had plans for the night, and her clothing played a part in it all.

The flowery dress was new, sheer and very daring, ending well above her knee. In the wraparound fashion, it buttoned at the side of her waist on the inside where no one could see. One button, the only thing holding the dress together other than the matching belt in the same material, which she'd loosely tied. Getting the dress off would be a very simple matter.

She'd left her hair hanging loose the way Nick preferred it. And this time, she had chosen red, strappy sandals with midhigh heels so she could walk without stumbling. She'd even painted her toe nails bright red. She'd set the stage the best she could.

Beneath the dress, she hadn't bothered with sexy garters or nylons; they would have been superfluous in this case. Other than her panties, she was naked.

She rubbed her bare arms, gave her image one more quick glance and went to open the door.

Nick lounged against the door frame. At least, he did until he saw her. Slowly, he straightened while his gaze traveled on a leisurely path down the length of her body and back up again. Without a word, he stepped forward, forcing her to back up, then kicked the door shut behind him.

"Damn, you look good enough to eat."

Her lips parted and heat washed her cheeks. He lifted one hand and traced the low vee of her neckline from one mostly bare shoulder to the other, then his hand cupped her neck and he drew her close. "Such a pretty blush. Whatever are you thinking, Josie?"

He must not have wanted an answer, because he kissed her, his mouth soft on hers while his tongue slowly explored. Josie gasped and clutched the front of his cotton shirt, almost forgetting what she intended. But she needed to wrest control from him, to play the game her own way before she lost her heart totally. As it was, her feelings for him were far too complicated. And Nick, well used to his effect on women, would recognize what she felt if she didn't take care to hide her emotions behind her strong physical attraction.

If he thought she was growing lovesick, he'd leave. And she wasn't ready for him to go. Not yet.

He slanted his head and the kiss deepened. One hand slid inside the top of her dress and when he found her bare breast, he pulled back.

"Damn." Hot and intent, his gaze moved over her mouth, her throat, the breast he smoothed so gently. "You're naked underneath, aren't you?"

"No." A mere squeak of sound and she cleared her throat, trying to sound more certain, more provocative— more like the woman who had attracted him in the first place. "No, but too many underthings would have ruined the lines of the dress." She tried a small smile, looking at him through her lashes. "I have on my panties."

"I'd like to see." No sooner did he say the words than he shook his head and took a step back. "No, we can't. There's not enough time. If I had you lifting your dress we'd never get out the door."

Josie tried not to gape at him, to accept his outland- ish words with as much disregard as he'd given them. The thing to do would be to laugh, to tease. Instead she straightened her dress, covering herself, and tried to find a response.

Such an assumption he'd made! As if she'd just lift her skirt at his whim. Of course, she probably would. Nick had a way of getting her to do things she'd never considered doing before. It was both unnerving and ex- hilarating, the power he seemed to have over her. Now she wanted the same power.

"Are you ready to go? I've made a few plans."

He'd given up so easily. She hadn't expected that. "What plans?" She crossed to the couch to pick up her purse and her wrap. The September nights were starting to get cool.

"It's a surprise." He lifted his brows and once again scanned her body. "Not quite as pleasant as your surprise, which almost stopped my heart, by the way."

Feeling tentative, Josie smoothed the short skirt on the dress and peered at him. "So you like it?"

"Honey, only a dead man wouldn't. And I swear, I appreciate your efforts. I'll show you how much later, when we get to the boat." He reached for her hand and pulled her to the door. "But right now we're running a little late."

She had hoped their only destination would be the boat. "Where are we going?"

He looked uncertain, avoiding her gaze. "I told you, it's a surprise. Trust me."

She tried not to look too disappointed. "What if I'd had other plans?"

He smiled as they neared his truck. "It's obvious you did. And we'll get to that before the night is over." He opened the truck door and lifted her onto her seat. His gaze skimmed her legs while she crossed them. "That is, if I can wait that long. You are one hell of a temptation."

Josie wondered at his mood as he started the truck and pulled away from the parking lot. He kept glancing at her, his dark brows lowered slightly as if in thought.

The sky was overcast and cloudy and she knew a storm would hit before the night was over. She could smell the rain in the air, feel the electric charge on her skin, both from the weather and the anticipation. She welcomed the turbulence of it, took deep breaths and let it flow through her, adding to her bravado.

She had to follow through, had to make certain she got the most out of this unique situation before her time with him ended. In a low whisper, she said, "I'm not feeling nearly so secretive as you." She turned halfway in the seat to face him, aware that her position had slightly parted the skirt of her dress. "Would you like to know what my plans were?"

"I have a feeling you're just dying to tell me."

His smile showed his amusement, but it wasn't a steady smile and seemed a bit forced to Josie. So be it. He wouldn't be laughing at her for long. "I want to have my way with you."

He hesitated, and his gaze flew to her again. "You care to explain that?"

Using one finger, she traced the length of his hard thigh. "If you think it's necessary."

"I believe it is." His voice was deep, already aroused, and she drew strength from that; it took so little to make him want her.

"Tonight I want to know what you like, what your body reacts to. I want to drive you crazy the way you did me."

He laughed, the sound suddenly filled with purpose. "Men are embarrassingly obvious in what we like and need, honey. Unlike women, who are fashioned differently, men need very little stimulation to be ready."

Used to his blunt way of phrasing things, Josie didn't mind his words. But she stiffened when they stopped at a red light and he was able to give her his full attention. His gaze was hot, intense. His hand slid over her knee and then upward and she sucked in a quick startled breath. "And you already make me crazy." He spoke in a low husky whisper, and his cheekbones were flushed. "You're so damn explosive. I've never known another woman who reacted the way you do. There's something called chemistry going on between us, and it works both ways. I've been different, too, if you want the truth."

"The truth would be nice for a change."

"Don't be a smart-ass." But now his grim tone had

lightened and he relaxed. "We're hot together, Josie. Believe me, you make me lose control, too."

She'd seen no evidence of that, but she wanted to. It was her goal tonight to make Nick totally lose his head. Exactly how she'd do that, she wasn't sure. For now, though, a different topic would be in order. The present discussion had the very effect he'd predicted. Her pulse raced and she knew her cheeks were flushed. She wanted him, right now, and she was too new to wanting to be able to deal with it nonchalantly. "Do we have much farther to go?"

"We're two minutes away from where I'm taking you." He gave a strangled laugh. "And the way you affect me, I'm going to need five times that long to make myself presentable."

She glanced at his lap, knowing exactly what he spoke of. His erection was full, impossible to ignore. And the sight of his need quadrupled her own. She leaned toward him, imploring, letting the thin straps of her dress droop and fall over her shoulders. In low, hopefully seductive tones, she said, "Let's forget your plans. Let's just go to the boat." She reached for him, but he caught her hand and kissed the palm.

His gaze strayed to her cleavage, now more exposed, and he let out a low curse. "Sorry. But we can't." Incredibly, she saw sweat at his temples and watched as he clenched his jaw. He turned down a long gravel drive that led to a stately old farmhouse. It was a huge, sprawling, absolutely gorgeous home that looked as if it had been around and loved for ages. Josie hadn't been paying any attention to where they were going, but now she realized they were in a rural area and that Nick was taking her to a private residence. Horrified, she stiffened her back and frantically began to remedy the mess she'd made of her dress, smoothing the bodice and straightening the skirt, retightening her belt. "Oh my God, we're meeting people?" She thought of how she was dressed and wanted to disappear.

He jerked the truck to a stop beneath a large oak tree and turned off the ignition. "Calm down, Josie. It's okay." But he sounded agitated, too.

She gasped, then swatted at his hands when he reached out to help her straighten the shoulder straps of her dress. "Nick, stop it, don't touch me." She glanced around, afraid someone might see.

Her words had a startling effect on him. He grabbed her shoulders and yanked her close and when her eyes widened on his face, he growled, "I'm going to touch you, all right. In all the places you want to be touched, in all the ways I know you like best. With my hands and my mouth. Tonight…"

Her stomach flipped and her toes curled. "Nick—"

In the next heartbeat he kissed her—hard and hungry and devouring—and she kissed him back the same way, forgetting her embarrassment and where they were.

He groped for her breast and her moan encouraged him. But before he made contact there was a loud rapping on the driver's door and seconds later it was yanked open. They jumped apart, both looking guilty and abashed. Josie felt her mouth fall open at the sight that greeted her.

Standing beside the car, his grim countenance and apparent age doing nothing to detract from his air of command, stood a gray-haired man in a flannel shirt and tan slacks with suspenders. His scowl was darker than the blackening sky and his bark reverberated throughout the truck.

"If that's what you came for, you damn well should have stayed home. Now are you gettin' out to say your hellos and do your introductions, or not?"

Nick took a deep breath and turned to Josie, who was still wide-eyed with shock. Sending her a twisted smile of apology, he said, "Josie, I'd like you to meet my grandfather, Jeb Harris. Granddad, this is Josie Jackson."

With sharp eyes the man looked her over from the top of her tousled head to her feet in the strappy sandals. Josie felt mortified at the scrutiny and did her best not to squirm. He shook his head. "You can be the biggest damn fool, Nick." Then he laughed. "Well, get the young lady out of the truck before you forget your poor old granddad is even here."

And with that, he turned and headed to his front porch, leaning heavily on a cane and favoring one hip. Josie noticed his shoulders were hunched just enough to prove he tolerated a measure of pain with his movements. The caretaker in her kicked in, and she briefly wondered what injury he'd suffered.

Nick cleared his throat and she slowly brought her narrow-eyed gaze to his face. "This is your surprise?"

He kept his gaze focused on a spot just beyond her left shoulder. "Yeah. Granddad called, asked if I could visit tonight." He jutted out his chin, as if daring her to comment. "I didn't think it would do any harm to stop here for a bit first."

She opened her door and climbed out of the truck

without his assistance. Nick was such a fraud. He didn't want her to think he was a softy, but the fact that he hadn't been able to refuse his grandfather only made her like him all the more. She glanced at him as he came to her side. "A little warning might have been nice, so I could have dressed appropriately instead of making a fool of myself."

"Josie, Granddad is getting older. He's not dead. He knows who the fool is, and he's already cast the blame. You he's simply charmed by."

Josie looked down at her dress, and decided there was no help for it. She sighed. "How do you know?"

"Because I know my grandfather." As Nick looked up at the house, Josie looked at him. There was a softness in his eyes she'd never seen before. "When I was a kid, I loved the times I spent with him here more than you can know."

Because he hadn't had anyone else. His mother had used him as a pawn and his stepmother and father had made him a stranger in his own home. She could have asked for better circumstances, but she wanted to meet his grandfather, knowing now that he was the only family Nick was close to.

Nick saw her frown ease and he leaned down to whisper in her ear. "You look beautiful. And I think you'll like my grandfather. He's the one who taught me everything I know."

Josie rolled her eyes. Somehow that didn't reassure her.

HE WAS LAYING IT ON a bit thick, Nick thought, as his grandfather said, once again, "Eh?" very loudly. Hell, the man's hearing was sharper than a dog's and not a single whisper went by that he didn't pick up on. But for some reason he was playing a poor old soul and Nick had to wonder at his motives.

At least Josie no longer seemed so flustered. She continued to fuss with that killer dress of hers—she'd almost given him a heart attack when he first saw her in it—but she had mostly relaxed and was simply enjoying his grandfather's embellished tales of life in years gone by.

The old bird was enjoying Nick's discomfort. The small smile that hovered on his mouth proved he was aware of Nick's predicament, but there wasn't a damn thing Nick could do about it. Not with Josie sitting there on the edge of the sofa, her legs primly pressed together, the bodice of her dress hiked as high as she could get it. She inspired an odd, volatile mixture of raging lust and quiet tenderness. It unnerved him, and at the same time, turned him on.

Right now he felt as if lava flowed through him, and the volcano was damn close to erupting.

He shot out of his seat, attracting two pairs of questioning eyes. His grandfather chuckled while Josie frowned.

"I, ah, I thought I'd go get us something to drink."

"Would you like me to help you, Nick?" Josie made to rise from her seat.

Before Nick could answer her, Granddad patted her hand and kept her still. "He can manage, can't you, Nick?"

"Yes, sir."

Granddad waved at Nick. "Fine, go on, then. Josie and I have things to chat about."

Exactly what that meant was anyone's guess. In the

kitchen, he filled some glasses with iced tea, then stuck his car to the door.

"I'm afraid you have the wrong impression, sir."

"Just call me Jeb or Granddad. I can't stand all that 'sir' nonsense."

There was a pause. "Really, Jeb, Nick and I are only friends."

"Ha!" Granddad made a thumping sound with his cane. "My old eyes might be rheumy, but I can still see what needs to be seen. And I ain't so old as to be dotty. That boy's got himself a bad case goin', and you're the cause. Probably the cure, too."

Nick groaned. At this rate, his grandfather would run Josie off even before Susan could. Josie didn't want the responsibility of another person, of permanence or commitment. This was her first chance to be free, and she wanted to widen her boundaries, to explore her sexual side.

Between Susan telling her how irresponsible Nick was and his grandfather trying to corner her, he probably wouldn't last through the week. The thought filled him with unreasonable anger. He didn't want things to end until he was damn good and ready.

His determination surprised him. He hadn't felt this strongly about anything since his mother had sent him home to live with his father, making it clear his presence was an intrusion. Not even Myra's ruthless attempts to alienate him had stirred so much turmoil inside him. Josie had tied him in so many knots, it was almost painful. But once he got her alone tonight, once he made love to her, everything would be all right.

"His mother and father are to blame for his wild

ways, too caught up in pickin' at each other to remember they had a son. And that witch Myra—she let
her jealousy rule her, though I doubt Nick knew that was
the cause. But you see, she knew I had cut my son out
of my will. After he married her, I left everything to
Nick. And it ate Myra up, knowin' it. She couldn't do
anything to me, so she took it out on the one person she
knew I really cared about."

Nick groaned. Not only had his grandfather's impec-
cable speech deteriorated to some facade of what he
considered appropriate dotage lingo, but now he'd
gotten onto an issue better left unaddressed. Nick still
felt foolish over his last bout of personal confession
with her. Josie didn't want to get personal, but his grandfather was forcing the issue.

"I hear you're a home health caretaker? Nick said
you run a nice little business called Home and Heart.
Could use someone like you around here."

"Are you having some problems… Jeb?"

"Broken hip, didn't you know? Busted the damn
thing months ago, but it still pains me on occasion.
Front porch was slippery from the rain and down I went.
Poor Nick near fussed himself to death—reminded me
of an old woman with all that squawkin'. Wouldn't
leave my side, no matter how I told him to."

"He did the right thing."

"There, you see? He knows right from wrong when
it matters. It's just the women he's got a problem with."

Nick closed his eyes to the sound of Josie's disbelieving laughter.

Granddad ignored her hilarity. "Now to be truthful, I'm
pretty much recovered, but I just don't get around the way

I used to. I could use someone to check up on me now and then, without me having to go all the way into town."

Nick used that as his cue to reenter the room. "Excellent idea, Granddad. Maybe Josie could help you out." If he got her involved with his grandfather, it would be difficult for her to dump him and find another man to experiment with. She'd be pretty much stuck with him, at least for the time being, until the excitement wore off.

Josie didn't look at all enthusiastic about the idea. "But don't you already have someone in place? I should think—"

Granddad waved her to a halt. "Didn't care for that woman they had coming here. She was too starchy for my taste. I discharged her. Told her to go and not come back."

Nick remembered the incident. Of course, Granddad had been officially released from care anyway, and the poor woman whom he'd harassed so badly was more than grateful to be done with her duties.

"I could find someone better suited to you if you have need of a nurse, Jeb."

Nick liked how she'd so quickly accustomed herself to speaking familiarly with his grandfather. He knew Granddad would appreciate it, too. It gave him a warm feeling deep inside his chest to see the two of them chatting. No matter how Granddad went on, Josie never lost her patience. She listened to him intently, laughed with him and teased him. Nick felt damn proud of her, and it was one more feeling to add to the confusion of all the others she inspired.

"Fine. Never mind. I didn't mean to be a burden."

Nick snorted, recognizing his grandfather's ploy, but Josie was instantly contrite. "You're not!"

"I know they said I was all recovered, that I didn't need any more help. And I live too far out for people to bother with. Should have sold this old house long ago."

Josie looked around. When she replied, her voice was filled with melancholy. "But it's such a beautiful house. It has charm, and it feels like a real home, not a temporary one. Like generations could live here and be happy. They don't build them like this anymore."

Nick wondered if it reminded her of her own home, the one she'd lost after her parent's death. He watched her face and saw the sadness there. He didn't like it.

Granddad nodded. "It is a sturdy place. But it's getting to be too much for me. And it was made for a family, not one old man."

"You know," Josie said, setting her glass down with a thunk. "I don't think you need a caregiver, I think you just need to get out more. And I have the perfect idea. Why don't you come to this party my neighbor is having next week? She's a wonderful friend and I have the feeling, being that you're Nick's grandfather, you might like her."

Oh, hell, his grandfather would kill him. Josie was trying to play matchmaker and that was the one thing Granddad wouldn't tolerate. Since the death of his wife, Granddad was as protective of his freedom as Nick. But to Nick's surprise, he nodded agreement. "I'd love to. Haven't been to a party in a long time."

Covering his surprise with a cough, Nick watched Josie, wondering if she would invite *him* to the party, too. But she didn't say a word about it and his temper started a slow boil. Damn her, did she have some reason not to want him there? Had her sister gotten to her already?

"It's nice to have a young lady in the house again. First time, you know. For Nick to bring a woman here, I mean. 'Course, I wouldn't care to meet most of his dates." He leaned toward Josie, his bushy gray eyebrows bobbing. "Not at all nice, if you get my meaning."

"Granddad." Nick's tone held a wealth of warning.

In a stage whisper, Granddad said, "He don't like me telling tales on him, which makes it more fun to do so."

If his grandfather hadn't recently had a broken hip, Nick would have kicked him under the table.

When the evening finally wore down, his grandfather was starting to look tired. Concerned, Nick took care of putting their empty tea glasses away and preparing his grandfather's bed in the room downstairs. He used to sleep upstairs, Jeb explained to Josie, before the hip accident. Now he did almost everything on the lower floors while the upstairs merely got cleaned once a week by the housekeeper.

"It's a waste of a good house, is what it is. I really ought to sell."

When Josie started to object once again, Nick shook his head. "He's always threatening that. But he won't ever leave this place."

By the time they walked outside, the sky had turned completely black and the air was turbulent. The storm still hovered, not quite letting go. Leaves from the large oaks lining the driveway blew up on the porch around Jeb's feet.

Nick watched Josie hug his grandfather and he experienced that damn pain again that didn't really hurt, but wanted to make itself known. Josie stepped a discreet distance away and Nick indulged in his own hug. He couldn't help but chuckle when his grandfather whispered, "Prove to me what a smart lad you are, Nick, and hang on to this one."

"She can't hear you, Granddad. You can quit with the 'lad' talk."

"I was pretty good at sounding like a grandpa, wasn't I? I hadn't realized I had so much talent."

"I hadn't realized you could be so long-winded."

"Stop worrying, Nick. I know what I'm doing."

Josie looked toward them, and Nick muttered, "Yeah? Well, I wish I did."

He took Josie's hand as he led her to the truck. The wind picked up her long hair and whipped it against his chest. "Are you tired?"

She smiled up at him. "Mmm. But not *too* tired."

Her response kick started a low thrumming of excitement in his heart. With his hands on her waist, he hoisted Josie up into the truck, then leaned on the seat toward her, resting one hand beside her, the other on her thigh. "What does that mean, Josie?"

"It means we made a deal earlier, and now I expect you to pay up."

He almost crumbled, the lust hit him so hard. It had been too long, much too long, since he'd made love to her. "It'll be my pleasure."

She shook her head and her fingertips trailed over his jaw. "No, it'll be mine. I want my fair turn, Nick. Tonight I want you to promise you won't move. Not a single muscle, not unless I give you permission."

He tried to laugh, but it came out sounding more like a groan. "Why, Ms. Jackson. What do you have planned?"

"I plan to make you every bit as crazy as you make me. This time I want you to be the one begging. Promise me, Nick."

He had no intention of promising her a damn thing. He wasn't fool enough to let a woman make demands on him. It would start with one request, and then she'd think she could run his life. He wouldn't let that happen.

Josie smiled a slow sinful smile, smoothed her hand down over his chest. "Promise me, Nick."

"All right, I promise."

CHAPTER EIGHT

"STAND RIGHT THERE."

Josie surveyed her handiwork and felt immense satisfaction at the picture Nick made. She'd stripped his shirt from his shoulders, unsnapped his jeans. He was almost too appealing to resist. Kneeling in front of him, she'd taken turns tugging his shoes and socks off. He even had beautiful feet. Strong, narrow. Right now those feet were braced apart while his hands clutched, as per her order, the shelving high above the berth where she sat. Her face was on a level with his tight abdomen and she could see the way he labored for breath.

She liked this game—she liked it very much.

Nick hadn't said much once he'd agreed to her terms. The storm had broken shortly after they gained the main road, lightning splitting the sky with great bursts of light, the heavy darkness pressing in on them. They'd ridden to the boat in virtual silence, other than the rumble of thunder and her humming, which she hadn't been able to stop. She put it down to a nervous reaction in the face of her plan. Nick's hands had repeatedly clenched the steering wheel, but he hadn't backed out, hadn't asked her about her plans. At one point he'd lowered his window a bit and let the rain breeze in on him. She appreciated his restraint, though now she hoped to help him lose it

He stared down at her, his expression dark, his hair still damp from their mad dash to the boat through the rain. For a moment, Josie wondered once again why he'd taken her to see his grandfather. He'd even suggested Jeb hire her, but she couldn't go along with that idea. If she got entangled with the one person Nick was closest to, it would make it so difficult to bear when their affair was over. She needed to keep an emotional arm's length, but with every minute that passed, that became harder to do.

Determined on her course, she blew lightly on his belly and watched his muscles tighten and strain.

"I feel I have to get this right, you know." She stroked the hard muscles of his abdomen. "I don't want to disappoint you, or myself."

He made a rough sound, but otherwise he simply watched her as if daring her to continue. She smiled inside, more than ready to take up the challenge. She wanted to get everything she could from her time with him.

Using just the edge of one fingernail, she traced the length of his erection and heard him suck in a breath. Speaking in a mere whisper, she said, "You look uncomfortable, Nick. I suppose I should unzip you. But first, I want to make myself more comfortable, too."

Leaning back on the berth to make certain he could see her, she watched his face while she hooked her fingers in the top of her dress and tugged it below her breasts, slowly, so that the material rasped over her nipples and tightened them. She inhaled sharply, feeling her own blush but ignoring it. "That's better."

Nick's biceps bulged, his chest rose and fell. She

cupped her breasts, offering them up, being more daring now that she could see how difficult control had become for him. She stroked her palms over her nipples and heard his soft hiss of approval.

"And back at the apartment, didn't you mention something about wanting me to lift my dress?" She flipped back the edges of the flowered skirt until her panties could be seen. "Is this what you had in mind?"

Nick's cheekbones were slashed with aroused color, and his eyes were so dark they looked almost black. The boat rocked and jerked with the storm, but he held his balance above her and smiled. "You're so hot."

"Hmm. Let's see if we can get you in a similar state." She eased the zipper down on his jeans and reveled in his low grunt of relief. "Better? You looked so… constrained."

His penis was fully erect and the very tip was visible from the waistband of his underwear. Enthralled, Josie ran a delicate fingertip over it and saw Nick jerk back in response, muttering a low curse.

She peered up at him, loving the sight of him, his reaction. "You didn't like that?"

He dropped his head forward, a half laugh escaping him. His dark, damp hair hung low over his brow. "That might not be the very best place to start." He looked at her, his face tilted to one side, and he grinned. "You're really pushing it now, aren't you?"

"Your control, you mean? I hope so."

"I meant your own daring. But have at it, honey." Though his voice sounded low and rough, his dark eyes glittered with command. "This is your show. I can hold out as long as you can."

"I'm so glad you think so." And with that, she leaned forward and this time it was her tongue she dragged over the tip of him, earning a dozen curses and a shuddering response from his body.

Holding himself still as a pike, Nick squeezed his eyes shut and breathed deeply through his nose. He seemed to have planted his legs in an effort to control the need to pull away—or push forward. Josie thought he was the most magnificent man she'd ever seen.

"Relax, Nick." She stroked his belly, his ribs, and his trembling increased. "It's not that I haven't enjoyed everything you've done to me. We both know I have. But I want to be free to do my own explorations."

He didn't answer and she grinned. "I think we need to get you out of these jeans. I want to see all of you."

He offered her no assistance as she tugged the snug jeans down his long legs. They were damp and clung to his hips and thighs. Crawling off the berth, she knelt behind him and instructed him to lift each foot as she worked the stiff material off him. That accomplished, she pressed her face to the small of his back and reached her arms around him. Using both hands, she cuddled him through the soft cotton of his shorts and discovered how nice that felt. He was soft and heavy in places, rock hard and trembling in others. She bit his back lightly, then one buttock, then the back of his thickly muscled thigh.

"You're so rigid, Nick. Try to relax." She couldn't quite keep the awe from her tone, or the sound of her own growing excitement. Her hands still stroked him, up and down, manipulating his length, until he groaned, his head falling back.

She let her nipples graze his spine as she slowly stood behind him. "I love your body."

"Josie…"

"Shh. I'm just getting started." She moved in front of him again, but this time she didn't sit. She insinuated herself in the narrow space between where he stood and the edge of the berth and she simply felt him. All of him. From his thick forearms to his biceps and wide shoulders, the soft tufts of hair under his arms to the banded muscles over his ribs and his erect nipples. She explored his hipbones and the smooth flesh of his taut buttocks. She pushed his underwear down and he kicked them off. "Do you remember what you did to me in my kitchen, Nick?"

"Damn it, Josie—"

"Shh. You said it was my show, remember?" She kissed one flat brown nipple, flicked it with her tongue and heard him draw in an uneven breath. "Tell me, Nick. Do you like that as much as I do?"

He narrowed his gaze on her face. "I doubt it. You nearly come just from me sucking your nipples. Not that I'm complaining. It really turns me on." His voice was low, seductive. "I've never known a woman with breasts as sensitive as yours."

Damn him, he made her want things just by saying them. Her breasts throbbed and her nipples tightened into painful points. She decided she wouldn't ask him any more questions. She could do better if he kept quiet.

"Maybe you're just more sensitive in other places." And that was all she said to warn of her intent.

She kissed his throat, breathing in his sexy male scent. "I love how you smell, Nick. It makes me almost light-headed. And it makes me want you, makes me feel swollen inside." Her mouth trailed down, over his ribs to his navel. She heard him swallow as she toyed with that part of him, dipping in her tongue while her hands caressed his hard backside, keeping him from moving away.

"Brace your legs farther apart."

He laughed, the sound strained. "You've got a bit of the tormentor in you, don't you, honey? It's kinky. I had no idea."

"Be quiet." But she blushed, just as he knew she would. She sat on the berth again, opening her legs around his, assuming a position she knew that would drive him wild, "I only want to try some of the things you've done to me. Why should you always be the one in control?"

"Because I'm the man," he said on a groan as she fondled him again, exploring, fascinated by the smooth feel of him, the velvety skin over hard-as-steel flesh.

"You certainly are. Do you like this, Nick?"

"Yes," he hissed.

She brushed her bare breasts against him. "And this?"

"Josie, honey…"

"And this?" Josie slid her mouth over him, taking him as deep as she could and his hips jackknifed against her as a deep growl tore from his throat. She loved his reaction, the way he continued to groan, to shudder and tremble and curse while she did her best to drive him insane. She'd had no idea it could be so exciting to pleasure another person in such a way. Before Nick, the thought of doing such a thing not only seemed incredible, but unpleasant.

With Nick, she felt as if she couldn't get enough—and she made sure he knew it.

His breathing labored, he rasped out rough instructions, unable to remain still. He strained toward her, hard and poised on some secret male edge of control. Josie had never felt so triumphant in all her life, so confident of herself as a woman. She drew him deeper still, using her tongue to stroke, to tease. She made a small humming sound of pleasure when he broke the rules and released the shelf to cup her head in his hands and guide her.

But seconds later he stumbled away from her. Josie tried to protest, to reach for him, but Nick wouldn't give her a chance. He toppled her backward on the berth, tore her panties off and shoved her dress out of the way. He lifted her legs high to his shoulders, startling her, frightening her just a bit. His mouth clamped onto her breast at the same time he drove into her, hard, slamming them both backward on the berth. He went so deep, Josie felt alarmed by the hot pressure, then excited. She cried out and wrapped her arms around him, already so aroused by his reactions, she took him easily, willingly. Within moments, she felt the sweet internal tightening, the throbbing of hidden places as they seemed to swell and explode with sensations. It went on and on, too powerful, too much. She bit Nick's shoulder, muffling her shocked scream of pleasure against his skin.

He collapsed on top of her, still heaving, gasping, his body heavy but comforting.

They both labored for breath, their skin sweaty and too hot.

"Josie."

He forced himself up, swallowing hard, and smoothed

her wildly tangled hair from her face with trembling hands. "Josie, honey, are you all right?"

She didn't want to look at him, didn't want to move. It was all she could do to stay conscious with the delicious aftershocks of her release still making her body buzz.

"Josie." He kissed her mouth, her eyelids, the bridge of her nose. Carefully he lowered her thighs, but remained between them, still inside her. "Look at me, honey."

She managed to get one eye halfway open, but the effort was too much and she closed it again. Seeing him, the color still high on his cheekbones, his silky dark hair hanging over his brow, his temples damp and his mouth swollen, made her shudder with new feelings, and she couldn't, simply *couldn't* survive that kind of pleasure again so soon.

Nick managed a shaky laugh and kissed her on the mouth, a soft, mushy kiss that blossomed and went on until it dwindled into incredible tenderness, to concern and caring. He rolled, groaning as he did so, putting her on top.

"You're a naughty woman, Josie Jackson."

She smiled, kissed his shoulder and sighed.

"I didn't wear a condom."

Her eyes opened wide and she stared at the far wall, her cheek still pressed to his damp chest. His heartbeat hadn't slowed completely yet, and she felt the reverberations of it.

"I'm sorry, honey. No excuse except that I went a little nuts and it was a first for me. Going nuts, that is."

No condom. *Oh God.* She hadn't even thought of that in the scheme of her seduction. Her body felt lethargic, a little numb, and she mumbled, "My fault," more than willing to put the blame where it rightfully belonged.

She had been in control this time, had manipulated the whole situation, and she was the one with no excuses.

Nick's arms tightened around her and he nuzzled his jaw into her hair. "We'll argue it out in the morning. Odds are, there won't be a problem. Not just that once."

She snuggled closer to him, her mind a whirlwind of worries, the major one being how she could ever let him go. For her, a baby wouldn't be a problem. It would be a gift of wonder, a treasure, a part of Nick. But she knew how wrong it would be and she couldn't help but shudder with realization. She'd set out to prove, to herself and to him, that their affair could remain strictly physical and she'd be satisfied. Instead, she'd proven something altogether different.

Damn but she'd done the dumbest thing. She'd fallen in love with Nick Harris, lady-killer, womanizer extraordinaire. Confirmed bachelor. Nick would probably never want a permanent relationship. And he might even see her forgetfulness with the condom as a deliberate ploy to snare him. So far, their time together had been spent on her wants, her needs, her *demands*. She'd gone on ordering him to show her a good time, on her schedule, without real thought to what he might want. But she knew; he wanted no ties, no commitments, a brief fling. She swallowed hard, feeling almost sick.

Now everything was threatened. If she hadn't pushed things today, the mishap might never have happened.

She realized where her thoughts had led her and she couldn't quite stifle a giggle. A possible pregnancy was far more than a mere mishap.

Nick lifted his head to try to see her face. "What tickles you now, woman? I hope you don't have more lascivious thoughts in your head, because I swear, I need at least an hour to recoup." The boat rocked with the storm and she could hear the rumble of thunder overhead. Nick held her closer. "I'm personally amazed that my poor heart continues to beat with the strain it's been under."

Josie kissed his collarbone. He didn't sound upset with her. So maybe now was the best time to find out if he planned to blame her. She didn't think she'd be able to sleep tonight if she had to worry about it. "Nick, I'm so sorry I forgot…myself. I should have been more responsible."

His hands on her back stilled just a moment, then he gave a huge sigh, nearly heaving her off his chest. "It probably won't even be an issue, Josie. But if it is, we'll figure something out together, okay?"

"I wouldn't want you to feel pressured. Or to think I did this deliberately."

"Hey—" he brought her face close to his and kissed her "—you're new at this. I'm the one who should have known better. I've never forgotten before, not that it matters now. But like I said, I've never felt quite this way before."

She wanted to ask him *what way,* but only said, "You're truly not angry?"

He smiled. "I'm not angry. Hell, I'm not even all that worried." His hand smoothed down her back to her bottom and he rolled to his side, keeping her close. They were nose to nose, and he yawned as if ready to sleep. "And I don't want you to worry, either. If anything comes of it, then we'll worry. But in the meantime, don't fret. Okay?"

"Okay," she said, but didn't feel completely reassured. Nick had never mentioned anything permanent between them, no matter how she'd wished it, and a baby would certainly be permanent. He was right, though. Worrying now was ridiculous. A waste of energy.

"Why don't you get this dress off, honey? You can't be comfortable like that."

She followed his gaze to where her dress was twisted around her upper arms and under her breasts. Her body was so numb with her release, she hadn't even noticed the restriction. She untied the belt, popped open the one button and slid it off. Nick took the dress from her and tossed it from the bed.

"That's better." He pulled her against his chest and closed his eyes once again. "Now let me sleep so I can recoup myself. There's the little matter of a payback for me to attend to, and I'll need some strength to see that the job's done properly."

To Josie's immense surprise, her body tingled in anticipation. She supposed she just had more stamina than Nick, because she was already looking forward to the payback.

NICK LOOKED AROUND the crowded room and wondered what the hell he was doing there. He'd get no time alone with Josie tonight. Every couch and chair was filled with an elderly person, and even standing room was limited. He'd barely gotten the door open and squeezed in past the loiterers.

He scanned the room, looking for Josie and trying to avoid all the prying eyes peering over the rims of their bifocals. It had been over a week since he'd seen her, a week since he'd given her control and she'd used it to drive him to distraction. But she hadn't tried in any way to abuse that control. She hadn't breached his privacy, crowded him in any way. He wanted to talk to her, damn it, but he doubted he'd get much private time with her here.

He headed toward the kitchen, hoping to find Josie there, and ran headlong into Susan. He caught her arms to steady her and accepted her severe frown. "Susan," he said by way of greeting.

"I want to talk to you."

He looked at her hands, which were behind her back. "What are you doing?" she asked.

"Checking for concealed weapons. I want to make sure verbal abuse is all you have in mind." He flashed her a grin, which only made her stiffen up that much more. Damn prickly woman.

"What are you doing here?"

He crossed his arms and leaned against the wall. "That was going to be my question to you."

"I was invited!"

"And you think I snuck in through the bathroom window?"

Her face went red and she looked around the room, then took his arm and dragged him a short distance down the hall. "You've been seeing my sister some time now."

"And?"

"And you've had ample time to decide if you're serious about her or not. I don't want you to keep toying with her."

He thought of how Josie had toyed with him on the boat and couldn't quite repress his grin. To avoid replying to her statement, he asked, "How's Bob?"

Susan blushed. "He's…fine, I guess."

"You haven't seen him lately?"

"I'm still angry because he lied to me, letting you work on my campaign when he knew how I felt about that."

"Yes, you weren't exactly subtle." Before she could blast him, he added, "He cares about you, you know. He just didn't want to disappoint you."

"He lied to me."

"Only so you wouldn't go away. But I'm thinking it might have been better if you had. If you don't care about him…"

She narrowed her eyes at him and almost snarled. "I didn't say that."

"Ah, so you only want him to suffer? This is one of those female games, meant to prove a point?"

She flushed, which to Nick's mind revealed her guilty conscience. "Not that it's any of your business, but I was planning to talk to him about it tonight. He's here at the party."

Nick felt his jaw go slack. "You're kidding?"

"No." Then she flapped her hand. "Josie insisted. She's got some harebrained scheme to get me and Bob all made up."

"Is it working?"

She chewed her lip. "I suppose. Josie already explained Bob's reasons for the deception. In a way, even I understand them. And I hate to admit it, but you really are very talented."

Nick's grin was slow, and then he laughed full out, placing one wide-spread hand on his chest. "Be still, my heart."

Susan looked like she wanted to clout him. "The

thing is, I don't know how to figure you anymore. Mrs. Wiley has been singing your praises ever since I got here. You're doing her work gratis, aren't you?"

"Our arrangement is private."

"Hogwash. Mrs. Wiley is telling anyone who'll listen what a *dear boy* you are." Susan stepped closer, causing Nick to back up until he hit the wall. "Well, *dear boy,* I want to know what your intentions are toward my sister."

Nick opened his mouth with no idea what he was going to say to Susan. Thankfully they were both side-tracked by his grandfather's booming voice coming from the living room. When Nick looked in that direction, he saw his grandfather standing next to Mrs. Wiley. He looked happy and he kept whispering in her ear, making her smack playfully at his arm. Nick shook his head in wonder.

"Your grandfather is charming."

"Ain't he though?"

"He's also very taken with Josie. He told me she's been out to see him twice this week."

That surprised him. No one had said a word to him, and his curiosity immediately swelled. What had they talked about? Him, no doubt. But what specifically? And where was Josie anyway? He needed to escape Susan's clutches. She wanted explanations, but he had no idea what to tell her. His arrangement with Josie was private; it was up to Josie to explain things to her nosy sister.

He nodded toward his grandfather. "I should go over and say hello."

"No need. He's headed this way." Susan gave him a

searing look. "You and I will talk again later." With that rather blatant threat, she dismissed herself.

"Well, boy, about time you got here."

"I really didn't expect you to show, Granddad." Nick saw how Mrs. Wiley clung to his arm, and he couldn't help but wonder what his grandfather had been up to. Not since Jeb had been widowed years before had he shown interest in any woman.

"Josie brought me. Which reminds me, I've been meaning to speak to you about her."

Dropping back against the wall with a resigned sigh, Nick prepared himself for another lecture, but his grandfather wasn't quite as restrained as Susan. The man had a way of making his feelings known on a subject and he didn't cut any corners. Mrs. Wiley stood beside him, nodding her agreement at his every word.

"If you have half the brains in that handsome head of yours that I've always given you credit for, you'll tie that little girl up right and tight and make sure she doesn't get away."

Attempting to ignore Mrs. Wiley's presence—not an easy thing to do in the best of circumstances—Nick tried to stare his grandfather down. "We've had this discussion before, remember?"

"Damn right I do. But this is different." Jeb's eyes narrowed. "This isn't one of those other women. I *like* Josie."

"Granddad…"

"So what's it to be, boy? What exactly do you have planned here?" He raised his hand as if to ward off any insult. "I only ask because I hate to see you ruin things for yourself."

Nick looked across the room and found so many eyes boring into him, he flushed. With the music playing, no one could hear their conversation, but he had the feeling every one of them knew he'd just been chastised, and why.

How the hell had he gotten himself into this predicament? And how could he tell his grandfather that he didn't know what his plans were because he didn't know what Josie's were? She had insisted their time together be temporary, no strings, simple fun. Of course, he'd never betray her by saying so.

He ran a hand through his hair and silently cursed. He didn't like being bullied, not even by his grandfather. "Right now, my plans are to find Josie and tell her hello. So if you'll both excuse me…?"

He stepped away and heard Mrs. Wilcy say, "Youth. They can be so pigheaded."

Jeb laughed. "He reminds me of myself at his age."

Mrs. Wiley cooed, "Oh, really?" There was a great deal of interest in her tone.

Nick finally found Josie in the kitchen. Once again, she took him by surprise with her appearance. He'd seen the sexy, femme fatale, the disheveled homemaker, the harried working woman…. Now she was the sweet girl next door. She wore a long tailored plaid skirt and flat oxford shoes. Her short-sleeve sweater fit her loosely.

She looked like a schoolgirl.

He grinned at the image and wondered what games he could come up with using that theme. She hadn't noticed his entrance. She seemed preoccupied, though she wasn't serving any particular function that he could tell. She stood at the counter, surveying the items Mrs.

Wiley had laid out in a large display. Without disturbing her, Nick looked, too. There was an assortment of fancy bottled lotions, scented candles in various sizes, pink light bulbs and music meant to entice. He thought of the advertisement he had planned and felt good. He hoped Josie would be pleased.

He slipped his arms around her and nuzzled her neck. "Thinking of buying anything?"

She jerked against him and gasped. "Nick, for heaven's sake, you startled me."

He could feel her tension, her immediate withdrawal. His jaw tightened. Trying to dredge up an air of nonchalance, he asked, "What do you think I should buy?"

"You don't have to buy anything. You didn't even need to show up."

She'd shown so much reluctance to have him there, he'd perversely insisted on attending. And to ensure success, he'd gone to Mrs. Wiley. He didn't like being excluded from parts of Josie's life. Usually, women tried to reel him in, not push him away. He didn't like Josie's emotional distance; it made him almost frenzied with need.

"Of course I'll buy something," he said while searching her face for a clue to her thoughts, but she was closed off to him. "Besides, I needed to be here to try to get a feel for the market I'll be appealing to. And I think I've come up with just the thing."

Slowly she started to pull away from him. He pretended not to notice. "Josie?"

Her smile was dim. "Tell me your plan."

He kissed her nose, her cheek. He couldn't be near her without wanting to touch her. He couldn't wait to get her alone. "I don't think so, not yet. I'll run my idea past Mrs. Wiley first. If she likes it, I'll let you know."

"I hate it when you're secretive."

She sounded so disgruntled that he kissed her again. He didn't want to stop kissing her, but he heard the sounds of the party in the other room and pulled back. Josie would be embarrassed to be caught necking in the kitchen. "How long do we need to stay here?"

If possible, she looked even more uncomfortable. "I'll be here till late. I want to help clean up afterward."

"I can help, too."

"No!" She looked at him then backed away. "No, you should head on home. I don't know how long it will take and there's no reason to waste your entire night."

Waste his night? His teeth nearly ground together as he pulled her close again. He tried to sound only mildly curious. Teasing. "Are you trying to get rid of me?"

Her head thumped against his breastbone, which offered not one ounce of reassurance.

"Hey," he said softly. "Josie?"

"The thing is," she said, her face still tucked close to his throat, "I'm a little indisposed tonight."

"Indisposed?" She was giving him the brush-off? Had she already found another man to experiment with? Anger and a tinge of fear ignited. He ignored the fear, refusing to even acknowledge it. "What the hell does that mean?"

He could almost hear her thinking, and it infuriated him. "Damn it, Josie, will you look at me?" It seemed so long since he'd seen her, anything could have happened. Her sister could have gotten to her, or his grandfather. Hell, it seemed all the odds were against him. His blood burned and he knew there was no way he'd allow her to go to another man. Not that he had any authority over her, but…

"I can't have any *fun* with you tonight."

She blurted that out, then stared at him, waiting. He had the feeling he was supposed to understand, but damned if he did.

Josie rolled her eyes. She turned her back on him and began straightening the items on the counter, even though they were already in perfect alignment. Nick thought she wasn't even aware of what she did. He felt ridiculous.

"Honey, I'd really like an explana—"

"I'm not pregnant, okay?"

He stilled, letting her words sink in and slotting them with everything else she'd said so far. Realization dawned. On the heels of that came a vague disappointment that he quickly squelched. "You're on your period?"

She gave him a narrow-eyed glare that could have set fire to dry grass.

"Josie, honey, for crying out loud, I'm thirty-two years old. I understand how women's bodies work. You don't have to act like it's some big embarrassment." He knew he sounded harsh, but in the back of his mind had been the possibility that she'd be tied to him, that he might have compromised her and in the process produced some lasting results. He'd never even considered such a thing before, and he hadn't really consciously thought about it until now. But he couldn't deny the damning truth of what he felt: disappointment.

"Well, then, given your worldly experience, I'm sure you understand that there's no point in us seeing each other tonight." She started to march away, but he caught her arm and swung her back around.

These overwhelming emotions were new to him, and he held her close so she couldn't see his expression or wiggle away. "I'd still like to see you tonight."

She forced her way back to look at him. "You're kidding?"

"No, I'm not kidding, damn it." He'd never had to beg for a date before. He didn't like the feeling. "I can settle for a late movie and conversation if you can."

She looked undecided and his annoyance grew. After what seemed an undue amount of thought, given the simplicity of his suggestion, she nodded. "All right."

He propped his hands on his hips. Her compliance had been grudging at best and it irked him. "Fine. And in the future, don't be so hesitant about discussing things with me. I don't like not knowing what you're thinking."

He waited to see if she would question his reference to the future. Their time together, according to her preposterous plan, was limited. At first, he'd been relieved by her edicts. But now, whenever he thought of that stipulation, his body and mind rebelled. Every day he wanted her more.

"I'll try to keep that in mind" was all she said. She picked up the tray of drinks and started for the door. Nick took one last peek at the display, decided his ad plan would be perfect and went in search of Mrs. Wiley. If everything worked out as he hoped, not only would Mrs. Wiley be able to expand her client list, Josie would also get some freed-up time.

Her dedication to the elderly who'd become her

friends was admirable and he'd never interfere with her friendships. He wanted to support her in everything she did, everything she ever wanted to do. But now he wanted her to have more time for him, too. A lot more time.

The thought only caused a small prickle of alarm now. He was getting used to his possessive feelings. She would get used to them, too, despite her absurd notions of sowing wild oats. She could damn well sow her oats with him.

He caught up with her in the living room just as she finished handing out drinks, and when two older men scooted over on the couch to make room for her to sit, Nick wedged his way in, as well. The men glared at him and he smiled back, then leaned close to Josie to gain her attention and stake a claim. Ridiculous to do so when he was the only man in attendance under the age of sixty-five—besides Bob, who sure as hell didn't count. He felt the need regardless.

"Your grandfather seems smitten with Mrs. Wiley." Josie had leaned close to his ear to share that small tidbit of gossip. Her warm breath made him catch his.

"Smitten?"

"That's his word." She took his hand and laced their fingers together. "Mrs. Wiley went with me the other day to visit him, and when I was ready to leave, he asked her to stay. He said he'd call a cab for her when she had to go home."

"That smooth old dog."

Josie laughed. "I think he's adorable. And a fraud. Do you know, there isn't a thing in the world still wrong with his hip. He was limping around dramatically right up until he spied Mrs. Wiley, then he looked ready to strut."

Nick laughed at the picture she painted. "His hip still gives him a few pains in the nastier weather, but he gets around good enough. As long as he doesn't try climbing the stairs too often."

"Mrs. Wiley told him he needed a condo like hers, instead of that big house. He's been considering it."

Shocked, Nick turned to look at his grandfather. Not only Mrs. Wiley had made note of him. He was surrounded by women, all of them fawning on him. But he kept one arm around Mrs. Wiley. Nick snorted. He'd never have swallowed it if he hadn't seen it himself. "I do believe he's fallen for her. In all the years since my grandmother died, back when I was too young to even remember, I've never seen Granddad put his arm around a woman."

"Mrs. Wiley won't take no for an answer."

Nick stared at Josie's upturned face, her neatly braided hair and her small smile. He decided it might be a good rule for him to adopt.

By the end of the evening he was the proud owner of new boxers he planned to gift wrap for Bob, and richly scented bubble bath for Josie. What she might have bought, he didn't know. She'd kept her order form hidden from him.

He and his grandfather helped the two women clean up, and he presented his plan to Mrs. Wiley. She was thrilled.

"Advertising to the elderly in the retirement magazines! It's a wonderful idea. I can travel to their residences and put on the displays, or they can order directly from me."

"I checked around, and almost all of the retirement

centers have a special hall for entertaining and events. We could call it Romance for Retirees. And each class of gifts will need a catchy name. Like I thought maybe the scented oils could be classified under Love Potions #99."

Jeb laughed. "And the silk boxers and robes could be listed Rated *S*—for seniors only."

Josie jumped into the game, her grin wide. "What about Senior Sensations for the candles. And the wines could be Aged to Perfection."

Nick looked down at her, one brow quirked high. "You're pretty good at this. You missed your calling."

Pride set a glow to her features, and that look, so warm and sweet, caused Nick's heart to thump heavily. He wanted to kiss her, to....

"Finish up the telling, boy, then you can see her home."

Roughly clearing his throat, Nick brought his attention back to Mrs. Wiley and his grandfather. "I thought you might want to make the parties a monthly event, open to all newcomers. That way more people would be inclined to join in and some of the retirement homes might be persuaded to make it part of a monthly outing."

Mrs. Wiley clapped her hands and gave him a huge grin. "That's wonderful! I love it."

"I can work up the ads later this week, then get them to you for approval."

Mrs. Wiley put on a stern face. "I'm overwhelmed. And I insist on paying you something. I can't possibly let you go to all this trouble for free."

"'Course you can," Granddad insisted. "Let the boy do what he wants. He usually does anyway."

"That's right. Stubbornness runs in the family." Nick

looked pointedly at his grandfather, then continued, "I'm thinking there's probably a lot of small, local publications where placing an ad won't be too costly, along with the insurance and retirement periodicals that go out. I'll call around on Monday and see what their advertising rates are."

Granddad took him by the arm and started leading him to the front door. Josie followed along, grinning. "You do that, Nick. Get right on it, Monday."

Mrs. Wiley was still thanking him when Jeb practically shoved him out the door. Josie cozied up to his side. "I think we need to get going, Nick."

"I think you may be right." As he finished speaking, the condo door closed in his face and he heard his grandfather's laugh—followed by Mrs. Wiley's very delighted squeal.

CHAPTER NINE

WHEN THEY REACHED Josie's condo, Nick offered to get the tape. "It's been a long day. Why don't you take a quick shower and get comfortable while I run down to the video store?"

Josie blinked up at him. "How do I know you'll pick out a tape I like?"

"Trust me." He tucked a wind-tossed curl behind her ear, struggling with his new feelings. He wanted to hold her close, keep her close. It was distracting, the way she made him feel complete with just a smile. "Give me your key and then you won't have to let me in."

To his surprise, she handed him the key without any hesitation. "I'll see you in just a little bit, then."

He rented two tapes, bought popcorn and colas, and returned not thirty minutes later to find Josie in the bathroom blow-drying her hair. She was bent over at the waist, her long red hair flipped forward to hang almost to her knees. Nick stared, mesmerized. She looked so young, with her face scrubbed clean and her baggy pajamas all but swallowing up her petite body.

She also looked sexy as hell.

Remarkable. No matter what she wore, what persona she presented, he found her irresistible. He wondered if she hadn't been dressed so sexily the first time he saw her, would he have reacted the same? It seemed entirely possible given the way his body responded to her now.

He stood there watching her for a good five minutes, wanting to touch her, to wrap her beautiful hair around his hands. Her movements were all intrinsically female and he loved how her bottom swayed as she moved the dryer, how her small bare feet poked out at the end of the pajama bottoms. Ridiculous things.

In such a short time, she'd come to occupy so much of his thoughts, and his thoughts were as often sweet, like Josie, as they were hot and wild like the way she made him feel when he was inside her.

She cared about people—her sister and her patients and even his grandfather whom she hardly knew. He hoped she cared for him, but he couldn't tell because she was so set on having a purely physical relationship. He'd encouraged her in that regard, but no more. Tonight would be a good place to start.

She turned off the dryer and straightened, noticing him at the same time. A soft blush colored her face. "Um, I didn't realize you were back." She started trying to smooth her hair, now tossed in wild profusion around her head.

Nick grinned, bursting with emotion too rare to keep inside. "You look beautiful."

"Uh-huh."

He crossed his heart and held up two fingers. "Scout's honor. I wouldn't lie to you."

She put away the discarded towel and started out of the bathroom around him. "You were never a Scout, Nick. Jeb would have told me if you were."

He followed close on her heels.

"True enough, but the theory's the same." He could smell the clean scent of her body, of flowery soap and powder softness. And Josie.

She headed to the couch, but as she started to sit, he pulled her into his lap, relishing the weight of her rounded bottom on his groin. The new position both eased and intensified the ache.

He caught her chin and turned her face toward him. Before he could even guess at his own thoughts, he heard himself ask, "Are you relieved you're not pregnant?"

He saw her chest expand as she caught her breath, saw her tender bottom lip caught between her teeth.

She looked down, apparently fascinated with his chin. After a moment, she whispered, "It's strange, really. I'd never before given babies much thought. There's always been a succession of priorities in my life that occupied my mind. Getting past my parents' deaths, getting through school, finding a job and then starting my own business. I suppose I'm fairly single-minded about things."

"But?"

Her gaze met his briefly, then skittered away. "There's really no room in my life right now for a child. But still, in my mind, I'd pictured what it would look like, if it would be a boy or a girl…"

He pictured a little girl who looked like Josie. An invisible fist squeezed his heart.

"Oh, good grief." She threw up her hands and forced a smile. "Luckily I'm not pregnant and so that's that. We've got nothing to worry about." Her smile didn't quite reach her eyes.

She was always so open with him. Yet he'd done

nothing but be secretive and withdrawn. He'd manipulated her at every turn, even as he worried about her trying to control him.

Ha! Josie was unlike any woman he'd ever known. She wasn't like Myra, trying to run his life, or his mother, rejecting him, or any of the other women he'd known who'd tried so diligently to mold him into a marriageable man. No, Josie hadn't tried to change his life, and he'd been too busy trying to change hers to notice.

He was a total jerk. A fool, an idiot.

He'd lied to her from the start in order to get his way. Then he'd continued to lie to try to keep her interested, claiming he agreed with her short-term plan, when even at the beginning he'd known something about her was special. He'd even done his best to alter her job, just to make more time for himself. He'd forced his way in with her friends, but never introduced her to his. He didn't deserve her—but damned if he was letting her go.

Pulling her close and pressing his face into her hair, he asked, "Can I spend the night with you, Josie?"

She tensed, and he hugged her even tighter. "Just to sleep. It's late and I want to hold you."

In a tentative tone, she said, "I'd like to see your home sometime."

He'd avoided taking her there. He hadn't wanted her to see the way he lived, with everything set for his convenience. Women didn't appreciate the type of functional existence he'd created for himself, which was the whole point. More often than not, his shirts never made it into a drawer. He laid them out neatly, one atop the other on the dining-room table. His socks were in the buffet drawer, convenient to the shirts. He never bothered to make his bed, not when he only planned to use it every night, and he didn't put away his shaving cream or razor, but left them on the side of the sink, handy.

His small formal living room had gym equipment in it and he'd never quite gotten around to buying matching dishes. He'd set himself up as a bachelor through and through.

Once a week, he cleaned around everything. He remembered now why he'd started doing things that way—to annoy Myra, and on her rare visits, his mother. He laughed at himself and his immature reasoning. For Josie, he'd even put away his toothpaste.

"Nick?"

"I was just thinking about your reaction when you see my house."

One hand idly stroked his neck. "What's it look like?" She was warm and soft and he loved her—everything about her. The notion of something as potent as love should have scared him spitless, but instead it filled him with resolution. Damn her ridiculous plans; she could experiment all she wanted, as long as she only experimented with him.

"My house is small, not at all like Granddad's. It looks like every other house on the street, except that I've never planted any flowers or anything. I bought it because it's close to where I work, not because I particularly like it. You'd be shocked to see what a messy housekeeper I am. I can just imagine you fussing around and putting things away, trying to make it as neat and orderly as your own."

She leaned back to see his face. "You're kidding,

right? I barely have time to straighten my own place. I'm not going to play maid for anyone." She kissed his chin. "Not even you."

Brutally honest, that was his Josie. He laughed, delighted with her. "So you wouldn't mind stepping over my mess?"

She stared at him, her expression having gone carefully blank. "I don't imagine it will be a problem very often. Do you?"

He didn't want to address that issue right now. He knew she wouldn't like his house because he didn't even like it. She wouldn't be enticed to spend much time there.

He kissed her again, then while holding her close, he said, "One of the movies I rented is a real screamer, a new release guaranteed to make your hair stand on end. What do you say we put it on?"

Greed shone from her eyes. "I'm certainly up to it if you are."

The movie was enough to make them both jump on several occasions, which repeatedly caused gales of laughter. At one point, Josie hid her face under his arm, her nose pressed to his ribs. They ate two huge bowls of popcorn and finished off their colas and by the time the movie was over, they were both ready for bed.

Josie looked hesitant as she crawled in under the covers. When Nick stripped naked to climb in beside her, she groaned and accused him of being a terrible tease.

It was the strangest feeling to sleep chastely with a woman, with no intention of making love. It was also damn pleasurable. Only Josie, he thought, could make a scary movie and popcorn seem so romantic, so tender. He pulled her up against his side, then sucked in his breath when her small hot fist closed gently around him. "Josie?"

She nestled against him. "I'm not a selfish woman, Nick. Just because I'm out of commission doesn't mean you should suffer."

He could find no argument with her reasoning while her slender fingers held him. "Sleeping with you isn't a hardship, honey. I think I can take the pressure."

"Nonsense." She kissed his shoulder, then propped herself up on one elbow to watch his face while she slowly stroked him. In a whisper, she told him all the things she wanted to do to him, all the things she wanted him to teach her about his body. "Will you groan for me, Nick?"

He groaned.

She kissed his ear, the corner of his mouth. She kept her voice low and her movements gentle. "I need more data for my experimentation, you see."

He refused to talk about that. If she even hinted at going to another man right now, he'd tie her to the bed.

"You can't continue to have your way with me without paying the piper, lady."

Her smile was sensual and superior. "Oh? And what does the piper charge?"

He ground his teeth together, trying to think through the erotic sensation of being led like a puppet. "I want a key to your condo."

Josie went still for just a heartbeat and Nick thought she would refuse. But she bent and kissed him, then whispered into his mouth, "Keep the one I gave you earlier. I have a spare."

"Josie…" He groaned again, wanting to discuss the ramifications of her easy surrender. Josie had other ideas.

And Nick, once again, gave her total control.

Almost two weeks later, he still had her key—and he'd all but moved in.

"GOOD GRIEF JOSIE, you should get dressed before you answer the door."

Her sister's comment might have been laughable if she wasn't so incredibly nervous. Josie looked down at her short, snug skirt, the same one she'd worn the night she first met Nick, and stiffened her resolve. She had a new plan for changing her life, and this one suited her perfectly.

Keeping the door only halfway open, more or less blocking her sister, Josie said, "Hi, Susan."

Susan leveled a big sister, somewhat ironic look on her. "Aren't you going to invite me in?"

"I…uh, this isn't the best time."

Susan stiffened. "Oh? Is Nick in there? Is that it?" Susan tried to peek around her and Josie gave up.

"No, Nick isn't here. Come on in."

Josie turned away from her sister's curious, critical eye and went into the kitchen. She had to keep moving or she'd chicken out.

Susan followed close on her heels. "Why are you dressed like that?"

Because Nick likes me dressed this way. "What's wrong with how I'm dressed? I'm rather fond of this particular outfit."

Susan eyed the short skirt and skimpy blouse with acute dislike. "What's going on, Josie?"

"Nothing that you should worry about." Josie went

through the motions of pouring her sister a cup of coffee. Nick would show up soon, and she needed to get Susan back out the door. What she planned required privacy, not her sister as a jaundiced audience. "So what brings you here on a workday, Susan? Is anything wrong?"

Susan chewed her lips, twitched in a wholly Susan-type fashion, then blurted, "Bob wants to marry me."

Josie stared at her sister, at first taken aback, and then so pleased, she squealed and threw herself into her sister's arms. Susan laughed, too, tears shining on her lashes, and the two women clutched each other and did circles in the kitchen.

"I'm so happy for you, Susan!"

"I'm happy for me, too, Josie! Bob is perfect for me. He's not the man I first thought him to be, but he's proved to be even better. And I love him so much." She wiped her cheeks with shaking hands and tried to collect herself, but she couldn't stop jiggling around. "He treats me like I'm special."

Josie knew the feeling well. Nick made her feel like she was the only woman alive—but he would never ask her to marry him. It was up to her to take the initiative. "You *are* special. Bob's a lucky man to have you."

"Bob told Nick this morning." Her tone suggested that Josie should be upset by that news.

Nick had gotten so comfortable with her, and every day it seemed he spent more and more time with her, sleeping with her at night, calling her during the day. He talked to her and confided in her. He'd taken her to his house and they'd laughed together at the unconventional steps he'd taken to simplify his life.

But inside, Josie's heart had nearly broken. By his own design, Nick had set up his life so there was no room for a permanent relationship. Jeb had warned her several times the effect his parents' divorce and his step-mother's spite had had on Nick. Not that Jeb wanted to discourage her from loving Nick. Just the opposite. Josie often had the feeling Jeb did his best hard sell on Nick, trying to maintain her interest.

"Don't you want to know what Nick had to say about it?"

"He's due home in just a little while. I'm sure we'll talk about it then."

Susan tilted her head in a curious way and then forced a laugh. "You say *home* as if Nick lives here now."

Josie sat in her chair, stirred her coffee, then put down the spoon. She looked around the kitchen for inspiration, but found nothing except her own nervousness.

"Josie?" Susan pulled out her own chair, then frowned. There was a heavy silence. Josie tugged at the edge of her miniskirt, knowing what was coming. Her relationship with Nick wasn't precisely a secret, not really. But it had been private.

Now, though, what did it matter? In a very short while, Nick would either decide to stay, or he'd go. "He's been sort of staying here, yes."

"Sort of? What the hell does that mean?"

Susan's voice had risen to a shout and Josie sighed. "It means I have my own private life to lead."

"In other words, you want me to butt out, even though I can see you're making a huge mistake?"

Josie refused to think of Nick as a mistake. He made her feel alive, special and whole. Even if he turned down her proposal, she'd never regret her time with him.

Josie was still formulating an answer when Susan's temper suddenly mushroomed like a nuclear cloud.

She launched from her seat and began pacing furiously around the kitchen. "I'll kill him! God, how that man can be so considerate and generous one minute and such an unconscionable bastard the next is beyond me!"

Josie glanced at the kitchen clock. She was running out of time. "Susan, I really can't let you insult Nick. It's not fair. We made an agreement and he's living up to his end of the bargain. I'm the one who stipulated no strings attached."

Susan slashed her hand in the air. "Only because you knew anything more was unlikely with a man like *him*." She thumped a fist onto the counter. "I asked him to leave you alone, but he wouldn't listen to me."

"You did what?"

"He told me he wouldn't hurt you."

"And he hasn't! Oh, Susan, you had no right. How dare you—"

But Susan wasn't listening. "And to think I was actually starting to like the big jerk."

"You were?" Then, "Damn it, Susan, don't change the subject. When did you talk with Nick about me? *What did you say?*"

In the next instant, Bob stepped into the kitchen. "I knocked, but you two were arguing too loud to hear…me…." His voice trailed off as he stared at Josie in her killer outfit. After a stunned second, he gave a low whistle. "Wow."

Susan whirled to face him. Bob took one look at her piqued expression, quickly gathered himself, then pulled her close. He glared at Josie over Susan's head. "What did you say to upset her?"

Josie's mouth fell open in shock. She'd never before heard Bob use that tone. Before she could even begin to think of a reply, Susan jerked away from him.

"Don't you snap at my sister! It's not her fault. It's that degenerate friend of yours who's to blame."

Throwing up his hands, Bob asked, "What did Nick do now?"

To add to the ridiculous comedy, Nick walked in. "Yeah, what did I do? And who forgot to invite me to the party?" He grinned, caught sight of Josie and seemed to turn to stone. Only his eyes moved, and they traveled over her twice before he frowned and lifted his gaze to her face in accusation.

"We're not having a party," Josie informed him, feeling very put upon with the circumstances. She pulled two more coffee mugs down from the cabinet. "I'm just trying to convince Susan that I know what I'm doing."

Nick advanced on her, his stride slow and predatory. "I see. And what are you doing, dressed like that? Planning to expound on your experiences? Planning to breach new horizons?" He pointed a finger at her. "We had a deal, lady!"

"What in the world are you talking about?"

His cheekbones dark with color, his eyes narrow and his jaw set, he waved a hand to encompass her from head to toe. "Were you planning to go back to the same bar? Have I bored you already?"

Her plans were totally ruined, the moment lost, and now here was Nick, behaving like a jealous, accusing ass.

Her temper flared. "Actually," she growled, going on tiptoe to face him, "I thought I'd ask for your hand— or rather your whole body—in matrimony. So what do you think of *that?*"

She heard Susan's gasp, Bob's amused chuckle, but what really fascinated her was Nick's reaction. He grabbed her arms and pulled her closer still, not hurting her, but bringing her flush against his hard chest.

"You what?" he croaked.

"You heard me. I want to marry you."

A fascinating series of emotions ran over his face, then Nick turned, still holding her arm, and practically dragged her from the room. Josie had no idea what he was thinking, because the last expression he had was dark and severe and forbidding. In her high-heeled shoes, which still hampered her walk, she had no choice but to stumble along behind him.

Susan started to protest, but Bob hushed her. Josie could hear them both whispering.

Nick took her as far as her bedroom, locking the door behind them. Josie jerked away from him, but he simply picked her up and laid her on the bed, then carefully lowered his length over her, pinning her down from shoulders to knees. Josie struggled against him. "We have to talk, Nick. I've got a lot to say to you."

Still frowning, he said, "I love you, Josie."

Her eyes widened. Well, maybe she could wait her turn to talk. "Do you really?"

"Damn right."

She chewed her lip. "Do you love me enough to marry

me?" Before he could answer, she launched into her well-rehearsed arguments on marital bliss. "Because I love you that much. I had planned to ask you properly, after a special night out. Even though I'm not the sexy lady you met that first night at the bar, I can be her on occasion. I just can't be her all the time. I realize that now. I knew something was missing from my life, but it wasn't what I thought." She touched his jaw. "It was you."

His Adam's apple took a dip down his throat, and then Nick smiled, his eyes bright, filled with fierce tenderness. "You are that same sexy lady, honey, and you make my muscles twitch with lust just looking at you. You're also the very sweet little sister who's spent years showing her appreciation, and the conscientious caretaker who makes people feel important again. I love all of you, everything about you." He kissed her quick and hard. "Were you serious about wanting to marry me?"

Josie threw her arms around him and squeezed him tight.

Nick laughed. "Talk to me, sweetheart. This is my first attempt at professing love and I'm in a welter of emotional agony here."

"You're very good at it, you know."

"At suffering?"

"At professing your love." She pushed him back enough to see his face. "Yes I want to marry you. And I want to buy a house and make babies and—"

"Whoa. About the house…"

His hesitation shook her and she cupped his face in her hands, hoping to soothe him. "A house is permanence, Nick, I know. But it's what I want. I don't expect you to change, to become someone else, because I love you just as you are. But you will have to meet me halfway on this."

"No more gym equipment in the dining room?"

"And no other women. Just me. Forever."

"I like the sound of that." He leaned down and nuzzled her chin. "Honey, we don't need to buy a house because we already have one. And no, don't look so horrified. I'm not talking about my house." He smoothed her hair from her forehead, his touch tender. "Granddad came to see me today. He's moving into the condominium with Mrs. Wiley and he wants us to have his house, if, as he put it, I was lucky enough to convince you to marry me."

The enormity of Jeb's gesture overwhelmed her and put a lump in her throat. She swallowed hard. "Oh."

"Granddad knows you love that house almost as much as he does. He insists it has to stay in the family, and he said it might help my case in persuading you to the altar. Wait until I tell him you proposed and all I had to do was say yes."

"So you are saying yes?"

"How could I not when I'm so crazy about you?"

Josie contemplated a lifetime with Nick and felt so full of happiness, it almost hurt. "I can't believe I'll get to do anything and everything to you that I've ever imagined."

He froze over her, groaned, then settled his mouth, hot and wet, possessively over hers. Josie had just decided she didn't care if Bob and Susan were in the kitchen when Nick pulled back.

"I have a few confessions to make."

She bit his lip, his chin. Her breathing was unsteady. "Not now, Nick."

He caught her hands and held them over her head. "It has to be now. I don't want to mess up anymore. So just be still and listen."

Since he wasn't giving her much choice, she listened.

"I didn't realize it at the time, but I took you with me to see my grandfather because I knew he'd talk me up to you. I suppose I wanted you to like me as more than a damn fling, and Granddad seemed like the perfect solution."

Tenderness swelled in her heart. "You've never needed any help with that one. I've always liked you."

"I wasn't thinking of anything permanent when I did that, Josie. I just wanted more time with you, and I knew I couldn't let you start experimenting with any other guy. The thought makes me nuts."

"I never intended to. I just told you that so you'd agree to hang around. I knew it was what you wanted to hear."

He stared at her with widened eyes. "You lied?"

"Mmm-hmm." She touched his jaw, his throat. His familiar weight pressed her down and had her body warming in very sensitive places. "I'd have done anything to keep you around a while."

"Damn it, Josie, do you have any idea what you've put me through?"

"Are you talking about on the boat?" She dragged one foot up his calf, then wrapped both legs around him. "I remember it very well."

His expression changed from annoyance to interest, then to grudging respect. "You know damn well that wasn't what I was talking about, you just said it to distract me. You're such a little tease."

"I learned from a master."

His grin was slow and filled with wickedness. "A master, huh? But I haven't even come close to showing you everything yet."

Though his words caused a definite hot thrill to shimmer through her belly, she hid her reaction and smiled. "And I haven't even come close to testing the limits of your restraint. Do you know what I'd like to do to you next?"

"I don't want to know. Not yet."

She leaned up and whispered in his ear anyway. He groaned, pressed his hips closer to hers and asked, "When?"

EPILOGUE

"NICK…" Josie's groan echoed around the large bedroom and Nick slowed his pace even more, loving the sound of her pleas, loving her. For almost six months now they'd been married and living in what he still called Granddad's house—and Nick knew he couldn't have been happier.

"Tell me what you want, sweetheart."

For an answer, she dug her fingers into the muscles of his shoulders and tried to squirm beneath him.

"Uh-uh-uh." He pressed down, making her gasp. "You promised to hold perfectly still."

"I can't, Nick."

His lips grazed her cheek. "You always say that, honey. I always prove you wrong." He chuckled softly at her low moan. "Trust me. You'll enjoy this."

He slipped his hand down between their bodies and pressed his thumb where she needed it most. "Easy…" But this time his words did no good. Josie arched off the bed, her head back, her cries deep and real and she took him with her as she climaxed.

Long minutes later, he managed a dry chuckle and a mild scolding. "You're too easy, Josie. And you need to learn to slow down. I'm going to get conceited if you don't stop trying so hard to convince me what a wonderful lover I am."

Without bothering to open her eyes, she lifted a limp hand and patted his cheek. "You're the very best."

He laid his hand on her belly and watched her shiver. "I love you, Josie."

A smile tilted her mouth. "I've been thinking about cutting back at work some. With the way Granddad and Grandmom run things, I don't need to make my rounds to visit nearly so often anymore. No one is lonely, not with those two always throwing a party of one kind or another."

Nick still had a hard time thinking of Mrs. Wiley—now Mrs. Harris—as *Grandmom*. But he called her that because she asked him to and because he loved the way she pleased his grandfather, doting on him and putting the glow back in his eyes. She doted on Nick and Josie, as well, treating them as if they were her own grandchildren. The elders had married about a month ago, and were the epitome of lovesick newlyweds.

Nick dragged his fingers down Josie's belly to her hipbones. He explored there, watching gooseflesh rise on her smooth skin. "If you want to work less, you know I won't complain. But why the sudden decision?"

She turned to look at him and she caught his hand, bringing it to her lips. "Susan is pregnant."

He stared at her for a long minute, then broke into a huge smile. "Well, I'll be damned. Bob hasn't said a thing."

"Susan was going to tell him tonight."

"He'll be thrilled. And Susan will make a wonderful mother. Maybe it'll keep her from checking up on you so often."

Josie smacked at him. "You know she's cut way back on that since we got married. She even likes you now."

"Yeah, but she pretends she doesn't. I think she just got used to hassling me."

Josie shook her head. "She knows how much you enjoy arguing with her." Then she bit her lip and tucked her face into his shoulder. "Nick?"

"Hmm?"

"What would you think about having a baby?"

His heart almost punched out of his chest. It took him thirty seconds and two strangled breaths to say, "Are you…?"

"Not yet. But I think I'd like to be."

He fell back on the bed and groaned. "Don't do that to me. I almost had a heart attack."

Josie didn't move. "So you don't like the idea?"

He came back up over her and rested his large hand on her soft belly. He stroked. "I love you, honey. I didn't think I'd ever feel this way about a woman, and now I can't imagine how I ever got by without you."

"Oh, Nick."

"And I'd love a baby." His rough fingertips smoothed her skin, teasing. "I'd love three or four of them, actually. God knows this house is big enough for a battalion, and nothing would make Granddad happier."

She chuckled and reached her hand down to his thigh. "Let's concentrate on just one, for now. I promise to make the endeavor pleasurable."

"I await your every effort."

Josie laughed at his hedonistic sigh. "You're so bad."

With one move, he flipped her over and pinned her

beneath him. "You just got done telling me how good I am."

She lowered her eyes and flashed an impish grin. "Hmm. Then that must mean it's my turn to show you how good I can be."

"You're not done experimenting yet?"

She trailed a fingernail over his collarbone. "Nick, I've barely just begun."

* * * * *

In summer 2011 New York Times
and USA TODAY *bestselling author LORI FOSTER*
returns with her trademark blend of scintillating storytelling and sexy heroes in a steamy new trilogy!
Read on for a sneak peek of
IF YOU DARE....

DARE CAME INTO THE HOTEL ROOM quietly, saw Molly curled on the bed and frowned. The towel barely covered her and her knees were pulled up—he would get one hell of a peep show if he moved to the foot of the bed.

Not that he would. In many cases he lacked scruples; it was a hazard of the job. But with women, with *this* woman, he wasn't about to take advantage. Despite her bravado and commonsense reaction to her nightmare, he'd never seen anyone more emotionally fragile.

Besides, the less involvement he had with her, unscrupulous or otherwise, the better. He needed to figure out what had happened to her, and the quickest way to safely remove her from his care.

He'd known she was spent, on the ragged edge, but the fact that she hadn't even pulled the covers over herself proved her level of exhaustion.

More than anything, she probably needed to eat. But should he wake her for that when she also needed sleep?

He wasn't a damn babysitter, but since he'd personally gotten her out of Mexico, he couldn't very well just dump her somewhere. By rescuing her, he had accepted an implied responsibility.

Trying not to rattle the bags, and juggling the food with his other purchases, Dare closed the door and locked it. A glance at the bedside clock showed the time at 1:30 a.m. He'd been gone only half an hour, tops.

Luckily the Walmart across the street stayed open twenty-four hours. He'd found not only clothes for her, but food, too. Dressing and feeding her would go a long way toward resolving her most pressing issues.

With barely a sound, he stowed the drinks in the tiny fridge and put her share of the food into the microwave to keep.

Removing his wallet, change and cell phone from his jeans, he placed them neatly on the desk. Next he took out his knife and the Glock 9 mm he carried, and set them beside his other belongings. He stretched out his knotted muscles. Too many hours without enough sleep or food, crawling over rough ground, ducking for cover and demolishing men had left him tense and weary.

After pulling out a chair from the round table, he opened the covering on his pancakes and coffee.

He'd taken only one bite when she stirred, sniffed the air and drowsily opened her eyes. Dare turned toward her.

She gave him a "deer caught in the headlights" look.

He studied her, a small bundle huddled tight on the bed, face still ravaged and eyes wounded. Never had he seen a woman look so vulnerable.

He swallowed his bite and, sounding as casual as he could under the circumstances, asked, "Hungry?"

She stared back, then struggled up to one elbow. Her expression changed, the wariness hidden beneath that intrepid bravado. "Starved. Literally."

With all the dirt removed, her big eyes dominated her small features. More marks showed on her fair skin—one on her cheekbone and under her left eye, one on her throat and a darker, angrier bruise on her right shoulder.

She breathed deeply, her eyes closing and her nostrils flaring. "That smells so good."

Out of his seat already, Dare fetched her food. "Do you want to sit here, or eat on the bed?"

She hesitated, looking down for a moment as if uncertain of her welcome, not wanting to inconvenience him. "Table, please, but…I should dress first."

"All right." He set the food on the table and opened the bag of clothes, pulling out a few T-shirts, panties and a pair of pull-on cotton shorts. "You can get more stuff tomorrow if you feel up to it. Something warmer, maybe, and nicer for the plane ride. But for now, I figured this would fit."

She didn't look at the clothes. The arm she leaned on barely supported her, and her breath went choppy with effort.

Voice weak, strained, she said, "I'm sorry, but…I haven't eaten in too long and I'm feeling kind of…faint."

Dare straightened, going on alert. Would she pass out on him?

"If…if you could help me into the bathroom, I'll dress in there."

Shit. He did not want her passing out alone, maybe hitting her head. "Yeah, no problem."

Dare moved to the bed and slipped an arm behind her, then drew her to her feet. She swayed into him, one hand clutching at his shirt and holding on for dear life.

She made no attempt to step away. He didn't ask her to. "What would you like to do?"

"I can't…" She choked, cleared her throat, and her voice was so low he barely heard her when she said, "This is embarrassing, but the shower…" She swallowed. "I think I'm depleted."

Easing her back onto the bed, Dare knew he'd have to be firm to get her agreement. "Okay, Molly, listen up." He kept his tone as impersonal as possible. "This isn't a big deal. I can dress you. I can even feed you."

She rolled in her lips with embarrassment, a habit he'd already noticed.

"It's nothing I haven't done before," he lied.

That brought her dark eyes up to his.

Damn, but her eyes could melt a man's soul. "I'm in the personal protection business. You're not the first woman I've rescued. You're not even in the worst shape." Another lie. Most women he retrieved were found in the first forty-eight hours before too much damage had been done—or they weren't found at all. "Okay?"

Still with her gaze locked on his, she nodded.

"Good girl." He grabbed the clothes from the bag, not really discomfited with the task, but he'd just as soon get past it.

Taking clothes off a woman—yeah, he had plenty of practice with that.

Dressing the near-dead…not so much.

REQUEST YOUR
FREE BOOKS!

2 FREE NOVELS
FROM THE ROMANCE COLLECTION
PLUS 2 FREE GIFTS!

YES! Please send me 2 FREE novels from the Romance Collection and my 2 FREE gifts (gifts are worth about $10). After receiving them, if I don't wish to receive any more books, I can return the shipping statement marked "cancel." If I don't cancel, I will receive 4 brand-new novels every month and be billed just $5.74 per book in the U.S. or $6.24 per book in Canada. That's a saving of at least 28% off the cover price. It's quite a bargain! Shipping and handling is just 50¢ per book.* I understand that accepting the 2 free books and gifts places me under no obligation to buy anything. I can always return a shipment and cancel at any time. Even if I never buy another book, the two free books and gifts are mine to keep forever.

194/394 MDN E7NZ

Name	(PLEASE PRINT)

Address	Apt. #

City	State/Prov.	Zip/Postal Code

Signature (if under 18, a parent or guardian must sign)

Mail to The Reader Service:
IN U.S.A.: P.O. Box 1867, Buffalo, NY 14240-1867
IN CANADA: P.O. Box 609, Fort Erie, Ontario L2A 5X3

Not valid for current subscribers to the Romance Collection
or the Romance/Suspense Collection.

Want to try two free books from another line?
Call 1-800-873-8635 or visit www.morefreebooks.com.

* Terms and prices subject to change without notice. Prices do not include applicable taxes. N.Y. residents add applicable sales tax. Canadian residents will be charged applicable provincial taxes and GST. Offer not valid in Quebec. This offer is limited to one order per household. All orders subject to approval. Credit or debit balances in a customer's account(s) may be offset by any other outstanding balance owed by or to the customer. Please allow 4 to 6 weeks for delivery. Offer available while quantities last.

MROM10R

LORI
FOSTER

| 77444 | TEMPTED | ___ $7.99 U.S. ___ $9.99 CAN. |
| 77382 | SCANDALOUS | ___ $7.99 U.S. ___ $7.99 CAN. |

(limited quantities available)

TOTAL AMOUNT	$ _____
POSTAGE & HANDLING	$ _____
($1.00 FOR 1 BOOK, 50¢ for each additional)	
APPLICABLE TAXES*	$ _____
TOTAL PAYABLE	$ _____

(check or money order—please do not send cash)

To order, complete this form and send it, along with a check or money order for the total above, payable to HQN Books, to: **In the U.S.:** 3010 Walden Avenue, P.O. Box 9077, Buffalo, NY 14269-9077; **In Canada:** P.O. Box 636, Fort Erie, Ontario, L2A 5X3.

Name: _____
Address: _____ City: _____
State/Prov.: _____ Zip/Postal Code: _____
Account Number (if applicable): _____

075 CSAS

*New York residents remit applicable sales taxes.
*Canadian residents remit applicable GST and provincial taxes.

HQN™

We *are* romance™

www.HQNBooks.com

PHLF0710BL